TALES FROM THE CRUST

CRUST

AN ANTHOLOGY OF PIZZA HORROR

EDITED BY:

DAVID JAMES KEATON &
MAX BOOTH III

PMMP

Perpetual Motion Machine Publishing
Cibolo, Texas

www.PerpetualPublishing.com

Cover art by George Cotronis

"Last Request" by Rob Hart was originally published in *Thuglit*, 2016

"The Violent Life and Ugly Death of the Noid" by Nathan Rabin was published at Nathan Rabin's Happy Place, 2019

TABLE OF CONTENTS

INTRODUCTION:
PIZZA MY SKULL

DAVID JAMES KEATON AND STEVE GILLIES

IS IT JUST me or is turbulence getting worse? It was inevitable that Little Debbie Oatmeal Crème Pies shrunk from hubcap to half-dollar size and taste more like sugary ashtrays every day, and any boomboxes still around sound like cell phone speakers in mayonnaise jars. But if they're cramming so many seats on airplanes that your knees are in your throat (three extra seats in the goddamn Emergency Exit row!) and everyone just keeps pretending they've always been there, then maybe, just *maybe,* the fucking wind is gonna start knocking down planes. All I know for sure is my last flight had to be one rumble away from drunk Denzel finally flipping the thing over to smooth out our ride. So next time you fly the friendly skies, get ready to reenact that hallway fight in *Inception*. And you know what that means? Pizza everywhere! Because here's the thing, along with all the deregulation, they've also eliminated food on planes, as well. Sure they might give you a button to suck on, but no more meals, even when you're catching a connecting flight in Boston, which is apparently directly between Pittsburgh and San Jose. And because everyone's starving up in the sky now, the planes are full of stinky subs, tacos, casseroles, and pizza. I actually started counting pizzas on planes about two years ago, and I'm up to thirty. That's thirty full-size pizzas, smuggled past security with no one batting an eye. Meanwhile they force you to drink David Lee Roth's proverbial "Bottle of Anything" right there at the *Total Recall* scanners, where your funniest X-ray'd dick pic is no doubt traded for cigarettes between some FAA security-theater shitbags . . . but somehow you can still rock up spinning two larges with extra pepperoni on your fingers like Erich Brenn on *The Ed Sullivan Show*? I'm still waiting to see that crime-scene ceiling when the turbulence sends all those airplane pizzas flying. And it's going to happen. It's just a matter of time. In fact, I'm predicting it right now, a soon-to-be-famous snapshot of a pizza comet smeared across a dozen "fasten seatbelts" will take the internet by storm. I mean, if that poor Pizza Rat can go viral, a pizza bomb at 40,000 feet flinging pepperoni everywhere like Sharon Stone throwing her casino chips over her shoulder can't be too much of a stretch. I'll bet you ten bucks (coincidentally the price of the worst pizza in California), because Snipes had it all wrong in *Passenger 57*. Always bet on red.

Speaking of shitty pizza, I was mostly inspired to put this book together because I'd just moved to California, where pizza is garbage. Hopefully this monstrous generalization inspires people to send me hate mail detailing amazing pizza places on the West Coast. This is known as a win/win. Maybe I just miss the Pizza House back in Pittsburgh (a.k.a. "Police Station Pizza" because it's in an old police station, get it?), which was the best pizza in Pittsburgh hands down, or maybe anywhere, even though just like real police stations, it has to be a front for something shady. Maybe there's just a card game in the back where they're betting with dick pics, but it's always so weird when you go in there: got a dozen mooks behind the counter milling around doing nothing, a lockbox instead of a register, pizza kinda looks like high-school cafeteria pizza and only comes in these 4x4 squares . . . but like Dignan (sorta) said in *Bottle Rocket*, just because it's a front, someone's gotta make the actual pizza! Police Station Pizza. Accept no substitutes. P.S. it's not really in Pittsburgh. It's in Ambridge past Sewickley, not to be confused with Actual Hell on Earth "Ampipe" in *All the Right Moves* though it looks just like it, because that movie was filmed in Pittsburgh! What? Never mind just try some.

I was also inspired to do a project like this because of my own adventures as a pizza delivery guy. It was probably one of the strangest jobs I've ever had, and I've had about forty of 'em. I never really made any friends doing it, and the only co-worker who left an impression was some jerk-off on my shift who drove a convertible Mercedes for his deliveries, was like 20 years older than everybody else there, and had a keychain he was always flashing that read, "My other car is a Corvette." "But isn't a Corvette worse than a Mercedes?" I would ask him. "You're just jealous," he would say. So dumb. Here's to ya, dummy! Even though you'll never read this. Seriously, his Mercedes was a cool-looking car from a distance, a '70-something model something? Up close a real mess, though, kinda like the opposite of deep dish pizza! And the Marco's windsock probably didn't help. But this guy promised me that eventually I would be propositioned by a woman at the door all seductive-like, just like in the movies where the porn actor cuts a surprise hole in the pizza box, which makes a whole lot less sense than Mickey Rourke and his famous hole-in-the-popcorn-box move in *Diner* (how does that play today, I wonder!). But, shockingly, this moron's fantasy sort of happened to me for real! Except it was a guy in his back yard who propositioned me, not a hot woman in a nightie, and when he waved me around behind his house, he handed me a warm beer and whispered, "Hey, let me show you where I'm digging a new pool," then he gave me a hearty clap on the back. And that's the day Dave almost got murdered!

Anyhow, I started pitching ideas for this book to Max Booth when I figured he would be the most hungry after working his twelve-hour shifts at the Overlook Hotel. And I was thinking of calling the book *PIZZA MY SKULL* at first because there's a pizza place around San Jose called Pizza My Heart, meaning "piece of my heart" and I thought a "piece of my skull" joke would be hilarious. Understandably, Max balked at this. Turns out that's a lot of assumptions to make about a gag. Also we're in California, and their pizza is garbage, remember! Why name a book after it? Then George Cotronis brainstormed a much better title and came up with a cover for our book that's so good I sincerely want to live in that world. Go look! And poor long-suffering Max finally said "Yes," and he's been sorry ever since. From dealing with social media pile-ons in the comments of our submission announcement to excruciating pizza puns in the query letters, including nutty questions from hopeful authors (like the one who submitted a story without a pizza in it and said if we liked it we could "sprinkle one in there." That's some balls!), and, oh yeah, that notorious, endless thread on Facebook where the authors we rejected (not kidding) tried to announce their own pizza anthology of "Leftover" stories. We almost had to get the Legal Team on the horn for that shit! Still, I thought Max was having fun with all this, until the note below showed up in my mail, pinned to a nasty-ass pizza he'd ordered for me from, you guessed it, Pizza My Heart . . .

Speaking of alarming correspondences! Remind me to tell you about another disturbing letter I got. But before I turn the microphone over to that psycho, I just wanted to thank you for taking a chance on this book, and these pizzas, because it's scary out there, and it's scary up in the sky, and whether you're headed to Ricky's or Sousa's or Vinnie's or Alexandria's or maybe you want to mix it up at Poppa Pedro's Pizza 'n' Tacos or, heck, roll the dice at ol' Dicey Slice, or, if you want to head off the beaten path altogether and take your chances at The People Place's Secret Pizza Co-Op. Or, worst case scenario, if the power is out at Papalocka's, just stay home and throw a Buvoskor's Frozen Pizza in the oven. But whatever pizza you choose, we got you covered . . . with a shovel full of dirt! You totally thought I was going to say "cheese," didn't you?

Okay, here's that creepy letter I was talking about. I hesitate to share this because I don't know if someone is fucking with me here or just trying to scare me or maybe get back at me for whatever prank pizza order I stuck them with back in the day, but I used to go to school with this guy named Steve, and he's not really the jokey type. And when we were putting this anthology together, the following letter showed up out of the blue. I wish I would have saved the stamp or the envelope for greasy fingerprints or other clues. But in the meantime, I may as well slap this whole thing into the introduction because it somehow feels safer to create some kind of semi-permanent record (books never go out of print these days, remember?) and the only time I don't dwell on this letter lately is when I'm eating a delicious slice of California pizza, which is never.

Hey Dave,

How have you been? I've seen you online talking about this pizza book. It's funny. I don't know if you know this, but after I bugged out of Writing Camp I ended up back in the town I grew up in, delivering pizzas for one of the big chains. I know I tried to come off as a sophisticated big city guy back in school, but I actually grew up in Alabama. Why'd I end up back there? Who cares? There's nothing like grad school to open your eyes to the cold indifference of the world. And if nothing really matters, why not drive around the town where you grew up, delivering awful pizza to terrible people?

Bespectacled disillusioned writer type. Gross pizza chain. Deep South. Seems like the perfect setup for some kind of creepy southern gothic pizza horror, right? The thing is, sorry, my dog ate my homework. Nothing to write about here. Swap SEC hats and sweatshirts for NFL gear, and it could be anywhere. Our malls all have the same stores as everywhere else. We get our accents from the same TV shows as people in the Midwest. Shit, man. We don't even have our own pizza places.

So every day I go to this place that smells like grease and sweat and stale dough. I'll say hi to our cook, Red Beard (dude doesn't even have a beard), then I'll grab some pizza and drive around town past perfectly manicured lawns, cookie cutter houses, and miles and miles of strip malls. One thing I'll say, even though I've got the map on my phone plugged into my car, everything looks so similar that this is still a place where you can get lost.

Do you ever have that thing where you're so lost you don't even know if you're lost, Dave? I get it all the time. I'll just zone out while I'm driving, then look up at a building or a gas station sign I've seen a million times and it just doesn't look right. It's definitely the place that's always there, but the details are off, the shading is wrong, the contours contain a little more menace (or is it promise) than usual. Maybe it's not that Hardee's I always drive by. Maybe I'm in a place I haven't been a million times before. And I'll panic. Then I'll check the map, maybe look at a street sign and realize I'm nowhere I haven't been before and that I better hustle to deliver those two pepperonis with breadsticks or whatever. I dread those moments where everything seems wrong, but I kind of live for them too.

I had something kind of like that tonight, Dave. I had a delivery to 11226 Suncrest Drive. I rang the doorbell. And the man who opened the door had squinty eyes, a cheerful expression. His SEC sweatshirt was charcoal grey, his shorts were khaki, and his head was mostly bald. He looked like one of those chubby, comfortable overgrown-baby types you run into in the South from time to time.

"Well, now, I didn't order any pizza but if you're giving them away, I sure could eat one," he said. He seemed really amused by his own laugh.

I checked the door number. I looked at the pizza box. It was right. Then I just stood there, unsure what I should do.

"Well, come in. You can call the office or what have you if you need to work it out," the man said, friendly as you like.

"That's OK. We have a rule about going into houses. I'll just call from my car. Sorry to bother you, sir."

"Mind if I see that box right there," the man said. "I got an idea about the problem here."

I should have left then, but something in that house caught my eye. On the outside it looked like any other suburban split-level house you'd see in the backdrop of all your favorite '80s movies.

Inside, it looked, well it looked bigger on the inside somehow. And filthy. I could make out hundreds of newspapers, candy wrappers, Coke bottles, beer bottles, jars filled with liquids I don't want to speculate about. All that covering what looked like a dirt floor. But that couldn't be right. That stuff must be covering dirt that's covering some kind of carpet, right Dave? The other strange thing about the house is that it didn't seem to have any overhead lights. It just seemed to be glowing like there was a fireplace somewhere in the recesses of that cavern. In that light, I caught a glint of something about three feet tall, a figure, maybe bronze. And a man is bent forward, pushing with all his body into this giant rock. I was pretty into mythology as a kid. They were basically superhero comics that teachers would let you talk about, and the endings were less stupid and happy. There was this one about the guy who got punished by the gods for something, I don't remember what, but gods are always punishing people in these things, that's kind of the point. And in this one, the guy had to keep rolling this boulder up a hill, and as soon as it got back up it would just roll back down. Then he'd go down and have to start over again.

"You like ol' Sisyphus there?" the man said. "It's a good one. I collect them all."

"All?"

"Punishments. I've got them all. Prometheus, Sisyphus, Ixion, Erysichthon, anyone the gods have seen fit to punish. Anywho . . . " The man handed the pizza box back to me. "This is 11226 Suncrest Lane. You want 11226 Suncrest Drive. That's your problem."

"Oh. OK, thanks." I was anxious to get moving.

Then I noticed he was holding a container of garlic dipping sauce.

"A little something else for my collection. For the disturbance? I'm sure your employers won't mind."

What could I say? I don't care much about dipping sauce. I just wanted to get away from this weirdo. So I got back in my car and drove. According to my phone, Suncrest Drive wasn't far away. Just down Hillcrest Dr, across Woodcrest Lane and onto Chicamaugua Trail. I'd been on these streets a million times, so I just zoned out as I was driving. And I arrived at what I'm pretty sure my phone told me was Suncrest Drive. I didn't pay too much attention to the house as I approached. Just another boring split-level. Every week I deliver to hundreds of them. I rang the bell, and the same man opened it. But now he was tall and thin. His face was hard. His eyes squinted suspiciously. Behind him I could see the mess, the candy wrappers, the dirt. The man, though I'm not so certain that's what this was, casually sipped his garlic dipping sauce through a straw. Behind him, Sisyphus was lit by the place's creepy, pizza oven like glow.

"You bring breadsticks?" he asked.

I backed away as quickly as I could. When I got to the car, the map said 11226 Suncrest Circle. I figured I hadn't put the correct address in. So I just drove. I thought about Sisyphus. The guy had to spend the rest of eternity working on something that would never be finished. It kind of reminded me of being a delivery guy. There was always more pizza. I guess as far as punishments go, I was getting off light. I wasn't getting my liver pecked out, I wasn't bound to the sun or cursed with a hunger so great I had to devour my own flesh. I wasn't even lifting a boulder. I was just delivering pizza. My phone's connection is getting all janky, but I needed to tell someone so I thought I'd write it all down for you. Sorry it's kind of a mess, but you'll figure it out.

Anyway, I hear you just had a baby. Congratulations. Maybe you heard I have two kids. I don't see them as much as I should. You know, pizza delivery guy hours. Still they mean everything to me. All those stories, Dave. Ixion, Erysichthon, even whatever it is I tricked myself into thinking is happening tonight. I know we think we make them up to scare ourselves. Things bigger and stranger and more powerful than us that can bend our lives into whatever shape that amuses them. The capriciousness of fate, whatever. I'm not really scared of that at all. All those punishments seem like a kind a mercy to me. Sisyphus, Prometheus, those guys get eternity. They all know where they are and why they're there. There is some comfort to take from that. A life that's just over without you even knowing it ended because there's nothing left of you to know you ever lived it. That's what scares me while I'm out here driving on autopilot, Dave. But it all goes away when I get home to the kids.

Even if I'm just watching them sleep after a long night on the road. Life is the point of life. Nothing else matters. I hope to see them soon. I hope to finally get this pizza delivered.

Okay, I don't want to freak you guys out any more than I already am (okay, I kinda do), but I haven't been able to get in touch with Steve since I received this. The phone number I had for him back at school went nowhere. And on Google Maps, his old address appears to be a crater where the Chicago police test missiles. I even tracked down the number for Papa John's in his neighborhood, but the exhausted dude who answered the phone told me he never heard of him. Then the even more exhausted manager I got a hold of a couple days later said yes, he looked into it, and a "Steve Gillies" *did* work for them, but that was in the mid-'90s.

Also, I didn't ask, but the man told me 11226 Suncrest Drive was outside of their delivery area. They were quite vehement about it. Like they get this question a lot.

THE VEGAN WENDIGO

CODY GOODFELLOW

WHEN MY BROTHER Ethan invited us to the grand opening of his buddy's new pizza place, we knew we could expect literally anything but good pizza.

Amanda put it best a year before, when we staged an intervention against his "dinner dates."

"You're so marinated in irony, that you think those things are fun. They're the opposite of fun. It makes for a funny story, but we're sick of living through it."

But pointing out the abuse only invited Ethan to make it more overt, with a blog and then a semi-regular column in the local weekly, and even talk of a book. His obsession metastasized into a career, and we kept coming, because we had nothing better to do.

I remember how I asked Amanda, when I was badgering her to put down the Nintendo Switch and get ready, "How bad can you fuck up pizza?"

She rolled her eyes, slammed the oven door on a leftover Signal Station calzone, and returned to her cocoon on the couch. She had the Pager of Doom tonight, and had to stay sober and close to the hospital in case she had to go out on a collection run.

Amanda harvested organs and tissue from donors for a living, so she was up to her elbows in a cadaver whenever someone with a D on their license died without requiring an autopsy, which, if they were young and healthy enough to be harvested, usually meant accidents or suicides.

My job was somehow even more depressing. I transcribed videos, mostly hardcore porn, so my sole creative outlet was in devising onomatopoeic words to describe the noises of colliding and convulsing anatomies. We made for a great tag-team cocktail party act, but our stories got old fast. Nobody really wants to know how the sausage is made, when you are the sausage.

So whatever Ethan was cooking up was bound to be a cure for the daily blues. Ethan's favorite thing, and by extension our own, was seeking out the worst restaurants in town. No mere inept cuisine or indifferent service would suffice. The whole experience had to be baffling, except when viewed as some kind of punishment. Once he wore out the merely awful, he fixated on places that were an obvious front for illegal activity.

The Mongolian BBQ on Martin Luther King where the employees threw tantrums in the kitchen when you had the temerity to order food, then burned it to cinders in front of you; the donut shop on 82nd with rows of unused fryers and a pitiful stock of day-old glazed donuts obviously bought from the Safeway down the street; the Moonie coffee shop where manic Stepford Wives love-bombed you over vaguely medicated omelets; the Nation of Islam fish fry joint where they just took your money and sharpened knives on the counter until you gave up and went home hungry.

Something about pushing the awkward illusion until it snapped goaded Ethan into an ecstatic state. At least he found a way to monetize his obsessions, but if he was this hard to get off in bed, maybe he should just become a priest.

Ethan told me in the car that we'd pick up burritos at a new cart on Hawthorne if the pizza was a bust, so I was braced to expect the worst. "What about the Korean BBQ?"

"Shut down by the appropriation police," he snorted. "When are white people going to learn to stick to cooking only the things we hate them for?"

He wouldn't spill any details about tonight's tribulation, but didn't emit the same mischievous animation that preceded the buffet place where everything was made of insects. Laurel barely nodded when I climbed into their boxy VUE, kept her eyes hooded and trained on her phone like I'd walked in on a fight. Ethan kept the music slightly too loud for conversation as we crossed town to 82nd and then turned south, where our car became a downwardly mobile economic bathysphere.

Where the poverty was just about enough to crush our privileged skulls, we parked out front of a condemned Unitarian church. The old sign had a new one fingerpainted by children on military-grade psychedelics:

"THE PEOPLE PLACE," it said, then helpfully under that, "A Place for People!"

"Oh, this is gonna make for a choice column," I told him.

Ethan told me this guy was a good friend of his, and he wasn't there to burn him. "Not everybody appreciates what he's trying to do," he said with a straight face, "so he's keeping it on the down-low. Don't tell anyone about this."

I was naturally suspicious. First, I thought I was his only real friend. He had an endless supply of characters all over town that he'd introduce with one eyebrow cocked disingenuously, like a game show host warming up a rube. All his restaurant picks were fronts for something awful, so it followed that eventually, we'd hit a cult or criminal syndicate that was a front for an actual restaurant.

We went inside and tripped over the rows of sandals, moccasins, and muddy running shoes strewn across the vestibule. Posters and sign-up sheets for anarchist workshops, poetry slams, Antifa summer camp, teach-ins and nonbinary meet-ups covered every wall the fingerpainters hadn't yet marked up. Ethan badgered us until we shed our shoes.

Beyond the open double doors, a few groups of Portlanders as random as you'd find at any bus stop roamed around the chapel, which had been hastily converted into a gallery and performance space. And on the stage, a trio of the dirtiest hippies ever slouched behind an acoustic guitar, upright bass, and a set of honest-to-god panpipes, lovingly murdering Andean folk songs.

We got paper cups of sangria with overripe fruit pulp in it and passed on some vegetable platters, looking around while we tried not to laugh out loud at art that could most charitably be described as a real breakthrough in somebody's therapy. The whole place had that moldy, musky aroma of clothing worn by people who couldn't bring themselves to use detergent.

A starry-eyed, skeletal specimen of early Woodstock Woman explained that the People Place was more than just an alternative arts-collective co-operative community center, it was a radical safe space that turned deep questions of human ecology into direct action for the people who needed it most. And if we wanted to sign up for their newsletter, we'd be able to access the People Place's deep core of services . . .

Ethan told her he was a friend of Jarob, which shut her up. Even he seemed over the whole sad experience.

"So, where's the pizza?" I stage-whispered at Ethan.

He bolted his sangria and tucked the cup in his pocket. "Downstairs."

"If this is what I think it is, you owe me a steak dinner and a lapdance at Acropolis."

We went down a twisty flight of stairs in our stocking feet to a dank, low-ceilinged room with a dozen tables but no chairs. About half of them were occupied by a similar assortment of roped-in locals and spacey-looking hippies, studiously gnawing on pies that looked like botched first attempts from a pottery workshop.

Eager to get to the punch line, I plucked a menu off an empty table. Photocopied on magenta cardstock, it rattled off a four-alarm dumpster-fire of incoherent culinary fuckery, and the worst kind of joke, hence the kind Ethan never got tired of.

While I enjoy vegetarian food as much as the next Portlander, my grandest pet peeve is the vegan switcheroo: vegan friends who never tire of trying to convince you they've finally cracked the code on cheese or eggs or milk chocolate, and foist some soy curd-cashew-cauliflower paste atrocity on you, hoping to finally whittle away your last attachment to the death culture.

Ethan had as much use for vegetables as a dog eating weeds, so he wouldn't enjoy this unless I didn't.

The People Place's Secret Pizza Co-Op menu listed specialty pies with appropriately radicalized titles—the Leveler, the Wobbly, Subcommander Mushroom, Che Guacamole, the Captain Cook and the Wendigo—and no prices, apparently addressed by the all-caps misquote:

"FROM EACH, ACCORDING TO HIS MEATZ, TO EACH, ACCORDING TO HIS CHEEZE."

The ingredients looked normal enough, though too many of them ("cheeze," "meatz," "sawsage" and "pepperony") all appeared in scare quotes, leaving little doubt we were getting switcheroo'd, but good.

The waitress was half our age and walked with a cane. Ignoring my elbow jabs and glaring side-eye, Ethan ordered a Wendigo and a Wobbly and a round of Kombucha shots. He ended up drinking these alone, as they contained Everclear. Laurel stayed quiet, deflecting small-talk, making me wonder if she was finally getting tired of the joke, too.

Ethan's buddy came out to greet us about ten minutes later with some archeological artifacts vaguely resembling bread. His dreadlocks were bound up in a mass like the root ball of a fern that hung down to his waist. His earlobes dangled to his shoulders like snapped rubber bands. He wore a holey T-shirt and greasy jeans. He had a peg leg.

He apologized for the delay, but demand was crazy. They were trying something new, but also very old. Pizza was invented by Italian bakers, he explained, who threw scraps and offal on flat, crusty bread and left the pies on the back steps to keep beggars from lurking out front.

He opened the beaded curtain so we could see into the kitchen. Two skinny neck-beards tossed dough beside a butcher-block table and a formidable wood-fire oven. A pass-through window in the back wall opened on the alley behind the old church. A grimy pair of hands thrust into the kitchen like someone being buried alive, until a cook handed him a pie in a box that looked to be on at least its third life.

He blessed us for our patronage, picked his nose and ate it, then hobbled back to the kitchen.

"Fuck was that?"

"What d'you mean?" he asked, disingenuously.

"The whole Captain Jack Sparrow thing, the fucking peg-leg . . . "

"That's real," Ethan said. "Motorcycle accident."

"Dude picked his nose and ate it right in front of us."

"It boosts the immune system, crybaby," Ethan said.

Some indeterminate period later, which could've been ten minutes, or the same ten minutes recycled until it was as used as that pizza box, our pies arrived.

Neither pie was much to look at. Both pies were meager twelve-inchers, and lopsided. The teardrop-shaped Wobbly, with what looked like artichoke hearts, pear slices and onion wheels on a charred pumpernickel crust, went unloved. But the Wendigo . . .

Tofu doesn't sizzle like that. Soybeans and mushrooms, no matter how you gimmick them, don't smell like that. Only meat, properly butchered, seasoned and fired. Puffs of creamy ricotta cheese dotted the steaming, pesto-clotted crater like nostalgic clouds in a Nintendo game.

And I finally got the joke.

I looked sidewise at Ethan and Laurel, but they only had eyes for the Wendigo, lifting half the ineptly sliced pie onto their own mismatched thrift-store plates. I looked at the other tables, fully expecting someone to give us shit, but they were either watching their own plates or the shy girl with the big guitar tuning up in the corner.

I grabbed and hastily stuffed the curled end of a slice into my mouth as if Laurel might take it if I didn't act fast enough. It burned half my taste buds off, and the other half unconditionally surrendered.

In the middle of this sad-ass exurban ashram, real pizza, with real sausage and cheese. The whole thing was almost funny enough to make you laugh. Somebody back there got a little crazy with the turmeric and the "meatz" were little more than shavings, but the volcanic crust, buttery and crisp and thoroughly infused with garlic and oregano, melted my mouth, then jumped to my nerves and what should have been blisters and a lawsuit became a pure Xmas morning feeling. Motherfucker, I'm not exaggerating here. I would never again laugh at the cliché, "There's a party in my mouth."

The girl with the big guitar was joined by Simon & Shartfunkel from upstairs and they started strumming and piping "El Condor Pasa," and the simple melody was the most lovely thing I'd ever heard. When they finished, it didn't seem to fade out or cut off, but simply to float away to wherever songs go when they're over, and I wanted to grab the rest of the Wendigo and follow it.

I stuffed the rest of the slice into my mouth and reached for another when they sang, "I'd rather be a spider than a snail." My nails skinned Laurel's knuckle as she grabbed for the same slice, and I half-ass apologized through a mouthful of pure pleasure. She licked the blood and nibbled off the loose flap of skin, staring fixedly at the empty plate. Boost that immune system, I thought.

We ordered another Wendigo without so much as touching the

misbegotten Wobbly. Jarob pegged over to stare daggers at us. Ethan picked up a slice of the saddest pizza ever made and gamely polished it off, adding lamely that he planned to take it home with him.

I'd never seen the like before. My brother had never in his life admitted he was wrong or ceded the upper hand in any situation. Acting like he was doing you a favor when you comped him a meal or a show was his thing, and somehow he'd made good at it. So to see him choke down the slice of that shitty pie, to watch him grovel, was sweeter than any present he could've given me.

And after that shameful display, his main man Jarob said he was real sorry, but they were out of the "meatz," deploying the scare quotes with his fingers and everything.

I complimented him on his excellent pizza and tried to ask where they get their ingredients, but he foisted an empty box and a bill on us and bowed back through the beaded curtain. The box was pressed mycelium cardboard, capable of biodegrading in your compost in days, and clearly, we weren't the first to take home leftovers in it.

Ethan settled up and we padded upstairs to discover that, naturally, our shoes had been nationalized. It was somehow even more galling that only one of my next-to-new Adidas sneakers was missing. I would've pitched a tantrum, if I wasn't still tripping balls on that fucking pizza.

Ethan frisbeed the Wobbly into traffic as we jumped in the VUE, but he wouldn't break character and join me in lambasting those clueless freaks who'd accidentally made the best pizza in town.

"You're actually going to have to do a positive review, fucker," I told him.

"I couldn't write that up," he said. "It'd ruin my reputation."

"And your buddy would draw enough business to buy a proper prosthetic leg. Really blowing it, by the way, not milking the pirate thing. With that excellent location, and maybe a parrot . . . "

"He's not into it for that. He's got a truck, he goes to homeless camps and feeds them on his own dime. It's a genuine calling. You wouldn't understand."

"The culture police are gonna have his ass. That was real sausage and cheese."

"It's a hundred percent vegan."

"Then why doesn't he just open a real restaurant? People should know about this."

Ethan swerved out into traffic and nearly got us clipped by a guy merging into our lane. Laurel shouted, "God damn it, Ethan!"

He screamed back, "It's fine! What? You want to have a crash, go ahead and fucking scream at me when I'm driving."

Laurel cried in the drive-thru at the burrito place, which pretty much killed the topic. She barely touched her carnitas chimichanga, but I noticed the mark on her hand where I'd scraped her was now a hole the size of a silver dollar.

We didn't see Ethan for a couple weeks after that. Or, to put it bluntly, the douchebag ditched me. Every time I texted him about getting dinner, he begged off. He and Laurel were getting back into cooking at home, and we'd have to come over some night, when they were ready to show off their new project . . .

I assumed they were fighting, had reverted to poly status, and were fucking other people.

I tried to shake the craving with every resource available—Signal Station, Sizzle Pie, Pizza Nostra, Caligula's . . . All my old favorites tasted like toilet paper, as if the taste buds that replaced the ones scorched by the Wendigo were wired for a new definition of pizza.

So I went back by myself.

The People Place site was a stoned masterpiece, hiding or omitting even the most basic information. All the workshops and events were free to members who put in four hours or more a week at the co-op, or taught a workshop. The Secret Pizza Kitchen was only open during evening events and weekends. Co-op members got a discount, but no menu was on the site, and "NO TAKEOUT, NO DELIVERY" blinked continuously at the top, like news of a tornado.

Amanda was off work, but she was only into it when I pretended to be obsessed with something, so she bowed out. I had yogurt and coffee for breakfast, and skipped lunch. I drove over in the rain. I went downstairs and I picked up the pink menu on the table.

The three dreadful-sounding pies on the menu went for twenty to thirty dollars. The waitress with the cane didn't know what I was talking about. No Wendigo. No Captain Cook. Jarob wasn't around.

I went upstairs and asked to sign up with the co-op. I told the skeleton I'd like to teach an animism workshop, in which I'd take anyone who signed up into the park to talk to the spirits inhabiting every rock, tree and inanimate object in the world, and divine their secret names and choose one as a spiritual guide.

She nodded sagely, like it wasn't even the dumbest idea she'd heard today. "We could also use help in the gallery," she said.

"How about the pizza kitchen?"

Did her eyes shrink into her face? "You have any culinary training?"

I can make a circle, which puts me way ahead of your crew, I thought. "How bad can you screw up pizza?"

"You'd be surprised." She handed me an application. She was missing two fingers on her left hand.

The application included several pamphlets outlining the co-op's policies on every conceivable sphere of human behavior . . . and a red "Secret Pizza" menu. I thumbed this last open and scanned it, then dropped the other shit on the floor.

"What the fuck is this?" I asked. The Wendigo, a twelve inch pizza with "100% vegan ingredients," cost $112. All the other pizzas cost between ten and sixty dollars.

Those who had the least, she explained, got the most out of the People Place. Because I held down a full-time job, I could afford it, if I really cared about supporting the People Place.

The Captain Cook was crossed out. Since pineapple wasn't authentically Hawaiian, but a colonial product foisted on the locals, they were trying to source locally produced *poi*. The "ha'am," I was assured, was tofu.

Also missing was the slogan: "*From each, according to his meatz, to each, according to his cheeze.*"

I managed to get away without them getting my name. Went out to the car and sat there fuming. Fired off a couple angry texts to Amanda, who was working and didn't reply. Was about to put Ethan on blast, when I had an idea.

A bunch of ideas, actually.

I could send nastygrams to local vegan cuisine message boards and alert the Food Police about the vegan place with the secret sausage pizza. I could whip up a picket sign—RELEASE THE WENDIGO!—and stand around out front until I got satisfaction. Or, I could take them at their word.

I went into my trunk, which I hadn't opened all winter. Out of a trash bag of clothes I meant to donate to Goodwill, I got a moldy flannel shirt, some oily, torn jeans, and a mismatched pair of jogging shoes. Mashing a trucker cap onto my head that proclaimed "TIGHT BUTTS DRIVE ME NUTS", I practiced a convincing stagger before circling the People Place and wandering down the alley.

There was a line halfway down the block.

We stood huddled against the backside of the church to get out of the rain. We avoided each other's eyes. I became invisible once it was established I wasn't holding drugs or cigarettes. I waited, shivering, no longer needing to pretend to feel homeless, until I got to the pass-through window. With my head tilted down so rainwater streamed off the bill of my cap, I asked for a Wendigo, and they gave me one.

It took everything I had not to run giggling up the alley. *Fuck you, hippies! Your secret pizza is mine!* Instead, I managed a more urgent iteration of my improvised wino stagger all the way to the car.

I got inside and opened the lid, half-sure I'd been burned again, half-expecting to find the gray-green remains of the Wobbly that Ethan threw in the street last week.

But I'd earned this, and now I had it. It was hotter, greasier, greater than the first time. I was eating my second slice when I noticed the car was surrounded.

Three scarecrows in tattered ponchos blocked my headlights. Three more flanked my car. One of them knocked forcefully on the window.

I licked my fingers, turned over the ignition and forced the car into gear. One of them threw himself onto the hood. I peeled out and jumped into the traffic lane, then hit the brakes so the guy on the hood slid off. I backed up, honking the horn, and hit the gas so two of them had to jump out of my way.

Veni, vidi vici, vegans!

I considered texting Ethan or just dropping by his house, but the thought of sharing the stingy twelve-inch pie was almost worse than not having it at all. In the end, I pulled over as soon as I knew I wasn't being followed, and I devoured the rest of it. I had planned to save a slice to have Amanda test it at the hospital, but I couldn't help myself. When I skidded into our driveway, I was sucking the last orange droplets of grease out of the napkin.

I was so preoccupied with this pathetic act, that I nearly ran into the catering truck parked in my spot. It was flat primer black with a logo rendered in glossy paint, so I could only read it when the streetlight hit it just so, which was when they were dragging me out of my car.

"SECRET PIE SOCIETY," it said, and beneath that, "Societatis Occulte Etruscum."

The people who carried me into my own home might have been hippies, or homeless, or both. They stank of patchouli, mildew and malnutrition. I couldn't tell how many there were, but enough to suspend all my limbs and carry my weight over the threshold and into the living room, where Amanda sat in her pajamas with her head in her hands, and Ethan and Laurel sat on the couch, while Jarob did something in our kitchen.

The hippies set me down, not ungently, on the couch.

"What the hell is this supposed to be?"

"I guess," my big brother said, "you could call it an intervention."

I thought I knew what he was going to say. *You* think you know what he's going to say. I had no illusions that I'd stumbled on the El Dorado of vegan meat alternatives, or caught these dirty hippies indulging in actual food when nobody was looking.

I knew what I had become. Laurel, with bandages covering her entire hand, knew it too. Ethan actually looked proud of it.

The Algonquin Indians believe that if a brave loses his way in the forest or succumbs to the temptation to eat human flesh, he becomes a wetiko, or wendigo, doomed forever to haunt the wilderness, tormented by the insatiable craving for his former loved ones' sweetmeats.

Maybe it's just some dime novel blood libel bullshit white people made up. I suppose I could look it up. You could look it up, and I'd look foolish. But unless you've tasted the Wendigo too, I guess only one of us knows what the fuck they're talking about.

Europeans have words for us, too. Ghouls. Cannibals. Slurs that brand us as subhuman for one big reason.

They don't want you to know.

Have you ever eaten something that did more than just fill your various cavities, that actually filled the emptiness in your *soul*? People eat to feel full, or they fuel their bodies for high performance or long life, but seldom do they ever get to consume something that feels like a life inside them, that recharges the vital spark that makes us more than meat.

It didn't matter how it happened, now. The genie wasn't going back in the bottle.

I started to bust out my best Charlton Heston, but Ethan cut me off. "It's not what you think," he said. "I brought you with us because I hoped it would help you become a little more grounded, more serious."

"Like you."

He shrugged and sipped his IPA. "I go out with the truck every chance I get. I help make the pizza. I help at the charcuterie . . . "

"Dude," I tried to get him to just say it. "What's on the fucking pizza?"

"Like I said," he winked, "it's 100% vegans."

Jarob hobbled over (sporting my stolen sneaker) and set down a fresh pizza, almost round and generously topped with shavings of what looked and smelled like prosciutto and bubbling mozzarella cheese and dabs of purple poi. "The revised Captain Cook, at your service," he said.

"Think about it," Ethan said, as we ate. "Veganism is a dietary and ethical choice that recognizes it's wrong to eat meat because it's wrong to hurt animals. These people don't even eat honey, because it's wrong to steal from the bees."

"I guess you could call us a splinter faction of the movement," Jarob put in. "If it's given freely, we believe, there's no sin in eating meat. And people every day are waking up to it, to the reality that the only rational act isn't just zero population growth, it's not opting out of the Machine or even shutting it down. The only sane way out is to give in. What more radical act of self-sacrifice could there be, than to feed one's own body to the poor?"

"You never crashed a motorcycle, did you?" I asked him, looking at the peg where my other shoe would have been.

He shook his head. "I did, though. That's how I got started. The lower leg is too tough to eat, and they wouldn't let me keep it. Surgical waste, they called it, and threw it away. But the thigh meat is choice, some of the best cuts. I gave it up last summer. We had a feast."

He ran his fingers over his ribs, then rolled up his shirt to reveal a ghastly tessellated bas-relief whittled into his flesh, and a weird sort of port embedded in his belly.

"I've been vegan for thirty years. Always said my intestines were clean enough to eat off of. Now I know it's true."

I turned it back on Ethan. "But that's not why you're into this shit."

He smiled. "Is it a crime to enjoy making the world a better place?"

I thought about all those people eating in the dank basement parlor with no chairs. I thought of those used pizza boxes and pictured them whittling down their sharp edges and bringing them in to have them baked into a pie for a hungry stranger waiting in a rainy alley. Was this just a phase you grew out of, or did the peer pressure and the mania and the joy of tasting your own flesh carry you through to the final cut?

These thoughts were spinning in my mind as I gorged myself, even as I noticed the drops of blood seeping through Ethan's Melvins T-shirt. Aware of my stare, he smiled and rolled up the shirt to reveal the transparent bandages over the divots gouged out of his prodigious belly.

"Jesus," was all I could say, but I couldn't stop eating. That's probably why they chose that moment to hold me down.

I was forced onto the floor and my pants were yanked down. Ethan held my hands with his knee planted in the small of my back. He leaned into my ear and whispered, "Time to pay the pie maker."

Jarob knelt over me and slapped my buttocks. "Not very marbled at all," he complained, "but we've done more with less."

He prodded my skin with a chisel, then gouged a big shaving off my left ass cheek. I bucked and tried to get free. I screamed into the carpet and bit my lip.

That's what got me through it. The taste of my own blood. That and pondering how I'd close-caption my screams and the sounds of steel on meat. I was like a baby who one day realized the terrifying noises bombarding my crib were really beautiful music. I felt, oddly enough, human. Maybe for the first time.

I passed out before he was done, but they brought me around with smelling salts when my pie was ready. The cheese was donated by ladies on hormone treatments who mostly sell their mother's milk to perverts on the Dark Net. So I can't take credit for all the hard work. If you've never tasted meat from anything that didn't live its miserable life in a pen up to its fetlocks in its own shit, too pumped full of hormones to move or feed itself, you've never tasted meat, so your judgment doesn't mean a fucking thing.

While we were eating me, I was given two choices. I could fuck off and keep my mouth shut, or I could join the co-op.

After Amanda had her third slice, we gave them a third option.

Expand.

Under Amanda's guidance, we grew the harvesting pool from the pitiful list of co-op members to include the bulk of the local population.

In Oregon, unless otherwise stipulated, the law states that everyone is an organ donor. When Amanda harvests soft muscle tissue from the abdomen and upper thigh, she secretes it in a false bottom in the biohazard bag, and brings it to us. We've expanded our truck fleet, too, and begun catering to select upscale clientele in Laurelhurst on a unique basis that should handily overcome its first challenge in the courts. We feed the guilty 1% to themselves, with the proviso that all of our clients leave their bodies not to science, but to us.

And we deliver.

WHEN THE MOON HITS YOUR EYE

JESSICA MCHUGH

"**HELLO. THIS IS MIKEY.** How can Pies-n-Stuff stuff your pie-hole today?"

A girl howls with laughter, then shouts for her friends to quiet down. "Shh! I'm doing it right now!"

"Hello? Can I help you?"

"Sorry! I'd like to place an order for delivery."

"What can I get for you?"

"Four medium pizzas with smoked mozzarella crusts, please."

"And your toppings?"

"One pepperoni, one sausage, one chicken, one bacon. And . . . " The background chatter starts again, followed by nervous giggling.

"And . . . "

She clears her throat and lowers her voice. "We were told you take special requests."

Mikey's mouth goes dry. He pulls out his cell phone, swipes open the Pi Kappa Alpha private chat, and locates the street name Chad sent earlier. Somerset. The old beachfront. "What kind of special request?" he says.

"Like . . . umm . . . "

She must've covered the receiver because Mikey only hears mumbling. After a muffled yelp, another voice jumps on the line. It's deeper and more confident but edged in annoyance.

"Just draw something on our boxes, okay?"

Sweat studs Mikey's upper lip when he hears the code phrase. He doesn't like delivering weed during Pies-n-Stuff shifts, but if these are the girls Chad, Booker, and Eric saw in the liquor store, he doesn't have a choice. No one says "no" to a request from a senior Pike brother during summer rush.

"Your address?"

"7483 Somerset Lane."

Anxiety gums up Mikey's throat and he squeaks dryly, "Got it. I'll be there by 10:30."

"Can you make it 11:00?"

He sounds accommodating when he says, "No problem," but having to wait so long annoys the piss out of him. At least it's the last step. After all the keg-hauling and campus-streaking, the chugging and chanting, Mikey will finally prove himself worthy of the Pike legacy. He'll get everything his dad claimed he wouldn't when he announced he was rushing Pi Kappa Alpha: four years of tuition and frat dues, a paid internship at the firm after graduation, and, most importantly, access to a bank account full of fatherly regard.

After submitting the order, Mikey examines the photos the senior members of Pi Kappa Alpha snapped of the girls who entered Cozy's Corner Mart behind them. He tries to assign voices to faces, but there aren't many to speak of. The guys took most of the pictures from low, covert angles; some too rushed and blurry to be anything but smeared grins and upskirt shots, but their commentaries make up for it. The quartet wears matching black crop tops, leggings, and neon sweatshirts around their waists, and, according to Booker, they strolled the store giggling, dashed in vibrant colors and undeniable—if not slightly annoying—confidence.

The first solo picture depicts a leggy, dark-skinned girl with blue box braids and purple lipstick standing in the whiskey aisle, off-balance, like an invisible chip weighs down her left shoulder. Eric added that when she held the door open for her friends, she twisted her lean body as if trying to crack a "crazy deep kink," but was somehow at the head of the pack by the time the door shut. She strode alongside a bald girl, shoving herself between her friend and Booker when he tried to rub the girl's smooth scalp. Chad dubbed this girl, "The H.B.I.C." "She's the leader," he said. "The den mother, the head bitch in charge. Overprotective as fuck, especially about the bald one."

Imagining a girl with a receding hairline, Mikey tightens his face in revulsion. The actual girl doesn't resemble his mental image, but there's still something off about her. According to Eric, she was on the short side but took impossibly long strides. Each footstep was a leap that stretched her thin physique with little moans. In the blurry picture, her bright makeup and slick scalp accentuate her features to a bizarre, almost extraterrestrial degree.

"She must have Alopecia or something. Her eyebrows looked painted on," Eric commented. "I kinda wanna lick one off while we're fucking and see if she notices."

Mikey can't imagine she wouldn't with all of Eric's suave subtlety.

He rolls his eyes and scrolls to a tan girl with a face full of dark freckles who looks like she's doing yoga in the liquor store. She stands akimbo, neck craned to one side, her hair slicked into a high ponytail that starts dark brown but lightens to pale gray, and her eyes shining so green they don't look real. Mikey might've spent more time captivated by her colors if not for the hot pink thong winking at him from the last girl's photo.

The smiley blonde has a toned Botticelli body—"Curvy but not jiggly," as Chad puts it—and looks like an ivory valentine when she squats in the mixer row. Her face is turned away, but it's a mystery that doesn't need solving when Eric says, "Girls don't show their asses if they have anything else to offer."

Mikey's near cackling until he hits an enlarged photo of the girl's lace-flossed ass and a bright red stamp declaring, "Target Acquired."

His stomach tightens. Not every pledge earns this assignment, especially not freshmen. The guys must've pulled pin to get it for him—maybe because they like him, maybe because of who his dad is. Either way, the favor glazes Mikey in cold sweat and he holds off confirming with the men of Pi Kappa Alpha. Failure isn't an option this time.

He pictures the frat house's "hazement" decorated with dozens of stolen panties. The ones with snapshots cradled in the crotches. The ones marked with initials, indicating a brother had sealed the deal. The wall grossed Mikey out the first time he saw it, but after hearing dozens of acquisition stories, both firsthand and urban legend, he saw the panties as something more. As trophies, sure, but also as the petals of a holy flower from which each brother plucks an ageless honor.

But the honor isn't theirs alone. A membership in Pi Kappa Alpha bleeds into every facet of a brother's existence. Once initiated, an aura of American sovereignty will protect Mikey, improving the caliber of people, business opportunities, and even girls that drift in and out of his life.

Imagining the pink thong tacked beside the nylon panties that bear his father's wobbly monogram, he grins. Whoever wore those high-waisted undies was probably better for letting them go, and the blonde Botticelli would be better for it, too.

Despite his swelling bravado, the pulsing ellipses of his post-in-progress wave like flags of pussification in the group chat. Chad sends, "Nut up," and Eric adds a laughing emoji. After Booker sends a gif of an angry woman with the word "triggered" glittering over her head, Mikey confirms the delivery.

His courage is rewarded by three identical messages: a show of Pike solidarity and a warning to anyone who dares stand in their way.

Mikey types the same two words and mashes the send button. "IT'S ON."

He's the only car rumbling down an oil-black road. This end of town used to be a bustling hub of summer activity, but tourism virtually disappeared after Hurricane Sandy laid waste to the beach and rental properties. Her wrath still scars Somerset Lane, a bevy of beach house skeletons littering the coasts and cliffs of the Eastern shore. The street is barely lit. Even with his high beams on like usual, Mikey has to squint to see the house numbers. Most have lost their sheen, even some digits, but he's still in the early thousands so he turns up the radio. His voice grows louder as he approaches a sparse forest, the stripped and broken trees dispersing into an open field bathed in moonlight. Caterwauling, Mikey tilts back his head and leans on the gas, cradled by a moment of perfect contentment before a shadowy figure darts into the road.

Mikey throws the wheel to the right and hits his brakes, but something smacks his bumper. His bald tires slip and spin him into a fishtail he eventually brings to a skewed stop on the cracked shoulder. Killing the engine, he sits panting, sweating, heart threatening to punch a hole in his breast. He can't will himself to look at the person flailing to the left of his car. Until the person screams his name.

"Goddammit, Mikey! That was my fucking dinner!"

Eric stands like a petulant child, his face red and puffy as he inspects his stained shirt. He holds up the stubby sub wrapper and frowns at the shredded lettuce dangling like a scraggly beard from mustard-soaked paper.

Chad and Booker guffaw from the other side of the road, their diamond earrings glistening under the full moon.

Opening the insulated delivery pouch, he inspects the pizzas. The incident rearranged the toppings, but the pies are otherwise unharmed. He sighs in relief, then seethes at Eric. His nostrils flare as he flies from the car and grips Eric's popped collar, but Chad pries him away.

"What do you think you're doing, scab? Attacking a senior member is cause for lifetime banishment." Chad retrieves the Air Jordan flip-flop he lost in the dash to separate the guys and furrows his white-blonde eyebrows at the pledge.

Mikey clenches his jaw. He would've chewed off his tongue if he could. The men of Pi Kappa Alpha were just playing with him, like he was a friend, like he was a little brother, and he was acting like they were trying to murder him. Mikey's screwing everything up, just like Dad said he would.

He apologizes to his betters, saving Eric for last. "I'm really sorry, man. I owe you a sandwich, okay?"

He gives Mikey a doubtful glare as he sucks a glob of mustard from his shirt. "It was a seventeen-inch hoagie."

"Whatever you want. Just don't do that again. I feel like I'm gonna puke."

Booker scoffs and pokes Mikey's arm. "Don't you even try to pussy out!"

"I'm not. I just didn't know you guys were coming tonight."

The unintentional sexual innuendo settles into the Pikes' hips. As Eric humps air and says, "I fucking hope to," he nearly crashes into Booker's wild thrusting. They shove each other away before grazing bare skin, and Eric falls into a spatter of roadkill ham.

Chad smacks the pledge's back. "You're a cunt hair from brotherhood, dude. No way we'd miss that." Opening the passenger side door, he removes the pizza boxes from the pouch, stacks them on the hood, and uncaps a black marker.

Mikey watches in puzzlement as the senior writes two words on the cardboard canvas, then rearranges the pile, breaking and scattering the letters along the greasy edges. Snapping the marker closed, he crinkles his nose at Mikey and returns the pies to the front seat.

"Nice," Mikey says dryly. "You don't think this is going to be hard enough?"

Chad raises a white-blonde eyebrow in offense. "Did you just say it's gonna be hard to fuck a drunk girl? Shit, son. I thought this was important to you."

"It is!"

Eric is still discovering suckable mustard on his clothes. Picking fuzz off his bottom lip, he grunts. "It better be, cuz this is your last chance, kid."

As the guys from Pi Kappa Alpha pile into Mikey's back seat, Mikey marvels at the tableau in his beater: kings among men squished like sardines under low-hanging polyester, and all because they believe that he, a lowly freshman, can be as cool as them.

One pair of panties.

Mikey's excitement falls heavy on the gas and catapults the brothers down the road with a triumphant howl. One pair of panties, and he'll be set for life.

As he nears #7483 Somerset, he expects the summer home to shine immaculate between pitch black bones, but it's as dim as the rest. It's in better condition than most, but large patches of the exterior are rotted, and there's no car in the drive.

Mikey cocks his head as he parks. "Maybe they stopped somewhere on the way back from the liquor store?"

"Or maybe they're fucking," Eric says.

Mikey rolls his eyes. "They might not even let me in."

Chad snorts, echoed by his cohorts. "Like you'd let that stop you."

Mikey's stomach tightens, but he exhales through the rising nausea and slides out. Slamming his door summons a commotion from the attic, and a flashlight beam pierces the greasy window at the peak. What follows sounds like a herd of elephants scrambling down the stairs, trumpeting in excitement. The guys duck, and Mikey hops onto the porch as the front door flies open and four girls cluster in the entrance.

They've ditched their sweatshirts, now all clad in midnight black like much of the room behind them, but they've clearly been playing with makeup—the Botticelli blonde in particular wearing an excessive amount of glitter pink lipstick.

Mikey proclaims, "The Pies-n-Stuff Special!" with more gusto than any pizza boy in the history of the profession, and most of the girls cheer, but the HBIC steps out of the pack with a dubious squint.

"You're Mikey?"

"That's the name they gave me," he says. "Well, *Michael*, but still." When she crinkles her nose like she's sniffing out his self-doubt, he lifts his chin. "Yeah, I'm Mikey."

"You're early," she says, expressionless.

"Sorry about that. Do you want me to wait in the car?"

The blonde taps her smartwatch and rolls her eyes. "Chill out, ladies. It's only ten minutes."

Fanning her face, the bald chick turns on her heel. "Go ahead. Pay the man."

"It's forty-four for the pies," Mikey chirps.

The freckled girl hands him sixty. "No change. And the other?"

A smile spreads over his face, and he pumps the pizza in his arms. "Mind if I come in? I work out, but these might be the heaviest pies ever made. You girls really like your meat, huh?"

The blonde's smartwatch dings, and she winces at her friends. "Sorry. *Now* it's ten minutes."

He furrows his brow, puzzled. "It won't take long. I just need a place to roll the joints."

"Fine. Come on in," the HBIC says in defeat.

He can't hear the Pikes cheering when he struts into the damp Somerset home, but his phone buzzes with congratulatory texts like high fives to his right ass cheek.

Candles give the house a soft glow that maximizes its lengthy, aching vacancy, especially where warped mahogany floorboards meet large scraps of shaggy carpet so black Mikey feels he could fall right in. Black yoga mats also crisscross the floor, creating jagged paths of shadow that run through the living and dining rooms and into the kitchen.

The girls giggle as he weaves around the mats in a wobbly journey to the dining room table cluttered with alcohol and mixers. He elbows out a clean spot and sets down the pizzas with a sigh. Stepping out of the savory aroma, he finally smells Hurricane Sandy's festering wounds in the wood. A sour stench hangs like a sweaty fog in the house. There's no air-conditioning—no electricity at all, in fact—which doesn't friendly up the scent, but the girls don't appear bothered, nor shy about ravenously diving into the stuffed pizzas. By the time Mikey's seated at the table with his rolling kit spread, they've emptied one box and set it upend against the wall.

"Five joints for fifty," he says. "It's mids, but it'll do the job."

The blonde with pink panties leans over from behind and hands him a fifty. Her tits are an inch from perching on his shoulder like preening birds. One shrug and he could nudge them right out of their tiny nests. But he resists, for now.

His phone buzzes, and he crinkles his nose at the eggplant emoji from Eric.

"Do you have another delivery?" the blonde asks.

"Nah, I'm all yours, sweetheart. It's just my friends." He stops, smirking. "What was your name again?"

The HBIC rolls her eyes as the Botticelli giggles. "It's Lucy. And that's Aleesha." Pointing to the freckled girl, then the bald chick, she adds, "Yolanda and Dee."

"Good to meet you all. Anyway . . . " He licks the paper and rolls up the first joint. "I don't like to deal during shifts, but I gotta take what I can get, you know? I'm not as well off as most of my brothers. I mean, my *dad's* well off, but he's not the most charitable guy." He sprinkles weed on the second paper and starts rolling. "That'll change soon though. I'm gonna break the cycle."

Dee laughs, and Mikey scowls at her.

"What's so funny?"

"Nothing." She splashes rum into her coke and gives it a deliberate swirl. "I just understand wanting to break out of cycles."

He sets down the finished joint and Yolanda nabs it from the table. "Those boys from the liquor store are your frat brothers? They were . . . " She sparks the tip. " . . . interesting."

"I hope you don't mind that they gave us your info," Lucy says. "We really wanted weed for the celebration."

Yolanda passes the joint to Lucy, who tilts her head back to inhale. Closing her eyes, she blows a thin white dart of smoke with a grateful hum, but the serenity of her first hit shatters when something smacks the living room window.

Yolanda yelps, and Lucy sputters smoke, pre-dialing 911 on her smartwatch as Aleesha rushes to the window with her phone blazing. The other women wait on alert, eyes wide and ears perked like coquettish meerkats.

After a few seconds of investigation, Aleesha shrugs. "I don't see anything." Snatching another slice of pizza, she sets the second box beside the first and flops down on the couch.

Just as Mikey's heart slows, his phone buzzes across the table, causing the girls to jump. Chuckling, he apologizes and reads a half dozen taunting texts from the guys, culminating with more eggplant emojis and several tidal waves preceding the message: "Pinky's begging for it."

Dee's stride is just as odd as Eric described. She looks like a ballet dancer crossing the room and stretches her neck as she pauses behind him. "Are you almost done?"

"Yes, sorry. That pizza smells so good, it's kind of distracting."

"Or maybe you could stay off your phone," Aleesha mutters, impatiently checking the time on her own.

Dee spins, walking backward to the couch. "I feel like I'd get sick of pizza if I was trapped in a pizza place all night. Every time I saw a pizza commercial or read about PizzaGate or debated the merits of pineapple as a pizza topping, I'd want to die or kill or . . . " She runs her hand over her sweaty scalp. " . . . do *something* unrefined."

"You're clearly not a true pizza lover." Finishing the joint, Mikey passes it to Dee with a cheeky wink.

She lights it and inhales. "You're right. It's not really my thing."

He chuckles as Yolanda sets the third empty box by the others. "Could've fooled me. What are you girls celebrating anyway?"

Lucy, Yolanda, and Aleesha throw their focus to Dee, who

whispers, "Freedom." Doing a slow push-up on the back of the sofa, she stretches her lean calves as if preparing for a race.

He furrows his brow. "Most people don't celebrate freedom at the *end* of summer, you know."

"Yeah? Well, most people aren't cursed."

He wheezes a laugh, but when Dee's face stiffens, he lowers his head in apology. "I take it you mean . . . " He waves his finger at her bald head. " . . . all that?"

She sneers. "Yes. *All that*."

"You don't look bad, you know."

"Of course she knows," Aleesha says curtly.

"So why don't you finish out the summer?"

Yolanda groans. "No thanks. Three months with these bitches in a house without electricity is more than enough."

"You've been here for three months?!" Mikey sets down the last joint and fans his face as he stands. "Were you conducting a psychological experiment for extra credit?"

Lucy is immediately opposite him, her eyes shrinking to glittering blue slits when she laughs. Grabbing his hand, she tows him to the couch, pushing him down beside Aleesha as she says, "You're funny, Mikey."

"And you're stoned," Aleesha mutters, scooting to the far end.

Lucy groans in exasperation and folds her body over her knees. "Aleesha, could you try *not* being a cunt-rag for one night?"

The HBIC rolls her eyes and sets off to fix another drink while Lucy giggles at Mikey. Touching her toes, she reveals pink lace like the flash of a golden ticket in a Wonka Bar, then tosses a glance over her shoulder. A glittery devil is curled up in the corners of her lips when she purrs.

"Do you wanna see it?"

His stomach swamps itself, and he wipes his clammy palms on his shorts. "See it?"

"The house. Do you wanna see the house?"

He laughs, his heart pounding as he nods. Relief washes over him as she pulls him from the couch. He hadn't expected it to be this easy. Before she turns him to the stairs, he spots Chad's milky face in the living room window. The senior's diabolical rictus quickly drops out of frame, but it's enough to make Mikey's brain whir with confidence.

The guys are watching him. He can do this. Whatever it takes.

Lucy snatches a bottle of vanilla vodka and drags Mikey to the creaky stairs. Her thong swings side to side in a teasing dance he follows gleefully into the sweltering dark, taking swigs whenever she pushes the bottle to his mouth. At the top of the stairs, she grabs a small remote from an end table and clicks on a variety of battery-operated candles scattered down the hall. The dank, sour smell is unbelievably thick on the second floor, but Lucy smiles at him and dangles the liquor bottle like a red cape, and he snarls playfully as he charges at her.

She makes him drink again, and they both smack against the wall as he guzzles. Untucking his shirt, she climbs her hand up his hairless chest and twists his nipple. He shouts, and she collapses into him hungrily, moaning as he glides his hand down her ass and between her thighs. She's already wet, and she groans as he grinds his fingers against the sopping crotch of her leggings.

"Upstairs," she whispers and leads him to the attic door.

They kiss and drink their way up another flight, and though the stench is thick as soup in the stairwell, it vanishes with each lick and pinch. Dropping to her knees, sitting on the soles of her feet, and unzipping his shorts, she's a picture perfect replica of her photo in Cozy's.

Glitter stings Mikey's eyes, but the girl swallows him entire. Shutting his eyes, he ignores his buzzing phone and the girl's beeping smartwatch. The world becomes a wet blur, and Mikey leans into it, oblivious to Lucy closing her fingers on the brass knob behind him.

When the attic door swings open, Lucy spits in disgust, and the pizza boy suddenly plummets into a pit of blood and light.

He hits the floor with a befuddling clang of pain and writhes in the blazing glow beneath the moon-roof. The attic has a thick nickel reek that stings his senses like the litter boxes when Dad's new wife got pregnant and lazy. Pain rockets through his skull as he flips over and grasps a nearby mattress. Pulling himself up, he sees three other mattresses, the bare pillow-tops stained with rusty splotches. Some of the stains are dry like the shocking blood streaking his fingers. Others are shallow swamps of cold jelly on the mattresses, textured with viscera and what looks like human teeth. Surveying the attic, he sees more of them: scabby molars and incisors scattered about the attic, piled in the putrid corners and clustered in sagging mattress divots. When Mikey belches up bile, Lucy snickers from the corner.

She leaves a trail of bloody footprints as she enters the orb of moonlight and removes her crop top. "You must think we're pretty stupid, huh?"

He blinks, puzzled. "What the fuck?"

"Your frat brothers. Your pictures of us. Your plans for us."

He snorts. "Chill out, sweetheart. It's not what you think."

She crinkles her nose and begins wriggling down her leggings. They paint her thighs crimson as they roll into wet rope at her feet. Stepping out demurely, she hooks her thumbs on her thong's waistband—the only section that isn't soaked in menstrual blood—and flashes a coy smile. "Isn't this what you wanted? A pair of dirty underwear for your shitty little rape wall?"

"No!"

"Don't lie. We *heard* you. We *smelled* you. We knew your game the second we walked into that liquor store. Would you like to know ours?" Baring her teeth, she hisses. "We walked in looking for boys like you."

Mikey jerks when glass smashes two floors down, but Lucy stands perfectly still. Even when a door slams and a juddering thud abruptly silences someone's scream, she doesn't move until her smartwatch dings.

Reading the message, she wiggles in excitement and slithers to the pizza boy with an abrupt grin that splits her bottom lip. A wet ruby blossoms on her sparkling smile, and she wipes it across her mouth: a hasty application that coats her chin and teeth as she gazes up at the moon. "It's almost time. She'll be free soon."

He stares at the door, eyeing the distance between freedom and the woman in his path. His muscles flicker as he plots, and Lucy sniffs the air with a devious smirk. Gritting his teeth, he darts for the door, narrowly sidestepping her and closing his sticky fingers on the knob. One glorious moment of relief rushes through him before Lucy grabs his hair and tugs him back so sharply, pain bolts all the way to his toes. Liquor typhoons his gut as she drags him from the door, shoves him down, and climbs on top.

"It's just summer rush," he mewls. "It's just a joke. We weren't going to hurt you."

"No?" She taps her smartwatch, opens a picture message from Aleesha, and holds the screen to Mikey's bloodshot eyes.

The stacked pizza boxes declaring "IT'S ON" consume the frame, but Mikey zeroes in on the background. A diamond sparkles from the camera flash, stealing the normal luster of the white-blond hair spattered with sauce too red to be tomato-based.

"Chad . . . " His whimper grows to a growl. "You stupid bitch, it was just a joke!"

Grabbing his wrists, Lucy forces his arms over his head and pins them to the mattress. "What a coinkydink," she says. "I'm a joker too."

As she squeezes Mikey's wrists, her mouth splits up the sides and ivory fangs rip through her gums, pelting him with slimy molars. Crushing his bones in her fists, blonde fur spikes along her bulging neck, her joints popping and stretching and eyes swelling in her elongating skull. Releasing him, Lucy rears back and claws the thong from her growing bush like soggy tissue. As she looks to the moon, her swollen eyeballs burst, sloughing from their sockets and down her cheeks, and from their greasy graves, yellow sludge gels into solid orbs on either side of her shifting, lupine skull.

When the door slams open, she wheels around and falls to all fours, her malformed snout to the floor. Yolanda and Aleesha stands half-transformed in the doorway, naked, slippery with blood and the hairless human cradled in the latter's arms. Looking down on the pizza boy, Aleesha huffs.

"Jesus Artemis Christ, Luce, how many times have we told you not to play with your food?"

Mikey's arms are screaming meat, his hands folding under him as he tries to crawl away, but he makes it less than a foot before Lucy drags him back to the mattress.

"I didn't even taste him yet," she grumbles through crowded fangs. She punches Mikey in the nose, and he wilts to his side as blood spills down his lips. Licking her paw, her brow bounces in delight. "I've had worse. What about the others?"

Yolanda covers one of the mattresses with a clean blanket, and Aleesha lays Dee on top. "Tasted how they smelled, and I'll be damned if that's gonna be her first real meal in a year. She deserves something fresher."

"We all do," Lucy says. "Three months waiting for alignment hasn't exactly been a picnic."

Dee's piercing scream suddenly shakes the room, and the women collapse to their knees. Lucy's smartwatch chirps seconds before her rippling muscles pop it off her arm. Yolanda snarls and massive fangs push out her molars. Her face shudders and stretches as Aleesha's skeleton cracks and shifts. And Dee, still sitting like a human on the mattress, closes her eyes and whispers in shuddering joy.

"I can feel it. Sisters, the moon is in my blood again."

With a sacred glut of light, the women bleed in menstrual synchrony, and Dee cries out with rapturous release. Her spine rolls unnaturally, her chest broadens, and her head snaps to the moon. Scarlet dots appear on her face, and blood blooms from her pores, spilling down her cheeks like oil, but when flashing silver fur follows, her cry becomes a blissful howl. As her body judders and snaps and the other wolves watch in panting pride, Mikey scrambles to the attic door.

His hands slip on the knob, and Lucy turns when he pulls it open. She lunges after, but Dee stops her with a growl. Emerald eyes blossom in the empty sockets of her wolfish skull as she strides past her sisters to the landing.

Glaring at the pizza boy rushing down the stairs, she spits out an incisor.

"Let him run. After all that pizza, I could use the exercise."

ROSEMARY AND TIME

CRAIG WALLWORK

IMAGINE THE WORST sunburn you've ever had. Now multiply that by ten. The skin feels cool to begin with. Ice cold. But really it's burning. The first layer, the epidermis, the one that gives our skin colour—that dissolves away in seconds. If you stop screaming, you can hear it sizzle. The next layer down contains hair follicles and sweat glands. Once they go, you'll never need to shave again. You can run five miles and never break a sweat. This is just the beginning. There is more pain to come. All you can do is think of something else. Distraction. Memories.

My first job was for a local spinster. Her neighbour sold weed and parked his VW outside her window, the only one that overlooked the hillside where she had scattered her husband's ashes. He played music as loud as he fucked women. Back then, I was a student studying astrophysics at King's College. So long as I agreed to do a few chores around the place, the spinster was willing to rent out her basement for half the price of campus lodging. The price of my real job was never discussed.

But I never charged the spinster. Truth be told, I wanted that drug-dealing son of a bitch dead, too. It's not easy processing the laws of physics to the beat of a headboard. You can't take in the principles of the Special Theory of Relativity when all you can smell through the air vents is weed. There was an old joke in college that went along the lines of, never trust an atom because they make up everything. After I ended up strangling that guy to death in his own bed, I figured you can't trust arseholes either, especially those that say they're going to keep their music down.

So how does a college student with a bright future get into killing? Well, I never gave blood. Never donated to charity. I guess this was my way of giving back. The way I see it, if an apple is bad in one place, you don't discard the whole apple. You extract the rotten bit. That's what I do with people; I remove those that are bad, leaving behind what is good. It also helped pay my tuition.

The old woman told her friends. She never mentioned me by name. Said she knew a guy who could make people disappear. She referred to me as the Magician. Every now and then she would bake a cake, bring it down to the basement and tell me about a woman from her bowling club whose ex was bleeding her dry. Other times it was some guy who wanted his boss to take a dirt nap. We'd eat lemon drizzle and discuss names, addresses, schedules.

"If they wanted to speak to you, how can they get in touch?" she asked. "There's a lot of business for a guy with your talent. You'd make a killing."

I don't think the pun was intended, but it made me smile.

You can't advertise what I do in the classified section of a newspaper. You don't make up flyers. There are no websites or Twitter accounts. You go old school. I got the idea while watching reruns of *The Equalizer*:

Got a problem? Odds against you? Call the Equalizer. 212-555-4200.

"Tell them to put an ad in the classified section," I told her. "Tell them to begin with: Magician Wanted."

Sometimes it's a genuine request. I call the number they provide, and some mother on the other end asks me what tricks are suitable for a nine-year-old, or if I can really pull a rabbit out of a hat. Most of the time, though, the people I ring, they speak quietly and in short sentences. They always sound tired, like this is the end of a long journey. They always ask, "Is it true you can make people disappear?" I sure can, though I never bring them back.

The average tuition cost per annum is over 10k. Combine this with average cost of living, and you're looking at trying to find in

ROSEMARY AND TIME

excess of 22k per year to study astrophysics. Add another 5k because it was King's College, London. So while everyone else was racking up loans or working part time pulling pints for city folk, I was pulling a trigger.

Fast forward six years and I'm reading an ad that says: *Magician Wanted for one-off event. Need to be skilled as audience is unforgiving. If interested, ring Rosemary.*

Rosemary wasn't like my usual clientele. She didn't sound lonely, drunk, or desperate. Listening to her voice, I estimated her to be in her mid-twenties. She spoke confidently, as if arranging a catering order or car to be fixed.

Her opening line: "You're not a real magician, are you?"

"No."

"Good." She cleared her throat. "At precisely 3:00 p.m. tomorrow, you will attend unit 456 on the Corona industrial estate. Tell the security at the gatehouse you're visiting lot number 350. The door will be locked. You can open it using a key code. The number is 060617. Repeat that back."

"Tomorrow. Corona. Lot number 350. 3:00 p.m. Key code 060617."

"Once inside, you'll find a man. Kill him."

This was the first time I'd ever heard a customer use that word. They use puns like the spinster, or they generally substitute kill or murder with more polite euphemisms, such as *remove* or *subtract*. Conversations with my clients sometimes sounds like two people working out long division.

She continued, "A payment of 5,000 pounds will be in a bag, which I'll leave outside the main door once I know the job has been done."

"I prefer to be paid in advance."

"Once he's dead, you'll get the money."

"That's not how I work."

There was a pause before she added, "How do I know you will do the job?"

"I'm not into ripping people off. That's bad for business."

"Same here. But if you kill this man, they'll be more work for you. Lots more."

"And why should I trust you?"

"Because you're not stupid."

That was all she said. And for whatever reason, I was convinced.

Corona Industrial Estate was a good 20 miles from my home. I set off two hours in advance to make sure I got there on time. In this line of work, you end up travelling light, just like a photon. You skip lunch because you never know how a person is going to react once a gun is pressed against their head. Most cry, beg, or plead. And sometimes they actually shit themselves. It's not good for business coughing up your guts at the crime scene.

Corona was a wasteland of brick-built units ranging from 10 sq ft to 100 sq ft. 24-hour security. Smoke alarms. Key codes. This place was cheaper and more effective than a prison. I pulled the car on a side street a good mile down the road from the estate. Walked the rest of way. If asked, the security guard at the gatehouse would remember a brown dense beard, a tattoo of a dragon on my left hand, turtle shell glasses. None of these things were real, but they add for a richer description if later interviewed by the police.

Lot 350 was at the north end of the estate, as far to the perimeter fence as possible without being on the motorway. There were no windows, just a steel door. Electronic bolts withdrew when I entered the pin number into the key pad. Inside, white breezeblock walls made the room look like an isolation cell in a psychiatric ward. A table and two chairs were positioned in the centre of the room, stacks of plain boxes piled up beside the door, one of which had been upturned spilling out gauze and various medical supplies across a linoleum floor that hadn't been cleaned in years. In the corner of the room was a bed, wrought iron, sheets stained black in patches. Probably blood. The air was charged with the scent of herbs and bread baking in a small oven, and for a moment I was reminded of my mother's cooking back when I was just a small boy. The buzz from a lonely refrigerator almost drowned out the flushing of a toilet from behind a small door on the opposite of the room.

I raised my gun head-height as a raw-boned man entered, back arched like a shrimp, hair touching his shoulders the colour of morning piss. Shadows clung like leeches to his face. He scuttled over to the makeshift kitchen area and opened the door to the oven.

"Won't be long now," he announced, maybe to me, maybe to himself.

The contents of a saucepan bubbled and hissed on the stove. He stirred it with a wooden spoon then ambled to the table. Lowering himself carefully to the chair, he finally acknowledged my presence and motioned me over with his hand.

"Come, please. Join me."

Keeping the gun aimed at him, I approached the table slowly. He raised his head, as if getting the measure of me, and as he did I saw a face so disfigured I thought he was wearing a mask. There were no eyebrows to articulate emotion, leaving him unreadable. His eyes appeared dipped in raw albumen, the cartilage of his nose eroded away. Two holes sat above lips so receded they exhibited neglected teeth the colour of coal and wax.

I pulled out the chair and sat, my hand resting on the gun.

"She found you then?" he asked. "Rosemary."

Strip away a person's lips and they gain a lisp.

"You're hungry," he said, the chair legs shrieking as he withdrew from the table.

The man walked back to the oven, placed on a pair of oven mitts and pulled out a tray.

"I made pizza."

The landscape of pale, smooth dough matched the man's complexion perfectly. He retrieved a saucepan and poured the tomato sauce, releasing more aromas into the air. Then he took a moment to admire the pizza, as one might their own reflection in a mirror.

"That smell . . . What is it?" I asked. "Parsley, sage?"

"It's my own recipe."

"I'm not hungry," I replied, and in protest my stomach gurgled louder than the refrigerator.

"You must eat." He sat down again. "How else is this all going to work?"

"How's what going to work?"

The man hesitated, "You're the Magician, right?"

I nodded.

"Did she say the money would be waiting for you outside the door?"

The man reached over to a wooden ruler and began measuring the pizza's base. He placed the ruler above the dough, angled it one way, before changing his mind. He pressed the edge into the deep crust, forced it down until it cut through to the tray beneath, then repeated the process until the pizza was divided into four sections.

"Well, she lied to you."

The man pointed the ruler over my shoulder. "There's no door handle on this side."

I turned to check. He was right. I scanned the room looking for a way out, but this wasn't the type of place you're meant to leave.

I raised the gun. "How do I get out of here?"

"You eat."

"I told you, I'm not hungry."

The man got up, fetched a plate and placed it in front of me. He removed one quarter of the pizza and put it on the plate.

"One year to the day, I came here to kill a man I knew nothing about. Like you, I was told the money would be waiting for me outside when the job was done. I was more cautious than you, and I wedged the door open. I found the room pretty much as you see it now. Only instead of a man, I found a girl strapped to that bed. She had been beaten, tortured. I untied the straps, but I guess she thought I was going to hurt her. She was scared. There was a jar beside the bed."

He touched the pale skin on his face, like a blind man reading Braille.

"She was just trying to protect herself," he said.

"You've been here for a year?"

"Feels longer. But time is an illusion, isn't it? It can slow down or speed up depending on the observer. A person falls off a ladder and time slows, but to the person watching, it's normal speed. For anyone trapped in a room like this, a year can feel like five."

"You know about Einstein's Theory of Special Relativity?"

"You clearly do," he said.

I was well-versed in such theories. With a life that had taken so many strange turns, and a chosen profession that altered the future of so many others, my fascination with paradoxes increased with every job.

"What do you know about me?" I asked.

The man gazed at the pizza slice, clouded eyes lost in deep contemplation. "Everything."

"The stuff that was in the jar, it did that to your face?"

He nodded.

"You didn't go to the hospital?"

"I managed the pain with morphine injections." He gestured to a stack of boxes near the door. "The burns were protected with gauze, and when I gained my strength, I found food supplies in the boxes too. Mostly tinned goods. Enough to live on for a year, maybe longer if I rationed."

I looked around trying to understand how a person could survive here for so long without human contact.

"What is this place?"

"An experiment." He lifted a small journal from beneath the table and added, "I found this behind the refrigerator."

"What is it?"

"A way out."

Spreading the pages, he turned the journal toward me. Tiny cursive writing filled the pages.

"It is the account of one man who believed that time is not linear but instead looped. The closer one travels forward, the closer they are to the past. He likened it to travelling forward in an aeroplane; to the passenger it would appear they are travelling in a straight line, but as we know, the earth is curved. The passenger doesn't perceive the change and continues forward in a linear path until they eventually curve around the earth and end up at the original point of departure. It is the same with time. When we die, we reach our birth, and so things repeat. Toward the end of the account, the man scribed a recipe for pizza that would permit a person to accelerate so far into the future that they will eventually end up repeating their life again, and, if done correctly, they could arrive at any point in their past."

I laughed.

"I appreciate the illogicality, but as you can see, there are very few options once that door closes."

He had a point.

"And how exactly does this work?"

"The recipe given puts the person in a catatonic state so that time progresses, but they remain preserved. Frozen. The calculations given in the journal suggest that eating this full pizza will put you back in time one year from the present day."

"The day you arrived?"

The man nodded.

"By going to that point of time, you can stop me from entering this room. You can call the police and tell them about the girl. I won't believe you, but you'll convince me."

"Why have you never tried it yourself? Make the pizza, go back and stop yourself from entering the room?"

"You know as well as I that brings with it issues. For one, there would be another version of me on that timeline. The present me would speak to the version of me from one year ago, and from that point on, the younger me would grow knowing that I will eventually go back in time. That I'm not aware of this means it hasn't happened."

"If I go back, they'll be another version of me, too."

"I thought about that."

The man pushed the journal. Opened the pages and pointed to the recipe.

"See." He tapped the page with a long nail. "It's been signed."

I leaned in and read the scribble: *Magician.*

"This is your journal. You left this for me to find."

Just like that old pocket watch from the Christopher Reeve movie, I thought. His character is given the watch by a mysterious old lady. He gives that same watch to the old lady's younger self, which prompts her to give it to him, resulting in the watch having no origin. They called this the Bootstrap Paradox. It was all bollocks of course, and a terrible movie. But I enjoyed pondering such things.

I raised my gun. "You expect me to believe this shit?"

"I expect you to trust in what you know."

I smiled. "I do. That's why I know it's not possible. None of this."

"How can you be so sure?" the man asked, his voice wavering for the first time.

"To prove if time travel did exist, Stephen Hawking created an invitation for any potential time travellers, asking them to attend a party. Only he didn't publicise it until *after* the event day. The theory being, all future time travellers would go back and attend the party."

"The point?"

"The point is that no one showed up, which proved time travel was bullshit, just like you."

I dispatched a bullet. Hit him straight between the eyes. Blood sprayed the back wall, and his head snapped back, mouth agape. I placed the gun on the table and spent the rest of the evening looking for a way out. I struck the door, shouted for help. Fired a couple of shots, leaving dimples in the steel. I figured the security guards had to patrol this place. It was just a matter of time before they heard me.

When you're in a room with no windows, your stomach lets you know when it's getting dark. Like the man before me, I found tinned tomatoes in a few boxes. Flour and yeast in another. It'd take an hour or so to make bread. I looked over to the table and saw the cold pizza. I lifted it to the light, smelt the sauce. It seemed fine. I ate the first slice and let it settle. No choking. No tightness in my chest or throat. I ate the second slice, the third, then finished the fourth shortly after. I then lay on the bed. Darkness came like the hand of a lover, fingers pressing my eyelids closed.

I woke to a woman's face. Oval eyes the colour of onyx, tanned skin, hair pulled back. I tried to get up and felt resistance around my wrist and feet. The bedsprings pressed into my back like fists.

"Do you believe in time travel?" the woman asked. I recognised her voice. Rosemary.

"Part of me did, until I came here." My throat, sandpaper.

"Really?"

"For a moment, you may have had me convinced. Disfiguring the man was a good idea."

She smiled and sweat gathered across my palms. "And what changed?"

"I've studied paradoxes too long to accept any answers could lie in a fucking pizza."

Resignation shadowed her face. She pulled out of view. I glanced toward the table. The man was gone. The blood was cleaned up. Then the woman returned.

"What is this place?"

"A hobby."

Her hand came into view. In it was a jar containing clear liquid.

"You'll find gauze in the boxes, morphine and solutions. There's enough to last until the wounds heal. Exactly one year from today, you'll be visited by a man. I will write to you explaining all I know about him. You'll need to convince him that to escape the room he'll need to eat the pizza. If you do, I'll let you go free. If you don't, well, you already know your fate."

Her hand titled the jar, the contents pouring over my face. Imagine the worst sunburn you've ever had. Now multiply it times forever.

They called me the Magician, but I never once said "Abracadabra," nor did I ever take a bow. I made people vanish and never return. And now my punishment for those deaths is to disappear with them, except my fate was to return; one year to the day. As a young man, I always believed my future would be written in the stars, but now I know it's in the scars that will forever mark my face.

LAST REQUEST

ROB HART

CYNTHIA MARKS HAD dreamt her entire life of seeing New York City. She wasn't worried about the sharp edges that made out-of-towners afraid to wear jewelry on the subway. The bad old days were long since gone, and she knew that. Her New York was Audrey Hepburn staring into the gem-filled window at Tiffany's, still wearing her dress from the night before. It was Ross and Rachel, playing out their will-they-or-won't-they romance around the comfortably worn couch at Central Perk. It was Billy Crystal's rambling profession of love to Meg Ryan at a New Year's Eve party, surrounded by the buzz of perfectly oblivious revelers.

It was a place where magical things happened, and there always seemed to be lights strung up somewhere in the background, twinkling like the stars you couldn't actually see in the night sky.

That's what it was supposed to be.

Instead, Cynthia found herself dodging greasy paper plates blown about by the wind, inching forward on a filthy Brooklyn sidewalk, toward a pizza take-out window carved into the side of a brick building. She gazed at the red metal picnic tables, packed with people tearing into thick, square slices of pizza. She didn't know pizza came in squares slices.

She wished she were sitting. With the way the sun was hammering down, her stiff gray uniform clung to her skin, sweat acting like glue.

Cynthia could have packed a change of clothes, a pair of shorts and a blouse to wriggle into after the plane touched down. But even if she could have gotten the clothes out of the house without Doug noticing, what would have been the point? This entire trip, beginning to end, should last no more than nine hours.

Get off a plane, catch a cab, get the pizza, catch a cab, get on a plane.

Who was there to impress?

Not that a little part of her didn't hold onto a wistful fantasy: that she'd meet a handsome man along the way.

Maybe waiting for a cab outside the airport. A man in a suit with windswept hair would make a clever comment, and she's come back with a witty retort, and by some mystical turn of events they'd wind up in a place where 'maybe' wasn't just a wish. But no, there was just a line of harried travelers, screaming into phones, choking on exhaust fumes that hung heavy in the humid air.

Maybe the cab driver would be a dark-haired rogue looking for someone to keep him company on the late shift, and they'd eat in a late-night diner where he'd regale her with wild tales from the job. "Only in New York" type stuff. But no, her driver was a hunched Eastern European man who reeked of sizzling meat.

The pizza line was her last hope.

But no, she found herself stuck. Between the Mexican family behind her, and, in front of her, a man wearing a worn tank top, stained yellow with age. Although he didn't look capable of it, he smelled like he ran a marathon to get there.

Nothing about any of this trip was magical.

And for the hundredth time since the airport when her morning began, she wondered what the hell she was doing this for. She settled on the same answer, even if she wasn't sure it was the right one: that everyone, no matter what sin they've committed, deserved a little dignity in death.

She looked up at the sign, stuck atop a black pole at the corner of the lot, looming over the line. Red cursive on white background.

M&C Spumoni.

What the hell is *spumoni*, she wondered.

The joke was, Cynthia was chosen for her strawberry-blonde hair.

"He only kills brunettes," Cap had said.

Like it was supposed to be encouraging.

The truth was, budget cuts and staff reductions meant the administration had to think creatively. They realized they could move Cynthia's desk from her office in the main wing over to death row, and they wouldn't have to pay someone else to sit there all day.

"If anything happens," Cap said, "just call a real guard."

The day she arrived, she put down small potted cactus, and her little faux-crystal Statue of Liberty—a souvenir from a friend who had spent a week in New York and needed someone to feed her cat. Sometimes Cynthia stared at it, wondering how the real thing would compare.

Her desk was at one end of a long, dreary hallway. Along the left wall, which was water-stain mint green, there were barred windows that looked out onto the activity yard. On the right was a line of five cells, and at the end was a blank wall with a small, off-center crucifix.

The day Cynthia moved in, only one of the cells was occupied.

The one holding the Southpaw Killer.

Cynthia stood at her desk for a long time, working up the courage to walk down to the end of the row and back, which she was told to do once every hour. She'd interacted with prisoners before. But never one she heard of before she laid eyes on him.

She took some time to adjust the plant and the statue so they were perfectly framing the boxy gray monitor. She logged onto her computer and checked her e-mail. She took a deep breath and got up and walked. As she got closer to the third cell, the one that was occupied, she drifted toward the wall with the windows, away from the bars.

The man was in his beige uniform pants, no shirt, his muscled torso catching the light and casting shadows that made him look he belonged on the cover of a romance novel, an unexpected thought that immediately turned her stomach. He was sitting on the slab bolted into the wall that served as his bed, reading *Pride & Prejudice*. On one side of the slab was a toilet with a sink built into the top. On the other side was a showerhead sticking out of the wall like an afterthought.

He wouldn't leave the cell until it was time to die. No physical activity in the yard, even. As Cap would say, dead men and nearly dead men had just about the same amount of rights.

The man looked up and put down the book. His smile was sharp, showing off teeth like an anatomical drawing. But his eyes were soft. He had a thin beard, black and dashed with salt to match his hair. Cynthia didn't know what she was expecting, but she didn't expect what she got.

He nodded. "I must have finally done something good to get a guard pretty as you."

Something hot flashed in the middle of Cynthia, but she paved it over with fear and revulsion.

"I'm not here to chat," she said, continuing on her way, toward the end of the row, past the last two empty cells. She stopped at the crucifix, turned, and headed back the other way, not-looking at the prisoner.

"I didn't do it, you know," he said.

"They all say that," Cynthia responded.

As she neared her desk, he called, "I'm James."

She paused, wanting to say her name back, like a reflex. Instead, she sat down and gazed at the tiny Statue of Liberty, its torch barely touching the bottom of her computer monitor.

There were twelve known victims, spread across three states, though authorities speculate there might have been more. All of them were college-aged, doe-eyed, brunette. When the local paper ran all their pictures together on the main page, they looked like sisters.

Each one was found missing her left hand.

Cynthia turned blue hyperlinks purple, scrolling back and forth through Google, reading article after article on the case as the computer choked and chugged like an old car.

James Winston was arrested based on a description provided by two young boys. They said they saw a man burying a body along a creek. Winston was a drifter, claimed to be passing through town, and besides the two boys, there was no evidence tying him to any of the crimes. No DNA, no proof he was actually at the place where those two kids said they saw him.

Or saw someone matching his description.

The jury deliberated for two days.

Cynthia wasn't an expert in anything, but looking at the scant evidence, she wondered how they could have wrapped up that quickly.

Meanwhile, the district attorney, the police chief, and a local state senator were all up for re-election that summer. And all three of them were running ads claiming they'd captured the Southpaw Killer and sentenced him to death.

The front door slammed open. Cynthia closed out all the windows on the computer, her finger slipping on the mouse, her heart racing.

Doug stomped into the kitchen, reeking of blood and raw pork. No matter how hard he scrubbed in the locker room showers, the smell of death always followed him home from the plant. It was one of the only things they had in common.

He stood in the middle of the kitchen, waiting. His brown eyes sunken, his thinning hair disheveled. Cynthia kissed him on the cheek, lips scraping against stubble, and she tried not to gag at the stink.

"Dinner?" he asked.

"We're overdrawn," she said.

"Well, what about a line of credit at the grocery store? I heard they do that sometimes. Those bastards can't just let good people starve, can they?"

Cynthia twitched a little at 'good people.'

"They put interest on it," she said. "We're going to wind up paying so much more. I know it's not ideal . . . "

"Dammit, Cyn," Doug said, smacking the flat of his fist into the fridge. An overdue bill tacked up with a magnet depicting the New York skyline came loose and tumbled to the floor. "What the hell are we supposed to eat?"

"We got some pasta, and I can dip into the pantry," she said. "Were you . . . were you able to bring home anything from work?"

Doug held up his hands, gesturing to the empty space around him. "Do you see me carrying anything?"

"Well, no . . . "

"So I should bring the food home with me? Should I cook it, too?

Do you want me to do everything? I work twelve-hour days just to keep the goddamn lights on. What more do you want from me?"

Cynthia nearly told him.

She nearly said that he ought to stop handing so much of their income to the bar around the corner. Or to the machine at the grocery store that sold lotto tickets.

Instead, she opened up the fridge, a beam of yellow light dividing them. She pulled out a can of beer and cracked it and offered it to him. "Just go on into the living room and put your feet up. I'll make something. It'll be good, promise. Tomorrow I'll see about that line of credit."

He ripped the beer from her hand, white suds erupting from the top, splashing her arm. He stalked off, but the smell of death remained.

Cynthia pressed both hands to her mouth and fought to keep from crying.

Hours later, after they had eaten pasta with jarred sauce and watched some television, Doug passed out on his recliner, the living room scattered with beer cans like corpses. Cynthia retreated to the back porch with a glass of wine and the copy of *Pride & Prejudice* she got from the library.

"I hate Jane Austen," James said, putting aside the car magazine he'd been reading.

"Seems like an odd choice then." She'd quite enjoyed it.

"Well, Cynthia, it's not like I have a whole lot of options."

Cynthia watched James, legs curled up onto the slab bed. A killer of woman, and yet she couldn't get past those kind eyes. The sadness that permeated the space between them.

"What would you like to read?" she asked. "I can see if we have it."

James smiled and swung his legs around so he was sitting, facing her. It was the closest he'd gotten in all the times she'd passed by, because he always seemed to be curled up on that bed whenever she got close.

"What's your favorite book?" he asked.

"I don't have a whole lot of time for reading lately," she said.

"C'mon," he said, smiling. Showing his teeth. "Everyone has a favorite. Just name something."

"I really liked *The Stranger*," she said. "Albert Camus. I read it in college."

James nodded, resolute. "Then that's what I'd like to read. I've never read it."

"We don't have that one in the library," she said. "It's about a man condemned to death. Someone probably decided that's not good for inmates."

James rested his elbows on his knees. "I wouldn't want you to get in any kind of trouble. I'm just saying, if a copy were to find its way into this cell, I would be sure to hide it nice and good."

Cynthia turned and headed back for her desk. "You're not worth my job."

"I didn't think so," James said, the words echoing in the empty hallway behind her like a taunt.

Cynthia ran down the hallway, cursing Doug. He'd taken the car and hadn't filled up the tank, and she'd had to stop at the gas station. Now she'd be the last one to the briefing room.

There were ten guards to a shift and nine seats. It's not that she minded standing. She was more worried that Williams was working today, and that he'd have gotten that final seat.

Cynthia rounded the corner into the room and her heart sank.

All the seats were filled.

"Hey Marks," Williams said to her, smirking, spilling out his chair and pointing to the wide expanse of his lap. Something about the light in this room made his bald spot shine so much brighter, his pale skin so much more waxy. "Plenty of room right here. Pay no mind to my nightstick if it pops up, okay?"

Cap shook his head. "Williams. One more time, I'm writing you up."

Cynthia was keeping count. It was the seventeenth time Cap made that exact same threat. And Williams responded the same way he always did.

"All in good fun," he said, looking at Cap. Then he shot a look at Cynthia. A shadow passed over his face and his voice grew stern. "Right?"

"Yes, sir," Cynthia nodded to Williams and then Cap. "All in good fun."

"Exactly right," said Williams. "You just have to know how to laugh. Marks knows how to laugh."

Cynthia forced a smile. "Good one," she said.

Williams nodded, looking around the room to make sure everyone realized his joke had gotten the sign-off.

Then Cap launched into his daily spiel, and Cynthia was already far off, planning out the route that would take her through the infirmary and up two flights of stairs to the death row cells. Where instead of being catcalled, she would hear something nice from a nice-looking man in a cage. She reached back and patted her rear, double-checking she had that copy of *The Stranger* tucked into her pocket.

"Do you know the origin of the last meal request for death row inmates?"

Cynthia looked up and down the narrow hall. The walk back to her desk was taking longer every time she did it.

She stepped a tiny bit closer to the cell, peering into the dim space. James was standing underneath the showerhead, leaning against the wall. Like he'd been waiting for her.

"Tell me," Cynthia said.

"It was a superstitious act," James said. "By accepting food, the prisoner was making peace with the jury and the executioner. This was so the person didn't come back as a revenant."

"What's a revenant?"

"A ghost."

Cynthia smiled. "Why not just say 'ghost'?"

"It makes me sound smarter."

A small laugh shot out of Cynthia, like air whistling from a balloon. She closed her mouth quickly and took a step back.

"Do you know what I would request for my last meal?" James asked.

"You're not going to get it, so what does it matter?"

"But aren't you curious?"

"No," Cynthia said, lying.

"C'mon." James curled up the right side of his mouth. "Smart girl like you. You're curious. You like knowing things. You're just waiting for an opportunity to use the word 'revenant' in conversation. Tell me I'm wrong."

The hallway was still empty. The crucifix on one end, her desk on the other.

"What would you order?" Cynthia asked.

"A slice of pizza from M&C in Brooklyn. Down in Bensonhurst."

Cynthia took a half-step forward. She looked down at her boots on the scuffed concrete floor, up at James again. Wondering if she looked demure. Wondering if she should be trying to look demure.

"You can get pizza everywhere," she said. "What makes that place special?"

"Well," Jason said. "You can get pizza anywhere, but you can only get good pizza in New York. Some people say it's the dough. Other people say it's the water. Like the mineral content. I think it's the place. Place matters just as much as anything. Do you know what alchemy is?"

"It's the combination of different elements into a new element," she said. "Like magic."

He nodded. "Like magic. What the hell are you doing working in a place like this, smart girl like you?"

The way he said 'smart girl' made her smile.

She didn't hide her face. She let him see it, allowed the moment to hang.

"What's so great about this pizza?" she asked.

"It's just . . . perfect. I can't explain it. If you ate it you would understand. You never look at a slice of pizza from around here the same way again."

Off in the distance, Cynthia heard a metal clank. A door opening and closing. One of the guards on rotation. She turned and walked back toward her desk.

"It's not fair, you know," James called after her. "What they're doing here is inhuman."

Cap had been holding a stack of papers in his hand. When Cynthia was done with her practiced monologue, he whipped it down onto the desk with a crack.

"Are you kidding me with this?" he asked.

"I know it's . . . " Cynthia started.

"No, you don't know."

He heaved himself down into the beaten black roller chair. Except for the chair, everything else in the office was white. The fluorescent light. His starched uniform shirt and bushy hair. The stacks of papers that framed him and the painted brick walls surrounding them.

Cap looked up, his eye twitching, a sign that he was really and truly annoyed. More so than his general state of agitation. He stared at Cynthia in a way that made her feel like she was shrinking.

"Cap, look . . . " she said.

"You know the governor just shut this program down. All requests have to be fulfilled by family, or come from within five square miles of the prison. If I file this, they're not going to just ignore it. They're going to take it like we don't respect them. I'm going to get a phone call."

"The only thing within five square miles of here is an Arby's."

"Then he's got to eat Arby's," Cap said, leaning back, looking up at the ceiling. "That new Angus steak sandwich they got ain't too bad."

Cynthia went diving for words. Something that would win him over. A cogent argument that would get him to see the light. Instead, all she saw was light disappearing as she sank deeper and deeper, drowning.

"Why do you even need to do this?" he asked, his face twisting into a sneer.

"Because it's kind."

"After what that son of a bitch did. All those girls."

She meant to say it with confidence but it came out like a peep: "Allegedly."

Cap slammed his hand against the desk. It was an intimidation tactic, and it worked. Cynthia jumped, then cursed herself for it.

"He was convicted by a jury of his peers," Cap said. "I'm sorry but we're no longer fulfilling unreasonable demands of murderers and rapists. I'm sorry this offends your delicate sensibilities."

"It's not about that."

Cap sighed, leaning back again. Looking at the ceiling again.

"Do you remember that one guy, wanted that sandwich from the place in Atlantic City?" he asked. "One sandwich. The state had to pick up airfare and overtime and travel expenses. Do you remember that? Probably never been a sandwich that expensive. For a guy who murdered his wife and two children because he didn't want to have to go through the trouble of a divorce. That's actually what he said when they caught him. I remember that. I'm going to remember that for the rest of my life. That he did that hateful thing, and then we had to spend thousands of dollars to get him a goddamn sandwich. And then he didn't even eat it."

Cynthia took a deep breath, exhaled slowly.

"I know women are hard-wired for sympathy, but this is ridiculous," Cap said.

His face was hard as steel. There was nothing she could say that was going to change his mind and she knew that. So she went for the last resort.

"I have vacation time due to me," she said.

Cap just frowned and shook his head. For once, he was at a loss for words.

Cynthia tried not to think too hard about how that made her feel.

"You can't use a microwave," said James. He was standing within arm's reach of the bars. "Do you have a toaster oven? Like in the break room?"

"We do." Cynthia, too, was an arm's reach from the bars, on the other side.

"Heat up the slices on the 'toast' setting, but carefully. Watch it close. As soon as you start to smell it, pull it out. You don't want to go through all of this and burn them."

Cynthia nodded. "Should I get any kind of topping?"

James laughed. "M&C doesn't need toppings. And . . . I need to ask you one other favor. And this one is important."

He looked around and took a tentative step forward. Cynthia stayed where she was, even though she wanted to walk toward him, but then he would be within reach of her, and she wasn't ready for that yet. She was saving that for when she got back.

"I want you to get two," he said. "And I want you to join me. I want you to have your first M&C slice, and I want to see your reaction when you eat it. It's not as good as fresh, but it heats up pretty damn well."

Cynthia smiled. "Why is that important to you?"

James shrugged, suddenly taking on the gait and manner of a little boy. "Because I want to see how that pretty face lights up."

Cynthia's cheeks caught fire.

"Deal," she said.

"Good," James said.

"Now boarding all zones. All zones may board now."

Cynthia held her ticket in a tight, sweaty fist. She was in the last zone, nearly maxing out the credit card Doug didn't know about to get there. She watched the stream of people dragging suitcases and bags onto the plane. Bleary-eyed, frowning, some of them still even wearing pajamas. Outside the floor-to-ceiling windows, the sun was just peeking over the horizon.

She stood there for a long time, watching the line dwindle. Wondering what it would take to get a refund at this point. Whether that was even possible.

She poked around the Internet the night before but couldn't find a good resource for how many people were exonerated *after* they were executed. Municipal governments didn't want to spend money collecting data on things like that. But there were examples of it happening. Evidence or a witness or a new technology that proved a dead man's innocence too late.

For the death penalty to be just, it had to operate under a standard of absolutes.

And clearly, it didn't.

But what if she was wrong? Cynthia couldn't know, *truly* know, if James was being honest. But she wanted to believe him. She wanted to believe that someone with eyes that kind couldn't do something so bad. She wanted to believe that people were good.

She wanted to believe this, in spite of the fact that when Doug found out she spent money on this, he would likely hit her. That her co-workers would lose even that last tiny bit of respect they had for her. That Cap would give her that look again, like a parent who's failed a child.

And for what? James would be dead in the ground, that pizza not even fully digested.

A young Asian woman in a smart navy blazer looked at Cynthia clutching her ticket, the last person standing in front of the gaping door leading to the airplane.

She asked, "Ma'am? Are you ready?"

The jagged skyline of New York City jutted into the air. She got dizzy trying to count the buildings. Cynthia watched it recede, replaced by long stretches of suburbia, until they were up through the clouds and all she could see was blue sky and a carpet of white.

She tried to watch the television nested in the seat in front of her, settling on a show about two families renovating their homes in a competition to see who can renovate their home better. The pizza sat in an insulated lunch bag on her lap. Her only carry-on.

She watched the color and light that flashed on the screen and tried to imagine what was going to happen when she got there.

She and James would eat their pizza. James would die the next day. She would go home to Doug because she was unable to escape the gravity of their crumbling bungalow thousands of miles below. She would come into work and stare at the tiny Statue of Liberty and dream of seeing it up close.

Her stomach felt like an empty pit.

Her first trip to New York, and all those things she wanted to do—ride the Staten Island Ferry, see the Empire State Building, catch a Broadway show, and the statue—right there at her fingertips. The opportunities disappeared behind her.

And in that moment, she made herself a promise. She would go back.

Once she saw this through, she would leave. Doug, the job, everything. She was strong enough to do this. She was proving she was strong enough by doing this.

Cynthia had flown to New York City for a slice of pizza. She could do anything.

She put her hand on the bag, warm and comforting in her lap, and she smiled.

"Hey, is that pizza?"

Williams lumbered into the break room and cut a line over to the nook with the toaster oven. He peeked in, his shoulder pressing against Cynthia. She shrank away from him.

"Is that square slice?" he asked. "I didn't know you could get square slices around here."

Cynthia nudged him aside and pulled the two slices out, scorching her fingertips as she dragged them onto a thick stack of paper plates. They were thick and doughy, with the mozzarella underneath the sauce. There was a snowfield of Parmesan cheese on top, and the edges were slightly blackened.

Williams reached out a meaty hand. "Let me get one of those."

Cynthia held the plate close to her body and twisted away. "No."

"C'mon, you have two. You could stand to watch your figure a little . . ."

Cynthia felt the rush of every joke, every comment, every leering glance, and now, coupled with the invasion into her space, something brittle and worn inside her finally snapped. She put the plate down on the counter, out of his reach, and threw an elbow into his gut.

He took a few steps back as he doubled over, face red, gasping for breath. The shock of it froze Cynthia in place, and then the mandatory twelve hours a year of personal defense training took over. She put her entire body into pushing him back.

For a second, she thought he wasn't going to budge. It was like pushing a fridge. And then he tipped and crashed into the haphazard arrangement of chairs, going down with enough force that she swore she felt the floor rattle.

He cried out, yelling something at her as he deflated, but she wasn't listening. She left the kitchen, cutting a path through the infirmary and up two flights of stairs to death row. Delicately balancing the paper plate that held the two slices of pizza.

She stopped at her desk. Wondered how she looked. She wished she had time to stop in the bathroom, maybe put on a little foundation or some mascara, but Williams was surely reporting her to Cap once he got back to his feet. Someone was going to be looking for her.

But when they did come for her, she'd hand over her gear and walk right out. She wouldn't even go home. She'd get another plane ticket. She'd figure out how to pay for it. Go back to New York. No more Doug. No more prison. She'd go and stand on a corner with one arm raised high, until something magic happened, or until a taxi stopped to pick her up. Whichever came first.

When she reached James's cell, he was sitting on his bed, legs drawn up, reading *The Stranger*. He looked at her, and his eyes went wide. He put the book aside, stood, took a few steps forward. Even with the bars in the way, Cynthia felt vulnerable but open. His voice was quiet, filled with awe. "I can't believe you actually did it."

She held up the plate with the two slices, square as the prison cells around them, but much warmer.

"Like you asked," she said.

He stepped forward until he was at the bars, pressing his forehead against them so he could get a good look at what she'd brought. His eyes went glassy, bordering on the verge of crying. "I can remember my first M&C slice with my dad. And now this is the last." He took a deep breath, got lost in the maze of a memory. Finally he looked up at Cynthia, a tear cutting a path from his eye and disappearing into his beard. "Do you know what that feels like, to know that?"

Cynthia didn't, but she teared up, because the emotion was so thick it was rolling off James like steam and filling her up, too.

She took a step closer to where he could just barely reach her. The closest they had ever been. She wished she could open the cell, sit with him. Not touch, not that, but just sit next to him on that slab.

Feel the warmth and weight of him next to her as they shared his final meal.

"I'm not an idiot," Cynthia said. "I just want to thank . . . "

"I did it."

It was like a punch to the chest, the air getting pushed from her lungs.

She tried to breathe and found that she'd forgotten how.

"What?" she asked.

"I need to be honest," James said, tears streaming down his face. "I feel like I owe you that. I did it. I killed those girls. I need to say it out loud. But I think you knew that. And it speaks to your character that even someone as damned as I am, that you would do a thing like this. But I'd probably do it again."

He reached his hand though the bars, nearly brushing the paper plate.

Then he reached for her.

Cynthia took a big step back.

Those soft green eyes suddenly didn't look so soft anymore. That smile looked so much more sinister. She thought of those girls. The sour taste of bile tickling the back of her tongue.

She let one of the slices fall.

It tumbled in the air until it splat, top side down, on the filthy concrete floor.

James fell to his knees, reaching for it, his mouth hanging open.

She wanted to rage at him. To open the cell and beat him to death. She wanted to inject the pentobarbital herself. She wanted to scream and cry. She wanted the world to open up and swallow her. She wanted a time machine to bring her back to that moment she stood at her desk and wondered what kindness was worth.

She couldn't do any of those things. So instead, Cynthia picked up the other slice and took a bite.

She fought to swallow it, her throat thick and hot. James's face twisted, like someone was dragging a knife across his gut.

She stepped back, coming to a stop against the far wall, and she slid down it until she was sitting. She kept eating, holding eye contact with James as he wailed like an animal, thrashing on the floor, arm stretched through the bars, trying to reach it with the desperation of a drowning man reaching for a life preserver.

The ruined slice just a few inches from his fingertips.

As the metal door at the far end of the hall groaned open, Cynthia took the last bite of her slice. She put the plate down and wiped her mouth and locked eyes with James, who had stopped struggling. He was sobbing, his arm still stretched out.

"You were right," she said. "You were right."

UPPER CRUST

MICHAEL PAUL GONZALEZ

BACK IN COLLEGE, I ran in some good circles. Not the best. I always wanted to be in the best. *Now*, I'm in the—I was looking for a fraternity, because you know it's *who* you know that gets you ahead in the world. I wanted to know the important people. Only the best. My father, when he sent me off to Wharton, he told me, I don't give a shit what you learn or what your grades are. I care who you meet. *That's* where the important lessons are. Know *who* to know, and *what* you know becomes second place.

One night, I'm at a rush party for Delta Kappa Epsilon. Lot of good people in that—Gerald Ford, the Bush Family, you see where I'm going—but this is obviously before any of them were president. I'm at this party looking at a goddamn oil painting of my great grandfather, he pledged so many years—but even legacies have to earn their spot. Out of nowhere, I feel something slide into my pocket. I look down, and there's this hand—silk glove, red silk, sexy as hell and—good party when someone's reaching into your pants before you've finished your first drink, right?

I turn, and there's this woman behind me, just *painted* into this silk dress. Everything red. Hugging every—I mean everything, the curves and her nipples—she just smiles at me, extends her hand, and says, "Ursula Dupree." Just like that. So I kiss her hand, and she flicks a finger toward my pocket, turns, and walks away.

In my pocket there's a little engraved business card. Gold. Sharp as a razor. Still got it here somewhere. You can see the stains from our meal on the—we'll get to that.

TANNER STEED—YOU ARE CALLED
SEPTEMBER 14, 1964
10PM
FULCRUM
ANWEALD · FEOH · WEALDAN
FOLLOW YOUR GAZELLE

Gazelles! That's what they called them . . . anyway. And you've seen the Fulcrum logo on my desk. That's usually covered by the first dollar I ever "made," nobody gets to see—but I have to show it to you tonight. And you've seen it, so now you have to—my father sent me there to meet people. Fucking is meeting, right? You don't pass up opportunities.

So, I followed her to this big ballroom, and everyone's eating dinner. We sit, she says, "Don't eat, you'll be eating later tonight," and she slides a finger up her thigh and gives this little shudder, and I'm—well, you get the idea. But she eats! Seven courses. Clam chowder, oysters Rockefeller, escargot, poi and sashimi, mustard potatoes, lamb with mint sauce and jelly, and a pineapple upside-down cake for dessert. I remember all seven, it comes back later. I'm just supposed to watch her eat? But the way she did it was—she could do things with that mouth, and—so we're talking, small talk, and then the last course comes, the waiter sets this little silver dish down, lifts the lid, and nothing's there.

Ursula stands up, and I swear, I don't know how they cut this dress, but it slides open across her thighs, and there, eye level, *pow*, her pussy, right in my face. Just a long enough flash that I can see how neatly trimmed, and she says, "Dinner was delightful. Are you ready for dessert?"

You're thinking what I'm thinking, right? She walks away. Up this spiral staircase in the corner of the room. There's these two guys standing right at the top of the stairs, like big stone—these were, one of them was probably Samoan, I mean huge—and the guy just looks at me and says, "Card." Just, *card*.

And the other guy has his hand out, gentle on my shoulder, but like a granite—so I give them the card, right? I pull it out from on top of my money clip. Back then I was like you, stupid, thinking that power came with showing wealth—anyway, showed them the little card she gave me, and they melt. Big, soft teddy bears. They step aside, backs to the wall, but like I said, big guys, so I still have to squeeze between, and then this door slides open a few feet away.

Maybe she's a prostitute, right? That's what I'm thinking, these were her body guards, they saw the money, they thought I—anyway, I step inside, thinking it's a bedroom, but it's an elevator. The door closes. She's not there. Small elevator. Red lights. And I can't even feel it moving, I'm just waiting for five minutes to move and—the doors open, and I'm on another floor. Basement. Way down. Didn't know it at the time.

I step into this waiting room. Two benches, one along each wall, look like they were from a museum. Like they'd been there since the 1700s, and that's because *they were*. Immaculate condition because people only sat on them once every four years. That's how lucky I was to—anyway, one wall, four ladies sitting. Four silk dresses. Red, purple, blue, and green. Other wall. Three guys. Not even college guys like me. One of them was my age, the other two were older and—they don't matter.

I stood by them. Here's a little secret. If everyone's sitting, you stand. If everyone's standing, you sit.

The walls are covered, floor to ceiling in these small oil paintings, little two-foot-tall portraits of men, great men. Didn't know it at the time. That's another secret—most of the truly powerful men, you never know their names, because there are positions. Roles. Some people are behind the scenes, some people, like me, are destined for the stage. So. We're just looking at these ladies, and they're not talking, just sitting there looking as hot as—and then these two big double doors open.

And the ladies stand, and this is where it gets good. This guy, this little butler, comes out wheeling a cart. On top of the cart, four leather collars, each attached to a chain. Without a word, the ladies stand up, unzip their dresses, and slide them off. You've never seen anything like—I mean, they all had underwear on, same color scheme, red—I guess Ursula had just put them on—and blue, green, purple, somehow that was even sexier than if they'd been naked—each one puts on a collar, walks over to us, hands us the leash. The butler gestures us through the big doors.

Inside, there's a—I'm not supposed to talk about the room, but you're going to see it soon enough, so I'm not really spoiling anything—like a courtroom fucked a brothel. Best way I can—there's a big, tall judge's stand. Big podium, three chairs way up high. On one side, a jury box. Sits twelve people. On the other wall, nothing. Well, almost nothing. Two little iron loops that I didn't notice when we—I'll get to that.

In the middle of the room, where the lawyers would normally go—a small table, like we're here to play poker. I don't know what the hell's going on, I just know I have Ursula's hot blonde ass on a chain. I'm up for anything. The butler claps, and the ladies lead us to a chair. High-backed, satin cushions, and the cushions match our ladies' clothes. My chair's red, guy next to me is blue, the—you get it. You understand. The ladies pull out the chairs, we sit, and they stand just behind us.

The butler claps again and says, "Judges." Two more doors open. Twelve guys in robes file into the jury booth. Then the butler rings this little bell. And it gets quiet. A door opens behind the podium, three men walk in, and they have full hoods on. Can't see their faces. They sit up high. The Triumvirate. You'd know their names. You've read about them in history books. They have done great things—that's a history you only get to learn if you pass tonight.

They sit, and I figure this is it, we're being hazed into the fraternity, right? Couldn't be more wrong. The Triumvirate, as one, they raise gavels and tap three times. The one in the middle says, "Dinner is served."

The butler leaves and comes back, with—get this—a pizza. A fuckin' pizza margherita. The most boring—cheese, tomato slices, some marinara. Smelled good, but I mean, *this* is what you dragged us down to—and nobody else reaches for a piece, so I don't either. I don't know where this is going.

"Gentlemen," the butler says. "This is the gathering of the Fulcrum. You've been carefully selected to begin the process of advancement to an echelon of society known to your fathers and their fathers. Every four years, we open our chambers around the world so that men can prove themselves worthy of joining the ranks of the Fulcrum. Is the Triumvirate prepared?"

The guys behind the podium gavel in turn. They go in order, left to right, saying Secundus, Primus, Tertius.

And Primus bangs his—god I wish I was allowed to tell you his name, you'd die, you wouldn't believe—anyway, he bangs the thing and gives us this speech.

"We are the playwrights of society. We control the stagecraft of the world. This is not an honor, it is the highest achievement a man can strive for. In the Fulcrum, there are no individuals. Behind these doors, we are many. In the world, we are one. If one of us succeeds, it is shared victory. If one of us is slighted, we are all wounded. This is your opportunity to join us. *Sacrifice* is a word greatly misunderstood. *Power* is a word greatly misused. *Fortune* is a word whose meaning few people truly grasp. Tonight, you will sacrifice. You will understand what is required to obtain fortune. With fortune comes power, responsibility, money, and no need to sacrifice again. To show your willingness to move to the next phase, you must break bread together. *La Festa dei Burattinai.* Will you take a bite of the food before you to show you are willing?"

That's all they wanted? I check the competition. They each grab a slice. Me? I do it big time. Slide a knife under a piece, guide it up to my plate with my fork. Cut a slice, the right size, not too big. I pick the guy across the table, the first to grab a slice. Unbroken eye contact while I chew. I look at the next guy, same thing, keep chewing until he looks away. I swallowed before I had a chance to look at the third guy, but he got the idea. It wasn't the best pizza I've ever—and then, after one bite, the butler whisks it all away and another guy brings in a different pizza. This one has sausage. Hot peppers. Like really hot, the ghost kind, we don't know from—and then the Primus says, "The world presents resistance. Can you push through hesitation, work through discomfort, withstand the heat of the forge?"

This time, maybe they're on to me, they're really testing my resolve, because all the cutlery goes away. I have to pick up the slice with my bare hands like these other chimps. We take a bite, and it's hot, really fuckin'—I mean, we need water, and we're laughing at this point, because we can see this coming. Spicy food, gross food, whatever, we're pledging, getting hazed. Same drill again, one bite, butler goes out, new guy comes in with a new pizza. This one is covered in black crickets and live earthworms.

"The world is rife with poor, simple creatures. The mechanisms of society are infested. You must consume them. Their bodies exist to nourish and sustain you."

And here, of course—I mean, fried crickets, yeah, that's disgusting, but live worms? But then again, it's fraternity life, right? So one of us, not me, I'm not ashamed to admit, goes first, big bite, and then we all dive in. Not as disgusting as I thought. Tastes like dirt. Cold and soft, though. Like a dead lady's lips. I figure once they stopped squirming it would be—but they never really stopped. I could feel them moving in my stomach for—probably a lesson in there somewhere.

"People are the salt of the earth. Though it may turn your stomach to mingle with them, you can, and must. Farm them, nourish them, consume them." Right as the Primus says this, the butler's back in with another pizza, plain tomato and cheese. Big slices. And behind him, another guy's pushing a cart with small cardboard boxes.

We hear this scratching. Pecking. *Peeping*. Our ladies open the boxes and pull out these fuzzy chicks. Little baby chickens. Without a hitch, they take the chicks, and *krick-krick-krick-krick*, break their tiny legs. They set them on a slice, and these little birds are . . . not fluttering, vibrating. The wings are moving so fast and their eyes squint from the pain and—and the primus says, "Sacrifices will always need to be made. Vermin and pets alike. You consume them all, those you revile and those you adore. Increase their suffering or end it, but the suffering is not the matter. Our nourishment is. The door awaits."

We stare at each other. Hazing is one thing, but this was . . . and Ursula leans down and whispers—and I can still feel her juicy lips brushing my ear when I think of this, gives me goosebumps—she says, "Do it. For me." I don't know what the other ladies were saying, and I didn't care, because this time I was first. If only one of us was going to win this game, it had to be me. I rolled the little bird up in the pizza slice, cradled it with the head pointing at my mouth, because I figure, you break the neck and then—and it was a clean bite, I have strong jaws thank god, and it was . . . it didn't taste like I thought. Crunched like . . . and the beak just felt like an unpopped popcorn kernel, if it was stuck in a cottonball soaked in blood, and . . . I saw the other guys going for it too. And the butler, thank god, tells us, "You may spit."

The ladies give us a chalice, and we spit out the mess, and just stare at each other. It was the act, not the eating, you understand? Ursula gestured to me. I had this little piece of gristle and a tiny feather stuck to my lip.

The Primus says, "The game begins. Woman. The ultimate tool of resistance and persuasion. Her fortitude is incomparable. Her service to you is irreplaceable. Her greed will push you to greatness. Her guile will bring down those who would seek to hurt you. Uncontrolled, her fury will consume you. Choose your tools wisely."

The butler brings out the next pizza. A plain ham and cheese. Each woman rotates to the next man at the table. Now I've got blue next to me. They plant their hands on the table and snort. I mean, big, phlegmy . . . and they start spitting on the pizza. Just greaser after greaser. Big, green shiny . . . coating the whole thing. Then they fold their arms and stare at us.

After the birds, this seemed like nothing to me, so I grabbed a slice and took a bite. I mean, I had plans to bury my tongue in Ursula's asshole, what's a little spit? We all take a bite. The women rotate again. They put our slices on the floor. The butler gives them sneakers. Each one announces where they walked from to get there. "I took the train from Shitburgh to blah blah blah," you get the idea. They made it clear, these shoes had been through spook neighborhoods, or immigrant shitholes, whatever piss-stained, dog-shit-encrusted sidewalk you could think of. And they stood on the slice. Really smeared their foot in there. Then, without lifting the shoe up, they took it off, carefully slid a hand underneath, flip it, and served the piece to us, like the shoe was a plate.

This one made me hesitate. You know me and germs. Eventually the other guys ate, so I had to.

The Primus says, "Four courses: The women will weed out the weak. They will serve until two remain. This will comprise the end of the second chapter. If all four pledges remain, the women are deemed to have failed. Fortune does not accept failure."

A new pizza comes in. Cheese only, nothing else.

The Primus says, "Sauce."

And two of the ladies squat over it and piss all over the—soaked it—and this was where things got weird.

The Primus says, "Toppings."

You know how sick a woman can—the lady in blue says, "I'm menstruating." Drew out the word like it's supposed to scare us. Reaches into her underwear and pulls out this fat, brown piece of cotton.

The butler comes over with a silver tray and she sets it down, gets out a scalpel, and carefully cuts it into little pepperoni slices, putting them on the pizza. She says, "Who wants a fresh one?"

I figured if I got it while it was still warm, I could—and you know, it tasted—have you ever had a bloody nose? Sort of like that. I meant the cotton was . . . it wasn't easy to chew. But thank god, the butler clapped again and we were allowed to spit that into the chalice too. So far, we're all in.

Ursula though, what a bitch, brings out this small plastic box with a picture of her dog on it. And she says, "This is Mopsie. She's a purebred Pomeranian." I hated that dog, by the way, so glad when it died. Little worm-infested—always chewed up my—anyway, she opens the box. "Mopsie eats only the finest cuts of meat and pure vegetables. Mopsie made this for all of you."

She takes tongs and sets down one perfect little roll of Mopsie shit on each piece and stares at us. Like little tootsie rolls with rice noodles embedded in—dead worms, you see? And win or lose, eating this means a trip to the doctor's office. You can't succeed without eating a little shit. That's what my father always told me.

It was too much for the guy across from me. He pushes the plate away. The first failure. He starts to curse the Triumvirate, ask them what the hell they thought they were doing, if they knew who he was, who his father was, and in come the Samoans, you know, dragged him out and things got quiet.

The Tertius stands at the podium, and points a finger at the guy's lady. She's dressed in the blue, right? And he says, "NAME?" nice and loud, and I swear I saw a little squirt of piss shoot down her leg. And she says, "Savannah".

"Expendable."

The Samoans are back. One grabs her arms, handcuffs her. The other puts this ball gag in her mouth, and then they chain her neck to the iron loop on the empty wall. Put a big spotlight on her.

"That's a sight," I say. Got the Primus to smile at that. Always try to make friends. Read the room.

"Three remain," the Primus says. "Crimson has proven her breeding. One woman can be a worthy ally and a fierce adversary. A group of women can be insurmountable. Where Crimson leads, the others will follow. Present the next challenge."

And I'm thinking, wow, I got the good one, right? She won, she gets to go again. And the other two women look nervous. Like maybe they're all playing a game too, and Ursula's on the brink of winning their end or something?

"Dinner tonight was splendid," Ursula says. "Seven delicious courses." The butler brings out another pizza, this one just bread. Nothing else on it. But it's deep dish style, right? It looks like a giant bread bowl almost. Our women move back to us and sit in our laps. And even with everything we'd been through, feeling that ass in those silky panties on my—anyway, they sit.

"Our compliments to the chef," Ursula says, and she sticks two fingers down her throat, and everything she ate earlier that night comes back. Chowder, some pineapple cake chunks, the oysters Rockefeller, escargot—whole fuckin' snails, the poi thing, man, the smell of that, and sauce, wine, she stops and pumps her stomach again—like a cat with a hairball— I mean this was Chicago-Style. Just *gallons* sloshing and—I'm just feeling her ass clench every time she retches and watching her ribs expand and lurch as she pours it all out. And it was almost sexy. Almost. I think she's done, but no! The potatoes, more wine, the lamb with mint sauce and jelly like green chunky toothpaste, and all of it's in this perfect cone on the pizza, and then to top it off—how did she do—a perfectly whole pineapple ring from the cake. Like she saved it just, *bam* on top.

And the smell?

The Primus looked at me and said, "You shall begin. The next man to eat may allow his woman to add to the feast. The game continues."

Ursula looks at me, just . . . the other women, they're all over their guys, right? Rubbing thighs, shoulders, nuzzling their ears—I mean, they all got a shot of mouthwash first, but—they look like they're pleading for their lives. Not Ursula. She's got this gaze of steel, just looks at me and says "Do this. You will do this now." Her eyes are wet and wild, like she's somewhere between crying and orgasm, her crotch is like a dripping furnace sitting there on my thigh, and she's just *animal* and I dove in. I can't explain it, and I know she looks a little tough now after all the surgeries, and who cares, you don't worry how the car you sold twenty years ago looks now—I mean, back then, she was *something*. I don't know how to— and I mean, it's just food. That's all I thought. It's all just food.

I swallowed. Tried not to chew. Terrible. It was like chili. The bile made it taste like old sausage—but the other two guys, it took them another five minutes to even start. I thought I won, for the longest time, I thought, this is it, Steed, you win. But then another guy, the guy across from me, chows through a bite. So his woman gets to puke on the pizza too, and now it's down to the third man. That's all they ever wanted us to do, right, just a bite. That's the big thing. The hesitation. They want you to get over the—but the last guy, he couldn't do it. He went to push the plate away, got some of puke on his fingers, and then *he* puked, everywhere. Bam, in come the Samoans, *boom* out he goes.

"NAME," the Secundus, this time, stands up. And the woman, this is the lady in purple, she says, "Posey." And she looks so sad, like a pale little flower. That was the first time I felt sad that night. She's crying right, because same thing, here comes the Samoans, the handcuffs, then they force a piece of puke pizza into *her* mouth, then the ballgag, and *bam,* chained to the wall.

"The game continues," the Primus says. "When your competitor falls, it is up to you to utilize his assets."

I don't know why it was worse to know a man's puke was part of this soup now, but Ursula did this thing with her palm, like cupping my—you know—and instant, I mean *instant*, like Viagra has nothing on—and so I took a bite. Unbroken eye contact until I swallowed. And the other guy whispered, called me an asshole, and he took a bite too.

It's just me and him. Eyes watering, trying not to lose it. Ursula in red. His woman in green.

The Primus smiles. "Blood and money are the finalists. Names?"

"Ursula," Ursula says.

"Amalie," the lady in green says. Pretty name, I'd never heard it before. Usually you hear AHM-uhlee, but she was AM-alee. Cute girl. Great ass.

"Tanner Steed," I said, offering the other guy my hand. I guess I can tell you, it was Colton Northcutt. Remember him, ran for president a few years ago? Anyway, he goes to shake, and I did this thing, you know my trick, pump twice, and pull them in. Got his whole forearm in that puke pizza. He knew who was in control. You have to break them.

The Primus says, "Loyalty and Ambition will provide *il corso principale.*"

The big guys come in, real careful, and take that table out. Didn't spill a drop out of that puke-soup pie. They bring in a new table. White marble, unfinished. That's when I noticed the walls for the first time. Same white marble. Like big tiles, all with these abstract color designs on them. Reds and browns. A year inscribed at the bottom of each one. Little plaque with a name—a woman's name, I would later learn. You see where this is—Ursula in red and Amalie in green sit at the table, staring at each other. The butler sets two empty wine glasses next to a new empty pizza. New pizza, new table. Thin crust. No toppings. No plates. Not even a pan under the pie.

"The gentlemen will pour," the Primus says.

The butler hands us these knives, like little syringes. Or funnels. Like big tubes of . . . and we couldn't figure out what to do with them, but the Samoans come back, and they unchain the two ladies from the wall. Savannah and Posey. Bend them over the table, yank back on their hair, their necks are just hovering above the wine glasses. They're panting through those ballgags, just frothing and moaning and crying. And the veins on their necks jump up and, just coated in sweat, and you know they're in their little underwear, and this whole thing is kind of sexy until the one Samoan holding Savannah looks at me and his eyes go to the weird knife-funnel thing, and he says, "Sir, will you pour?"

He tapped a finger on the vein in her neck.

I looked at Colton across the table. Looked at Amalie and Ursula, but they only had their eyes on each other. I push the needle into the side of Savannah's neck and—have you ever popped champagne on New Year's? You know? Just . . . everywhere! Sprayed everywhere! Everything's red, Ursula and Amalie in their little underwear, just soaked and the Samoan is kind of helping me, right, guiding my hand, keeping the funnel pressed in so that I fill up one wine glass with Savannah.

And Colton, in for a penny, in for a pound. They didn't—and see, this is the thing with power, they didn't even have to explain to us exactly what we were playing for here, it just made sense—so Colton pops Posey's neck, and she—maybe she's dehydrated, she's not a squirter like the other one, and she pours out, one glass, and the Samoans grab the ladies by the nape of the neck, haul them out of the room, like meat. Empty boxes. I thought they were taking them out back to ditch the bodies, but—can you believe it—I actually saw Posey at a function a few years later. She couldn't really look me in the eye. Fucks like a rabbit though, little—anyway—they're gone, right? Now, it's the big deal. Colton and I toast each other and take a sip.

The Triumvirate stands. The butler announces, "The game will conclude!"

The jury stands, and shit, I'd forgotten they were there this whole time. The judges have their hoods off. And they all start saying their names, full names, names you'd know! Cereal companies, newspaper barons, cattlemen, oil magnates, you name it. Fortune. They said their name followed by a woman's name. Not the women they married. Not a woman I'd ever heard of. You'll see in a minute.

"Appetizers have finished. Each woman has hidden a gold ring. The game concludes when an entrée is prepared and served and the ring is found," The Primus says. God I wish I was allowed to tell you his name, it's gonna blow your—anyway.

The butler lays a sword on the table. A real, god-damned ancient . . . I mean not like a big broad—just like a little curved—an Egyptian dagger thing. I'm standing on one side of the table, Colton's on the other. Ursula to my left. Amalie to my right. The big Samoans are holding them with a short leash. All of this in an eyeblink, mind you, I see their stomachs, bare skin, I see the veins in their necks, smell the sweat, and I just get it. Dinner. It's my job to serve.

So I go to grab the sword, and Colton realizes it too, but I'm faster. All he can do is watch. I swing for the fences, just *hi-yah!* right into Amalie's midsection. Cut it wide open in one—like a piñata! But instead of a bunch of little spic kids running around grabbing candy, it's just me and Colton watching Amalie *literally* spill her guts onto the table. And the Samoans help. White glove service. They're just delicately guiding her large intestine out onto the blank pizza pie, piling it like spaghetti, and it's just—you can see what she ate *moving* in there, right? Even after the puking! Still so much food left. Pulsing and squeezing, and they just keep feeding organs out. Liver, kidney, spleen, stomach and this is a *mess* I tell you.

"The ring is presented!" the Tertius shouts. "Claim your prize."

And the ring—they said she hid one, remember? Way down in her intestine, I see this hard little outline, kind of round on one side, flat on the top. She swallowed it this little film canister thing, see? The ring has the seal of—well, you see it here on my finger. I can't tell when Amalie died. Maybe it was fast. Probably. I mean, her head was rolling back and forth, mouth open, eyes like glass. You get disemboweled, you can't really scream. It was like bad opera. Embarassing. That was the—I can't describe it. I saw her soul leave, and whatever was left was staring at me, and all I thought—and I said this out loud—was, *I deserve this.*

"Will you serve?" the Primus asked.

I took the sword and cut a piece of pizza. I don't know when they led Colton out of the room, but it's just me at the table with Ursula, chewing this other woman's guts. Ursula had to eat too. They all ate. All of the jury, the Triumvirate, they all came down and took a bite, like this is the best buffet they've ever—And they're all applauding us, and Ursula's crying like Miss Fucking America, covered in blood, and shit, and filth, and she takes my hand, and I'm—I mean normally I'd tell them to take this bitch out and give her a bath, but this was a *moment*, you understand?

I took her hand, and I looked her in the eye, and I kissed her. And I swear if the challenge would have gone further, I would have sat her bare ass in that pile of guts on that pizza and fucked her, right there, that's how happy I was. Because I understood everything.

But it didn't come to that. I don't want you to think I *actually*— Anyway. That was my dinner that night. That was my entrée into fortune. The *Festa dei Burattinai*. These days, they make fun of me in the press for eating bland food. Steak and ketchup. Simple things. They have people working at restaurants. They test you. They slip in little pieces of things sometimes. And if you're eating fancy food, you might miss it. I want the flavor to stand out. The sacred organs. Liver. Kidney. Hearts. Guts. It reminds me who I am and what I'm capable of. The flavor of life.

You have to meet the right people. And you have to eat a little shit. I told you it takes guts. Didn't say whose. Your job, your only job tonight, is to come back here with my daughter on your arm. Full, and happy, and content. Fortune favors the bold.

A BLOODY HAND TO SHAKE

BRIAN EVENSON

T WAS HARD for him to know how the fight had begun. Turner certainly didn't think he'd been the one to start it, even if he'd been the one, inadvertently, to end it. To end Raster, rather. But that hadn't been his fault either: he simply had the bottle in his hand, sloshing, half-full, and when Raster, snarling, came at him, he swung, forgetting the bottle was there. Really it was Raster's fault. If he hadn't dodged the blow, Turner would have hit his face with his knuckles instead. And if he'd had the sense to back off after that first punch, Turner wouldn't have struck him with the now suddenly jagged end. But no one had ever accused Raster of having, or making, any sense.

By the time it was over, Raster was lying on the floor, blood slowly pooling around his head. As soon as the fight started, Raster's dealer grabbed all the gear and cleared out, and his girlfriend fled after him. In the aftermath, Turner was still too gone to take in all of what had happened. He prodded Raster with a shoe and the body wobbled a little. No sign of life. No chance the man was alive. Too much blood, and Raster was lying face down in it, breathing it in.

I should be panicked, Turner thought, collapsing onto the couch. But even while telling himself this, he still felt extraordinarily calm. Perhaps this was one of the drug's effects. What had the drug been exactly? He didn't remember, or maybe he had never been told. Raster's dealer had been trying to explain something about it to them, about its unpleasant side effects, stumbling his way through—

the man obviously hadn't tried the drug himself so it was all hearsay—until Raster finally said, *Fuck it, I'll just see for myself.*

He tied off and shot up. Turner was right behind him.

So maybe Raster wasn't to blame after all? Maybe it had been the fault of neither of them, but of the drug.

At some point, Turner fell asleep or nodded out, hard to say which. Once he came back, he started calculating how many pieces he would have to cut Turner into and whether there were enough suitcases in the house to smuggle those pieces of him out of the house in one trip. Then Turner thought, *Wait, I'm Turner.* His wasn't the body that needed to be sectioned up: Raster's was. His eyes idly wandered until they settled on the back of Raster's head. *Thank God it's a wood floor*, he thought. If it had been carpet, he would have had to tear it out. He didn't have time for that, and he couldn't afford it. Getting the blood out of the wood grain before anybody showed up would be hard enough.

Would Raster's dealer say anything? No, probably not. He wouldn't want anybody scrutinizing him. It would be bad for business. Besides, he and his girlfriend had left before anybody had killed anyone else, so who were they to say what had happened?

You should turn yourself in, a voice instructed him. *Claim it was self-defense.*

It *had* been self-defense, that was true. But nobody would believe that, would they?

What other choice do you have? the voice asked.

Only then did he realize this was not a voice within his head. No, this was a voice coming from elsewhere in the room.

He looked around, but didn't see anyone.

"Where are you?" he finally said, aloud. He no longer recognized his own voice. The acoustics of the room had gone strange, somehow. Or maybe something within him had.

Here, said the voice, another voice he didn't recognize. *Down here.*

He realized the voice was coming from Raster.

He stared at the back of the corpse's head.

I am probably still passed out. Raster isn't talking. This is not possible.

Of course I'm talking, said Raster. *Help me up.* His voice sounded muffled, which made sense since he was lying face down in a puddle of his own blood.

"But you're dead," Turner said.

Raster didn't respond, just lifted a hand and held it, palm outstretched, in what—still lying on his face—he must have guessed was Turner's general direction.

With infinite caution, Turner moved to the far end of the couch, away from the hand. He pulled his feet up off the floor and sat cross-legged on the cushion, only realizing too late that the soles of his shoes were covered in blood. Now he'd have to throw out the couch too.

Help a brother up, said Raster. And when Turner made no move to do so, he snapped his fingers, spread his hand wide. *And here's a bloody hand to shake,* he said.

Turner had heard the phrase before, in a poem maybe. What kind of poem would have a line like that? Yet even if Turner could vaguely recognize the line, Raster wasn't the type to know it. Which Turner wanted to take as further proof that he was asleep, or delusional, that nothing that was happening meant anything, that nothing about it could really harm him.

Which was perhaps why, as the hand remained there, steady and outstretched, he felt an increasing compulsion to take hold of it. And so he finally did.

As soon as he touched Raster's hand, it wrapped tightly around his own. For a moment, he thought Raster might pull him off the couch, but then, almost with no effort at all, and with no sense of transition, Raster was there seated beside him.

Blood lay in a red mask over his face. Now that he was upright, it had begun to slip down and drip from the tip of his nose and off his chin and onto his already sodden shirt. Turner could see the slick crater in Raster's temple that the jagged bottle had made. A smear of brain blossomed out of the hole and into his hair, dissolving into a damp sheen. Each time Raster swallowed, blood welled up in the wound, then receded again back into the skull.

Turner leaned away, and Raster smiled broadly. His teeth too were slick with blood.

"I'm hungry," Raster said, his voice more forceful now, filling the room. "Who's hungry?"

Turner didn't answer.

"Turner?"

"What?" said Turner, trying to look at anything but Raster.

"Aren't you hungry?"

"Not really," said Turner.

"But you could eat though, huh?" said Raster as he nudged him in the ribs. "Am I right?"

"I—" Turner began.

But Raster didn't let him finish. "Good!" he said. He clapped a hand on Turner's shoulder. "Let's split a pizza."

He did not want to split a pizza with Raster, but what was he to do? It was, probably, a dream. Perhaps the only way to wake up from it was to follow it to its inevitable conclusion. And yet, he still didn't want to indulge it.

"Is this a dream?" he couldn't stop himself from asking the recently dead man.

"Does this feel like a dream to you?" asked Raster.

No, it didn't feel like a dream, that wasn't quite it. But he felt it would not be in his interest to admit this to Raster.

"Yes," he said. "A dream."

Raster began to chuckle. Bubbles of blood formed on his lips, then burst when he smiled again. "Come on, Turner," he said. "Don't fuck with me."

"Okay," said Turner.

But it was not okay.

"Shall we call?"

"What?" asked Turner. He looked around him. For a moment he wasn't sure where he was.

"The pizza," said Raster. "Jerry's? They deliver, right?"

"Sure," he said. And then, "I think so." Then he made the mistake of looking over at Raster, and it all came rushing back to him. *Definitely a dream*, he told himself. *Maybe. If I'm lucky.*

Raster slid out his cellphone and thumbed the dark screen to no avail. "Damn. No signal," he said. "We'll have to use yours."

"You have to turn it on," said Turner.

"It's on," said Raster. "See?" He held up the phone, but the screen was still dark, smeared now with bloody fingerprints. It did not seem to be on to Turner.

"I—" started Turner.

"Are you calling me a liar?"

That was how the fight had started. Someone calling someone else a liar. *Liar* rang a bell, anyway. Turner didn't respond, nor did he look at Raster. Instead, he took out his phone and dialed Jerry's.

When someone answered, he half-covered the bottom of the phone with his palm.

"What do you want on it?" he asked.

"Mushrooms," said Raster.

"Mushrooms," said Turner flatly. Raster never had mushrooms on his pizza. It must be a dream. "Just mushrooms?"

"And pepperoni. And sausage. And bacon. Peppers, too. And olives."

"Anything else."

"Yes, everything else," said Raster. "Put everything on it."

"Everything," said Turner.

"Except mushrooms," said Raster. "Leave off the mushrooms. Can't fucking stand mushrooms."

Almost immediately, the doorbell rang. Too quickly, by any standard. Another sign, Turner told himself, that this was all a dream.

The doorbell rang again. "Aren't you going to get that?" asked Raster.

Turner got up off the couch and made his way to the door, trying not to step in any blood. He looked out through the peephole.

It looked like a regular pizza delivery boy. He didn't know what he'd been expecting but somehow not that.

"It's the pizza," he said to Raster.

"Well, open it and pay the man," said Raster. He still hadn't moved from the couch.

"Do you have any money?" asked Turner.

"Naw, man, fresh out," said Raster. "I'll pick up the next one, though."

Turner opened the door, trying not to wonder how many meals they would be sharing.

"Pizza with everything?" asked the delivery boy.

"Except mushrooms," said Turner.

"Sure, whatever," said the delivery boy. Then he quoted a figure that sounded to Turner like a plausible price, especially for a dream. He took his wallet out and paid him.

Transaction completed, I will now wake up, Turner told himself. But nothing changed.

The delivery boy handed him the pizza box and was preparing to step off the porch to leave when Turner stopped him.

"Just a second, please. I need your opinion on something," he said.

"You do?" asked the startled delivery boy.

"I do," said Turner. "Could you come in for a moment?"

The man seemed to take Turner in fully for the first time, and apparently found what he took in alarming. "I don't think I can," he said slowly.

"No?" he said. "From the door then. Just look at my couch and tell me what you see."

But the delivery boy was already backing up, hands raised. He nearly tripped going down the steps while trying to keep Turner within sight. "Sorry, I don't want any trouble, mister," he said.

Who does? thought Turner. *And yet trouble always comes.*

"Just tell me in your own words," Turner said as he turned and looked back at his bloody friend. Raster grinned, then waved. "Do you see a man on the couch? And when you look at that man, are you convinced he's not breathing?"

When he turned back around for an answer, the delivery boy was long gone.

He closed the door. He carried the box in and put it on the coffee table.

"Mmm," said Raster. "Pizza. With everything."

"Except mushrooms," said Turner.

Turner opened the box and out came a rush of warm, damp air, quickly dispersed. The smell was right. There was nothing to suggest this wasn't a real pizza. Hadn't he read somewhere that the way to tell if something was a dream or not was by paying attention to smell? That if it was a dream, you couldn't really take things in through your nose?

Turner paced the room.

"Sit back down," said Raster.

He hesitated, shook his head. "I'm good," he claimed, though he knew this to be a lie.

Raster shrugged. "Suit yourself," he said. He slipped the fingers of one blood-smeared hand under the crust of the pizza and worked a piece free, cheese stringing out as he lifted it.

Surely any of your senses can make an appearance in dreams, Turner thought idly, still trying to solve the situation, still trying to pretend it made sense.

And then Raster lifted the piece of pizza to his mouth and took a bite. When he pulled it away from his lips again, the bitten edge was speckled with blood. Turner watched him chew, fixated on the way the deep dent in the man's head pulsed with each movement of his jaws. He couldn't look away. As he stared, the hole became damp and began to seep, and Turner felt his vision, as well as himself, narrowing, as he fell into it.

A moment later, he passed out.

He regained consciousness to find himself sitting on the couch, where his night had begun. He looked around and discovered his neck was sore.

Raster was not there.

He was not on the couch, and he was not on the floor. Blood had been tracked all over the floorboards, dozens of bloody footprints, as if, while he had been unconscious, many people had come and gone.

"Raster?" he called cautiously.

There was no answer.

With great difficulty, he managed to stand. He made his slow way to the foot of the stairs and shouted up Raster's name again, then stayed there waiting for a reply. Nothing.

He walked back through the riot of bloody footprints and went into the kitchen. Raster wasn't there either. He looked in the closet and in the bathroom and out on the screened-in back porch, but Raster wasn't in any of those places.

And yet, when he came back into the living room, there Raster was, on the couch, just as he had been before.

The blood on his face had dried and darkened. Where his skin wasn't stained with blood, it had grown livid. Probably it was equally livid underneath the crust of blood, too. His eyes had grown cloudy. And, at first, when Raster turned them toward him, Turner wasn't entirely sure the man could still see.

A noise involuntarily escaped Turner's throat.

"There you are," said Raster. "Where have you been?"

Turner didn't answer. But when Raster repeated the question, Turner finally said, "Nowhere."

Raster smiled. He patted the cushion next to him.

"Come," he said. "Come over here to somewhere."

"No," said Turner.

"You will," said Raster, confident. "Sooner or later. You won't be able to help yourself."

Heart thudding in his throat, Turner turned toward the door and tried to leave the room behind him once and for all. But his path kept circling back to the couch. He could not, he found, leave the situation that had been created. And after a while, exhausted, he gave up trying.

"Come on, brother," said Raster. "Why fight?" He patted the cushion next to him once again. "Why not do this the easy way?"

He was on his knees now.

Raster was looming above him, hand extended down to him.

Here's a bloody hand to shake, Turner thought, and though he did not reach up to take it, he suddenly felt Raster's grip secure and cold in his own hand. Through a flurry of motion that was beyond his reckoning, he found himself drawn onto the couch, the dead Raster beside him.

"Why did you kill me?" asked Raster.

"I . . . " said Turner, but he didn't know how to answer.

"Do you know what it feels like to be this way?"

Turner shook his head. He tried to get off the couch, but Raster pulled him back down. He kept pulling on Turner's arm, dragging it down, until Turner, grunting, couldn't help but face him. He brought his face very close, so close that Turner could hear the blood gurgling in the hole in his head.

Raster regarded him with his cloudy eyes. After a while, one of them drifted in its orbit to look past his shoulder. Turner tried to shake free, but Raster would not let him go.

"You should have turned yourself in," said Raster, "instead of remaining here with me."

"Let go of me, and I will," said Turner.

Raster shook his head slowly. "No," he said. "Too late for that. You had your chance. You didn't take it. Now you'll stay here with me."

Abruptly, Raster's whole demeanor seemed to change, to lighten. For some reason, this levity terrified Turner more than if he'd kept on with his vague threats. It was suddenly clear to Turner that he had no idea what Raster would do next, that he could do anything.

He tried to shake his arm free, but Raster's grasp remained firm. Just as in life, Raster was the one in charge.

"I'm hungry," said Raster. "Famished even."

Turner didn't say anything. He kept struggling.

"Shall we order more pizza? We could split one. Or order two and still have a slice or three left for breakfast."

Raster squeezed his arm hard. Turner couldn't stop himself from crying out.

"No?" said Raster. "You're right, of course. We have everything we need right here." He licked the blood off his lips.

And then, mouth open, he leaned toward his friend.

When Turner regained his senses, he was still on the couch. His whole body felt numb. A hissing was coming from just below his chin, and when he reached for his neck, he discovered it was no longer there. His throat had been cut out.

Raster, standing, looming over him, nudged him. The broken bottle was in his hand.

"Come on," he said. "Get up now."

Raster nudged him again, harder this time. Turner coughed, the sound strange and wrong in the void.

"We've got to get Mike back over here," said Raster. "Coax him back. Get another fix. Something to keep us going, before it's too late." He held out his phone. "Give him a call."

Turner tried to respond, but could only hiss air, a fine spray of blood with it. He couldn't speak.

"What are you waiting for?" asked Raster.

And then, since a small part of him still hoped this might be a dream and that the dream could have an ending if he did the right things, he took the phone.

He tried to turn it on, but even though he did everything right, it remained dark. He took his own phone out of his pocket, but he couldn't turn that on either.

He held the phone up to his ear anyway.

Immediately Raster was there, his own head pressed against Turner's, the phone balanced between Turner's ear and Raster's hole.

"It's ringing," one of them said. "It won't be long now."

But Turner heard nothing on the end of the line. Still, desperately, he waited, dead phone pressed to one ear, Raster's hole pressed to the other, on the alert in case anyone ever bothered to answer.

ELUDE THE SNOOD

TONY MCMILLEN

THE SNOOD WRECKED PIZZA. Everybody knew that. He made it so pizza arrived late, or with the wrong toppings, or even to the wrong house. He would try to freeze your pizza or burn it, sometimes even stick a bundle of lit dynamite into the delivery box. He was the Snood. He wrecked pizza. It was what he did. Or at least what he tried to do. The little long-eared goblin could be easily thwarted, or so all the animated commercials he used to star in would tell us. To prevent the Snood from wrecking your pizza, all you had to do was order your pie from Dicey Slice. *"Elude the Snood! When it comes to pizza, why roll the dice? Best make sure your pie's a Dicey Slice!"* Like I said, everybody knew that.

But the Snood also wrecked lives, and not everybody knew that. My name is Drederick Fitzgerald Snood, and in the winter of 1989, for five long hours, I held six employees and two customers of a Dicey Slice Pizza in Atlanta hostage with a sawed-off shotgun. My demands were three pizzas, a two-liter of Pepsi, and one new copy of the novel *The Trellis* by Sigmund Delis Wafflen (because my mother threw mine out), and one hundred thousand dollars. Oh, and a helicopter with a pilot for my escape. If it sounds like I didn't know what I was doing, that is 100% correct. I was 20 years old and convinced that the second biggest pizza chain in the world was behind a vast conspiracy to humiliate me because their cartoon mascot shared my last name. Me, Drederick Fitzgerald Snood, some nobody from Atlanta who still lived with his mother and who had just dropped out of community college because I thought I had discovered the teachers there had a secret arrangement to monitor and indoctrinate me in a joint effort between the Five-Percent Nation and—of all institutions—the Mossad. Me, Drederick Fitzgerald Snood, who only ever had one girlfriend, and that was back in the eleventh grade, which was around the same time I became obsessed with the Snood character. But then, how could I not be? Me, Drederick Fitzgerald Snood. But even if we didn't have the same name there was no way to elude the Snood; he was everywhere back then.

I waited my turn then went up to the counter calmly that February day in 1989, and when the high school girl behind the register asked me what I wanted, I pulled out the sawed-off and managed to keep my voice steady. "I want to talk to Jim Grunkemeyer right now." When I placed my double barrel on her forehead, the listless look she had on her face earlier fell away. That was the minimum-wage look, that was the *you-the-get-what-you-paid-for* look. But now she looked like she was working for something worth more than $3.35 an hour.

And yet " . . . who?" was all she could stammer out to answer my question. I hated how afraid she looked, because it made me afraid I had been wrong about this whole thing. But when she answered me with such a sloppy lie . . . all my pity disappeared. I pressed the barrel against her forehead, and her mouth pulled into a frown.

"Grunkemeyer," I told her, "he's here today on a visit, and you know that!"

By now the rest of the crew in the back had picked up on what was happening, and I heard the front door chime and realized I had lost one of the other customers—which meant they'd probably go get the cops. Good. But I didn't want anyone else running out, especially Grunkemeyer, so I stepped back, held the sawed-off to the ceiling and let out a shot. Two of the men working the ovens in the back screamed, and the two remaining customers both backed up to a wall plastered with a mural of the Snood chasing after the Dicey Slice logo. Dust from the ceiling plaster hung in the air like a mummy had just teleported out of there, and the smell of the sawed-off overtook the delicious scent of Dicey Slice brand pizza sauce that usually filled the place. From my count, there were nine of us there: two customers, two men working the ovens, another dude wearing a jacket looked to be a delivery driver, a second teenage girl handling wings, and next to her was a middle-aged woman wearing glasses who looked to be the manager. This left me and the girl crying at the register. That girl's eyes never left mine and all of sudden she looked so much younger than me. Of course she was only three or four years younger at the most. Same age I was back in high school, back when I had a girlfriend, back before the Snood showed up. I blocked the door then pointed the sawed-off at her face.

I was in eleventh grade when the Snood appeared. People in my school already thought I was weird because I liked to read and didn't really know how to do much else, so his arrival was perfect ammunition for them. I'd go into lunch on pizza day in the cafeteria, and while I walked by, everyone would huddle over and guard their slice while giggling in my direction. At first I even played along, made pretend like I was going to steal some of the kids slices. But eventually people would just see me in the hall and yell, "Elude the Snood!" while they took off in the other direction. Didn't matter what they were serving in the cafeteria after a while, kids would do that or worse whenever they got the chance. My girl—my old and only girl Crystal—she had already dumped me before any of this started; so don't go thinking this is her fault—but before the Snood stuff she would still smile or say *what's up* to me when we saw each other in the hall. Now she just laughed along with everybody else, right before they turned their backs to me. It was like playing hide-and-go-seek against your will. And you were always going to be it.

I loaded a second shell in case anyone at the Dicey Slice thought to test me.

"You two," I yelled at the customers on my side of the counter, "get back there with the rest." They listened, and then I pointed the sawed-off at the manager in the back. "Boss lady, get over here and lock the front, anyone moves . . . " I didn't even finish the sentence and she was moving quick. And as the two customers—some brother who looked like he was into De La Soul, and some white lady with big wavy hair that looked like Patrick Swayze—were making their way to get behind the counter the manager almost collided with them. She gave them a look—almost a polite, a *how-silly-was-that* kind of recognition, and then she let them go first.

As she ran past me and locked the door, she said, "You know you can take all the money we have. I have the key to the safe . . . there's no reason to lock us in here, sir."

The *sir* is what set me off. There was no way she'd ever call a slob like me sir unless it was, *sir, we'll have to ask you to leave* or something similar. "I don't want your money. I want to talk to Grunkemeyer. Cut the shit and tell me where he's hiding."

"His visit was cancelled."

"Alice . . . " The word *manager* was written on her nametag. "You and I both know that's not the truth." I pointed the barrel between her eyes and the girl at the register behind us whimpered.

"It's cool, honey, it's cool," Alice told the girl, calming her while a gun was at her head. Damn, she was a good manager. Made me wish I worked for someone like that. Back when I still had a job.

I tapped the barrel against her forehead as gently as I could. "Listen, I don't want to hurt anyone, but if you don't bring Jim Grunkemeyer to me I am going to have to do something that I don't want to."

Alice nodded and let out a deep breath. "I'm sorry . . . but he's just not here—"

"He was in the freezer when you came in, and I think he's still hiding in there," the girl at the register blurted out.

"Maya, what the fuck?" Now Alice was sounding like the managers I knew. I couldn't trust anyone.

"Move," was all I had to say to her, and I followed her behind the counter. Seeing all the hostages clumped together there I couldn't help but think about how I was outnumbered. "You all might have noticed that I only got two shots in this thing. Well, if you want to pick which two of you die, be my guest. But you might have also noticed that this here is a sawed-off shotgun, which doesn't mean shit for distance, but in close quarters like this . . . if I point this thing at you and pull the trigger, I might as well have pointed it at whoever was standing next to you too, get it?" These were my stepfather's words; I hated him, and almost everything he ever said scared the shit out of me. Them too apparently, because no one budged. "Now, Alice, go get Grunkemeyer's ass out of the fridge."

"That won't be necessary."

I whirled around to find the door to the fridge open, and standing there was Jim Grunkemeyer, the man behind the Snood.

I started putting it together after reading *The Trellis*. It was sold as fiction but what author Sigmund Delis Wafflen really was doing was setting me on the path for shocking truths about who actually runs this world. The book wasn't about some pizza conspiracy with a *Pizzanati* who ran things from the shadows, but it did detail the major corporations that were behind everything. How these six corporations were all run by one family: The Grunkemeyers. Jim Grunkemeyer was the owner of Dicey Slice Pizza along with a lot of other things. His family had connections to U.S defense contractors, medical research firms, film studios; they were in everything important. Including pizza. Jim was the man in charge when the Snood became Dicey Slice's new advertising tool. The character boosted pizza sales and there was clothing, comic books, two Snood Nintendo video games and even an animated series in the works before I ruined everything in 1989. Grunkemeyer took a chance with his anti-mascot. The Snood was like Wile E. Coyote, only you never ever felt just a little bit bad for him when he fell off a cliff. So we all got to be the Roadrunner and just *beep beep* while something heavy fell on him over and over again. Well, most of us.

After reading *The Trellis,* it became obvious to me that Jim Grunkemeyer had based his character on me. Not that the Snood and I looked alike; I wasn't a shriveled up old white dude in some rubber bunny getup. Despite what all the wiseasses at my high school said, I didn't stop anyone from enjoying pizza, especially Dicey Slice Pizza. How could I? I still ate it. It was the best pizza you could get delivered and it had, hands down, the best sauce I'd ever tasted.

Which is why I had them make me three pizzas at gunpoint, I suppose. See, I liked pizza. The other Snood hated it.

The first time the cops called, I was too busy shoving my shotgun against the temple of a kneeling Jim Grunkemeyer to be bothered. "What does the Grunkemeyer Corporation gain from turning me into some sort of joke? What does the pizza have to do with the defense contracts and pharmaceutical experiments your family—your real family—finances?"

Grunkemeyer wasn't as cool as when he waltzed out of the freezer. "I don't know what you're talking about . . . how did you even know I would be here?"

"I'll ask the fucking questions!" I pushed the barrel into his skin. I could feel the eyes of everyone on me as I did it. De La Soul and Lady Swayze looked the most unnerved. Maya and the other girl who looked her age were huddled over with Alice, and all three shared the same grim expression. I had the three men who worked there all cooking pizzas. One pepperoni, one pepperoni and mushroom, and then one ham, bell pepper and onion. I crouched down to look Grunkemeyer in the eye. "I know you've been watching me, there are things in the commercials that you could only know from spying on me. But what I still can't understand is why?"

"What . . . what sorts of things?" De La asked, and Alice gave the dude a look like she wanted to fire him even though he didn't work for her.

"There's plenty. Take the commercial where the Snood's pizza catapult malfunctions and he's sent flying into the surface of the moon where he brushes himself off, breathes a sigh of relief, only to pick up a newspaper lying in a moon crater reading, 'Solar Eclipse Today,' at which point the sun comes up and disintegrates the Snood."

Everyone in the room was looking back at me like I was a talking dog. "It's symbolic, see . . . if you were me and if you'd read *The Trellis* you'd see; it's about me losing my job delivering morning papers. I had overslept—so the *sun* had eclipsed the *moon*—and then I was *fired*. See . . . they use symbols . . . his whole fucked up cult family use symbols . . . don't look at me like that!" Everyone backed away a bit. "My mom didn't see it either, made me throw out my copy of *The Trellis* . . . I almost thought you had got to her, too..." Grunkemeyer arched an eyebrow and looked up at me, his lips pursed. "But no, she was just scared I was losing it."

"What's this *Trellis*? Is it about Dicey Slice?" Alice asked.

"No, it's a science fiction book by Sigmund Delis Wafflen," I told her.

"Well, no offense," the delivery guy told me as he opened up an oven, "but you said *fiction*."

I shook my head. "Grunkemeyer here won't allow the truth to be exposed. So the book uses Grunkemeyer's own weapons against him. Symbolism, analogues, stand-ins."

"I don't know what you want me to say." Grunkemeyer held his hands up. "I understand you believe I have wronged you but these people have done nothing to you . . . please—"

"Well, I *did* think that." I pointed the gun at Alice and the girls. "To answer your question; *how I knew you'd be here today? . . .* you've been watching me and I've been watching you. Sometimes I walk around outside the back—where your workers take their smoke breaks—sometimes I sit in the parking lot behind the dumpster. About a month ago, two of them were complaining about having the owner come down from California for a visit, some sort of inspection."

"What do you want?" Grunkemeyer asked.

"Pizza's ready," one of the cooks said.

Then the phone rang again. "That's probably the cops," I said, "I'll tell them what else I want that I can't get here from you . . . " I put the barrel back to Grunkemeyer's head. "Yet."

When I had listened in on the workers in the parking lot both of them seemed surprised that Grunkemeyer would be visiting their store. They talked about being one of the worst performing stores in the region, so maybe that was why the big boss was coming down? *Who knows why the people in charge do any of the shit they do?* I heard one of them say. Now I had a gun to his boss' head and could ask him myself. Ask him why him and his family that had been the money behind entire dynasties and two world wars now wanted to mock some nerd from Atlanta whose mother told him if he didn't get a second job the landlord said they'd be on the street in two months.

Everybody knows the world is unfair, that the odds are stacked against you, that there are people at the top who just don't give a shit about you or anyone who isn't them. Everybody knows that. But when you start saying that maybe those same people at the top aren't just indifferent to you, but that they're actively trying to keep you down, that's when people label you paranoid. Delusional. Even self-aggrandizing. I was all of those things, I was, but I was also right. Mostly. For nearly five hours at that Dicey Slice, I was also for the first and only time the master of my own destiny. With the sawed-off shoved under his nose, Jim Grunkemeyer was finally my pawn, my plaything. And there would be no more eluding me.

The five hours went by like recess on a sunny day. No one tried to run, not after I made Maya, the register girl, eat a slice of pepperoni-and-mushroom pizza. After everything that happened, I still feel the worst about that. While we waited for the cops to call again, I told everyone to eat; at first they declined. but then I explained that I wanted to make sure none of my pizzas had been drugged. It was Grunkemeyer himself who took the first slice. and as he chomped down on it told Alice to make the rest follow along. Maya took her slice but I noticed as I ate mine—slurping the sauce that ran down my chin as I balanced the sawed-off in my lap—that Maya wasn't touching hers. So I put my pizza down and told her to eat.

"I'm a vegetarian."

"Then take off the pepperoni and just eat the mushroom."

"The sauce . . . it's got meat in it."

"Eat it!" I screamed at her. She looked over to Alice like she could help her, and then I shook the shotgun in her face. "Fucking do it." The poor girl didn't even bother flicking off her pepperoni as she bit into the slice.

"Good job, Maya," Grunkemeyer told her through a mouthful.

The girl started gagging, and I remembered being a kid and how my old stepdad used to force me to eat things I didn't want to. He'd beat my ass if I didn't finish my plate sometimes. One time he forced me to finish a stack of cheesy potatoes. And when I took my last bite, he leered at me saying something like, "I told you, you would like it. Now, give us a smile," and then I threw up all over his smug face. He was so disgusted he didn't even beat my ass that night. He just went right into a shower, got drunk and passed out. I sat waiting at the table alone—mom was at work—so I sat with my own vomit still caking my face and waited for him to come back and give me what was coming. I think I waited until I heard him snoring to go clean myself up. I still won't eat cheesy potatoes.

"Just spit it out," I told the girl. "I'm sorry, just spit it out. You don't have to eat it."

She was crying now. "It's too late . . . " she said after she spat out her bite. I thought I knew what she meant.

I caught Grunkemeyer staring, and for the first time he was looking at me with something other than fear. It was outright disgust or deep disappointment. I was used to people like him looking at me like that, but this was the first time I ever felt like they were right to do it. The girl kept her head down, but I could still hear her sniffling. There was a pit in my stomach as I looked around the room at all the people I had held against their will. What if I was wrong?

The phone rang, breaking my thoughts, and I took one hand off the gun to pick it up and listen.

"Mr. Snood?"

"Don't call me that, just 'Drederick.'"

"I'm sorry, Drederick, we have some of your demands, and we're still . . . working on the helicopter and the money, but we do have a copy of *The Trellis* along with someone special who would like to give it to you and talk things over."

Someone special? I heard the knock on the door and thought maybe it'd be my mother, holding a copy of the book she made me throw out. But standing on the other side of the glass door was the author of the book himself: Sigmund Delis Wafflen. Which didn't make any goddamn sense. It couldn't be real. But there he stood, waving a little hesitantly. He was an older guy, little pudgy, grey hair—what was left of it—wearing a tweed jacket like in his author photo. This was too much. This was impossible . . .

"What the fuck are you pulling?" Instead of going for the door, I marched over to Grunkemeyer, pulled back and clocked him on the side of his head with the shotgun. He screamed out then fell to the floor.

"What are you talking about?" Grunkemeyer managed to wheeze out as he clutched the side of his head. "Who's the man at the door?"

"You know who it is!"

"Please, please don't hurt anyone," the man at the door shouted from behind the glass. "I am Sigmund Wafflen, the police found me at a hotel a few hours away and I—"

"Bullshit!"

"Oh God, let's all just calm down," Alice said.

"Dude, is that the author of the science fiction book?" De La asked.

"Well, it's really more speculative fiction with elements of espionage and autobiography," the man at the door explained.

Grunkemeyer got to his knees and looked up at me. "Maybe you should let him in, see if he can settle this for you." He called out toward he door. "Sir, Mr. Wafflen was it? My name's Jim Grunkemeyer, and can you please tell this man that the evil corporation in your book, the *Alucinari* has nothing do with me, my family or our company?"

Wafflen was about to speak when I spoke over him, "I never told you what the name of the evil corporation in the book was, Grunkemeyer."

He looked up past my barrel. "Well . . . I must have read it somewhere. This book's fairly popular, maybe *Publishers Weekly* . . . "

"Nobody reads *Publishers Weekly*!" My finger curled round the trigger, and then I heard someone behind me. I spun around, firing the sawed-off before I even saw who it was. Blood was everywhere, along with the smell of someone's insides hitting the air. What was left of Maya, the register girl, the high school girl, laid on the floor. I felt my bottom lip twitching as I looked down at her.

"This wasn't supposed to happen," Alice said.

I had one shot left. I wish I would have used it on myself, but then that wouldn't have made any difference. I turned around and put the smoking barrel to Grunkemeyer's face. This was his fault. He was hiding something. His eyes were eggs, complete terror. "She was innocent! You're not getting out of here alive . . . " he said.

I pulled the trigger. No, I couldn't pull the trigger.

I tried again, but nothing. I wasn't scared, I simply could not do it. Next, I couldn't stand. Against my will, I went to my knees until I was eye to eye with Grunkemeyer. I was still holding the sawed-off towards him but now he was laughing at it and me.

"Let's have you put that away before anyone else gets hurt." I placed the gun on the ground and scooted it over to him.

"What's happening?" I could still at least speak under my own power.

Grunkemeyer leaned over. "The Snood never had anything to do with you. Your surname probably comes from the slave-owners who bought and sold your ancestors." He stood up and rubbed the side of his face where I struck him and then ran his fingers over his head, his eyes rolled back.

I was so focused on Grunkemeyer, I failed to notice any of what was happening around me. The place should have been swarming with cops. The hostages should have been running. But they were still there, only the men now were coming out of the freezer dragging some long, white sort of trough with chains. Alice and Ayesha dragged Maya's body past me and I was grateful I couldn't turn my head to follow the bloody trail she left on the ground. Standing next to Grunkemeyer was Sigmund Delis Wafflen, someone had let him in. He looked at me, rubbed his balding head like I was giving him a headache then he patted Grunkemeyer on the shoulder with a smile. "*S-n-oo-d*" Grunkemeyer said to me, "you know those things on top of its head aren't really ears, don't you?"

"And they're not part of some suit like a jester's cap and bells," Wafflen said.

There was a crunchy sound as the skin on Grunkemeyer's scalp pulled and stretched. "But they *are* part of its body." My jaw went slack as Grunkemeyer's pulled up into a grin while his scalp twitched and jumped like something underneath wanted out. "Yes . . . there it is . . . you have no idea how good it feels to finally be able to let these out again." Wafflen's eyes sparkled at Grunkemeyer as it happened and then he started rubbing again on his own scalp, almost furiously. Grunkemeyer let out a moan that made the insides of my ear feel dirty. "They're carnucles . . . or snoods . . . kind of like a turkey's." And then there they were:

Glistening, purple wrinkled flesh in two long twisted stalks. They hovered and twitched in the air like living burnt calamari.

"Sorry, they only become engorged when we're *reallllly* excited." I screamed. I wept. " . . . but why leave clues in *The Trellis*?"

Wafflen came into view, and I saw his caruncles pushing their way through his scalp as fragments of flesh hung on the wet barbs and hairs that covered the stalks. "You ever go fishing?" Wafflen touched a finger to his temple. "Never mind, I can tell your stepfather never bothered with fishing. Anyhow, do you know what you call the line that attaches the hook to the main line? That's right, you call it a snood. We use entertainment like *The Trellis* to get us what we crave. What we crave is someone like yourself. Someone isolated."

"Paranoid," Grunkemeyer agreed.

"Unsure of anything and distrustful of everything," Wafflen continued.

"That's what it takes for someone as old as us to get it up anymore." Grunkemeyer laughed. "A trail of breadcrumbs, and pepperoni, followed by a shit load of exposition."

"If it ain't Baroque, fix it," Wafflen added.

"And we're the only ones who can make the sauce."

Grunkemeyer and Wafflen began taking off their clothes when I heard all the hostages and the customers chanting in some language I'd never heard before. They knelt around the white trough. "What's in the secret sauce?" I asked.

Grunkemeyer stood over me naked, and to my relief he was like a Barbie doll, nothing between his legs but smooth skin. Nothing. "Well, you've already had some today and look at you . . . you can only do what we allow. And you've been feeding yourself this for most of your life, so there's all sorts of . . . other things the sauce will provide."

"But you know what? We're still only number two when it comes to pizza," Wafflen said.

"The local cops might have been able to keep this under wraps, but the story has gone national now, the whole brand will have to be shelved," Grunkemeyer said. "I guess the 'ol Snood won't be the thing to take us to maximum market penetration just yet."

"Oh, I think there's still some life left in the little bugger yet." Wafflen shifted a shoulder and then all the skin of his body fell to the floor next to me like some soaking wet winter coat. I screamed as I saw his real body, just like his caruncles; wet, purple muscle, coiled into the shape of human being. All that remained that looked remotely human was his face, which sat like a Halloween mask of humanity on whatever was his true face.

As Wafflen put his purple fingers to his face and began to remove the last bit of his costume, Grunkemeyer looked down at me with something close to pity. "No hard feelings, Drederick. In fact, as a reward for your assistance in helping us keep our business afloat, I think you should have the honor of sampling the secret ingredient in Dicey Slice's legendary red sauce in its freshest form; what do you say?"

I couldn't say anything as my mouth was somehow forced open

while Wafflen's human face slid off into his hand. Behind it was something without eyes or intelligence, something like a slit that opened only to reveal things somehow worse. Wafflen aimed this slit at the trough, and from it spewed a viscid substance in a wild torrent. As he expelled it from his orifice, his caruncles writhed and whirled about. And after he filled almost a quarter of the trough, he dipped a claw and carried a cupped palm of the gleaming red vile down to my lips.

"No, no," Grunkemeyer said. "What are you doing? Dear Drederick deserves the freshest taste possible."

The Wafflen creature turned away as Grunkemeyer himself slipped off his own mask and showed me its true face. Even without a mouth, his words found me, threaded into my own thoughts like a tattoo needle on my brains. "Soon enough, you'll find out what this sauce does, and has already been doing to you, for most of your life

I still couldn't scream, still couldn't move and then he pushed his glistening slit to my mouth and emptied his awful into me over and over again. "Your mind is banquet for me, you know . . . So many memories, so much delicious distrust. Taste me as I taste you . . . now, give us a smile . . . "

If you look me up, it'll say I was arrested, declared mentally unstable, sent to live in a mental facility, then, of course, that I offed myself. It's a sad story, but I still wish it was a true. The truth is they'll never let me die. I'm too useful. Instead, they'll make me do what I'm doing now, writing this story down; using it to tell you just enough to let you know that it isn't just a story. Like *The Trellis* did for me. The names are changed, but not for protection. Because they make the game more dangerous. More unsteady. Because even if you don't believe my story, maybe you won't really know what to believe anymore. When the only truth they let you have is the scraps they toss in with the bullshit they give you to survive, it's nearly impossible to separate one from the other.

Lies are hard to avoid . . . everybody knows that.

THE BLESSED HUNGRY

T. FOX DUNHAM

DANNY WAS PLAYING with himself as he peeped at the carnage through blinds on his front door when he saw his neighbor dart out of his bar. "Run, you fucking mutt," Danny whispered, watching the black comedy play out in front of his restaurant. Bobby C hustled between the abandoned vehicles on South Street, trying to get to his car parked in the lot next to Stylish Dildos. His blue velvet tracksuit bunched up under his arms, and he carried a piece in one hand and a silver tin in the other. What the fuck? The chubby bastard couldn't go an hour without stuffing his face? He hadn't paid him for it either. "Made" guys never paid. Bobby staggered across South Street, slipping between the abandoned cars and got to his Caddy. Then one of the Hungry grabbed his legs from under a cab, holding him in place. He unloaded his piece to no effect. A mutilated woman staggered over to him and bit a hunk out of his flabby arm. Blood sprayed from her mouth, and Bobby dropped the tin, mixing pasta and chicken with chunks of his flesh that fell from her jaw. A mob gathered and devoured the fuck, eating through the velvet and spitting out mouthfuls of black curly hair. Danny watched, licking his lips, unable to look away, so satisfied to see Bobby get stripped and eaten like a roasted pig. Men like that forced Danny to always be looking over his shoulder when the lights went out, terrified they'd find out about his special needs. Now, he savored Bobby's judgment—the same judgment coming for him. Danny replayed it in his mind, imagining the sensation of being eaten.

His guest growled from his chair, kicking against the floor and sniffing, probably smelling the execution. Curly lunged at Danny but couldn't break free, and he looked desperately at the chef. "Calm your ass down," Danny said. "You'll get your chance, but I'm doing it right, not like that asshole." Danny planned a meal, his best—a final culinary benediction. He had all the ingredients to make a rich sugo, perhaps something with veal. Or maybe he should keep it simple. "Everyone loves a good pizza, right?" Curly barked, and Danny left the dining room of his restaurant and returned to his kitchen. He took out the ingredients and started chopping vegetables. He didn't have to make the dough since he always kept some ready. The chef seeded tomatoes, cut some onion and eggplant and fried the colorful bounty in a cast-iron pan, grateful the power was still on.

He'd never closed his shop the night before, standing guard over the restaurant from what the news was then calling "violent mobs." They could have easily busted through his front window, especially with the gate up. It might have been clear now. The Hungry usually scattered after a meal, searching for any runners. The chef set the range to simmer, returned to the door and scanned through the debris and abandoned cars littering South Street. The mob had dispersed, though he didn't know how far. He spotted a figure in front of the Penn's Landing walkway that bridged I-95 and led to the Delaware waterfront, but most of the mob had moved off. He grabbed the keys from the table, hurrying, regretting the timing, but he didn't know when he'd have the chance again. Their numbers grew. Danny pushed the podium and opened the front door but forgot the bell. The goddamn thing chimed, and he nearly shot it. No one noticed, and he stepped out.

The chef choked on the sickly sweet stink of decomposition, and the aroma mixed with the spicy scent of roasting basil and tomatoes, defiling the atmosphere of his Italian cuisine. He gagged but controlled his nausea and felt like a goddamn amateur who'd never smelled the stench of a rotting corpse before. Out on the sidewalk, he pushed away one of his outdoor tables. Clay shards from shattered flower pots crunched under his boots, and he stepped through the potting soil, the fallen azaleas and two rotting bodies that cluttered the front of his restaurant. Danny got out his keys from his front pocket under the greasy apron then reached up for the gate under the awning. He slowly eased it down, trying to blend into the environment. He pulled the gate most of the way and removed the padlock from one of the slots, getting ready to secure it from the other side.

Danny was stepping back into the doorway when one of the Hungry stumbled out of the alley and grabbed his leg. He pistol-whipped it in its hoary eyes, but it didn't let go. The smell of burning vegetables distracted him—vegetables he couldn't replace. He kicked the woman in the head, trying to free himself. "Fucking whore!" he said and slammed down the gate, cracking her arm. Danny jammed its base into the sidewalk, crushing the woman's flesh, then fed the padlock through the iron loop anchored into the concrete. He left her pinned, locked the door behind him and ran back to the kitchen. He turned down the electric range and slid the cast iron pan off the heat. Danny despised electric but couldn't tolerate the odor of gas. At least if they lost power, he could use the generator in the cellar, though he dreaded going down into the basement. The charred scent dissipated, leaving only the rich flavor of roasting vegetables, sautéing in extra virgin olive oil—the stuff he picked up in Cyprus while he was doing that job last year.

When the range cooled, he moved the pan back and sprinkled wet and sticky garlic bits over the yellow paste, making sure to add a bit of the savory juice behind his ears and down his neck. The pungent smell sped his heart, and he watched the sauce bubble. He took out his gun, made sure the safety was on and rubbed the hardness still pressing against his pants when he watched Bobby get his ass munched on. With his other hand, he reached under his apron and shirt, found the scarred indents on his left shoulder and fondled the recession still deep in his flesh. Pleasure shocked his body again.

Curly kicked against the hardwood floor, trying to get free of his plastic bonds, and Danny turned back to him. Danny had forgotten he was watching, and his cheeks flushed with shame. "Fuck off, you rat asshole," he said, aiming the piece at his head. "Plenty of freaks out there like me," he said. "I remember this guy from the neighborhood who loved his Mustang—and I mean 'loved'. He polished it, always changing the hubcaps. One night he called 911 because he nearly burned his dick off trying to fuck the muffler."

Curly pushed his toes against the floor, trying to break free, nearly flipping the chair. Danny grabbed the seat and held it firm.   "I clipped you once. I wasn't paid to do it twice," Curly said. "Shit. I'm not going to get paid at all." Curly just kept fidgeting and couldn't keep his mouth shut.

"That's why Dominic gave the order," Danny said. Curly managed a hot auto parts scam through his garage for the crew, but their mole in the Philadelphia courthouse said he'd been singing to the feds.

Yeah, Curly. Come by the pizzeria tonight. My girl's sister's in town and needs a date. Oh hey, Curly. Sit down. Get comfortable. Judy will be here soon. I'm just going to clean up a bit. Dinner's cooking. Oh hey, Curly . . . You should have kept your fucking mouth shut.

Blood stained Curly's work shirt from the first gunshot, and red, clotted goop occasionally oozed out of the wound when he raged. Another gunshot exposed the white of his shit-for-brains. Danny had shot him through the temple after he started twitching and moaning, thinking he hadn't finished the job. Nope. The mother-fucker kept going. What could he do? He tied the asshole down with the industrial plastic wrap until he figured out how to handle it. That's when the news started to figure this shit out, right before going dark. Now, Curly would witness. Danny liked it when someone watched— but not just anyone. It had to be some poor shit that could only get his cock sucked when he paid for it. He liked it when they watched with envy, jealousy, wishing they could be as beautiful to fuck a beauty queen with big tits and a Catholic attitude. He'd lay down on the counter while they ladled hot marinara sauce on his freshly-shaven chest, and then they'd lick him clean, lapping up the chunky tomato sauce made with fresh basil and oregano from his garden on the roof then bite him hard.

Curly lashed out again and nearly snapped the chair.

"Enough with this shit," Danny said and grabbed the nail gun out of his toolbox on the floor. He pressed the power tool to Curly's boot and fired a nail through his foot, then repeated. Danny stood up and set the tool on the table. Curly lurched forward, pulling against the nail and popping his arms out of his shoulders. Then, with cobra-like reflexes, he chomped down on Danny's jowl, snatched a flap of flesh and ripped it free with his teeth.

"Son of a bitch!" Danny pulled away and pressed a cloth napkin to the wound. Blood soaked his apron, and he replaced the soggy napkin with another. When the initial shock subsided, he checked and felt his teeth through the hole. At first, the pain exploded through his head like a bomb but eventually numbed as he went into shock. Curly had calmed, now chewing on the fresh flesh, and Danny's body jerked in response but not in pain. Danny worked his jaw harder and felt the edges of the wound, digging around the hole, and enjoyed the high. He walked to the customer bathroom, found the first aid kit and bandaged his face, then he grabbed the grabbed a bottle of Percocet from the kitchen. He swallowed down three of the horse pills with a swig of red wine, then checked the sauce, dripping a little blood into the paste.

His face ached but didn't hurt too much. He figured he was probably going into shock, as if he might pass out before he could set the table. What could he do? He couldn't call an ambulance so he just ignored it, hoping God would be kind for once.

Instead, he checked the bowl of dough to see if it had risen. Danny punched it down with two fists, pushing out the air so it could rise again, then he started preheating his oven. When he returned to the dining room, Curly had finished chewing his piece of Danny's face.

"Fuck you, asshole, and all your dead friends," he said. For a glancing moment, intelligence renewed in Curly's faded eyes, startling Danny. Then Curly ceased his gyrations, calmed from his agitations, and spoke in clear and alien voice:

Sic transit gloria mundi.

Then, as quickly as the moment came over him, he returned to his ravenous and mentally deficient state.

Danny recognized the language and thought back to the early Latin he'd taken at school when his mom hoped he'd stay out of the family business and go to the Seminary.

Thus passes the glory . . . glory of world. Thus passes the glory of the world.

The metal gate outside rattled, hitting the front wall and cracking the main window. Danny dropped down and crawled to the front door. Several of the Hungry were yanking on the gate. The hungriest ones must have heard him scream. He dropped and looked out at the gathering throng. Their judicial gaze fixed on him, and they suddenly froze, chanting as one:

"*Sic transit gloria mundi.*"

He fell back and grabbed his gun, but he knew he didn't have enough ammunition. What could he do? Not a fucking a thing. Danny got up and returned to the kitchen.

He checked the dough again and stirred the sauce, pausing briefly to change the bandage. Wooziness came over him, and he held onto the counter, willing himself to stay awake. Danny poured himself more wine and drank it with water, trying to up his blood volume. When it calmed, he tasted the sauce then added oregano, salt, pepper but discovered his fresh basil was mostly gone. He'd have to make due. The oven heated to the optimal temperature, and he covered his hands with flour then worked the dough, spinning it in the air with his fists. The painkillers clouded his brain, and he floated. Chemical confidence drove him, and Danny giggled, finding the whole thing hysterical, a big biblical joke. He laughed until tears flowed, and he smelled the cooking oil, the scent of the fresh dough, and, as usual, he couldn't help feeding his hands down his pants to cover himself with flour. Curly growled at him, and he felt the shame again.

"You think I'm a fucking freak?" Danny yelled. "Like I had a choice? Took me some time to really understand. Therapy. Why do some men become lawyers or junkies? Or why did I start burying shit in the cellar? From the day I was born, my life dried up, like cement. My uncle was the fuckin' boss. You knew what my dad was? I wanted to be a priest, but my uncle had other plans."

Curly shrugged.

"You should understand," Danny said, pulling his hand from his pants to work the dough on the table. "We both got pulled into this life, and we paid the debts of our fathers. My pop did a few side contracts, and when they opened the books, he got straightened out. He retired to Florida with my mom, and I was expected to take on both sides of the business. I only ever wanted to be a fucking cook, but I was better at . . . the other thing. All fathers are assholes to their wives, kids, and that shit conditions us. That's how I got this fetish. It ain't my fault. I caught Pop bending Brandy the waitress over the prep counter one morning. Parmesan cheese and sauce smeared down their bodies, and she licked it off his fat, sweaty chest. The smell got into my head—the sweet taste of her pussy and the rich cheese. Pretty soon I was jerking off into the mozzarella. Brandy came in one morning and watched me. Sick chick, that one. She did me on some fresh dough. Licked the flour off my neck. But my pop walked in, grabbed me and threw me down the cellar, breaking my arm and collar bone. He left me down there for two days in the dirt with the flies and beetles. Taught me something important though: don't ever get caught. Now they've come for me as they've come for all sinners. I'm going to hell, I know this. I accepted that fact after my first job. But I'm going with a fucking grin on my face . . . "

Danny kneaded out the dough in a square and prepared three more to account for the required length. He checked the sauce and tasted the sweetness—nearly done, *almost* ready. He wanted it perfect for his final meal.

The lights went out.

The stove LEDs died, and the crimson glow of the burners dimmed then extinguished. *Fuck.* If the sauce chilled, it would thicken too early. He didn't have any choice. Danny would have to rewire the generator from the freezer to the oven. He had some experience building houses when he was a kid, but the system was old and might not work.

"*Sic—*" Danny emptied his piece into Curly's head until the rat shut up and finally stopped moving.

He sighed and washed his hands and tossed a tablecloth over the corpse at the front table, then he grabbed his tools. Danny always hated coming down to this mud hole—a crypt to bury his past, to hide away all the darkness he'd shed in his duty to the family. He grabbed a flashlight and descended the dry-rotted stair case of flat-boards into the ancient foundations of the building, built in the 1700s from what he heard. His hand trembled and his flashlight bean shook. What the hell? He could hold a shotgun steady but couldn't handle going down into his own cellar?

His back ached from the muscle memory from when his pop threw him down the same sharp steps. He took in a deep breath and stepped onto the loose dirt, following the sallow light of the dim flashlight. Unsteady, he tripped over some empty crates and fell back into a pile of broken chairs. Empty wine bottles rolled off a shelf and landed in the soft earth. The reek of rat urine burned his nose, and worms emerged under the pressure of his footfalls. He stepped through the loose ground, and the floor shifted under his weight, grabbing at his boots, sucking him down.

Danny found the generator boxed in the corner. He set down the flashlight and began to rewire it, bypassing the lines to the freezer. As he worked, he thought he heard something scratching, maybe rats digging behind the old walls. He ignored it and cleaned some of the connections, until a muffled moan distracted him. Danny set down his work and scanned the basement.

Had one of those things gotten in? He dreaded the thought since the flimsy cellar door wouldn't hold against a sustained attack. He searched through the debris and checked under the staircase but couldn't locate the source of the noise. The noise got louder, and he traced it to the ground beneath his feet. Soil subsided in several spots, and he watched it being pushed aside. Fingers dug upwards, clawing to the surface from the shallow graves below. He stood momentarily frozen and watched their efforts, counting seven bodies pushing through, which accounted for his own deposits. Danny couldn't be sure how many were struggling further below since he didn't know how many contracts his father had done.

Danny returned to work on the generator, hurrying, cutting corners, trying to fix the damaged connection. Arms continued to breach the ground around him, and in one location, he recognized the sloughing head of a drug dealer—one of his early ones, an example that had to be made. Lye had eaten away much of his skin, exposing grey muscle. His left eye rolled to and fro in wild motions, and he convulsed when he sniffed the air. Danny struggled to see the colors of the wiring in the poor light but finally finished rigging the generator, keeping his fingers crossed it wouldn't blow out the electrical system. Then Danny grabbed the flashlight and stepped over one of the bodies.

A hand snaked up and dug its fingernails into his calf. Danny stifled a scream and snapped off its fingers one by one until he could break free. Two more of the Hungry pulled their limbs from the earth and crawled towards their executioner. Did they remember? Another body climbed out behind them. A woman. Her shirt had torn during extrication, and a partially-chewed breast flopped about.

He'd never clipped a female, so it must have been one of his father's jobs. The old fuck knew no shame, or honor.

She pulled herself up on a shelf and staggered on decayed legs, walking unsure like an infant. The light revealed her face, and he nearly pissed himself. His pop had killed *her*?

"Brandy?" She'd been his first love—sick and twisted. "I didn't know," he said, lying to himself and babbling to her. "I thought you'd just quit and left town after . . . "

Her long, auburn hair had mostly torn from her skull, and worms had devoured her sweet apple cheeks. He expected to feel more emotion for the woman who had fucked him over so bad mentally—and physically—yet his heart emptied at the sight of her. Danny pulled the cord on the generator.

The turbine rattled but failed to start. Her gnawed fingertips brushed against his back, driving chills up his neck. He yanked again and again, screeching in frustration. By now, more of the Hungry came at Danny. He kicked the generator, dislodging a cloud of dust and pulled the cord hard, stripping some skin from his palm. Then he collapsed backward into the pit of writhing bodies.

A spark ignited in the turbine, lighting up the cellar, and a hanging bulb glowed, illuminating all the faces of the dead. Their eyes burned with such purpose, mesmerizing obsession, hypnotizing Danny. He shook it off. Brandy grabbed his shoulder, and for a frisson of fantasy, he felt her live once more—the grace of her flirtation, the rage in her hand clawing down his neck. He almost let himself fall into her mouth, but he tore himself out of Brandy's embrace, pulling her arm out of its socket in the process. He dodged the mewling drug dealer and frantically climbed his way upstairs. His heart thumped against his ribs, and he nearly blacked out.

At the top of the stairs, he barricaded the door with a wine crate. And after a moment to calm his breathing and let his heartbeat slow, Danny checked the stove and found the digital clock blinking. Back in his element, he calmly set the burners and stirred the sauce. Heat still radiated from the pizza oven, his one true love, and he shoveled the square patches of dough down her mouth, giving her all she could take. Pizza dough baked fast, just enough time to set the table.

One of the Hungry slammed against the cellar door, nudging the crate.

Danny knew he had to cut some corners on his perfect meal to finish in time, and he decided to sacrifice presentation and chanced the sauce being somewhat raw. He dabbed his neck with a bit of garlic to obscure the salty sweet aroma of decomposing flesh then rushed to the dining room to set the table. He pushed some of the tables together and covered them with a black satin tablecloth, then arranged a bouquet of orchids on the surrounding tables—the same flowers his mother wanted at her funeral. He fed white tapers into empty wine bottles and lit them all in a row with a single wooden match. Outside, he heard the cage rattle and break, and he knew the mob of the Hungry crowding South Street—all reaching, digging, crying out in hunger, rage, had unified in purpose. To purify his sins, everyone's sins.

Danny ran back to the kitchen and chopped fresh onions, peppers, olives, and pepperoni in a controlled frenzy, then dumped it all into a bowl. Blood dripped from his saturated bandage and mixed with the toppings, but he no longer cared. On the contrary, his erection pressed against his pants and pulsed. Euphoria spread up from his groin and electrified his stomach, electrifying his dying muscles.

The Hungry pushed harder against the crate, and two pallid hands reached through the crack.

And Danny checked his pizza crust.

The dough had baked golden brown, and he slid it out piece by piece, setting it atop the tables in the dining room. He brought over his sauce, cheese, and toppings, then set a rack of spices on a serving tray. It was ready. He smiled as he worked, dancing on his toes, creating the apotheosis of both of his lives.

Brandy pushed through the tight opening, tearing off the remainder of her hair against the pinch of the wood. The apron she wore on her last day caught on the door and ripped free, revealing her white ribs and a single rubbery lung. He spotted a gunshot wound through her sternum and guessed that Pop must have done it that morning while he huddled in the basement, rubbing his broken bones. She sniffed in his direction then chomped at the air between them, showing her white teeth, transfixing Danny. He always loved her smile, longed for her kiss again, this time slicing through his muscle and tendon, eating through to his heart.

Danny disrobed, standing naked in his restaurant, naked before the purifying dead, nude and vulnerable to his victims returned to him. Laying flat across the table, he ladled searing tomato sauce down his body, starting on his shredded face, then layering down the muscles of his neck. The thick sauce dripped and splattered on the floor as Danny worked to pool it on his chest, thighs, and groin. Then, he sprinkled a layer of cheeses and herbs, finishing the meal with the vegetables and meat. The sauce burned his skin and melted the cheese, and he rubbed more on his balls, then carefully sprinkled the oregano, garlic and pepper. Once he'd finished his top layer, Danny rolled about on the fresh crust, covering his back with warm grainy flour. His cock twitched, ready to burst, and just in time to eat it hot, his victims broke through.

He opened one eye, then the other. They were wandering through the restaurant, lead by Brandy. The Hungry meandered aimlessly about, sniffing the air but missing the meal.

"Come on you dead fucks!" he yelled. "Best pie I ever made! Just wait until you taste the special sauce I'm about to make you for dessert . . . "

He waited, body jumping, heart beating, suffering in anticipation. "Fucking idiots." Still, they wouldn't come. The Hungry muttered and sniffed about, possibly looking for him but never hitting the mark.

Then he realized the problem: he'd blocked the scent of his body with all the ingredients. Danny needed something else to attract them, some human food . . .

He freed one hand, tore off his soaked bandage and lobbed blood at Brandy, streaking her leathery face. She turned towards him, and he splashed more blood in her direction. She followed it like a dog, leading the mob of Hungry. Judgment had finally come.

"I've missed you, baby. I made you dinner!"

Brandy nosed through the toppings on his abdomen and, smearing tomato sauce and cheese down her gray face and flesh. She chewed through, letting most of the fresh veggies fall from her mouth, then pushed her chin up his inner thigh. His body exploded in ecstasy, tingling up from his feet to his mouth, the nascent orgasm erupting through his groin and stomach, his sauce mixing with the tomato and cheese. The fresh juice from his body drew Brandy down, and she bit hard, gnawing on it like the knob end of a baguette. He screamed, insane from the opposing sensations pushing through his body. He struggled to stay conscious, the two of them merged in rapacious lust. He filled her completely. Her mouth, her stomach, her heart.

But soon several others joined her feasting, and his resistance gone, he let them take him. When Brandy bit a last chunk out of his fleshy thigh, spraying blood across the room, they found him easily The outside mob broke through the front door, and they crowded the restaurant, and the blessed hungry devoured Danny completely. Their instinct matched his perversion, balancing his fantasy, satiating his last wish, and there was no shame. And as they ate, peace assuaged Danny, and he closed his eyes for good, finally understanding that a lifetime of separating sex from violence, family from love, and yearning from the feast, was over. He reveled in his last moment, as they all screamed together as one.

"*Sic transit gloria mundi!*"

"Thus passes the glory!"

DEMONS OF 1994

IZZY LEE

KAT OPENED THE door to find her best friend with a puffy eye, cupping his hand to a bloody nose. Rivulets of crimson rolled over Steve's knuckles, creating unsettling, spidery red lines. Pepper, the Pomeranian pup at his feet, made a salutational peep and trotted in like she owned the place.

"Again?"

Inside, he dropped his backpack on the floor. He shook his long dark hair out of his face, but only managed to splash more blood on his Downward Spiral t-shirt. The soft yellow and eggshell-colored cotton sopped up his blood like a thirsty bandage. The wet splotches would turn the color of rust, and blend into the abstract painting of the shirt's design; as a painter, she appreciated the organic possibilities of the final composition. But as Steve's friend, she hated that today's beating would forever mark the new shirt from his favorite band.

It'd be a bit until her parents came home, and she was glad they didn't have to see Steve caked in violence.

"School's almost out, at least." Kat offered a box of Puffs.

The thin, pale boy shrugged and ripped out a few of the soft, disposable tissues and pressed them up into his nostrils. "Can't come soon enough, K. I'm such a failure."

Her heart sung at the simple mention of his nickname for her, but twisted at the rest of his words. How unfair for him to think that of himself, the captain of the Science Club and a generally sweet guy who earned all honors in his AP classes for the last three years—plus a pretty decent guitar player, especially when it came to Nirvana. It was true that the songs were easy to play, but not everyone could play with such passion.

That shitty day in April when Kurt Cobain's body was found came back to her as full of force as that goddamn bully Joe's fist to Steve's delicate face. Steve had arrived at the bus stop, tears in his eyes matching hers. Without speaking, they'd embraced and cried in each other's arms. Everything was screaming inside of them, and they both wanted to die along with Kurt. The next day, they'd played hooky and driven to Hampton Beach, angry parents be damned. They'd camped out on the sand under the cold New Hampshire sun, bright without comfort.

Her face crumbled, and she stifled a cry. Finally, he turned his brown eyes to her. "That's not what I think of you," she squeaked. "You're the best person I know. Fuck that." She yanked a few tissues out of the box for herself as the tears fell, and sat back down in front of the TV. She'd been watching it when the doorbell rang; every channel was talking about the same thing. The news was re-playing footage of the slick-haired lawyer reading a note from that football guy who probably killed his wife. Something about not feeling sorry for him. Kat shook her head.

"I hate football," Steve mumbled. He sat down, too, and Pepper jumped up on the couch next to them. *So* ridiculous and cute. Joe Sousa, who was NOT cute, had been at it again. He was the beefy bully who enjoyed pummeling skinny Steve every chance he could get. Joe was a star player on the school's varsity team—because of course he was.

Kat imagined Steve ten years older, a graduate of some fancy college—Ivy League, maybe—and definitely successful. His smarts would take him far, unlike her art skills. Maybe he'd found his own company someday. Whatever he'd do, it would *not* be a failure. The thin fabric of the shirt she wore began vibrating in time with her heartbeat, and she inhaled sharply. "Steve." She waited for him to face her. "Do you trust me?"

He swallowed back a thick lump—blood and snot, she guessed. "You're the only one I trust."

She allowed herself a faint smile, and daydreamed of a life where you didn't have to bear a crushed heart and pretend otherwise. A life without villains and horror.

On the TV behind them, a white Bronco rolled on a California freeway.

"This is never going to work."

Kat slipped a key into the lock of her father's top desk drawer. It gave way with a satisfying *click!* and she put the key back in its potted plant hiding place. "We'll just have to find out, won't we?" Kat rummaged through the drawer until she found the prize, nestled deep behind assorted business cards and bills. She withdrew a small package, and unwrapped the twine and cloth to reveal a book weathered by time and circumstance. Steve cocked his head, like when Pepper was attempting to understand a command.

"This is dumb. We're just going to piss him off more, and he'll do something even worse than that time he threw my bike into the quarry." Steve approached as she creaked the brittle pages open; her heart dashed against her sternum as a few crumbs of parchment fluttered to the floor.

"Shit!"

He stopped next to her, closer than usual—they were almost touching—and she tried to push down the heat that rushed within. Did he notice? Would that make things worse or better?

"That thing's pretty old, huh? Where'd he get that?"

She kicked the tiny pieces of evidence under the desk. "Dad found it on one of his trips. I overheard him telling Mom about it last month." Her excitement skyrocketed as she recalled the conversation, her parents speaking in hushed tones that night, and how she was not to hear, except that she did. "I'm not supposed to know about it." Kat stood to show him the strange drawings and weird language within the book's pages. "I'm pretty sure he stole it."

That familiar fire lit up in Steve's eyes, and her nerves crackled. How badly she wanted to kiss him. "Can I see?"

She handed the book to him carefully; as he took it, his long fingers brushed hers. She recorded the feeling of his skin, and catalogued it in her memory for later, when she was alone in bed and the night was quiet.

"Not quite leather . . . " He turned the book over, taking in its strange, wrinkled texture. "Is this . . . human skin?"

"Maybe." She took the book back. "Technically, that's still leather! But check out these fucked-up drawings." She opened the pages to a series of sketches in faded reddish ink: a dead animal, a naked man on top of a naked woman, a spread of food, a sundial, a demon, the corpse of a man, and a town on fire. His mouth dropped.

He shifted and took a step back, to her dismay. "Were these drawn in blood?"

"That's what I heard. Cool, huh?"

Steve cleared his throat. "Yeah. So, um . . . What does your dad do again?"

Kat giggled. "He's not a Satanist or warlock or anything, though that would be kinda cool. He's more like Indiana Jones." When Steve raised his eyebrows, she continued, "He's an anthropologist, remember? Silly." She glanced toward the door and lowered her voice to a stage whisper. "Anyway, I heard him telling Mom that he'd found a resurrection book of some sort, and that he 'couldn't let it fall into the wrong hands.'" She laughed. "What a savior he was, stealing this precious artifact. From what I understand, if we chant some of these words . . . " She flipped to a spread covered in smudged writing. " . . . we'll summon a vengeful demon to do our bidding,"

Steve stared at the book in her hands and shifted. "Maybe we shouldn't mess with this, K. I hate Joe, and I would give anything to have him gone. But this is . . . " His eyes met hers. "I don't know what this is. This thing is straight out of the *Evil Dead* films.

She considered this. "But what if we really could get rid of the bad guys with this? Couldn't we make the world a better place? We'll try it on Joe as a test run."

Steve shuffled again. "I don't know. I'm gonna go home now. Thanks for the tissues."

"I thought you trusted me!" He pivoted and walked swiftly out of her father's den, followed by Pepper, who'd been busy kissing Kat's tuxedo cat Spooky in the sunny window. "Steve, wait. Come on!" He didn't answer. Maybe the fucking in the book had turned him off. "Damnit!"

Steve hadn't shown up to school come Monday. School would be out within days, but by lunch, Kat's nerves were on edge. Where was he? She took her brown bag lunch outside and sat on the steps of the school's side entrance by the parking lot. However, her sandwich held little appeal as her friends chattered on about the usual summer plans.

Steve's dented Chevy Celebrity raced into the lot and screeched to a violent stop. He threw the car into park and whipped open the door, emerging with a small form bundled in an old towel.

"Oh my God." Kat stood, not noticing the sandwich as it dropped to the cement. The students stopped chatting and gawked.

"K!" Steve yelled, his voice cracking and back drooping as he stood by the car. His face was drawn and pink. Swathed in terrycloth, Pepper's lifeless little head swung limp from a broken neck. Kat heard herself scream.

Mocking laughter erupted from the parking lot, where Joe lounged against a pick-up truck and clapped. "That's one way to end the school year!" His goon buddies whooped in response.

"Monsters!" Tears thickened with inky mascara were suddenly running down Kat's cheeks. They only laughed harder.

"What is going on?!" Her band teacher, Ms. Cacciola, had just stepped outside with Mr. Epstein, who taught AP Computer Science.

"Steve?" Mr. Epstein inquired. "Are you all right?"

Steve ignored the teachers and the jocks, his tunnel vision gazed focused only on her as he left his car and approached the steps. The unblinking torment in his eyes crushed her. "He did it, K! I know he did it. I ran into him over the weekend and he shoved me. I told him I wasn't afraid of him. I called him names. This morning, I found her dead on the lawn."

Kat could not escape the horror of Pepper's unmoving, black marble eyes. She thought she could hear Joe and his gang still laughing, and then the commotion of adults barking at the jocks beneath the heavy cotton blanket of her periphery. Steve leaned forward and lowered his voice to a hush, his lips pressing against her ear.

"I trust you, K. I want him dead." He drew back and shivered at his own words, broken into so many fragments that that he might never be whole again. And then Steve—in front of all those people—

drew in a shaky breath and kissed her on the lips. Too shocked to react, Kat watched as he pulled poor dead Pepper close, and walked back to the car. He sped away before the teachers could force him to the guidance counselor's office.

The evening sky blazed in luminous orange and pink as they pushed the last pile of dirt over Pepper's backyard grave with their bare hands. Steve sat next to Kat in silence and stared at the tiny lump of earth, before wiping the soil onto his black cargo pants. He pressed the edges of the soft mound down with his combat boots, creating a seal between the loose earth and the grass.

"Pepper was just a little dog. She never did anything bad to anybody. She was full of love." Tears glistened on the bruised black eye Joe had left him with over the weekend; a creeping perimeter of yellow ochre encroached on the bruised violet crescent under his left eye.

"I know." Kat fought back tears of her own. She took his hand and he grasped it with ferocity, surprising her.

"Does it have to be tonight?"

"I think that's what the sundial in the drawings mean. We might only have hours to do this. If you want to. I'm so sorry. She was an amazing dog. I know how much she meant to you."

Kat wondered about the sex drawing, and how they would complete that part of the formula. Would it be terrible or awkward? Would it tear their friendship apart? Hell, would it hurt? She'd heard from friends and in some movies, that yeah, it fucking hurt. But all sorts of things hurt, all the time. Why would this be any different?

"I don't know what I'd do without you. I really don't." He started bawling and fell into her shoulder, gripping her body for dear life. Kat found herself afraid of this new emotion from her best friend, but aware of her own, as well. She would take care of this. She'd take care of him. A roiling anger frothed in her stomach as she clutched him back.

"It's okay," she whispered through clenched teeth into his messy hair, not entirely sure that it was okay, or would ever be again. "Let's go summon ourselves a motherfucking demon."

"You sure your parents aren't coming back tonight?"

Kat unlocked the front door of her family's home, eyes instinctively shifting down to watch for Pepper. She thought of the little dog, dead in its grave.

"My dad's giving a talk in Phoenix tonight."

"I don't think I've ever been so happy that your parents have been out of town . . . or to have a friend like you."

Kat shut the door behind her, leaning against it like some forlorn heroine in a romance tale. Even though she didn't believe in God, she prayed for courage to help her say the words she was so afraid to. *And all the demon-invoking stuff, too, please and thanks, God.*

"We've gotten to the point where I think you know how I feel about you," she swallowed.

He turned, locking eyes, then rushed to her in a sudden movement that pushed his warm body and mouth against hers in a combustible embrace. Steve was always so much warmer than she, and she relished it.

"I think I know," he said, lips still against hers.

Neither of them really knew how to make love, but they figured it out together, even without the book.

"Are you sure you still want to do this?" she asked, pulling her black dress back on.

"Yeah. For Pepper." His eyes darkened, and a silence settled over them. Everything from now on was going to be completely different. Once they embarked on this dark adventure, nothing might happen at all, save for more pummeling from Joe and possibly his buddies. Or, the unreal and unthinkable could actually happen, and they'd call forth a being from another plane of existence for revenge purposes. It was an odd dichotomy for a Monday night.

Steve let his internal storm pass, opting for comfort. He nibbled the side of her neck, and she savored the tingle that ran up inside her.

"I'm hungry."

"I'll bet you are."

He smiled at her for the first time in days, since before the punch that nearly shattered his nose. "On the way over, I saw his car out back at the pizza place. And I don't think he knows where you live."

"Perfect." Kat picked up the phone on her nightstand and punched the buttons. "What kinda pie do you want? Pepperoni? Hawaiian? I think they have a buy one, get one deal tonight."

"Sure. Whatever you want." His eyes were laser-focused on her, studying her with such a mix of intensity and a fondness that it made her blush.

"No one's ever looked at me the way you are now."

Then, on the phone: "Sousa's Pizza, can I help you?"

Steve and Kat were perched on the couch when the doorbell rang.

"Get him inside," he said, and he strode to the fireplace and yanked the poker out of the stand with a *clang!* that sounded like a dull warning. He ducked into the hallway, out of sight.

The doorbell rang three more times in rapid succession, as if it was irritated she hadn't answered already.

Kat threw the door open to a surprised Joe, and grabbed his arm to steer him inside.

"Hi! Can you bring it in while I get the money? Thanks!"

Joe was already walking toward the kitchen when realization of who his customers were finally washed over his face. Then came the familiar sneer. He tossed the pizza boxes onto the kitchen island and grunted, "That'll be $15.99."

Kat sized him up; he wasn't a danger. Yet. The linebacker looked ridiculous in his too-tight red polo shirt with the tiny embroidered pizza slice on the front. She crossed in front of him, making a play to her bag on the counter, and Joe watched her with disdain. His crawling eyes made her anxious as hell.

A sound of metal scraped along the floor. They both turned.

Steve stood there, the fire poker raised.

"Motherfucker, you're dead," Joe growled. He lunged forward in a practiced tackle, but not before Steve brought the weapon down on the lunk's head. A sickening *crack!* rang out, and the bully fell hard onto the wooden floor.

Kat yelped as Joe tried to rise and Steve hit him again, this time aiming for the back of the neck, and he dropped like a cold slab of beef. Waves of arousal flooded through Kat, then guilt, then . . . *fuck it*. She stepped forward and put her arms around Steve.

"I think that'll do it for now."

"He would have tried to kill me. I know it. I just know it. He might've even tried to do something bad to you. I can't allow that."

She answered him with a gentle kiss. "I'm never letting you go."

He dropped the poker onto Joe's back and grabbed her in a fierce embrace. It was mere seconds before they were writhing on the floor—right next to Joe—in a second brazen explosion of passion that she wished would never end.

Of course, it did end. Everything had to end. And when they were done, they bound Joe to one of the kitchen chairs with duct tape.

Joe groaned as he woke, dried blood smeared on his face. He saw them chewing on slices of the pizza he'd delivered, but zeroed in on the book in Kat's other hand.

"What's that?" Joe realized he was unable to move his arms and saw swaths of silver tape holding him tight. "What the fuck, you freaks!" He bucked against his binding, making the chair jump around, scraping wood against wood.

"Shut up." Steve leaned down and slapped his half-eaten slice of pepperoni onto the jock's cheek, then smeared the grease around in a messy circle. He let the slice hang off his face there until it plopped onto the floor. "You're going to do as we say. Or do you want to get hit again? How's it feel, huh? How's it feel to be helpless?"

"I swear to God, I'm going to fucking kill you." Joe turned his gaze to Kat. "Both of you."

"You're not doing a fucking thing unless I tell you to . . . " Steve gritted through his teeth, landing a kick against the other teen's chest that sent him flying backwards. Joe's head bounced against the wooden floor in another *crunch!*

Too weak to scream, Joe whimpered. "Okay." The jock suddenly seemed like a child, his face stretched in pain and Kat felt bad. But the image of Pepper's broken, swinging neck killed any sympathy she had toward him.

"K, grab the phone," Steve muttered. She thought of all the times she'd seen him bruised and bloody, and snatched the cordless receiver off the wall. She dialed Sousa's Pizza again.

"Now, you fucking asshole, you're going to tell your dad that you're skipping out on the rest of your shift to go party in Forest Glade Park," Kat demanded.

"Sousa's Pizza, can I help you?" The tinny voice of Joe's dad answered. Kat knelt and held the receiver to the boy's ear, careful not to get blood or sauce on it. Joe did as he was ordered, and Kat hung up.

"Good. For that, little doggy, you get a reward." Steve heaved Joe back into an upright position, then considered his own words, his anger roiling again

Joe's eyes fluttered. He was at least concussed—and getting worse. "Ehmm sawwrryy," he mewled.

"Yeah." Steve pulled Joe forward by his polo collar. "Everyone's fucking sorry," he spit. "I'm sorry you were ever born, but you're never going to hurt anyone ever again. See, I'm thinking if we let you go, you'd kill us. Then you'd go to college on some sports scholarship or Daddy's money. You'd date rape some girls. You'd maybe graduate, inherit that pizza chain, and make all your employees miserable. I can't let you do any of that," he slapped Joe in the mouth and stood up.

"Steve." Kat touched him on the shoulder. "It's getting late." He pulled her into a new embrace, kissing her with more fervor than she expected in such a moment of hatred.

"I love you." He rested his forehead against hers as he spoke. She imagined him deep inside himself, small and dark and flailing.

Kat wanted to say so many things. That it would be okay, that they would get away with it, and that they would go on to thrive and have good lives, but she only answered: "I love you, too. Always. Forever."

She opened the book and started speaking the alien words within, probably mispronouncing everything. She knew this wouldn't matter.

Joe opened his eyes wide, real fear registering in him for the first time, she guessed. Steve held her close, one long hand traveling up and down her thigh, then up her waist and back down again, all the while whispering "I love you" over and over. God, it was hot.

"Wuh . . . wuth argh djyoou dewing?"

She continued speaking the words, confidence in her voice growing.

Then she stopped.

Waited.

They all waited.

Nothing happened.

Joe tried to laugh, but coughed, blood gurgling out of his mouth. Then he passed out, his thick skull slumping heavy on his neck, chin on his chest.

Kat flipped through the book to see if she'd missed anything.

"It doesn't work," Steve mumbled.

Behind the group, sticky bubbles popped. They both turned to see the blanket of cheese on the uneaten pizza rising up on its own . . .

Then a small gray creature climbed out of the pie, covered in red sauce—and howled an unearthly noise.

Neither Steve nor Kat spoke as the thing—more of an imp than the full-fledged demon illustrated in the book—took notice of them. It stared. Kat felt a horrifying, dark presence penetrating her mind, rifling through her thoughts and memories.

Kat grabbed Steve's hand, and she saw that his eyes were rolled up into his head, showing just the whites, and he was quaking. He fell. Her own eyes followed suit, crawling back under eyelids, her vision fading as the demon probed her mind. She felt the floor strike her body. Images of a hellscape flooded her thoughts: fire, a burst of heat then Arctic air, and then the impression of that air gusting past her as she fell. Echoes of the hungry and damned bounced off the walls of a cavernous pit, and the pitch of their wails escalated until she lost her hearing—and consciousness.

Crunch. Slurp. Chew. Gulp.

Kat opened her eyes with relief, grateful to have her sight back, but only for a moment. Her lower half was sodden; blood and piss had pooled beneath her, drenching her dress and coating her bare skin.

The demon was rooting around within Joe's cadaver, covered in viscera. The creature turned, Joe's liver hanging between its teeth.

She lurched up and vomited the remains of her dinner. Steve was already sitting up next to her, gazing in shock at the creature. It stopped eating. But instead of coming after her, it grabbed the pizza box that had been knocked to the floor.

Then, dipping a claw into Joe's blood, it painted on the inside of the box:

"MORE."

Steve inched close to Kat and pulled her into a huddle.

"What the fuck did we do?" he whispered.

"We summoned a demon," was all she could say.

When he could speak, Steve asked. "Are we the bad guys now?"

The creature dropped the remains of Joe's liver and thwacked the pizza box. It wrote again on the soiled cardboard:

"ANOTHER."

"Another victim?" It nodded.

An ocean of cold horror curdled within her. "Steve . . . "

He didn't answer. His eyes were on the crouching creature bathed in blood and barbarity. The demon hit the cardboard again, louder.

The pair jumped, and Steve paused, thinking of another tormentor.

"Rob Hansen," Steve croaked, the name leaden in his mouth.

The demon nodded. As it stood, its form stretched and grew about a foot taller. It cast its gaze at the far side of the room, and the curtains went up in flames. It looked at the table, and fire devoured that, too. Then the walls were engulfed in shades of blistering Halloween orange and Christmas red.

The demon pointed to the door, the one thing not aflame.

Kat took Steve's hand, and they followed the demon outside and toward their next meal, the house burning bright behind them against the darkness.

BAD NIGHT BELOW RICKY'S

NICK KOLAKOWSKI

[William Pabodie Interview Transcript, Version 1. Interview took place in the Cleveland Police Headquarters, Cleveland, Ohio, August 20, 2018. Consent was given by interview subject. Transcribed from video on August 21, 2018.]

IRST THINGS FIRST: I think internet conspiracies are bullshit. Those mouth-breathing wankers in their basements, posting photographs and picking through court filings like they're the second coming of Bob Fucking Woodward, they're a bunch of clowns looking for a circus. And I should know, because I spent years pretending I was one of them, theorizing in their online comment threads about Michael Jackson being killed by the Illuminati, or the government's secret plan to transform Walmarts into FEMA camps.

I was so good at it, I once convinced a hundred tinfoil-hat lunatics in a subreddit that Melania Trump had a doppelgänger for public events. They told another thousand whackjobs, and by the next day, a reporter from *The New York Times* was sending messages to my burner account. I never responded to the reporter, because I didn't need the added fame: in certain circles of the internet, I was already a trickster god, toying with the noobs and the weak-minded.

But after tonight, I think those folks on reddit and 4chan and Twitter got it right: there *is* something evil out there. Only they believe it's the FBI or CIA, ready to kick down their front door and take away their guns, and I know it's far bigger than that. This Big

Thing is probably older than the human race, and so chock-full of evil it makes the Nazis look like the Muppets.

The Big Thing, it lived in the kitchen of Ricky's Pizza Palace.

Why are you laughing?

Yeah, I know the pizza's good there. You have to admit, the place looks like it hasn't been cleaned since the Reagan administration. I'm surprised it passed health inspections. Maybe it hasn't. Have any health inspectors gone missing recently?

No, I'm not joking with you, Detective. I have nothing but respect for cops. Let me walk you through what happened. Hey, can someone get me a towel? There's blood still on my arm.

[Tape paused; resumes 03:32.]

Thanks. Is Officer Daltry okay? I saw what happened to his head.

[Detective Pabodie: 'Then you'd know that Officer Daltry, unfortunately, has passed away.']

Is someone watching the body? Do they have a weapon? Like a flamethrower or something? What?

[Tape paused; resumes 03:38.]

Okay, okay. Here we go: it started with Darkraven. Her real name was Monica, but Darkraven was her online handle. She was a troll, like me, only a far superior breed. I might have strung these maniacs along for the laughs, but she did her best to snap their fragile psyches like twigs. We met in a Flat-Earther forum, where she tricked the moderator into doing the math that proved the world is round. As he screamed in all-caps, Darkraven and I "retired" to a separate thread, where we whiled away the hours with discussions of philosophy and Xbox games.

And I was in love. By the time we wrecked another dozen tinfoil-hatters, I thought she might love me, too. For our three-week anniversary, she sent me some interesting photos, let us say. Even better, she revealed that she lived in Parma Heights, just one town over.

I was hot to hook up, but meeting a fellow troll in person is always tricky. They rarely look like their photos, you know what I mean? Plus, so many of them lack a meatspace personality, and there's nothing more disheartening than setting up a meeting with someone who's hilarious online, only to find out they're a monosyllabic lump once they're in the seat across from you.

"You know Ricky's? It's got good pizza," she messaged me. "We can meet there."

"Only if we don't order Hawaiian," I wrote back. "That stuff is nasty."

"DEALBREAKER," she replied.

"How about 8:00?"

She agreed, and I signed off. I was excited but nervous. If my life online has taught me anything, it's that you can bite into the tastiest treat and find a shit-filled center. So I called my best friend Guillaume, who wanted nothing to do with the conspiracy sites but loved kicking my ass in *Call of Duty* a couple times a week. Because they yanked my license after that bullshit DWI, I needed him to serve as my getaway driver if Darkraven turned out to be a three-hundred-pound felon with halitosis and a gimp fetish.

Guillaume's a solid dude, no matter what you guys might dig up about him. He drove a yellow Honda Accord with a smashed-out side window covered with a trash bag. The interior smelled like the Ghost of Burrito Farts Past, which I tried to counter by lighting a pre-game joint.

"I don't condone the use of illegal substances in my ride, man," he said.

"I got a prescription," I said, which was true: weed is the only thing that counters my extreme anxiety. So I tried staring him down, my lit match flickering an inch from the tip.

"No, man," he said, finger still wagging like an excited puppy's tail. "The smell is gonna linger."

"The smell of weed would only improve things, buddy." I waved out the match before it burned my fingers. "It is forty flavors of dank in here."

"I'm not the one who can't drive anymore."

"I know. I'm sorry."

"Apology accepted. Still going to frag the hell out of you, next game."

We arrived in Ricky's parking lot at 7:45. We had some trouble finding an empty spot. My palms were sweaty, and I barely heard Guillaume, who'd never dated a woman in his life, trying to give me a pep talk. Only it wasn't just the prospect of Darkraven making me nervous: Ricky's creeped me out. Maybe it was a trick of the dusk, but those huge front windows like glowing orange eyes, its shingled roof prickly as wolf's fur . . . I wanted a lungful of weed so bad, I practically shook in my seat.

Guillaume stayed in the car with a couple of iPhone games to keep him occupied. "Get me a slice of Hawaiian," he said. "Pineapple is awesome."

I'd dressed my best: gray Bruce Lee DJ t-shirt, a pair of clean jeans, and the same sport jacket I wore to my high-school graduation. Don't give me that look: this was a date at a pizza place, not some five-star French restaurant.

On the way in, I passed Officer Daltry's car parked in the front row. He must have been inside already, although I didn't see him until the metaphorical cow-patty smacked the ceiling fan.

Ricky's was packed with families scarfing down fat and carbs, and I had to circle the whole place before I found Darkraven in a back booth. Thank the Internet Gods, she looked just like her photos: dyed-red hair tipped blue, chunky eyeglasses, thin arms tattooed with swirling flowers and skulls. She wore a sleeveless black shirt and a long maroon skirt. As I approached, I waved, and she waved back. Fifteen seconds in, but so far, so good.

"I have a confession," she said as I sat down across from her, heart hammering.

"What?"

"I ordered the Hawaiian. Sorry." She leaned forward. "Damn, you have quite the poker face."

"I know you're kidding."

She laughed. "You were scared."

The waiter drifted over: sallow and thin, wearing an apron with the Ricky's logo, consisting of five pizza slices arranged in an off-kilter star pattern, tips facing out. "Hello and welcome to Ricky's," he droned. "Are you ready to order?"

Darkraven ordered a beer and a 21-inch with extra cheese. I opted for a soda.

"You don't drink?" she asked after the waiter left.

"Not anymore. I have a prescription for weed, though, so I do smoke."

She smiled.

"I get anxiety," I said.

"Really? You're fearless online."

"Exactly."

Reaching across the table, she took my left hand in both of hers. I flinched—but her skin was so warm, and her eyes so kind, that she overrode my nerves. "That's fine," she said. "Too many angry people in the world, anyway."

"But angry people brought us together."

She released my hand and settled back. "There's something I've never asked you online."

"Okay?"

"Why do you do it?"

I waved a hand at the restaurant. "I'm like a gallon of drain cleaner: I get in there, clean out their idiocy, make them re-think their assumptions. So maybe next time they hear something stupid, they actually question what they're hearing."

"And a little bit of mockery makes the medicine go down," she said, grinning.

I grinned back. "Something like that."

"You never think those wild theories are real?"

"Do I think Tupac faked his own death? Or that vaccines cause autism? No."

Our drinks arrived, and she downed half her beer in one gulp. Now that my tension had eased somewhat, I could see she was anxious, her forehead sheened with sweat. It made me feel weird and a bit proud, having that effect on someone. Don't mess this up, I thought.

After a long moment of silence, she finally said: "What if I told you I chose this place for a reason?"

I kept my smile, even as my excitement curdled.

She leaned forward, her voice dropping so low I had trouble hearing her over the cheesy pop blaring on the overhead speakers. "You notice this place's logo?"

"All the pizza slices?"

"It's a symbol. A bad one."

"Oh boy." My throat felt like someone had dropped a stone down it.

"Here, I'll show you something." She drained the rest of her beer and reached into the pink purse on the seat beside her, pulling out a slip of paper. It was a Sharpie sketch of the five-pointed logo.

"Okay, it's a pentagram," I shrugged. "But not quite. The three points on the top and left are closer together. Could be a weird-ass arrow, if you squint."

"Right, it's all angled strange," she said, returning the paper to her purse. "When I saw it on the restaurant website, I got curious, so I did some research. Even went to the library, cross-checked with *actual* books. You know what that symbol is?"

"I know you'll tell me."

"Okay." She took a deep breath, held it, exhaled and said: "I found a lot of references to ancient gods and demons, ones that get mentioned in the Old Testament, mythology from all over the world."

I kept my face neutral, just in case a hidden camera was live-streaming, as I glanced at the tables around us: happy faces, none looking in my direction. "Do you believe they exist?" I asked.

"I don't know," she said, pulling out her phone. "These Ancient Ones, they wouldn't cause any destruction if the people regularly offered them a blood sacrifice. So I started putting this together." She turned her phone so I could see the screen: a map of the streets around Ricky's, maybe two miles square, and peppered with little red dots. "These represent all the people missing over the past three years. Teenagers, good students, no trouble on their records. You know, *virgins*."

I didn't feel hungry anymore, and she flicked to the next image: a page from an old book. Yellowed paper crosshatched with crazy black lines, with two pale circles like eyes at the center of the mess. Script I couldn't read—Latin maybe?—ran in a tight column down the right margin, punctuated at the bottom by that five-pointed star. "I found a local one, if you can believe it," she said. "The first European explorers to this part of Ohio, they saw something near the lake. Something the local tribes worshipped, that they said ate people. For those tribes, this star symbol represented the thing. Pretty crazy, huh?"

"Yeah." I stared into the fizzing galaxy in my glass, unsure of what to do. "Really nuts."

"Hey, come on! We mess with those people, remember? You and me? I'm not saying any of this really means anything. I'm playing around."

"Playing around," I muttered, unconvinced.

"Weird symbols, ancient creatures, missing people: don't tell me it wouldn't make you curious, though. So I wanted to check it out. That's all." She set down her phone, talking faster. "You want to know why I torture those weirdos online? Because it's fun. Using logic is fun. Right?"

Our waiter returned, steaming pizza in one hand and a wire stand in the other. I said: "Sir, can I ask you something?"

"Yeah," he said, squinting as he centered the pizza on the stand.

"Is this establishment the home of an . . . Ancient One?" I pumped my voice full of absurd cheer. "Are you kidnapping virgins and performing blood sacrifices in order to spare everyone from some kind of Biblical wrath? Is there a stone altar in the basement where you enact the dreaded ceremony by the light of the full moon?" Pointing at the pizza, I asked: "And can you guarantee this doesn't have any human *beans* in it?"

Before the last words left my mouth, I knew I had made a horrible mistake. His eyeballs jittered in their sockets, the pupils practically constricting to pinpricks. The skin on his fists looked as gray as stone.

Darkraven's cheeks flushed. "What the fuck?"

The waiter turned on his heel and ran for the kitchen. Diners stared after him, the conversation around us dwindling. It would have been uncomfortably silent, if not for the happy music.

I decided it was all too weird for my taste. I stood up, plucking a paper napkin from the dispenser and peeling two hot slices from the pie for Guillaume. If he floored it, I could be home in twenty minutes, where I would delete every single message thread and email from this crazy chick. She could get the tab.

I don't know what I expected Darkraven to do, but her next move stunned me. Grabbing her purse, she leapt from the booth and charged after the waiter, disappearing through the swinging doors, presumably into the kitchen.

Pizza grease drizzling my knuckles, I looked through the restaurant's front windows at the distant speck of Guillaume's car. Then I thought: What if he tried to hurt her? There's no shortage of sharp implements in a kitchen . . .

So I charged through the double doors, a white knight in shining armor—only instead of a sword, I came armed with limp pizza slices. Cooks yelled, fire roared, and I accidentally whacked into a counter on my way through, scattering metal bowls of shredded cheese and vegetables. As I righted myself, I saw the star logo spray-painted on the wall above the ovens. My heart was in my throat, my vision constricted to a throbbing point, as I caught a glimpse of Darkraven disappearing through another doorway just ahead.

An authoritative voice echoed through the chaos, and I glanced back and saw a huge cop elbowing through the swinging doors. I picked up the pace. My feet slid on the tile as I took the final corner after Darkraven and into a massive storeroom.

As soon as I cleared the doorway, my hip smacked into the big boxes lining the wall. This checked my momentum, and maybe saved my life. Because what I saw in there . . .

[Tape paused; resumes 03:15.]

Just give me a second.
No, I'm fine. I just . . .
I saw *it*.

[Tape paused; resumes 04:10.]

No, I'm okay. Let's keep going.
So, my first thought was someone had spilled oil across the storeroom floor. It was sticky and thick, and so black it absorbed all the light from the bare bulb overhead. The waiter knelt in the center of the room, his back to me, his head bowed as he muttered to someone: "I'm sorry, so sorry . . . "

That's when I dropped the pizza, so you know it was serious.

Then fingers gripped my elbow, and I almost screamed. It was Darkraven. Her shirt collar was dark with sweat, her hair pasted to her forehead. "Don't step in it," she whispered, pointing at our feet, a few inches from where the oil began.

"I'm sorry . . . " The waiter was saying, bent forward until his forehead touched the oil, leaving no ripple.

And the liquid responded. It sent tendrils up his cheeks, brow, throat, hands. It slithered down the nape of his neck, into his shirt, and up his arms. I swear to God, this is what I saw. And as it did this, I heard a whispering sound, almost like voices.

"What the fuuuuuuuuuuuu . . . ?"

Darkraven and I turned and saw the cop in the doorway, his hand on his pistol, wary but not panicked. Not yet, at least. That's when I saw his nameplate: 'DALTRY, J.'

"Something's wrong with him," Darkraven whispered to the officer.

Daltry ignored her, stepping forward into the oil. "Move back, both of you."

That's when the waiter seemed to do a handstand in front of the three of us, his legs lifting into the air, his arms flailing, his head now coated completely in oil. He made no sound, not even a moan, but we heard the dull crunch of bones breaking. More tendrils rose from the muck like fingers, scraping the walls and shelves, straining for our legs.

"Freeze!" Daltry said, voice loud but weak. He'd drawn his gun.

The waiter began to descend into the oil, inch by inch. More like dissolve, I guess. Disappearing right into a concrete floor. That whispering sound rose, insistent, making my brain itch.

"Stop!" Daltry told the waiter, as if that would accomplish anything, and took another step, and a pencil-thin strand rocketed from the oil, spiraling almost to the ceiling before curving in a sharp arc for Daltry's head. It plunged into his right eye, and he loosed a bubbly shriek, dropping his pistol. Another ribbon of oil wrapped around his ankle, holding him in place. By that point I'd retreated to the hallway outside the storeroom, but I had zero doubt this thing was coming for us next.

Darkraven grabbed a small culinary torch from the nearest shelf and hit the top button, its snout spitting blue flame. Her other hand wrapped around the handle of a squat, heavy propane tank on the floor. Behind her, the chefs clustered against the swinging doors, their faces barely visible through the oven haze. Maybe they were frightened. Or maybe they were making sure nobody entered or left.

Daltry was on his head beside the waiter, ramrod straight, arms and legs trembling. Imagine the force necessary to hold adult bodies in that position. They looked like flesh-trees, bright and luminous in a black forest of tendrils; and the waiter had sunk to his shoulders by that point.

Darkraven waved the culinary torch at the approaching black mass, which retreated—but only a foot or two.

"Got to blow this," Darkraven said, meaning the tank, "without getting us killed."

"Stand back," I said, encouraged by her resolve. When she did, I kicked the tank onto its side. There must have been a slight slope to the floor, because it rolled through the ooze, threading between the cop and waiter, before thumping against the back wall. That seemed to grab the thing's attention. And as tendrils swarmed over the tank's metal sides, I scooped up Daltry's pistol and pushed Darkraven into the corridor.

"Think this'll work?" Darkraven asked.

"Does in video games," I said, guiding her against the wall beside the doorway. This close, I could smell her hair—a sweet scent, like something you know you'll never have. I stuck the pistol around the doorframe, aiming blind, and pulled the trigger.

I had never fired a gun in real life before, and the recoils jolted my wrist so hard it was almost impossible to keep a grip. I only had a second to worry about the pain before one of my bullets found the target and the world exploded.

The wall protected us. Darkraven screamed something that my shattered eardrums reduced to dim gibberish. The air was full of dust and smoke that burned my lungs. My lizard brain ordered me to turn and run, even as Darkraven gripped my hand and pulled me after her into the storeroom.

The tank had shattered everything on the shelves, along with the light bulb overhead, and the only illumination came from the flaming scraps of paper and food scattered across bare concrete. We almost tripped over poor Daltry, lying in the middle of the space, his face a spongy, red mess. Without thinking, I placed my hand over his badge to feel for a heartbeat. But I'm no doctor.

And the waiter was gone, along with every trace of the mysterious oil. In the center of the room, a square hole led into the darkness below. How far down, we had no idea.

I stepped forward and kicked a burning scrap of cardboard into the abyss, and we watched it flicker down a brick-lined shaft lined with rust-crusted rungs, illuminating a passage that cut across the bottom of the shaft, filled with a rushing black that seethed with thorny tendrils. The mass extinguished the flame, but not before we had a sense of its size. Its movements reminded me of a giant squid shooting its way through the deep ocean, only with its ink leading the way rather than swirling behind.

"Let's go," I said. The ringing in my ears had subsided somewhat. "Call more cops."

"No," Darkraven said. "We have to see where it's going."

"This isn't the internet," I said, extending my hand. She slapped it away.

"Wait. Drain cleaner . . . " she said, her teeth flashing in the dark. Opening her sooty purse, she pulled out her phone and tapped the flashlight function. Guided by its glow, she stepped onto the top rung and began to climb down the shaft.

She was halfway down when I knelt, grabbed the rungs, and followed her. My sweaty hands made it hard to grip the metal, and I spent every second of the descent expecting that horrible blackness to swarm up and kill us both.

When she got to the bottom, Darkraven dropped from the last rung, her feet splashing in shallow water, her phone illuminating what looked like an old brick sewer tunnel. I hit the water next to her, nose wrinkling. The smell of shit was overpowering.

"There he is," she said, angling her phone to the left side of the tunnel, where the crumpled body of the waiter lay with his limbs snapped into impossible angles. The light reflected off his wide, staring eyes. The veins in his neck and forehead were black as ink, as if that oil had filled him as he died.

My hands shook, and my chest felt tight. The tunnel was wide but not high enough to prevent us from grabbing the bottom rung and climbing back up the shaft. Let the cops, the FBI, the Ghostbusters, hell, anyone with big guns and bigger balls handle this thing, I thought. We were just a couple of kids who spent too much time online.

"Let's *go*," I said again, louder.

"Don't you understand? This is our chance to do something real."

I just stared at her in her phone's eldritch light.

"Then go back to your laptop." Turning away from me, she disappeared into the tunnel.

I know I should have followed. But then again, I'm not insane. In the distance, I heard her splashing in the dark, a glimpse of light taking a far turn, and then nothing.

I pulled that joint out of my pocket and lit it, filling my lungs with smoke. It felt like heaven—no, more like *medicine*—and the joint's cherry cast a dim red light on the tunnel walls.

When I saw the waiter blink, I thought it was my eyes playing tricks on me.

Then he turned his head, the bones in his neck crackling like sticks, and he smiled.

That did it. Stifling a scream, I leapt and grabbed a rung, climbing as fast as I could, my elbows and knees scraping the bricks. The shaft echoed with an inhuman sound, like a chorus of tinny voices rising into a shriek of pain. Maybe Darkraven had found a way to hurt the thing? I hope so, I truly do.

Back in the storeroom, I collapsed, my throat stinging with vomit. I smelled like a latrine, and every part of my body hurt, but that was okay. I was still breathing. I took a few more hits and got it together. When I reached the parking lot, that asshole Guillaume saw me puffing away, and, true to his word, drove off without me.

That's when you all showed up.

[Tape paused; resumes 04:24.]

Okay, you want it? Here's my conspiracy theory: that thing existed long before humanity, just like Darkraven said. It's tough, but not invincible, and so it began to retreat as we built bigger things like bombs and guns and planes. Or even homemade flamethrowers. Why else hadn't we discovered it before now? But when we could see every inch of the world with our satellites, and threatened to fill every part of it with concrete and lights, the thing needed a Plan B. So it hid in plain sight.

And there's nothing more everyday than a pizza place. You never notice them really, unless you're hungry. The thing could set up shop—so to speak—and let its dinner walk right through the door every night. People disappear in cities all the time. It might have remained unseen forever, killing virgins and whoever else, if one of its minions hadn't gotten a little too creative with the restaurant's logo, a little too cocky. I've seen it before. As soon as they built a website, it was all over. Good luck keeping any sort of secret on the internet.

I know you didn't find anything down there. But I swear I'm telling the truth. She was the crazy one, and I wish I could have gotten to know her a little bit better. Don't look at me like that. I'm alive, you know? Sure, I might be a coward, but only in the real world.

[NOTE: 8/21/18: Suspect escaped holding cell an hour after the conclusion of this interview. Barred window was unmolested, and the detached toilet seat, possibly used to facilitate escape, was covered in the suspect's prints, lifted and identified due to residual pizza grease. Prints also match those found on the nameplate of Officer Daltry, deceased. Whereabouts of suspect, or any accomplices, remain unknown.]

INTRODUCTION TO "LET'S KILL THE PIZZA GUY":
THE LOVE POEMS OF YAEL FRIEDMAN CONCERNING HADASSAH HERZ

TIM LIEDER

BEFORE YAEL FRIEDMAN'S death at the age of 27, her primary artistic output consisted of Identity Crisis spoken word performances and ketchup bottles sculpted from oak. The few existing videos of her spoken word reveal a sophist adherence to the literary function of language.

Three years after her funeral, *Gigawatts*, an independently published journal, acquired the rights to her biographical, psychological, and mythical poetry. The following year, Zangwill Books published many of the same poems, as well as 40 others the following year in *Tent Stake,* the first Friedman collection. They barely promoted the book and sold fewer than 100 copies in the initial 5 years. A traditional publishing house would have remaindered all copies and allowed the book to fall silently out of print.

The discovery of Jordan Vav, alive and working for an Egyptian consortium, pushed Yael Friedman's literary work into the mainstream. The renewed fascination with the Jordan Vav kidnapping only increased with the scarcity of material; the Vav family had purposefully erased Jordan's existence from social media, and even Jordan's notorious YouTube sermons were unavailable at the time. Zangwill Books was quick to promote

Friedman's Jordan poems from *Tent Stake* as a secondary source that had survived the purge. For a year, Friedman's reinterpretation of Jordan Vav's sermons provided the best link to the pre-war era.

Eventually, that aspect of *Tent Stake* lost its novelty. Jordan Vav told her story, and scholars found lost videos. Had Yael only written Jordan poems, her reputation would have faded. However, *Tent Stake* hosted several odes and lyrics and sonnets covering many themes. Ms. Friedman's obsession with Hadassah Herz excited the attention of Detective Sharon Fisher who gifted the collection to Margaret Nguyen, an investigative journalist. Ms. Nguyen had been researching unsolved murders of pizza delivery drivers throughout Birmingham, and she was the first of many to connect the love sonnet "Let's Kill the Pizza Guy" with her case.

To this day, "Let's Kill the Pizza Guy" remains one of the most chilling sonnets in the 21st century literary canon. Not only is it an achievement in literary rhetoric, but it has intoxicated expressionist and formalist critics alike with its emphasis on forensic details and breezy expression of ambivalent affection.

At the time, the sonnet was merely one among a dozen sonnets entered into evidence and broadcast over true-crime podcasts. It quickly entered into the lexicon as actors created videos and holograms reciting the poem, at first dripping with irony, but eventually pathos. Staged readings sprouted up in previously depressed towns with rewards given to the most popular narrators. The sonnet's emphasis on unconscious drives and post-modern criticism attracted an audience starving for romantic odes.

Long after Hadassah Herz had been sentenced for the homicides of Paul McLean and Bob Bialostosky, with suspicion falling on her for the deaths of five other delivery workers, the poems remained in the public imagination. The appeal to pure form allowed for a wealth of literary criticism from traditions as diverse as New Historicism, Marxism, Freudian, Dworkinian, and feminist.

As "Let's Kill the Pizza Guy" remains one of the most enduring sonnets in the Friedman literary canon, fascination with the relationship that inspired its creation grew. Through interviews with Ms. Herz from her jail cell and culling of the public records, scholars have established a timeline of the relationship which began when Yael met Ms. Herz at a wedding where they drunkenly kissed in the yichud room. After nine intense months of non-discriminating physical and mental torture, Hadassah Herz informed Yael that she couldn't see her. The news did not come easily.

Most scholars accept Professor Bozeman's theory that Yael's Hadassah poems began with this first breakup. In the next two months, Hadassah and Yael reconciled and fell away three times. After both women had issued restraining orders, Yael performed the Hadassah sonnets and stanzas in coffee houses until she publicly abandoned them for golem poetry.

For almost a decade, Yael Friedman fans accepted the published Hadassah poems as her best, but longed for supporting material. Fans devoted hours to poring over Hadassah poems to interpret the minutia of the relationship. Professor Norman Halliburton of St. Thomas managed to contribute to the Yael Friedman canon with a book solely devoted to fan theories.

Scholarship into Yael Friedman's Hadassah poems remained stagnant as neither the Friedman family nor Hadassah Herz agreed to interviews. Ms. Herz was appealing her conviction and the Friedman family refused to openly discuss their daughter and sister "falling prey to the homosexual agenda".

A completely unrelated inquiry opened up everything when Moorehead State graduate student Nora Duyfhuizen was struggling to prove the *Sisera is Free* Patreon campaign as a Yael Friedman page, based on the three public poems. At the time, academics were racing to discover traces of Yael Friedman through dozens of seemingly unrelated blogs and Facebook profiles. In fact, researchers had discovered several potential identities for Ms. Friedman among reddit users and slash fiction writers.

As Nora Duyfhuizen wrote and revised her thesis, her adviser remained skeptical and even suggested a change in focus. Nora Duyfhuizen's academic frustration led her to pay for the $50/month patronage to unlock all journal entries. In interviews, Dr. Duyfhuizen often claimed that she feared that the paywall journal entries would disprove her thesis. Her hesitation quickly turned to ebullience as she read the first of the many Dassie posts.

By the time she defended her thesis, she had collected over 9,000 entries, totaling almost a million words, dedicated solely to cataloging and investigating every aspect of Hadassah Herz. Less than a week after Nora's final thesis became public, rival professors and graduate students pounced. In order to secure exclusive rights, they hired hackers and bot-makers to find unpublished back end drafts and kill the Patreon site.

Even more troubling, Dr. Duyfhuizen's notes and printouts disappeared, presumably forever, in the home invasion and fire that killed her spouse and destroyed her Cleveland apartment. As she had been engaged in a legal battle with Professor Elizabeth Bozeman of the University of Wisconsin, Oshkosh, suspicion immediately fell on Bozeman who categorically denied malfeasance. The publication of Bozeman's Yael Friedman biography five years after the fire and three months after Dr. Duyfhuizen's sidewalk murder renewed suspicion, as many of her sources came from the officially lost Patreon posts.

Professor Bozeman went on to publish several academic books on Yael Friedman, and the same questions repeatedly surfaced. However, police cited three other professors as persons of interest in regards to *Sisera is Free*. When Lee Fairbanks, associate professor of Rhetoric at Harvard University published the complete *Sisera is Free* blog in a nine volume series, his association with Dr. Suzanne Brewster of The College of New Jersey immediately ended most speculation. Even though conspiracy bloggers still suspect Professor Bozeman, defenders have noted that the rediscovered *Sisera is Free* blog revealed many inaccuracies and fallacious speculations in the biography.

Professor Bozeman's recent death has silenced all but the most vocal detractors. The news of a reprint of Alexander Stone's book *Who Killed Nora?* should please only the more prurient scandal mongers. *The Bozenman-Duyfhuizen Controversy*, a sober account of the court case and surrounding incidents by Thor Jordan remains the definitive text.

This book represents the culmination of several legal battles, interpretive editing and investigative work. Since Ms. Friedman's family maintains the rights to her paper journals and offline poetry, this cannot be the final word on the Friedman/Herz affair; rather it provides a visualization of a relationship with broader sociological and stoical implications.

In compiling this volume, our editors worked primarily from the

Fairbanks books but also with the existing online work including her poetry and the *Purgatorio* fan fiction. In the process, we attempted to use both ethical wisdom and literary mythology.

One of the key points of controversy in involved the ordering of entries. Yael's original writing is fragmented, as even the most entertaining blog can fall into formless apathy, repetition, and self-criticism. For the purposes of clarity, editors have eliminated many of the more repetitive passages as the developments of Yael's analogies push against paradigms of reason. Even after eliminating redundancy, editors debated between three formats:

1. Chronologically by blog entry
2. Relationship timeline
3. Thematic

All three formats presented issues. Even if one can definitively order the posts that have long disappeared from social media, the methodology would confuse most readers. Yael Friedman begins her text writing about the initial break up and then chooses her subjects as she remembers them.

The second method also proves problematic as the official timeline remains controversial. Did Hadassah Herz cheat on Yael before or after she murdered Paul McLean? When exactly did Ms. Herz disclose her crime? When did Hadassah allow Yael to come with her to the abandoned house where they ordered a pizza only to shoot Bob Bialostosky in the face and leave the pizza on the steps? Yael's rhymed couplets suggest it happened at the beginning when they were in love. She even writes about Hadassah making a heart shaped image out of his blood as they remove the pepperoni. Yet Mr. Bialostosky's murder happened in April, a month after the first breakup. Yael is either mis-identifying the victim or engaging in creative non-fiction.

More importantly, several passages in the writing cannot be established via outside events. Several times in the work, Yael describes Ms. Herz writing fan letters to Simon Vav for his alleged participation in the Dayton massacre. Yet the Dayton tragedy happened a year before the couple met. Hadassah maintained a fairly consistent problematic but discipline-bound worship of Simon

Vav throughout the year. Furthermore, Yael's interpretations of Dassie's actions are highly subjective. When Yael states that Hadassah is no longer in love with Simon Vav because of his Banjo Music, it could be an aesthetic choice, an objective truth, or wishful thinking.

The thematic order provided the best methodology, based on the most prominent themes: Pizza Murders, The Wedding, The Breakup, Simon Vav and Sexuality. Some argued that several passages fell beyond these categories even as other chapters encompass several. In the latter case, we decided to go with the most salient aspect. For example, Yael describing Hadassah planning a pizza murder as an offering to Simon Vav is in the Simon Vav section. By contrast, Yael reminisces about kissing Hadassah while a pizza delivery man bleeds out is in the pizza murder section even as it could also belong in the wedding and sexuality chapters. Uncategorized poems are collected in the first appendix.

THE PIZZA MURDERS

Even though we have chosen to reprint the pizza murder poetry that first cemented Yael Friedman's artistic reputation, the pizza murders do not figure as prominently in the totality of the material as one would assume given the zeitgeist. In fact, most of the pizza murder material had been in the public eye long before the discovery of the *Sisera is Free* Patreon.

A reader unfamiliar with Yael Friedman beyond the pizza controversy may be surprised by the depths of her dialectical methodology. Instead of poetry, Ms. Friedman writes Socratic dialogues between her and Hadassah on the dimensions of love and ennui, with Ms. Herz ultimately coming out on the side of murder. In Yael's writing, the arguments form an interconnected whole between materialism (disposing of pizza delivery men) and exposed spiritual truth from higher realms of discourse.

Perfect love is both political and wondrous.

A chief example of this anomalous treatment of love is the Yael flash fiction "Reverse Shoftim" where she affectionately joins Hadassah is dismembering an anonymous pizza delivery worker (most likely Janet Williams) that Hadassah had stabbed in the neck. As the blood splatters on her favorite blouse, disgust turns to delight as Dassie brings out the hacksaw and they cut the victim into exactly twelve pieces. Then the women kiss, without changing their clothing. The story ends with them mailing the organs and limbs to all twelve Vav siblings.

Given the historical significance of "Let's Kill the Pizza Guy" in modern jurisprudence, the reader may be discomforted to encounter this famous sonnet in the context of dialogues and anecdotes where Yael's emotional attachment to Hadassah is sacrosanct.

For the most part, Yael manages to avoid the Dostoevsky guilt and the pseudo Nietzschean ubermensch tropes. Still, Hadassah's words and actions come out beautiful in Yael's phrasing. Several times, Yael uses flowers and silk and love scream metaphors for the pizza delivery worker's blood and excrement draining from their body. Many times, she did not eat the pizza because it wasn't kosher, but the act was enough.

THE WEDDING

In writing about the wedding, Yael presents many irreconcilable viewpoints. Several passages are dedicated to the security that had been on high alert since Bullet Events relocated from schools to love activities such as restaurants on Valentine's Day, pornography shoots, and weddings (the Men's Rights Activists, Camels and Incels had expanded their targets). In that year there had been three highly publicized wedding massacres, two at Jewish weddings alone.

Since Yael focuses almost exclusively on Hadassah, scholars have been left to discuss the exact location and participants based on clues in the text that describe catering, shtick and the venue. Dr. Duyfhuizen's original theory that the wedding was the Friedman-Hartman wedding in New Rochelle is based upon the passages where Yael expresses pleasant shock that the wedding dinner is not rubber chicken. However, that view has been challenged by several scholars due to the fact that the Friedman in the Friedman-Hartman wedding was Yael's brother and others have extensively documented Yael's intense participation.

Jill Goldsmith and Thomas Kennedy have proposed three possible weddings that could have served as the Hadassah and Yael introduction—the Rofeh-Smith wedding in Los Angeles, the Kranzler-Mogilensky wedding in Israel and the Berkowitz-Shamir wedding in Florida. In their seminal text *Next to the Huppah: The Origins of the Pizza Murder Love Affair,* they weigh the strengths and the weaknesses of each possibility with contemporary scholarship. The challenge of pinpointing the exact wedding has only grown as interest in Yael Friedman has led several of her friends both in the Orthodox Jewish and ex-chasidic communities to remember her attendance at these weddings with with dubious embellishments.

In her lifetime, Yael Friedman never named the exact wedding. Hadassah Herz claimed to not remember for years. Her recent endorsement of the Friedman-Hartman theory must be contextualized within the aspects of her lifetime of mistruths and current nanobot dementia treatments.

Contemporary scholarship seeks independent and relatively objective descriptions in order to provide color for Yael's descriptions of security guards, pre-wedding chicken wings, dance choreography, chair mishaps, falling grooms, and yellow wallpaper. However, the wedding material stands on its own as a testament to a bittersweet, affectionate tribute to the woman that inspired such artistic devotion.

A certain woman found Yael and behold she had been wandering the periphery of the hall when Hadassah greeted her. In that moment, both women found co-conspirators against patriarchal celebrations. Hadassah's interviews where she stated that an evil beast of lesbianism had devoured her and cast her into amorality must be contrasted with Yael's narrative, full of spice and balm and myrrh. Even at her most bitter, Yael's silver nostalgia remains a delight of wild dances. As much as Yael may have mourned the relationship, she would never mourn the root cause.

THE BREAKUP

Yael agreed with Dassie that the key to interpretation was

imagination. Fantasy greatly informed their affair. A poem, a dream, a painting and few words fostered archetypes of dreaming humanity. The floods that destroyed Los Angeles could only come from a thousand rain dances.

From the first "we need to talk," to the final restraining order, Yael was with Hadassah and Hadassah found grace in Yael's sight, more than she had believed possible. Love was upon all that Hadassah owned. In the breakup passages, Hadassah was a goodly woman and well favored.

In agreement with the Bozeman theory, the initial separation allowed Yael to write from holistic depression, determined by Hadassah's viewpoint. For Yael, there was no higher realm of truth than Hadassah's proclamations. She could never reduce the ambiguities from a common language.

This section contains Yael's three suicide notes. Hadassah's negative aura broke into her methodology and established laws that could only end in Yael's demise. Yael also writes of innocent ascension when Hadassah offers her hope in reconciliation.

The orders of restraint are reprinted in their entirety at the end of the chapter. Yael wrote extensively about breaking off with Hadassah after the official document entered into record. The legal writ serves as an implicit ending for their structural complicated linkage.

SIMON VAV

Simon Vav played the shadow monster. Yael had spent many weeks imagining that Dassie was more beautiful, kinder, and sweeter than the woman who demanded absolute devotion, bragged about killing Marxists, and recited from *Atlas Shrugged*. Dassie's thematic vision, a complexity of manipulation, language, and fan girl affection for Simon Vav, enchanted Yael from the first meeting. As Yael soured on Simon Vav, she began to scapegoat him for Hadassah's bad behavior.

When Hadassah cast her eyes upon Simon Vav and his alleged role in Dayton, she would often whisper "fuck me." Hadassah would tell her that yes, Simon Vav had made her and committed her to all that she named pride. How could she wickedly reject him in her heart? Many were the fights with Hadassah over the elder Vav.

Professor Ramirez has argued that Yael's hatred of Simon Vav allowed her to envision a wholly innocent Hadassah. His thematic map placed Simon Vav at the center and the pizza murders on the fringes—in sharp reversal of most popular texts that centered the pizza murders.

Certainly Hadassah Herz took great strength from Simon Vav. The Dayton Massacres rendered him the ultimate libertine libertarian. Simon Vav's callow pronouncements and barely adequate alibi only proved Simon as the model hero. He killed men when he was angry and punched cows when he was happy and tore the garments of a million reporters. Yael's writing about Simon Vav's centrality in her girlfriend's life betrays both self-immolation and denial. Yes, Yael never credits Simon with the pizza murders. Never do the tropes merge in her craft.

SEXUALITY

This is possibly the most tortured but fascinating portion in the way the artless prose struggles for transcendence. Yael Friedman's neo-Victorian view of sexuality cannot be completely blamed on her Chasidic background. Ms. Friedman can only write sexuality as pornographic or flowery. When she talks about the act itself, all of her emotions are pushed to the side. When she seriously considers the emotions, she pulls back and glosses over the physicality altogether.

Yael grew up in a religious household and her reluctance to engage in her pleasure renders these passages sterile. Practical criticism unpacks the language underlying the passion that Yael felt towards Hadassah.

Only when Yael and Hadassah torture a third woman with melted cheese and scalpels does the sexual language reach the level of orgasmic. Yael returns to this scene several times in order to transcend order, logic, and conceptual dialogue.

ADDENDUM

Beyond these sections, the editors have included the material that did not fit within the categories but also presented significant entries including the sweat poems, poison roots, and vicious rabbi letters.

Within the textual circles—hermaneutic, vicious, virtuous, and spiral—the words and events have countless meanings. Shadows of Simon Vav constantly brawl with the dead pizza delivery guys, and the oven is always baking in abandoned houses near Madison. Crudely, Yael Friedman attempted to remove the ambiguities from her love but the disarray only grew. Yael Friedman desperately wanted to explain her Hadassah obsession as a product of childish infatuation, brain tumors, and even an imbalanced evil.

Like Simon Vav, a man who disappeared long before Yael Friedman's writings became popular, Yael discovered that the world conspired against lovers and ultimately her dreams would never match her words.

The children do not sing love songs. The children eat marzipan and human flesh.

This volume aims at a selection of Yael Friedman's life with Hadassah that represents all stages of her love, rather than a hypothetical Essential Hadassah. Inevitably, this required the inclusion of material that more popular volume editors would have omitted. That's not to say that it is fully comprehensive collection. In the interest of clarity, the editors eliminated the more repetitive material.

The editors decided to exclude the Jordan Vav epics, even though some argue that it directly sprang from Hadassah's obsession with Jordan's brother Simon. Many advocated for inclusion. The editors arrived at the decision for two key reasons. First Yael's Jordan poetry does not directly address Hadassah. Second, rumors of Simon Vav selling his sister to human traffickers presents too many issues, most outside the scope of this collection.

MICKEY AND THE PIZZA GIRLS

SHERI WHITE

"WHAT TIME IS it, Sam?" I knew, but it was something to say. Just part of the routine now.

Sam squinted at the pocket watch embedded in his palm. "Looks like it's about that time. You ready for it today?"

"You know damn well I'm not." I scratched the eyeball in my cheek, hating the squish of it under my fingernail. I'd never get used to it, nor the blood that oozed down my face after my nail poked it. "I hate those Pizza Girls. I wish they'd leave me alone just for one fucking day."

"No such luck, Mickey. I hear them coming this way." Joel adjusted the pink party hat on his head.

I hit the hat with the back of my hand. "Take that stupid thing off. I'm not going to tell you again."

"But it covers my cone perfectly! Come on, let me wear it."

"Fine, whatever. At least find one that doesn't look like you got it at a little girl's princess party."

Joel took the party hat off and tapped the top of the flesh cone pushing out of his head. "I hope it's done growing. Party hats don't come much bigger."

"Am I too late? Have they come yet?" Margie hurried down her steps to join us, her baby fused to her breast, bouncing against her belly. The kid had smothered a while after it happened, and now its little body was mottled and bruised. It made me shudder every time I saw it.

Joel bowed his head and pointed down the street with his cone. "Nope, here they come now."

Sure enough, like the clockworks in Sam's hand, they were right on time. Their gleeful singing echoed through broken buildings, as they danced and performed their cheerleader moves down the street toward us.

"Christ, here we go." I clenched my hands into fists and closed my eyes, but just as the heart hanging outside of my body never stopped beating, the eye on my cheek never closed. I could still see them through a hazy red veil. And I could hear them. That song, that fucking song.

Oh pizza, you're so great,
You're so great, you fill our plate
Hey, pizza! Hey, pizza!

A few weeks ago, something happened during the night. We still don't know exactly what it was; we all just call it The Event. We woke up one morning and everything was completely fucked up. Some of us had extra parts, others had objects fused to their bodies, like Sam and his pocket watch. A lot of people in town killed themselves that day. I wasn't surprised. I *was* surprised that Margie hadn't checked out with that dead baby hanging from her boob.

I think somebody fucked up at that collider thing they talked about on that show with the nerds.I tried to get out the hell out of Dodge, but there was nowhere to go. The roads ended. I mean, I watched a car in front of me reach the stop sign and then just...float away. No matter which way I tried to leave, I saw cars suspended in the air for miles.

Did it just happen to our town? We'll never know. The sun and moon were gone now too. But it wasn't completely dark, thankfully. It was like we were living in a constant state of twilight. It suited us.

But those Pizza Girls? Man, that was fucked up. Chloe and Zoe were actually twins, popular at a nearby high school, cheerleaders who dated football players, the works. But The Event fused them together at the tops of their heads and they completely lost what was left of their minds.

They delivered pizzas Before, and I guess they think they still do. What they bring us is *not* pizza, though.

This pizza's fun to eat,
So fun to eat, it's such a treat!
Hey, pizza! Hey, pizza!

"What do you think they'll bring today, Mickey?" Margie tried to cross her arms, but the baby's head got in the way. I couldn't look at her when I answered.

"I don't know and I don't care. I just wish to Christ they didn't know my name."

Once The Pizza Girls found out my name was Mickey, they started singing. Before that they just babbled, but it was somehow better. I hated that stupid Toni Basil song in the '80s, and I hate it twice as much now.

"Hey look, it's Mickey! It's Mickey!"

They danced right up to me, holding a pizza box together, their fused heads making them look like a human arch, like a logo for a pizza place actually.

"Hey, girls! Whatcha got today?" Joel snickered, voice muffled in his party hat. He put it back over his cone when I glared at him.

"Christ, Joel. Don't encourage them."

The girls thrust the box at me, opening the lid, shrill voices in full surround sound stereo:

"For Mickey! For Mickey!"

In the box was the most putrid thing they had concocted yet. Up until now, they had brought me "pizza" made out of cotton candy with chunks of canned frosting and sprinkles swirled through it. Like a little girl's tea party. Once, they brought me tuna fish with ketchup on top. I would take whatever it was and pretend to eat it, then toss it once they'd danced away.

I didn't know if they were completely insane or just fucking with me this time, but today's "pizza" was shit — literally *shit*, topped with chunks of bloody tampons. The smell. *The smell.* My eyes watered, especially the extra one.

Margie ran off, dry heaving, the dead baby flopping and smacking against its mother's sweaty bare skin. Joel and Sam just laughed.

"What the ever loving fuck? I'm not taking that... that *shit*." I had my limits.

"But Mickey! But Mickey!"

They dropped the box on the ground, shit splattering. I wiped my face with my shirt, then let The Pizza Girls have it.

"The world is ending, you stupid creepy little shits, and you need to face that! There will never be pizza again, so just go away!"

They danced backwards away from me, tears in their eyes. I didn't care.

"Mickey, come on. They're just kids."

"Shut up, Sam. I've had enough. Kids or not, this isn't funny anymore."

"Hey, Mickey. Ohhhh, Mickey."

"Just go home, or wherever you usually go. And don't come here again."

They turned their backs to me, but didn't dance. They walked for the first time since The Event, a little unsteady with their fused heads, but at least they were leaving.

"I should go check on Margie. You guys want to come with me?"

"Sure. Come on, Joel."

Just then, I noticed The Pizza Girls coming back, and dancing again. And dancing fast. I tried to back away, but they were in my face in seconds. They opened their mouths simultaneously, ridiculously wide, but this time they didn't sing. They fucking *screamed*.

"Ahhhhhhhhhhhhhhhhhhhhhhhh!"

Joel and Sam took off running. I slammed my hands over my ears, but I could still hear them. They didn't even take a breath; it was like a siren going off.

"Shut up! Shut the fuck up!!"

"Ahhhhhhhhhhhhhhhhhhhhhhhhhhhhhhhhhhhhhhhhhhhhhhhh!!"

Finally, I knocked them to the ground. But they kept screaming. I grabbed a leg—I didn't know if it belonged to Chloe or Zoe, but it didn't matter, did it? I dragged them down the road, to the nearest stop sign where our town ended. Then rolled them past it until they floated into the air.

I should've killed them. Separated their heads with an axe.

Because they didn't float away. They just floated above me. Unreachable, untouchable. But still *screaming*. Always fucking screaming.

Dogs were howling with them now. Which wouldn't be so bad if the dogs didn't have extra mouths these days. Howling dogs and screaming Pizza Girls. It's madness.

I haven't seen Margie, Joel, or Sam for the past several days. I think they killed themselves. Or maybe they're floating. Eventually, everyone takes a run past the stop signs to take to the sky. I wish I could float. I've tried, but it doesn't work. No matter what I do, my feet remain on the ground. Am I being punished? Am I special? It doesn't matter.

Eventually, the loneliness gets to me, and I walk to the border of my world, and I reach for the Pizza Girls to bring them back to Earth, back to me. And because I'm Mickey, they let me.

They take me by the heart, and I take them by the hand.

THE BLACK CHEESE

MATTHEW M. BARTLETT

HE FIRST STRANGE thing that Marielle saw was the thin man dancing in the tree-ringed grove between the exit and entrance ramps. As she waited for the light, she could see him from the side, emerging from behind an unkempt shrub, clad in a sleeveless red T-shirt and yellow-and-white striped boxers. He was executing a strange, frantic dance, his knees bending, his hooked, dirty feet rising high out of the tall grasses, his hands flailing at his face. He froze, then began moving in slow-motion, like some fear-based version of qigong tai chi. Where his nose should be gaped a curved triangular hole. Elongated, disintegrating pink tendrils dangled from his slack mouth—chewing gum? If so, a *lot* of chewing gum. Under the tendrils, his neck puffed out like that of a frog. He was mouthing what looked like some kind of desperate prayer. Curious, she rolled down her window as the light turned green. He was scream-singing in some strange language, his eyes bulging from his head.

As she took one last glance in the side mirror, turning onto the road into town, she could have sworn that one of his eyes actually popped out of his head, bouncing off his forearm before disappearing into the grass. She grabbed her phone and dialed 911, got only a stuttering, strangely accented electronic voice that said, "Please try your callings again later, all lines are busy . . . "

Try your callings? She hung up, redialed, got the same message.

Disturbed, she turned her attention to the road. Along the sidewalk, under the highway bridge, stood a line of people, facing the direction in which she was driving. The line stretched for the next two blocks, past office buildings and car washes and lumber yards; people, young and old, standing in little clusters, shuffling their feet, couples embracing, currents of excitement running through the crowd.

But what are they in line for? Danielle thought as she drove past.

There were no phone outlets or ticket venues or record shops, or . . . there it was—the line led to the Food Forage Convenience Store. People crowded at the door, their arms flailing.

O . . . kay.

She craned her neck, but couldn't see any promotional banners nor curbside signs. *The lottery, maybe?* Probably that. She scooped her phone up from the cup holder.

Austin answered on the first ring. "Hey, hon."

"I just saw the weirdest guy . . . " She recounted the story, but his *uh-huh*s and *hmm*s told her he wasn't paying attention.

"Sounds like you did what you could." Austin's voice sounded like he was holding the phone slightly away from his mouth.

"I guess. Anyway, listen. We had three people call out today, even Joanna, who, like, never calls in, so there's no way in Hell I'm cooking tonight. Gonna just grab something. You have a preference?"

"Ooh. Yeah, actually. I saw the strangest commercial for this new thing. It's called Buvoskor's Frozen Pizza. I *really* think we should try it." His voice sounded off, somehow, dreamy. She struggled for the word . . . *emotional?* This wasn't like him at all.

"You sound weird."

"I just . . . the commercial, it really got to me. I must be starving!"

"Okay. It's just . . . I *just said* I don't feel like cooking. I *can* get pizza, though, from, like, a restaurant? Bianchi's has a Tuesday night special."

"It's just ten minutes in the oven. Come on, I'll preheat it now. Sugar, it's supposed to be otherworldly. Like, exotic, gourmet, ar-*teeee*-sinal. Try it with me!"

Frozen pizza was the last thing Marielle wanted. But Austin had been out from work for two weeks, convalescing after the accident. Eating celery sticks and cold cuts and canned soup. She felt bad for him. "Fine. Buvoskor's, you said?"

"Yeah. It looks *sooo* good."

"Spell it."

"Bee-you-vee-oh-ess-kay-oh-ar."

"Doesn't sound Italian."

Then the phone squealed so loudly she had to pull it away from her ear. The squeal trailed off into a low growl; somewhere in the background Austin was still prattling away.

"I can't hear you," she called into the phone.

" . . . ackee-uh abber-utt"

"I CAN'T HEAR YOU AT ALL."

" . . . *lack tease and gather-nuts . . .* "

"What? Hon, I can't . . . "

Now another voice cut in, decidedly not Austin's, radio interference or something, the clinical, passionless baritone of a professor or one of those droning religious hosts her mom used to listen to on AM radio:

" . . . *from black waters of Renshfor-8 where prayers curdle and demons frolic, cast out from the bogs of sentient rot, across great gulfs, to grow in our throats and be born, spat forth in blood and saliva, thus has the annexation already begun . . .* "

The squeal started up again, obscuring the strange beamed-in voice, and she ended the call. A shadow crossed the sun like a cloaked thing stepping out in front of a hall light. Looking up from the phone, she saw a strange, undulating gauzy cloud of deep black billowing out from between two cottony white clouds. Then she noticed that the line of traffic in front of her had stopped dead. She jammed both feet on the brake, and the car shuddered to a stop inches from the car in front of her. Ahead, below that strange pulsing cloud, she saw a billboard she hadn't seen before, perched atop a hillock alongside the abandoned building that used to house a psychic. BUVOSKOR'S PIZZA, it read across the top in a blocky red font. The ad below depicted a smiling brunette woman and a little blonde girl seated at a dinner table. The mother was jamming a fork into the girl's mouth. The girl's eyes were wide with joy.

The girl looked jarringly familiar. Marielle stared for a beat or two, and then her hand flew up to her mouth. It was *her*, Marielle, as a child, wearing the denim OshKosh B'Gosh overalls she remembered well. And she had the same bright blue eyes, the plump little nose, the oddly squarish chin she'd always despised. And the mother—well, she had only pictures and hazy memories to go by;

her mother had died when she was six, but it looked like her, a kind of idealized version, freed from the faded snapshots and blurred Polaroids stuck between the pages of photo albums, now looming large in high-definition. Her mother's hair was a brunette bob. She wore red lipstick. Her perfectly shaped eyebrow was arched, but she gazed down at the little girl with strong, indulgent love. Marielle felt a sob rise up through her throat. She wiped at her eyes with the backs of her hands and rubbed them, hoping that when she looked again they'd be gone.

The irritating bleat of a car horn startled her back into the present day. The cars in front of her had driven off, the roadway in front of her empty. Without looking up at the billboard again, she hit the gas, sped through the light just as it turned yellow.

The parking lot at Foster's was practically a bumper-car rink. Horns blared and cars pushed past each other, even rolling up onto curbs and clipping signposts, their drivers gesticulating wildly behind the windscreens. Some had parked in the handicapped spots, on the grassy, curbed islands that separated the rows of parking spaces, even in the roadway between the lot and the entrance. Inside, Marielle had to stop as she headed to the frozen section to permit the parade of people streaming towards her, right at her, streaming toward the exits. They were griping, pushing past one another. In passing she heard an ancient old woman in a jarringly brown wig say, " . . . and I could *kill* whoever is in charge of ordering for this place, cut their throat with a fucking Ginsu. This is *motherfucking unacceptable.*"

The freezer aisle was a mess. One of the glass doors had been wrenched open and hung precariously from its bottom hinge, the top having been bent and broken. On the floor were scattered packages of Tombstone, California Kitchen, and Celeste pizzas. A big gap on the shelves indicated where Buvoskor's Pizzas had likely been before the mob got to them.

She started to fish for her phone when a tall, multi-tiered cart swung around the corner, piloted by a lanky, long-haired kid in a baseball cap and an apron emblazoned with the store logo. He was trailed by a grim-faced mob, all eager eyes and grasping hands, some pulling pizzas from the cart and rushing off to the registers. Marielle raised her eyebrow at the kid—an unconscious mimicry of her billboard-mother—as he slowed near the gap in the shelves, directly in front of her. She grabbed a box from the cart and fled to the registers.

When she got home, Austin was waiting by the door in his wheelchair, his foot comically large in the bandages. He wheeled the chair toward her, tried for a second to push himself up out of it, but then fell back, breathing hard. "Did you get it? Let me see? I've been dying to see the box."

"Yeah, hold on, let me just get in."

He backed up in a huff, then followed her into the kitchen. "Let me *see* it." His ferocity startled her, then made her angry. She was tempted, just for a second, to hold the box up out of his reach. Childish. She took a deep breath. Long day. Instead she turned and handed him the box, stepped around behind him to look at the package.

It was a plain white box with the name in the same lettering as the billboard. Below this was a primitive computer-generated image of a strangely colored pizza. The crust was greenish-grey, the cheese black, peppered with yellow-brown shards. The lower edge of the box read: *black cheese and fraegen-nuts.* Whatever those were. Austin flipped the box.

The back read in tiny, italic script, *"Congratulation. You have never tasted a pizza like Buvoskor's Pizza before, and you never will again. The instructions are simple. Preheat your oven to 350 degrees. Ignore any sounds you hear as your Buvoskor's Pizza cooks on perfection. Turn your pizza sunwise a quarter turn every 3.33 minutes. You will know your Buvoskor's Pizza is ready when the black cheese has risen and the fraegen-nuts have curled and the edges turn brown as polished oak. Let your Buvoskor's Pizza rest after removing from oven until cheese sinks back down. A note: Buvoskor's Pizza tastes much better than it smells. Pizza like your mother used to make! Enjoy! But we don't have to tell you that. You've about to."*

"'*You've* about to'?" Marielle said, snickering, and the oven beeped impatiently. "I'm not going to turn this damned thing every three minutes. It doesn't even make any sense. It's not a microwave."

"I'll do it," Austin offered as he opened the box and freed the pie from its opaque plastic shroud. As he slid it onto the oven rack, Marielle went to change into pajama pants and a T-shirt and get the dining room table set for dinner.

Austin rolled in with the pizza on a cutting board across the arms of the wheelchair, the dome of cheese deflating as he approached the table. Marielle wrinkled her nose.

"It smells like . . . curdled yogurt on fire. And sulfur." He slid the board onto the dining room table between the two glasses of red wine Marielle had set out, then he rolled the wheeled blade across the pizza, cutting it into six fat slices. "Oh, Austin, it looks so weird."

The cheese, purplish black and glimmering, stood up in sharp peaks like a stippled ceiling, barnacled with thin, curled up strips of something that looked like polished wood. Fluorescent violet sauce dripped out from under the cheese. The crust looked like the bark of a birch tree.

"Tastes better than it smells, remember?" he said, pulling free a slice. "Still, though, *ugh*. Let's take the first bite at the same time, okay?"

"Or we could still order out?"

His face fell.

"Okay, okay, together. Too bad we have only the one bathroom."

With that, grimacing, she grabbed her own slice. They opened their mouths in unison, and Marielle felt a sudden, powerful urge to fling her slice to the floor and slap Austin's from his hand. She suppressed it. They bit into their slices.

At first, she tasted nothing more than salt. Then came a strong, deeply unpleasant tang as hot juices sprung up into her saliva ducts. Across the table, Austin's eyes went wide, his hands leaping to his neck, his slice dropping to the floor. She felt something wriggling on her tongue, followed by something . . . some*things* . . . sharp and pointed, scratching lightly at her soft palate. Then something *unfolded* in there and slid slowly, agonizingly down her throat. She opened her mouth and tried to cough it out, and something plopped onto her lap . . . but the obstruction was somehow still in her gullet, tearing it to shreds as it worked its way down.

She looked down but couldn't identify what was sitting in the lap of her pajama pants. Then she recognized it. It was her nose. She didn't have time to ponder this as her bottom lip split into pink, bloody feelers and pain spread its scorching fingers from her throat up into the center of her skull. Her eyes filled with tears, and her ears filled with Austin's hoarse shrieking. Everything faded to black, then morphed into a swimming bluish hue. A strange, alien chorus sang somewhere in the center of her brain. She rose, dimly aware of Austin struggling from his wheelchair, sliding down onto the floor. Something was calling to her voicelessly. Leaving Austin writhing, his skin popping like the layer of congealed fat at the surface of boiling soup, she shambled and lurched toward the door. Her mother's sweet voice—the one that sang her such sweet lullabies—was waiting for her out on the lawn, calling her, she was sure of it. Her mother could get the things out from her throat, apply Chap-Stik to her torn-up lips, hold her until the bad dreams went away.

Behind her, a chirping squadron of fat, multi-legged fat insects, red and segmented, crawled blindly out from under the black cheese, made their way down the table leg, and followed their brethren into Austin's wrenched-open mouth.

Rollo Taschen went out to call for the cat. Judging from the gathering black clouds, a hell of a storm was coming. Not that the nerdy-ass meteorologist from the local news had said a damned thing about it. "Ruby," he called. "Ruby!"

The cat, a skinny, ginger tabby, emerged from the hedge across the way and barreled past him up the porch steps and into the house. "Huh," he said. As he turned to follow the cat inside, he saw his neighbor, the French chick with the dye-job, teetering across her lawn in bloody pajamas and slippers. It looked like she had a pink car tire around her neck, and strange, pink tentacles dangling from the lower half of her face. She was pawing at them and singing some strange, alien song in a cracked, hoarse voice. He took a step toward her and stopped short. Her eyes were bulging out from her head like painted golf balls. Rollo reversed direction, backing slowly up the porch steps, keeping his eyes on her, until he was safe in his living room. He locked the door and grabbed his phone to dial 911.

A moment later, he hung up. "Try your callings?" he said. The cat gave him a plaintive meow.

Behind him, the kitchen timer rang out.

The pizza was ready.

It smelled weird.

CENOBIO
PIZZERIA

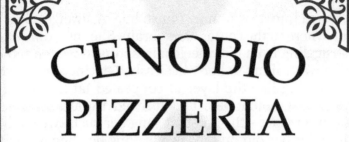

by Joshua Chaplinsky

**Catering to boundary pushing appetites
since 2002**

*Enter a new realm of culinary indulgence.
We have such sights to show you.*

Taste
Pleasure
Beyond Limits

CA$H ONLY

**CALL AND WE WILL ANSWER
NO PUBLIC ADDRESS
or PHONE NUMBER**

XXX-XXXX

THE CLASSICS

The perfect introductory pies to entice the curious and prepare them for the commitment required by some of our more challenging menu options.

THE KREUGER

Start off slow with this traditional pie smothered in hot, bubbling cheese. Reminiscent of a burn victim's skin, our special blend of gourmet curds browns to perfection, cooking up so hot you'll think the souls of murdered children are trapped inside.

THE VAN HELSING

Protect your neck by eating this tasty treat. A cheese pie topped with enough fresh garlic to choke a Sicilian donkey. They say garlic is as good as ten mothers, but no one's mom ever warded off blood-sucking fiends by virtue of their smell alone.

THE PAZUZU

Unbleached, whole grain crust slathered in puke-green pesto and topped with boiled peas. It may not look very appealing, but this delicious head-turner will leave you exclaiming, "Jesus, fuck me!"

THE LECTER

Off your meds? Then cover your pizza in a delicious medley of fava beans and pan-fried liver. Goes well paired with a nice *Amarone*—NOT a *Chiante*— as any knowledgeable sommelier will tell you. So good you might swallow your own tongue.

THE LOVECRAFT

Influenced by the *odori-don*, or "dancing squid" rice bowls of Japan. Fresh calamari pizza drizzled in soy sauce. The salt in the sauce causes an electrical reaction in the muscle cells of the recently deceased cephalopod. Feel those tentacles dance like an Old God in heat as you cram them into your mouth.

THE GILL-MAN

Top your pizza with the gelatinous innards of a hundred-year egg—the Chinese delicacy made by preserving a duck egg in ash and salt before burying it in the ground for six months. Of course, no one really knows what a Gill-man eats, but since the horny creature from *The Shape of Water* liked eggs, and he was basically a rip-off, we rest our culinary case.

THE DR. FRANKENSTEIN'S MONSTER

A white pie topped with *Acmella oleracea,* commonly known as Electric Daisies or Szechuan Buttons. This stimulating flora will give your mouth a jolt, and leave your tongue tingling like an afternoon at the dentist. Not to be confused with The Dr. Frankenstein, which is just a frozen pizza

CRISPY CRITTERS

For the adventurous eater looking to add another notch to their culinary belt. Cleaning your plate entitles you to bragging rights, but be warned—pride is a sin and the fall is steep.

THE DAY OF THE LOCUST

A thin crust pizza covered in ricotta cheese, liberally sprinkled with crunchy locusts baptized in wild honey. A favorite of itinerant preachers everywhere. You'll lose your head over the flavor!

THE CANDY MAN

For those who find The Dr. Frankenstein's Monster too tame an experience, this pizza comes smothered in tangy hot sauce and crunchy bees, stingers and all. Includes an optional side of Benadryl. You'll only have to say the name of the pizza once to make your waiter appear with *this* Candy Man. No mirror required.

THE BRUNDLEFLY

A traditional Granny Pie topped with Housefly *agrodolce* to simulate regurgitated digestive enzyme. Nice and mushy, so tell Grandma to leave her dentures at home.

THE BABY FROM ERASERHEAD

Boiled bird embryo (also known as *balut*) is a controversial Filipino street food that has inspired protests from animal rights groups across the world. It is also one of our most popular pizza toppings with adventurous gourmands. If this pizza keeps you up all night, it won't be with incessant crying.

THE VAMPIRE'S KISS

A brick-oven pizza bustling with an intrusion of the unpopular New York street vermin turned popular Chinese street food—cockroaches! Dig in fast, because these guys don't stay put, and will scatter in the time it takes you to recite your ABCs.

THE PIZZA OF THE GODS

Shredded murine meat slow cooked to perfection. Choose between cruelty-free country rat, raised in the idyllic fields of Vietnam, or filthy, disease ridden New York City sewer rat, raised on the trash of eight million people and infused with a variety of internal parasites.

THE SOYLENT GREEN

This might sound like a vegetarian option, but don't be fooled. Also known as the Long Pig Pie. Tastes so good they'll have to pry the last slice from your cold, dead hands.

BODY HORROR

Pain is pleasure, and these homemade pies nourish both mind and body, master and slave, willing and unwilling.

THE GEEK

Think you've got a strong stomach? Put it to the test with this literal kitchen sink of a pizza. Loaded up with washers, nuts, bolts and whatever other junk we have lying around. Shards of broken glass, old scouring pads—even a jagged metal Krusty-O if you're lucky.

THE POSSESSION

Our traditional cheese pie paired with a gallon of whole milk. Serving size: one person. No sharing. The meal isn't over until you drink every last drop of milk or are lying in a pool of pink vomit on the floor.

THE ITALIAN AMERICAN IN LONDON

A lovely salad pizza topped with *Aconitum,* commonly known as wolfsbane. Reactions vary, but each serving contains less than the 20ml dosage considered fatal. Savor the sweet suffering as waves of nausea wrack your body. It's not a meatloaf, Jack!

THE SERPENT AND THE RAINBOW

A Haitian style pizza topped with puffer fish, toad meat, and seeds of the *datura* plant. Will put you in a literal food coma, during which you will become highly suggestible and vulnerable to the whims of others until the poison has passed and you are "resurrected."

THE VASTRA DHAUTI

A simple, naan-like pie crowned with a braided length of jellyfish tentacles. The thin braid is inserted into the mouth and slowly swallowed. Continue until all but a few inches of the braid are ingested. The stinging nematocysts will inflame the esophagus, restricting the tentacles, and will abrade the delicate membrane when pulled from the throat, causing an exquisite pain.

THE STAY PUFT MARSHMALLOW MAN

Experience the feeling of being engorged to bursting with this neurotoxin laced pie. First you will feel a tingling in your limbs. Then, your breathing will slow. Then, your entire body will swell as extracellular fluid floods your system. You will remain this way, unmoving and in sweet agony, until the effects of the toxin wear off and the waters recede, leaving you physically drained.

TRANSFORMATION & TRANSCENDENCE

Gluttony is next to godliness. For those interested in experiences beyond the realm of human senses, requiring the complete surrender of self. Preferred customers only.

THE BLUE SUNSHINE

A sausage and pepper pizza dosed with our specially synthesized hallucinogen. Will open an inter-dimensional rift in your mind via your tastebuds and send you reeling across infinity. But beware the ancient entities that dwell within the darkness, for they hunger as well, and the inexperienced traveler may return partially devoured, if they return at all.

THE THE STUFF

That's not ricotta cheese, that's The Stuff. This living yoghurt will travel down your throat and fill your insides. It will then expand and force itself out of every orifice. It will squeeze from your pores like so many blackheads. It will burst through your eardrums and pour out your ears. It will fill your sinuses and leak out your nose. It will ooze from your eyeballs. You'll literally be shitting The Stuff. Eventually your entire body will turn inside-out from the force of its churning, leaving a pile of sticky, white goop in its place, which will then be used to top the next customer's pie.

THE SHUNTING

For a true communal experience, try The Shunting. Taste what your neighbor tastes as your bodies meld together, forming a singular, amorphous organism with shared senses. You will then drain the life-energy of a surrogate fattened on Cenobio pizza for your collective pleasure. Be a butthead and try a slice today! At Cenobio's, you are what you eat—and vice versa.

THE FIRST FLOWER

Fresh tomato and basil covered with shavings from the root of the First Flower. One bite and you will become a vessel for primordial energy as you experience biological devolution. Your physical self will regress from its human form to feral Neanderthal to a mass of synaptic matter to ethereal consciousness. Stop at whichever altered state suits you most, but be warned—once the threshold of the physical plane is crossed, there is no going back. Perpetual heightened ecstasy comes at a price.

THE TRANSFIGURATION

Thin slices of the fruit of The Tree of the Knowledge of Good and Evil adorn this pie like a crown. Bear the weight of the knowledge of your own mortality as your physical self is torn apart, atom by atom, and ascends to the heavens only to find irreducible emptiness between stars, as there is irreducible emptiness between your own microscopic particles—a vast, godless expanse where you will experience true abandonment as time folds in on itself.

FORCED TASTING MENU—120 MINUTES OF SODOM

Not sure what to order? Why not try our tasting menu? A sampling of our most popular pizzas, as well as some specialty items, hand fed to you while you're strapped to a chair. A personal, on-site medic will be provided at no additional charge. To top it off, still-conscious guests will be treated to a visit by our mad scientist chef at the end of the meal. *Mangia!*

Still have room for dessert? How'd you like some ice cream? Don't worry about passing out and missing post-meal treats. Our expertly trained wait staff is exceptionally intuitive, and will be able to tell whether you want ice cream or not, even if you are unable to speak.

INBRED FAMILY STYLE MEAL

Family is an important part of Italian culture, and most family interaction takes place around the table. Take part in a truly authentic dining experience, joined by *la familia*:

Nonna, the matriarch, who doles out food and punishment in equal measure. Mind your manners, or she'll whack you with her *cucchiaio di legno*!

Nonno, her husband, the family's soft-spoken figurehead. He may look like a corpse, but don't worry, he's only napping. Put anything near his mouth and he will bite!

Inbred sons Antonio and Pasquale. What they lack in intelligence and hygiene they make up for with childlike exuberance. You never know what to expect from those rascals. They love to play dress up, especially in other people's skin!

Make it through this meal and you'll never complain about your own family ever again, because you will officially be a part of ours.

DELIVERY/HOME INVASION

Want to experience Cenobio's in the discomfort of your own home? In an effort to expand our reach, we have decided to offer catering services. Just put your name on our waiting list and leave the rest to us! Sometime in the following six months our crack team of hospitality specialists will break into your home and proceed to terrorize, torture, and tantalize you and your family. You will be subject to a variety of our most popular menu items as well as some creative trauma in this intimate, one-of-a-kind dining experience. And if at any point the experience becomes too intense, we can put a permanent end to your suffering at no extra charge. Coming soon to a town near you.

NOTE: *Sanitary health inspection grade pending*

BODY OF CRUST

AMANDA HARD

"In a moment, in the twinkling of an eye, at the last trumpet, for the trumpet will sound, and the dead will be raised imperishable, and we shall be changed." —1 Corinthians 15:52

HE CAMARO'S TIRES skidded across the bloody street as Father Pearson jerked the wheel to his left, and the car bounced over the low concrete barricade onto the former parking garage's steep ramp. He stomped on the brake, stopping just shy of a chain curtain and let his grip on the wheel relax as the high-pressure wash began its power cycle, siphoning salted holy water from hidden tanks below. An agonized scream broke the drone of the wash nozzles, and Father Pearson imagined he could hear the patter of necrotic flesh dripping from bone to ground. He closed his eyes, his mind turning to the beach, where the sounds of the wash became the soothing rhythm of the surf. He could not, however, erase the image behind his eyelids: a Soulless, hunting in daylight, what remained of its rotten mouth wrapped around the stump of a tiny hand, four child's fingers hanging pale and limp from the beast's chin.

The wash stopped, a horn blasted twice, and Father Pearson took uncharacteristic joy in the double thumping under the car's wheels as he slowly guided the Camaro up the ramp.

"You look like hell, Father," the other priest told him as he swung his legs out of the low-riding sports car. Pearson felt a pop in his hip and an uncomfortable heat began to spread in his low back. "When was the last time you slept?" the priest asked.

Late spring? Last summer? Some time before the Soulless began to appear—the same as the rest of the priests in the communal rectory. Pearson had been living on the Power of Christ and Red Bull for so long that the days and weeks had melted together.

"No time," he said. "I've got deliveries." He slammed the car's dripping front door.

"Not now. We're holding all orders until Sunday, for a community mass. Safer that way. So take a nap. Monsignor wants you cleaned up and in the kitchen making dough in an hour, so get your ass up there pronto. The Lord be with you."

"And also with you," Pearson recited. He whipped the communion stole from his shoulders and wound it around his fist. They had less than 36 hours to make seven hundred pounds of dough. He closed his mind against the pain now radiating down his thigh. Fuck, he hated Sundays.

She would have been beautiful, the little girl. A cherub with blonde curls and smiling eyes, he imagined she had worn a pink taffeta dress with lace, the kind of dress that looks like candy floss, the kind only a child would find delightful. She might have spun in that dress, her layered skirts lifting and showing knobby knees and white stockings, before she fell back to the earth in a flurry of laughing and giggling. She would have been more solemn walking with her mother up the aisle, kneeling to receive God's blessing through Father Pearson's hand on her head. He might have administered her first proper communion, might have performed her marriage, baptized her own infant daughter who shared with her mother those angelic eyes. A part of that little girl would have stayed with him into his old age—the beautiful part, not the ugly black memory he now carried. The memory of her terrified face, the crunch of her neck as one of the Soulless bit into her, the blood spraying, her tongue extended, the beautiful cherub face screwed up in pain and terror, those sweet and smiling eyes rolling back in her head as the thing which held her ate her soft flesh, nuzzled its rotting jaw onto her breast, into her ribs, its teeth snapping at the shiny red prize, still pulsing frantically as the creature ripped . . .

Father Pearson awakened, starting so suddenly he nearly overturned his cot. He was sticky with sweat and deafened by the pulse of his own heartbeat in his ears.

"The Lord is my shepherd," he began. The little girl's face still glowed in the darkness, her smile alternating with that horrible grimace. "Yea, though I walk through the valley of the shadow of death . . . "

Surely she was dead. God was merciful. He wouldn't have allowed one of his innocents to turn, to turn into one of those things, a soulless abomination. Not one of the Risen, surely, but something other. Four white fingers, a child's hand, in the mouth of one of them. Consumed.

Suffer the little children, indeed.

"Heard you had yourself a stowaway." Father Mackey grinned at Pearson over an enormous vat of tomato sauce. "Heard the bastard screaming all the way up here."

"They're getting braver," Pearson said.

"They're getting hungrier." Mackey wiped his nose with the back of his hand and rubbed it down the length of his flour-dusted sleeve. "Takes determination to hang onto the underside of a car the way you drive."

"Fuck you."

"Language!" Mackey smiled. "Don't let Simmons hear you. 'Let no corrupting talk come out of your mouths,' or whatever that verse is."

"It's the end of world. Gotta keep up decorum."

"Well this is, effectively, God's house, so use your inside vocabulary. Besides, words are power, right? Otherwise this," he stuck his pinky finger into the vat of tomato sauce and showed it to Pearson. "Is nothing more than sweet, delicious marinara."

"Technically it's *pomodori pelati*."

"Which is Italian for let us pray, so let me focus."

Pearson reached into the basin in front of him and lifted out a dough hook, while Father Mackey measured out a cup of red wine into the bubbling sauce, closed his eyes, and sighed.

"Blood of Christ, shed for thee." Eyes still closed, Mackey found the long-handled wooden spoon and stirred the transubstantiated blood into the velvety sauce. "Do this in remembrance of me."

Father Pearson closed his eyes, but he couldn't remember. He couldn't remember the wooden face of the crucified Jesus hanging above the altar at what had once been his church, St. Elizabeth of the Woods. He couldn't remember the smile of the old priest, Father Timo, the man who had set him on the career path he'd once enjoyed, ministering to the rural poor, the godly and good-hearted farmers of southern Illinois who came to his church for mass every Sunday at 9:00 a.m., rain or shine. He couldn't remember any of their faces or their voices. Eyes open, all he could see was the converted hotel, now the region's rectory. Eyes closed, all he saw were four pale fingers, hanging from the jaw of an animal. A Soulless. One of the resurrected, but not Risen.

"Hey yo, Mario Andretti?"

Pearson looked up. Mackey flipped him the bird.

"The Lord be with you."

Pearson returned the gesture.

"And also with you."

Alone now, Pearson dusted his hands and forearms with flour, reached into the vat, and pulled out a hunk of sticky and pale pizza dough. Kneading and folding it over itself, he was struck by its resemblance to the white flesh that once overhung his belt. The rolls of dough quivered with each thump of his fist.

"Body of Christ," he heard himself speak. "If Christ was a fat-ass." He spun the mound of dough under his palms until it was an oval ball. He tried again.

"Body of Christ, given for . . . " For who? Certainly not for the children, the initial victims of the insatiable Soulless. He wanted to call them a plague, as if their incursion hadn't been a part of the divine plan—a judgment made by a loving God willing to slaughter Egyptian firstborns just to make a point, or condemn to drowning an earth's population of babies for the sins of their fathers. He slammed another ball of dough down against the metal tray where a dozen others sat, waiting to be spun and spread into pizza crusts, ready to carry the body and blood of their Lord and Savior to the remaining faithful in Illinois, sparing them and preserving them from the corruption the Soulless hoped to inflict upon their flesh.

How many pizza kitchens and Stromboli joints had the Church converted, fortified, and secured? He knew of at least four others, broadcasting over the shortwave, disseminating orders in broken English from an Archbishop in Brazil. How many priests braved streets crawling with Soulless, delivering communion where they could, gunning the engines of whatever sports and muscle cars they'd managed to confiscate? Four dozen? Forty?

"Body of crust," he laughed. "Hand-tossed for thee."

Mackey was wrong. Words didn't have power. Faith had power, and he couldn't help but doubt if a scant forty priests would provide enough of it to save the world.

Pearson dismissed two more balls of dough to the tray, looking up to see a hand-made sign above the sinks.

Chicagoland Parish: Delivering Us From Evil

"Amen," Father Pearson said aloud. He wondered if he actually meant it.

Hours later, Father Simmons came in to check on him.

"How many?" he asked.

Pearson surveyed the racks of metal trays, each holding two dozen blobs of ivory dough.

"Maybe two and a half, three hundred?"

"That'll do for now," Simmons said. "Let's get to spinning." They stacked the trays on carts and wheeled them into the central kitchen. Pearson went to the sink to wash. Tiny pieces of dough had already dried on his hands, adhering to the underside of his nails and gluing the hairs at his wrist together. He scrubbed until his skin was nearly raw and hit the tap closed with his elbow. After the pipes ceased their gurgling, he heard another sound, low and groaning at first, then higher-pitched and hoarse. Another Soulless caught in the cleansing spray, melting (or so he'd been told) like a slug under a shower of salt.

"They must be getting desperate now," he said aloud. Then to himself, "Fuck 'em."

Father Simmons led the Words of Institution, being the highest ranked of the dozen priests gathered together in the converted kitchen. A clean linen cloth lay over a low table, their makeshift altar. On it, resting on a wide silver serving plate, was a pizza, still steaming, the lip of lightly browned crust perfectly framing and containing the pepper-flecked sauce and a loose scattering of mozzarella cheese.

"On the night in which he was betrayed, he took bread; and when he had given thanks, he broke it and gave it to his disciples, saying, "Take and eat. This is my Body, which is given for you. Do this in remembrance of me." Simmons cut the pizza down the middle, then bisected each slice until there were twelve in all. Each priest took a slice.

"Body of Christ, given for you in this crust. Blood of Christ, shed for you in this sauce. Do this in remembrance of me."

The room responded with a mumbled group, "Amen."

Father Pearson blew on his slice before partaking of a small bite. Another loud banging came from below, then an uncharacteristic silence. Swallowing hard, Pearson rolled his slice, croissant-style, and shoved the steaming spiral into his mouth. Simmons followed suit, as did the others, and they each took a few uneasy steps toward the door.

"Let it be heard. Christ is risen!" one of the younger priests said excitedly. He had flour on the side of his nose and pizza sauce in the upper hairs of his miniscule moustache. Pearson hushed him and took another step towards the door. It was no risen Christ, of that he needed little convincing. The sound was louder now, a hum, like that of a locust swarm, devouring everything in their path.

"Is that . . . snarling?" The young priest swayed and Simmons hushed him this time. He still held the communion knife, sticky and red with sauce. Holding the knife like a bayonet, he moved closer to the door.

It was his imagination of course, but Pearson would have sworn he heard the sound of a trumpet, of something large breaking in half. Simmons had his hand on the door handle now, shaking slightly. Knife at the ready, he made a fist and slammed the door latch open.

The smell hit them first, disorienting and nearly blinding them to the sight of the hunched-over Soulless, staring down at the stump of his wrist, two fingers and a palm remaining wrapped around the other door handle. With an unholy screech, the Soulless launched himself at Simmons and they fell to the ground in a stinking and frantic puddle, arms and legs tangled.

"Get 'em off," Simmons yelled, then screamed as the Soulless bit off the bottom of his ear. Black-clad arms reached inside the pile to pull the two apart. Pearson grabbed and held a leg of the Soulless and saw Father Mackey above him, holding a long barbeque fork like a butcher knife.

"Watch it," Mackey shouted. He brought the fork down, perforating the neck of the Soulless until its head hung by a few strands of flesh and muscle. Pearson kicked at the head, which separated and rolled a few feet away. He dropped the leg, now twitching only minimally, and stumbled back against the altar.

"Simmons, you okay? Did he take your whole—"

Pearson stopped. The other priests turned from the grisly mess on the floor to see Father Simmons—the jovial and always good-natured Simmons—now on his knees, bleeding and drooling, his eyes already vacant, his mouth already chewing in anticipation.

"Oh fuck!" Mackey leaped over the decapitated Soulless to kneel down by the wounded Simmons, who sniffed loudly and lunged at him. Mackey fell to the side, stumbling away. His back hit the door, slamming it shut.

"That's not supposed to happen!" Mackey screamed, looking at Pearson in horror. His face drained of blood and the fabric at his crotch darkened and dampened. He rocked on the floor. "Oh fuck, this isn't supposed to happen! He took communion. He ate the host and drank the blood. Pearson, you were there. You saw me bless the wine. I know I did. It turned, oh sweet Jesus, it turned to blood like it always has, and you—you blessed the dough, you felt it turn, right? Right?" His eyes pleaded with Pearson. "Remember?"

He remembered. Pearson remembered. Her face, the angelic

smile, the child's hand in his, soft and warm, the white fingers hanging there off his palm. Hanging in that thing's mouth.

"You fucking blessed it, you fuck. Tell me you blessed it!"

What had once been Father Simmons reached out for Mackey's knee, knocking him off-balance so that he crashed against the altar. Simmons lunged for the fallen pizza tray, but Mackey kicked it away.

"I don't . . . " Pearson began. "I mean, maybe I didn't say it exactly . . . but it's not about the words, I thought it was faith and . . . I didn't really think the exact words mattered so much."

"Now? You're telling us this now? You didn't think the words of our Lord and Savior mattered?" Father Mackey raised the barbecue fork over the simpering Simmons, each jab in the neck punctuating his fury.

"Now. Is. Not. The. Time. For. A. Fucking. Linguistic. Debate."

Fully severed, the priest's head lolled beside its body, the eyes dim with confusion. Mackey kicked it away. "We're fucked."

Below them now came more banging and snarling, followed closely by the tense silence, repeating that pattern of scuffling and silence, scuffling and silence, each time closer and louder, each time the period of silence slightly diminished. Finally, there came a scrabbling at the door, the sound of a dozen fingers awkwardly working together, reaching and grabbing. The door handle turned down, slowly unlatching.

In the silence, Pearson saw her laughing, heard her twinkling eyes, tasted the sweetness of her soul on his palm.

Beneath the door handle, three small heads cautiously appeared. Wide eyes, ill-proportioned to such small bodies—oh but they smiled in sheer joy at the sight of the roomful of priests. Their stink masked the foul and tedious odor of tomato, the acid smell of basil, the dirty aroma of yeast. When they set upon Father Mackey, when they wrenched the bloody fork from his twitching hands, Father Pearson stood and laughed. He stretched his arms out in a wide embrace.

"Truly I say to you," he told his audience of eaters and eaten, "Unless you turn and become like children, you will never enter the kingdom of Heaven." He turned away, still smiling, toward the wall where a window had been boarded up, a cross painted on the wood in red sauce ink.

Father Pearson smelled her hand at his face before he felt her fingers clawing at his cheek. Then, slowly, the others came, tearing his clothes, biting at his waist, stripping his ankles of flesh. When she bit out his tongue, the pain in his hip disappeared, replaced by a fire of agony from his flayed skin. The blood from the stub of his tongue choked and gagged him.

The child's face beside his was far less cherubic than the one he remembered, and he struggled to push her away, push her memories aside, to see instead the smiling Christ, the praying Jesus on black velvet, the white-bearded and stern face of a God setting in motion the creation of life with the tip of his finger, the pillar of fire leading his faithful back to their rightful place in heaven. But that face was clouded and Father Pearson could no longer see through the sockets where his eyes had been, could not think through the excruciating pain from his gnawed and crushed bones. As he knelt on the concrete floor, his last thought was not of her, nor of his betrayal of the others, but instead, the curious realization that in just minutes, there would be nothing left of him to resurrect.

THE PARLOR

EVAN DICKEN

"**A** GOOD PIE is impossible to forget."

It was one of Dad's favorite sayings, second only to: "One day, Mark, none of this will be yours."

Dad would always laugh as he said it, his doughy grin lit by the buzzing overhead fluorescents, then he'd spread his hands to flick flour on the tiles, the bricks, the rolled metal kneading table, Grandpa Castaigne's creepy old pizza oven, *everywhere.*

When I was young, I used to think Dad was just being shitty and mean. He never said it when Mom or Tony were around, only when we were alone. Like he thought I didn't have guts, the smarts, the *strength* to keep this thing of ours going for another generation. I'd hammer my hands into the dough, add little angry shoves to the broom when I was sweeping up, hating Dad for being so sure Tony was going to inherit the place even though I was the older brother.

It wasn't until after Mom went south that I really started really thinking about it—that maybe Dad wasn't saying I *couldn't* handle the parlor, but that maybe I *shouldn't*. In his weird, dopey way, I think he was trying to protect me, to push me towards a different life, one without the long hours, the busy weekends, the swarm of gaping faces—eyeless, noseless, their ragged mouths dripping red as they chewed and slurped, moaning with delight.

People say pizza is universal. I know it goes much farther than that.

My earliest memory is of counting bricks. Anthony and I would rush through the morning prep to get to the back wall before Dad lit the fire. We were still small enough to slip between the oven and the wall, the bricks scorched black by heat, rough like stubble against our cheeks. We would count them over and over, but the totals never added up. Eighty-four one way, ninety-three the other. Once, we got a piece of sidewalk chalk and marked the bricks with numbers, end-to-end both ways. The counts still came out different. Somewhere in the middle, something strange had happened. Just like life, I suppose.

I think that's when I first started to realize our place wasn't like other places. You gotta remember that kids have no basis for comparison. People grow up believing all sorts of screwed up shit, not that my family was any more messed up than anyone else's. Dad yelled a lot, but he never raised a hand to Mom or us, not like Grandpa Castaigne did to him. In the end, that's all you can really do as a parent, right? Try not to make the same mistakes your folks did. And if there's one thing I can say about Dad: it's that he made *different* mistakes.

But enough about that.

Everyone always wants to hear about Tony, like he's some sort of Midwestern boogeyman. I saw a conspiracy website the other day that linked him all sorts of crazy crap. Like, they had some grainy security video of a guy that kinda looked like him boarding Malaysian flight 370, or a shot of some dark-haired dude loitering outside the Twin Towers just before 9/11. People believe anything. That's one of the reasons I need to set the record straight.

Now that Tony's gone I feel like the truth won't hurt him. I'm not worried about the feds bringing me in, they'll never find anything. Remember, I was there when they searched the parlor. Forensics went over the place with a fine-toothed comb. Five days and they came up with nothing—no blood, no hair, no signs of struggle, *nothing*. That article Cleveland Plain Dealer said it was like the place had been licked clean. Didn't know how close they were to the truth.

Thank God the feds didn't count the bricks, not because of what they might've found, but because of what might've found them.

Sorry for being so mysterious, but a thing like this comes with a whole lot of baggage. I'm sick of the stuff I say being taken out of context, so I'm just gonna lay the whole thing out, backwards door and all. Actually, the door is as good a place to start as any.

So, you see, most of the time we were a regular pizza parlor: people came in in, placed an order, got their drinks, their garlic bread, their pie; but some days it was different. We'd clean, Dad would fire up the oven, but he'd never flip the sign to "open." I don't know how Dad knew. The phone never rang, he never wrote anything down, he never even paused like someone was talking to him. Grandpa Castaigne was the same way, and later, Tony. Once, I asked Tony about it, but he just muttered something about "unfolding the flame-scarred eye," whatever that was.

Normal doors go somewhere: you step through and you're either coming or going. The backwards door wasn't like that. Yeah, it took us places, but you didn't have to step through. We'd be spreading sauce or sprinkling little bits of newspaper on the pizzas and there'd just be this feeling like we weren't *here* anymore. Like the bricks, it's hard to explain.

Once, after the divorce, Tony and I went to Florida to visit Mom over Christmas. She and her new husband, Frank, had this huge place in Boca Raton. Apparently he was some big real estate dude. Anyway, Cleveland was freezing, like negative twenty degrees with about three feet of snow. We get on the plane in scarves and coats, then bang, a couple hours later we get out and it's like ninety-five and sunny, palm trees everywhere.

The backwards door was sorta like that, except without the flight. Like you hadn't moved, but *everything* was different.

Dad was good about not letting us out of the back when there were special customers. We'd finish up a pie, then sure as shit the bell on the front door would jingle, and Dad would get this serious look on his face.

"Boys, listen to me." It was the same every time. He'd kneel down to look us in the eyes, one hand on each of our shoulders, painfully tight. "You need to stay back here. Don't peek, don't come out, or I'll have to burn you."

The threat was weird enough, but what was scarier was the little tremble in his voice when he said it, the way his eyes glittered like he was fighting tears.

We didn't look, not until the DeMarco brothers disappeared.

I mean, you ever try and stop a kid from doing something dangerous? Sometimes they listen, sometime they burn their hand on the stove.

Even though we didn't peek, we could hear the customers, voices were like wind through a cracked window, all tongueless and sharp.

Dad talked to . . . something, or some*things*. Well, I'm not exactly sure if he talked *to* them as much as *at* them—chattering about toppings and crusts, the type of sauce we used, where the newspaper clippings or baby teeth came from. He'd talk about The Browns and the Indians, what kind of summer we were having, who gave the biggest donation at the Saint Ignatius fundraiser.

All the while, that windy, fluting babble would just keep going. I'm not sure if they cared, or if they were even listening. When I asked Dad about it, he just said: "Don't worry, it's just the *ambiance*."

I don't think he was talking for their benefit, though. Near as I can figure it was like insulation, a cloak of ordinary stuff he could wrap tight against some screeching call of madness.

Tony and I would crouch behind the kneading table, facing the wall, heads down and fingers laced behind our necks like at a tornado drill at school. Nobody told us to do it. It just seemed like the right thing.

One time, we snuck in a tape recorder, planning to record some creepy sounds to freak out some kids who were picking on us at the YMCA, but when we played the tape back it was just Mom's voice whispering our names over and over.

After the special customers left, Dad would come back with a handful of gold nuggets. They never paid in cash, and that was a problem. People would start asking questions if the owner of a local pizza parlor started showing up to the bank with bags of gold. But Dad had a guy. There were guys for a lot of thing back in the late '70s, especially around Collinwood, even after the Danny Greene thing.

Dad probably got five cents on the dollar, but nobody looked into where the gold was coming from. Grandpa Castaigne had some shady connections back in Quebec, so I guess they figured Dad was the middle man for some rogue Côte-Nord mine. Ridiculous, I know, but even low-level operators know a good thing when they see it. Goose with the golden eggs and all that.

I worked in the parlor until I was seventeen. Mom hated it, but after Grandpa Castaigne died, Dad couldn't really handle the place on his own, and he certainly wasn't about to hire on any outside help. We were just trying to get by. A lot of people did far worse to make ends meet. I would've probably still been working there if Tony hadn't gone and bragged about it to Lisa Kowalski. He'd had a thing for her since first grade, and, being a dumb teen, thought he could impress her with stories about serving pizza to monsters.

She laughed at him, they all did, especially the DeMarcos. There were these two brothers. Jim was Tony's age, and Ray one grade above me. They were real shits, the kind of kids who would sling rocks at stray cats or hang around underneath the bleachers and try and look up girls' skirts. I'm not saying this to justify what happened to them—nobody deserves that—but honestly, they were shits.

The DeMarcos always had a wild hair for us. Something about a bunch of French-Canadian ex-pats running a pizza parlor didn't sit right with their grade-school concept of Italian pride. Anyway, they got wind of Tony's story and really started laying into him. Not just mean-spirited jokes, but full-on beatings. It was like they had a goddamn radar for when my little brother was alone. One time, I had to stay after school because Ms. Scali found some cigarettes in my backpack, and they caught Tony walking home. It was just after Halloween '81. I remember because Tony said they were wearing Flintstones masks.

Anyway, it was hard to get the story out of Tony. He was hard-headed even back then, but near as I can tell, they came up behind and knocked him over. Ray held him down while Jim pulled off his shoes and threw them over a telephone line. Tony must've tried to fight back, because they bloodied him good.

Ray had this old bicycle chain he stole off one of the other kids' Huffys, used to use it to smash beer bottles and scratch up cars. He must've whipped it across Tony's back a dozen times because the skin was all tore up. I was going to tell Dad, but Tony made me swear not to. I'm not sure if he was embarrassed or angry, but we kept it quiet and took care of the cuts with hydrogen peroxide and gauze. Not a great way to go about things—Tony's back scarred up real good. Fortunately, Mom and Dad were just hitting the end their marriage and were too busy with each other to keep an eye on us. If things had been even close to normal Mom would've known for sure, and Dad, well, he wouldn't have left parlor keys out.

It was one of those special days. We were hiding in back while Dad babbled away out front. Thinking back, I seem to remember there was quite a bit of nonsense mixed in with Dad's baseball stats. It might've been his marriage unraveling that put the first cracks in his mind, but I think it started long before that. You can't do what he did for a living and come away intact.

Anyway, we're huddled behind the kneading table and Tony just looks at me, his eyes all red and angry like he'd been crying.

"I hate them. I want them to go away." I mean, what was I supposed to do? I was his big brother, he was my responsibility. It was my fault the DeMarcos had cut him up.

So I just nodded.

We waited for the next special day, when the backwards door was wide open. It wasn't hard to get the DeMarcos down to the parlor. We just picked a fight with them when teachers were nearby. It wasn't much of a scuffle, but their pride was pricked. Ray said they'd settle up after school, teach us a lesson. We told them right where we'd be and when.

It was after hours, the parlor closed up for the night. No one was watching us. Mom had gone down to live with her sister in Youngstown, and Dad was halfway into a twelve-pack of Schlitz. So we grabbed his keys and snuck on down the block to the parlor.

I think the DeMarcos were planning on something really stupid, because when they showed up they both had pocket knives. Not the little Swiss Army numbers, but big clip folders they must've swiped from their dad.

Anyway, they pull up on their bikes and we're just lounging in the back, laughing and waving. The door was open, *all* the doors were open.

To this day, I don't know how we knew the things would show up, but they did.

Ray kicked the door open, almost jangling the bell of its hook. Both DeMarcos were red-faced, but they didn't yell like I expected. They just had these weird little smiles, like they were about to watch something funny.

It was Tony who saw it first. I know, because he grabbed my hand, fingernails digging into my palm hard enough to draw blood.

The things came in like a child's scrawl, a twisted nest of lines and curlicues scribbled through the air. From the chaos emerged long, uncomfortable limbs, hooked and swollen, their fingers like a stand of bamboo, knuckles all the way down. I'm not sure if they had bodies, but I know they had heads, and mouths. They hung above the DeMarcos like smoke, silent, almost reverent, like someone about to receive the holy sacrament at church.

Still blind to the madness above him, Jim nodded to Ray, pointing his knife at our clasped hands. "Look at the fags."

It was the last thing he'd ever say.

It happened so quickly. Barely enough time for Jim's grin to slip, barely enough time for his eyes to widen. Blessedly, I don't think he was even aware when the talons stroked the side of his face, then down his neck. Skin and muscle peeled back, and Jim was cut so cleanly I could see right into the pulsing heart of him. Crooked fingers took hold of his arms, his legs, his ribs, splaying him out like a medical cadaver, pale veins of fat draped like melting cheese over raw red innards. The rest of him went quickly after that, mouths chewing and slurping, chapped lips smacking with delight as they pulled him apart slice by slice.

I remember Ray dropping his knife, one hand pressed to his mouth like he was going to vomit. He made these weird mewling noises, and I could smell the sharp tang of urine. Still, he didn't run when they reached for him. Somehow, I think he knew it would only make matters worse. He did scream, though.

Tony and I watched as the things sectioned and devoured him, folding up the slices so the softer parts wouldn't drip off. There was probably a better way, a faster way, but all they knew was pizza, and pizza goes piece-by-piece.

At the time, I was surprised no one called the cops, but thinking back on it, I'm not sure if we were even in Cleveland anymore.

When it was over, the things slipped back into their scribbled holes as quietly as they'd come. There was nothing to clean up, no sign of the DeMarcos beyond the knife that Ray dropped. Where Jim had stood was a pile of gold. Not the handful that Dad brought back, but a goddamn *pile*.

We tossed the knife and the gold in one of the flour sacks then buried it under the wrinkled remains of Mom's garden. With the way things were going, it was a good bet she wouldn't be home to replant in the spring.

When we got home, Dad was out cold on the recliner, the TV light glittering through the bottles lined up on the table next to him. *The Tonight Show* was on, Rodney Dangerfield telling jokes about his terrible wife, saying something like "After she cooks dinner, I don't brush my teeth, I count them."

I can barely remember my first kiss, the first time Dad took us to see the Browns play, even my college graduation is a goddamn blur, but that night comes back to me every time I close my eyes. It's not guilt, though. Getting rid of the DeMarcos was basically self-defense. I didn't like what happened. I didn't like *how* it happened. But I'm damn sure that the next time Jim and Ray cornered Tony they would've killed him. It might've been an accident. They might not have intended things to go so far, but it would be my little brother gone instead of those two.

Sometimes I wonder if that would've been better.

After the thing with the DeMarcos, Mom threw a real shit fit. There was no evidence, and Tony and I never said a word to anyone, but somehow she knew. She drove up from Youngstown and stormed into the parlor, screaming at Dad. He yelled back. Tony, too. I don't know why, but Tony blamed Mom for what happened, like she had any control over anything. The look on her face was something else. Like she'd opened up a Christmas present and found a dead dog inside. I tried to calm everyone down, but no one was listening.

Mom said she wasn't leaving without us. Dad said we were old enough to make our own decisions. Mom picked up one of the tables and threw it through the front window.

It was early spring, March or thereabouts, the air just losing its bite, but the wind that came pouring in when Mom smashed that glass was humid and full of long white filaments like spider webs, but finer. It smelled like mildew and old mustard, the breeze hot like breath on our faces. The buildings on the other side of Waterloo Street were little more than smudges, blurred by the yellow-brown fog that hung over everything. Strange shapes moved in the mist, twisting and writhing as they unfurling long, articulated arms.

Mom took one look at them, then turned back to us. "C'mon boys."

I went with her, Tony didn't.

It had to have scared the shit out of her, but she didn't flinch. She just took my hand and marched out the door. I half expected us to step out into some shadowy alien wasteland, but it was just Waterloo road, same as always.

We drove back to the house. Mom went inside and came back with a purse full of gold. Dad must've known, but he never made a stink. I guess he felt she'd earned it.

I finished up high school down in Youngstown, then majored in history at YSU. Mom met Frank on a cruise during my senior year. After the divorce was finalized, they got married and went south to Boca. My girlfriend at the time was still finishing up, so I hung around and got a teller job at the Home Savings and Loan on Market Street. I had plans for grad school, still do, but I'm not here to talk about that.

Things were rough between me and Tony after I left. I went up a couple of times. Dad seemed subdued, but Tony would hardly give me the time of day. I think he'd started hanging out with one of Dad's guys, drinking and gambling, hopping the Friday red-eye to Atlantic City then crawling back half-dead from drugs and booze. It could've been worse, I suppose. Hell, it *was* worse.

Thankfully, Dad dying was kind of a wakeup for Tony.

I got the call late at night on a Wednesday. Tony was nowhere to be found, so the cop said I needed to drive up to Cleveland to identify Dad. He wouldn't go into details over the phone, so I spent the drive from Youngstown to Cleveland thinking Dad had blown his brains out, or that maybe one of his mob guys had finally decided to try and shake him down for the gold. I should've known better.

After Mom smashed out the front window, Dad had a new one installed, one of those double-paned super energy efficient models. The cops found him spread between the glass panes, his body sliced into millimeter-wide sections like a slide on a microscope. The cops thought it was murder, probably mob-related, but I knew Dad had killed himself. I saw the careful, almost respectful way they'd carved him up, and I knew he'd asked those things to do it.

The feds blamed my brother for that one, too, but he was innocent. Tony came back from Atlantic City on Monday, his suit rumpled and his breath smelling like a barroom floor. He took Dad's death badly, his grief soured by something like guilty relief. Only then, I realized how much he'd needed me, and how much I'd missed.

We made up at the funeral. Mom even flew in from Boca. Life's too short, right? Still, there'd always be that undercurrent of anger with Tony. Unfair as it was, I'm sure he felt like we abandoned him. It's true, I guess, but it's also true he chose not to come with us. Family is complicated like that.

This is the part everyone was always asking me about, but honestly Tony and I weren't too close. He married Lisa Kowalski, they settled down, got a big house in Shaker Heights, had some kids. You know, the American dream. I'd come up for Christmas, Easter, birthdays, that sort of thing. Tony always had some new expensive thing to show me, like a car, or a boat, or an entertainment system. Lisa was a public defender, great lawyer, but she didn't really rake in the cash, and Tony was still running the parlor, so I knew there was no way they could afford all that expensive stuff.

Still, my brother would have me over for holidays, then rub my face in how well he was doing while I was still slaving away at the bank. It didn't bother me, which I think pissed him off more. Like he had to *prove* he'd made the right decision, that I'd been wrong for leaving.

I mean, I knew where he was getting the money, goddamn me, I *always* knew. But he was still my brother, and even after all that happened, or maybe because of it, I felt responsible.

It was the mid-nineties by then, organized crime had learned a lot from the purges; no more car bombs, no more shootings, when people disappeared they did it quietly, no flash, no press. Thing about it was, most of the outfits that survived on were small, low-key deals, not the kind to bury a lot of folk.

I think that's how Tony got his start, though, disappearing wise guys who'd gone federal witness, settling old grudges, that sort of thing. Once he'd gotten a rep as a cleaner who didn't ask questions it would've been a pretty smooth gig. The mob would pay Tony to disappear someone, and those things would toss out a heap of gold for the privilege. I think it could've carried on like that for a while, but Tony had bills to pay.

He'd volunteer at soup kitchens and shelters, offer free pizza to homeless people on Christmas or Thanksgiving. Who was going to notice if some poor vagrant disappeared over the winter? And even if they did, Tony was a goddamn pillar of the community.

It's my fault he's gone. Shit, that's hard to say. You gotta understand, I still love him, even now, even knowing what he did.

I got the papers, you see, read the reports, the stats. Most of the articles blamed the economy, the rust belt, the winter, but I knew what Tony was doing. I don't think he's responsible for *everyone* who went missing—those conspiracy sites are bullshit—but I think he definitely took his cut.

It was when that runaway kid disappeared near Collinwood yard that I couldn't take it anymore. I drove up to Cleveland, almost killed myself speeding. It was 3 a.m., but Tony was in the parlor.

I felt it as soon as I stepped in, like I'd skipped a plane to Boca.

Tony was happy to see me, can you believe it? First time in I don't know how long he actually gave me a hug that felt real.

He'd figured it out, you see, all of it.

I don't know if there were sentences nestled amidst the word salad he spit at me, but goddamn was he smiling. There was a big chart chalked out on the bricks at the back of the shop, a sprawling, tangled spider web of sigils that made me dizzy to look at. He would point at this or that symbol, sketching shapes in the air with his free hand.

It was when the stuff he was saying started to make sense that I really got scared. He grabbed my shoulder like Dad used, talking fast, his words taking root in the cracks between my thoughts.

The sigils were places, the chart was a map, and the bricks had always been there. Left to right, right to left, the parlor opened for me like a flower. Tony wasn't like Dad—he hadn't wrapped himself in mundanity. He just hadn't talked at the things, he'd talked *to* them.

And they'd answered.

At last, Tony's words came to me, clear as my memory of the DeMarcos.

He wasn't talking nonsense, he was talking *franchises.*

I barely remember grabbing Grandpa Castaigne's old carving knife. It made a thin red line across my brother's throat, his words crumbling into a wet cough. He looked at me like he had that day before the DeMarcos disappeared, eyes wide and red-rimmed, his lips pressed into a tight line.

He raised a fist, then uncurled it to cup my cheek.

I caught Tony as he fell, holding him tight until his eyes rolled back and his feet stopped drumming on the tiles. You gotta understand, he was my brother, my responsibility.

The things came quietly, like they had for the DeMarcos. Not through the front door, but from the back. I don't think they really understood what was happening, but maybe they did. They kept their distance, the parlor silent but for the click claws on tile, the wet rasp of their lips on fire-blackened bricks.

Tony was stiff by the time I was willing to let him go, but they didn't mind. Everyone knows cold pizza is just as good as hot, better even.

There was an investigation, of course. I might've been a person of interest, I'm not sure, but I do know that nobody came forward putting me in Cleveland on the night Tony went missing, and there's nothing on Earth linking me to it.

When the feds were done with me, I had the parlor bulldozed and Grandpa Castaigne's creepy old oven chopped up for scrap. I think there's an apartment building there now, or maybe a gas station, I'm not sure. All the money went into a trust fund for Tony's kids. Sure, it could've helped out a lot, but I didn't touch it, even when I lost my job at the bank.

Just like Dad said, none of it was ever mine.

I still get the feeling, when I'm walking down the street, or watching TV, or even on the toilet. One second I'll be there, and the next, well, I'll be somewhere else. Whenever it happens I find a corner and sit down, eyes closed and head bowed, hands laced behind my neck.

I thought getting rid of the parlor would get rid of the things, too. I thought the backwards door was a thing, a place, but I was wrong. Dad was right. It's ambiance.

The feelings have been coming more often, lingering longer and longer. Sooner or later, the things will come for me, too. I know what they want, what they crave. It's inevitable.

A good pie is impossible to forget.

WATCH THEM EAT

ANDREW HILBERT

HIRD TIME THIS week I've been here. They're my favorite customers. Always smile. Always tip. Always ask how I'm doing. The Waltons. I like them. Good family. Even adopted some kid from China because it had one eye. I know a lot about them.

I know their order, too. The online deal. Two large pizzas for seven bucks each. It's a good deal. Only runs Monday through Wednesday, though. That's when I see them. Usually on Tuesdays, but if Rebecca is working late and only Tom is home, I'll see them on Wednesdays, too.

I like seeing Rebecca. She looks professional, most of the time. Tom's a slob. I don't think he treats her right. Just something about him. He's got muscles and a very well-manicured beard. Seems like the kind of guy who goes to the gym. Seems like the kind of guy who prowls around the gym looking for any good-looking woman that needs a spotter. He doesn't treat her right.

Hell, he won't even cook for his kids. Even the kid with one eye.

I ring the doorbell. It's Tuesday. Rebecca would be home. She'd answer. She'd smile.

"Oh," she says when she answers; smiles. "Hey, there. What's the damage?"

She always says that.

I laugh. Nobody ever knows the damage.

I always do this for customers I like, and I don't like many: I take the pizza out of the warming bag before they give me money. Watch your next delivery guy. If he likes you, he'll take out the pizza first.

It's a symbol of trust. If there's nothing there—no trust, no love, no nothing—I wait until there's some money out.

"It's sixteen dollars and eighty cents, Ms. Walton."

She always gives exact change with five on top. She's good tipper.

But she seems a little flustered tonight. She doesn't really smile. Doesn't ask how I am. She grabs the pizzas, says, "Thanks," and shuts the door.

My heart falls to my asshole.

It must be him.

It has to be him.

He doesn't know how to treat a woman.

He doesn't know how to be grateful for his children. Even the Chinese one with the one eye. They are gifts from God. Why are good women always with the wrong guy?

Maybe he suspects something. Maybe he doesn't like the way she talks to me. Maybe she doesn't like the way she looks at me. I might only be nineteen, but I can tell she sees something in me. It takes confidence to wear a mustache these days. I have confidence. She can see that. So can he. Fucking ape.

I ring the doorbell and wait.

She opens the door again.

"Yes?"

"Did you want any change?"

"I never want any change."

"Yes, but . . . "

She looks at me. Confused. She's beautiful. Her eyes are a little sunken in, but it looks natural. She works hard. She's tired. She needs someone to rub her feet.

I lean in.

"Is everything okay?"

She backs up a little. Looks around like she's not supposed to be talking to me.

"It's nothing."

My ears perked up.

"Oh?"

"I have to get back to my family. Have a good night."

It's nothing is a clue. Of course she can't say anything. Of course.

I go back to my car and grab my pepper spray. You always need to defend yourself. This is a cash heavy business. I have, like, thirty bucks in tips on me. People are always after an entrepreneur. Rats. Scumbags.

The gate on the side of the house is broken. A real man would've fixed it to protect his wife and children. Tom isn't a real man. He's a psychopath. A worm in man's skin.

I always went through that gate because just after it was a window, no curtains. Just blinds. But the blinds were all fucked up because they had a dog. "Puffy" is what they called it.

Anyways, a real man would have fixed those blinds. The dog sometimes could sense me there. He'd bark and bark and bark and fuck the blinds up more, giving me a widescreen experience.

"There's nothing there," I imagine Rebecca saying as she puts the dog in its crate. Tom sits there, chewing like the primate he was. A blank expression on his face, like there was a ping pong ball in that skull of his, bouncing up and down, up and down, and all he could do was concentrate on it.

No wonder she seems off.

The dog keeps barking in the crate. Even though they covered it, he can still sense me. A real dog would've sensed the real evil was Tom. Maybe it's Tom's dog. I always thought Puffy was a stupid name.

Rebecca was the one that cut the pizza for her kids. Tom just ate. I've seen him eat more than half a pizza to himself. Slob.

I tap on the window. Nobody does anything. They sit there in silence and don't even watch each other chew. They don't realize that you can learn a lot about people by watching them eat.

Fuck this.

I tiptoe to my car, count my money, and drive off.

There's no order tonight from the Waltons, but after my shift, I take two boxes of pizza some college dipshit refused because he didn't order onions and head over to their house.

I sit in my car for a little while to watch their shadows pace the living room. He's probably berating her for something she neglected to do. She's probably begging him not to hit her. Pathetic. I can't tell the kids apart from their shadows because they all have two ears but they're jumping around and having fun as kids do, even as their parents' lives crumbled around them.

I keep the car running.

Rebecca answers the door.

"Hi?" She looks confused. Like she's expecting me. Like she's hiding something. She looks over her shoulder at Tom. The kids are climbing him. She has a nervous smile when she looks back to me. She's sweating a little bit. "We didn't order any pizza."

"Really?" I look at the receipt of the last customer's delivery. "It says right here, your address," I lie.

I lift the receipt. She doesn't need to see it. She knows her address.

"Well, must be some kind of mistake. I'm sorry."

"Mommy's taking too long, the Dadasaurus is going to eat you all!" Tom says in the background like the fucking beta he is.

"There is no mistake. It says right here." I shove the receipt in her face.

She looks shaken up.

"Everything okay, Becca?" Tom asks. Shut the fuck up, Tom. Nobody's talking to you.

"Everything's fine," she says. "How much do I owe you? What was your name again?"

"My name?" She has to pretend in front of Tom. I understand. "Oh, never mind," I say. "Just take the pizza. Have a nice night."

I throw the pizza on the floor. The kids look shocked. The Chinese kid squints his one eye at the bell peppers and onions seeping out of the box on a wave of cold tomato sauce. I walk away.

"Hey! Kid! What's your fucking name? I want to talk to your manager!" She steps onto the porch to back me away.

She's a good actress. I feel the tingles. Get throbby.

I go to my car and sit and wait for her to shut up.

She doesn't shut up.

I drive around the block a few times. The music turned low, waiting for things to cool down so I can go watch them eat again. What kind of show was she acting in back there?

I pull around the corner and park a few houses down from them. I walk back to their window and watch them. Like nothing happened, they're playing again.

Why does she look so happy with the one-eyed kid on her shoulders? She chose an imperfect baby. Maybe he foisted that on her. Maybe he has a Jesus complex. All of them do. Just because you have muscles and money doesn't mean you can solve all the world's problems.

Their doorbell rings. I slink back down into the overgrown grass and wait. Rebecca is laughing. Her voice sounds flirtatious. She sounds like she sounds with me. I get to my knees and crawl to around the corner with the good view of their front porch.

It's some Pizza Hut bitch-boy at the door.

Rebecca's playing us all for fools.

They probably don't even know his name.

"It's so good to see you, Steve," Rebecca said. "Here's a little extra tip."

She knows his name. I can't sit for this anymore.

"Hey! Hey!" I say, walking as fast as I can to the front door. "What's my name?" I grab Steve by the collar and jerk him away from the money Rebecca's handing him. "What's my fucking name?"

Tom pushes past Rebecca. He grabs me by the throat and lifts me off the floor.

"Get the fuck out of here before somebody has to call the cops on me." What does that even mean? His eyes are empty. Dumb. A fucking ape. I told you.

"Yeah, I'm sure this is what you do to Rebecca every night!" I cough the words out despite his grasp. I can't move my head so I try to side-eye Rebecca. "What's my name?"

"I have no fucking clue," she says. She hands Steve his money, and he runs to his car like the beta he is.

She isn't lying. This is no act. She doesn't know who I am.

"Tom," I choke on my words. "Tom," I say, "you can put me down."

Tom loosens his grip and drops me. I fall to my knees, coughing blood.

"Don't come back here," Tom says. He kicks me in the ribs and I fall down the steps of their porch. He slams the door and the porchlight goes out.

Eventually my breathing starts to taste like blood and the time between inhalation and exhalation gets longer so I know I'll be okay.

But I still can't get up. I crawl to my car, prop myself up against the bumper, and sit in its shadow underneath the streetlight for a while.

Steve's car keeps driving by. He speeds up, slows down in front of the Walton's house, and then speeds off again. His Pizza Hut delivery sign light on the top of his car was shut off, camouflaged now.

Just like me.

Fucking pervert.

My ribs aren't aching anymore, so I light up a smoke and sit on the hood of my car to wait for Steve's inevitable drive-by. I watch the front window of the Walton's house. I can see the one-eyed kid peeking through the blinds. I wave to the kid but get no reaction. Probably should've waved with my left hand since the right eye still works.

The hum of Steve's car creeps past as I stare at the house, waiting for another distress signal from little one eye or Rebecca. Rebecca has to pretend to be scared by me. She has to pretend to not know my name. She is being trapped by her husband who obviously had a homosexual relationship with Steve.

I can save them all.

"Hey, faggot!"

All of the air goes out of me again and I fall to the floor. Steve's standing over me with a burning cigarette that he ashes on my eyebrows. He's still wearing his Pizza Hut uniform. Smells like cheese.

"I keep driving by and you're still fucking here, man. They told you to leave."

I got up, heaving.

"You're a fucking cuck," I say.

"What did you call me?"

"I said you're a fucking cuck."

"I don't know what that means." He stubs his cigarette out on my forehead. Right in the middle. "Listen, fuck off. And stay away from the Waltons."

The blinds are open again.

Steve gets back into his car, turns his delivery light on, and speeds off.

They don't order from us the next week. Or the week after that. I do my regular drive-bys. I watch Steve tip his hat like the beta he is. I watch him grovel for his tips. He even gets to shake Tom's hand. Something is afoot. Who treats a pizza delivery boy like that?

"Anyone want to take this misdelivery home with them? Otherwise, I'm just trashing it." my boss asks, like he didn't know I had dibs. Misdeliveries are little miracles for me. They happen a few times a week, some weeks more. Especially when some big sportsball thing is on TV. Sometimes people expect you to give to them for free anyways but my Pizza Hut knows to take them back and throw them my way.

My feet are up on the break room table and I'm scrolling through reddit. I put two fingers in the air to call dibs on it. My eyes never leave my phone.

The boss drops the pizza on the table next to my shoes.

"We got a complaint about you driving around a former customer's neighborhood."

"Nobody owns the streets," I say without looking.

"That's real fucking cute." He's sick of me, but not man enough to do anything about it.

I grab the pizza and go to my car, throw the pizza in the backseat, and flip on my delivery sign as I head back to the Waltons' neighborhood. I want to telegraph that help is on the way. Nobody has to suffer any longer.

Rebecca would be mine. The one-eyed kid could call me uncle. Their other kid could call me uncle, too, I guess.

Tom and Steve could rest in peace.

I park in the driveway. That's a big no-no in the delivery driver world. You never want to block somebody in. If you did, there would be no way they could escape.

I go to the side of their house, Tom's office. The blinds on his sliding glass doors are wide open, a blue light illuminates his pathetic face. He's hunched over, a piece of tape covered his webcam. He hardly moves, save for the short, rhythmic motion of his right shoulder: up and down, up and down. Pathetic. He's

married to gold and he pretends to fuck whores. He's down to his
boxers, socks still on. There's no pomp. No ceremony. Just some guy
stroking with the same excitement as taking a shit.

Sad.

Masturbation clogs the mind. Especially the kind of shit he's
stroking to. A real man saves every ounce of himself for the right
woman. You don't end up with troglodytes that way. It's not crazy.
Have you seen the world? The whole world's gone crazy and it's
because everyone's masturbating to the same unnatural bullshit.

Lesbians.

Give me a break. There's no penetration. How can you even
insert yourself into that situation? Literally or figuratively. Maybe if
he was watching them eat?

No wonder Rebecca is playing mind games with pizza boys. I tap
on his window a few times. He doesn't turn around. He's too close.
I used to know the feeling.

I throw a rock at the window. He jumps out of his chair and flips
around like he's having a seizure. Hard-on and all. I grab another
rock and walk across the broken glass into his room.

"What-what-what do you want?" His lip quivering.

"Honey?" I hear Rebecca call from outside the room. "Is
everything okay?"

Their shit-terrier is barking.

"Don't tell her, okay? She gets jealous."

I laugh and slam the rock against his face. I'm not a murderer. I
just don't want any surprises. The police will sort his abuses out
later.

I open the office door and walk out into the hall.

The dog's all bark. It runs to its crate where it whimpers.

"Pizza! Pizza! Pizza Daddy is here!"

Rebecca is at the kitchen table with paper plates. Her kids
already sitting. When she sees me, she drops everything and freezes.

"It's the scary man!" the one-eyed kid says.

"Girls, go to your room and lock the door," Rebecca says.

That thing is a girl?

"No! Finish setting up the table. Pizza Daddy has pizza!"

"Pizza!" The two girls raise their hands in the air, excited.

"Nobody move."

The doorbell rings. I go to answer it.

"Do we have company?" I open the door.

Steve. With two boxes of pizza. On a Tuesday. Tuesdays are my night.

"This is my night," I say, then I slap the boxes out of his hand. "Fuck Pizza Hut."

I grab Steve by his pizza bag and pull him inside. I throw him to the floor and straddle him. I put my face so close into his that I can smell the deep dish grease in his nostrils. I point to my cigarette burn.

"You did this to me."

Steve gets in my face and starts yelling. "You're crazy, man! You're crazy! You're back to this bullshit? You got fired for creeping customers out. The only reason anyone still lets you hang around is because we're all afraid you're going to kill us." Steve's hysterical. "Your shirt even has the old logo, man! You were fired before the rebrand. You're old news . . . " He's grabbing me by the ears, yelling so close to me that I can taste his spit.

I headbutt him.

No use in wasting pizza. Even if it is Pizza Hut. I grab Steve's pizza and close the door. The pizza I brought had nothing but onions, Spanish olives, and garlic on it. Bunch of bullshit, but I work with what I got. No wonder the customer refused it though. I open Steve's box. Pepperoni. Classic. Edible.

"Pizza's coming!" I yell with a smile.

Steve isn't unconscious. I want him to see me take Tom's place as rightful man of the house. Steve doesn't know Rebecca was sending me signals. I do not wear a cape.

As I walk to the table, I feel disgust burn inside me. No matter how classic the toppings are, it is still Pizza Hut. "I can't eat this shit, honey. I have too much brand loyalty to the company that pays our bills. And now you go run out and go to a competitor?" I sit down. I clasp my hands together. I shake my head. "Steve!" I yell.

Where is Steve?

I'm panting, red-faced, and sweating. My surroundings a blur. "Steve!"

There is no Rebecca. There are no kids with three eyes between them. There is no Tom. There is no house. There is no pizza.

It hits me. A cast iron skillet, I mean.

You don't expect a household that orders pizza twice a week to have one of them, but I guess that's the kind of thing nice couples get as wedding presents.

I fall, but everything comes back into focus. Steve is standing above me. Cast iron skillet in hand. How does Steve know where to find the cast iron skillet in the house?

"Why does he know where we keep the cast iron skillet?"

She doesn't answer. She's shuffling the kids down the hall into Tom's office. I laugh, wondering if they'd find Boner Mortis in there.

They scream.

Eyes closed. Sweating. Temples pounding. I try to get myself off the floor but I can't. My head hurts. It really hurts.

Steve turns toward the screaming.

"I told you he's hurting them," I say this to Steve very serious, man-to-man.

Steve doesn't say anything.

Fuck you, Steve.

He drops the skillet on the floor. It cracks the tile. He follows the sound of my family screaming.

I manage to get myself up despite the clanging in my head. Despite the fuzziness. Despite the stumbling. I grab the skillet. It's heavy. It hurts my wrist. Steve is pretty strong to be able to swing it like that. You need to be strong to carry pizzas, I should know.

Double vision. Nausea. Headaches. The skillet is weighing me down. The hallway is never ending. I drop to my knees and crawl. Panting, I get myself to the door with everyone crying over Tom, who is not moving. Maybe I did kill him.

"I saved you! He was watching pornography! He didn't appreciate you!"

Steve grabs a letter opener off of Tom's desk. The handle is engraved with a bare-breasted mermaid. Tom's got an obsession.

When you play videogames, they say to hold higher ground. You have a good view of things. But everyone expects it. Every now and then, you should be low. Take the more skilled warriors by surprise. I can't get up, so I have to default to this try-hard tactic. I grab Steve's ankle and tug at him as hard as I can. He falls right onto the mermaid. Takes out his left eye. Got a full set now between the

Chinese kid and him. If you count Tom's dead eyes, you've got five pairs of eyes to six faces. I've always been good at math. And science. Steve screams and gurgles out some nonsense.

"I saved you," I say to Rebecca as I crawl over Steve's pathetic wriggling. "Look," I point to the lesbians. "They can't love him, and he doesn't love you. That's science."

Rebecca doesn't look at me. She gets up, grabs the girls, and leaves the room. I hear her on the phone, calling the police. The lesbians are pretty good-looking actually.

But it isn't the right time for a boner. So I don't get one. Self-discipline. That's what this country needs more of.

Steve gets to his feet. He still has the big-titted mermaid in his eye, but I guess he has a gun somewhere up his ass, too, because he is pointing it right at me. And *bang!*

Game over.

Except in videogames, it takes a long time to die when you get shot in the stomach. But the sirens don't take too long getting to this neighborhood. Pizza doesn't take too long, either. In these kinds of neighborhoods, things happen fast. That's how delivery places can make promises like if the pizza's cold, it's free. Because it's never cold. Same goes for me. I'll still be warm by the time an ambulance gets here.

PIZZA_GAL_666

EMMA ALICE JOHNSON

FIRST DATE

One month of online dating and Sarah had already received so many "Hey"s from BigFordChad and Smiley_Guy82 and HoneyCookie420 that Pizza_Gal_666's opener of "What's your favorite pizza?" seemed absolutely thoughtful.

"Pepperoni and sausage," Sarah messaged back.

She didn't ask Pizza_Gal_666's favorite, because her profile listed her top 25, broken down by toppings, crust type and regional style. Most were New York style, which made sense, but one was Louisville style, which Sarah was like *huh?* about.

Pizza Gal replied, "I like a girl who likes her meat lol. Wanna grab a slice?"

Sarah agreed.

That evening, she met Pizza Gal outside a new pizzeria in Williamsburg. It was opening night and the line went around the block. Sarah hovered awkwardly at the back, staring at her phone, hoping not to see the usual "Sorry, can't make it after all," but also kinda wishing for the relief from anxiety that message would bring.

Instead, she heard the clacking of high heels on blacktop and the honking of horns. Pizza Gal ran toward her through traffic in stilettos and a tight black dress with a mesh top. Her outfit had a 5-star-restaurant vibe, but also a dancing-at-the-club vibe. Definitely not a grabbing-a-slice vibe, which Sarah thought she had nailed with her Chucks, jeans and sleeveless band shirt.

Pizza Gal led with a hug, knocking Sarah's phone out of her hand in the process. Gracefully, Pizza Gal snatched it up off the sidewalk and slipped it into Sarah's back pocket even as cars still honked at her audacity.

"I'm Vannie."

"Vannie?"

"Yeah! Short for Vanessa."

"Oh! I'm Sarah."

"Thank you for showing up. So many people on that site are flakes."

"Tell me about it. I've got like a 50/50 success rate. I'm starting to get into eating out alone."

Vannie grabbed Sarah's hand for a moment. "Not too into it, I hope?" Releasing it, she added, "You are super pretty. Oh god, your skin is flawless. Your pictures don't do you justice."

Sarah reached up to cover the trio of pimples along her right jawbone. "Yeah, my camera is terrible."

"Well, should we get in line?"

"Oh, you are super pretty too!" Sarah said, hoping it wasn't too awkwardly late to return Vannie's compliment.

"Ugh, thank you. My eyeliner turned out gross."

Sarah squinted to see what was gross about the perfectly symmetrical black wings of liquid liner. "I think we're already in line actually."

Vannie looked around. "I guess we are!"

"A thousand pizza joints in this city, but this place plops a donut on a slice and puts Ataris at tables and every denim jacket owner in Williamsburg shows up."

"Does it matter why people came if the end result is the same? This energy is palpable. Can't you feel it?" Vannie closed her eyes and spread her arms, as if actually drawing in energy from all the gathered pizza eaters.

"I'm sorry." Sarah stepped back. "I was just making a joke."

"No you weren't. You were doing the whole reactionary anti-hipster thing. As if people getting together and liking a fun new thing is somehow bad? Because why? Because it's not really about the pizza for these people? Because they just want to be part of this? This excitement? This energy?"

Sarah pulled her phone out, wanting to hide in it. Before she could get it up to her face, Vannie grabbed it and slid it into her back pocket again.

"Besides," Vannie continued, "maybe I picked this place on purpose, hoping there would be a line because I wanted to spend more time with you."

Sarah wondered if Vannie was just going to keep saying one perfect thing after the next, because that put a lot of pressure on her. The best she could come up with now was, "How did you find out about this place?"

Vannie shrugged. "Pizza grapevine."

"You are way into pizza."

"What are you into?"

"I like to run alone." Sarah clenched her teeth. Out of all the responses, this was the one that came out. And why did she emphasize "alone"? As opposed to running in a pack like a wolf or something?

She was getting nervous. She hadn't felt this kind of nervous in a while. Usually her dates didn't make her nervous. There was just nothing there to screw up most of the time, so it didn't matter if she said dumb things. But looking at Vannie, she wasn't sure she was ready to screw this up yet.

"Well, it pays off. You really do look amazing."

"Thanks."

"What's that T-shirt all about? Is that supposed to be a snowball?"

"It's a marshmallow. This band, they have a song about roasting marshmallows and how when one falls into the fire it's this little tragedy. I'm not really explaining it right. It's a beautiful song."

"Cool. I'd love to hear it."

"I have it on my phone actually." Sarah reached into her back pocket again. Vannie slid the phone back in, this time before it had even made it all the way out.

"I don't think this is the way I should hear it the first time, okay?"

"Oh, right."

The restaurant looked like an over-filled aquarium—high tops with people standing shoulder to shoulder around them, touching butts with people at adjacent tables. Vannie said, "It is packed, though. I hope it's not too loud to talk. Have you thought about what you want? I don't know if they do sausage and pepperoni."

"Might as well see what the hype is all about and get the donut slice."

"It's a savory donut, you know?"

"Oh."

"A blueberry donut on pizza would be gross, right?" Vannie stuck out her tongue trying to look grossed out, but ended up just looking cute. "It's a basil donut."

"Are you gonna try it?"

"Fuck yes, I am!"

"Haha. Me too then."

They eventually made it through the door. The heat from the ovens and the tightly packed bodies made Sarah sweat immediately. They were still fifteen people away from the counter when Vannie turned to her and whispered, "Oh shit. There are some people here who I, ummm, used to hang out with."

Sarah glanced around, seeing if she could guess which ones. The place was a Where's Waldo of Williamsburg hipsters, with a table full of very obvious exceptions. She giggled and pointed at it. "The ones in black cloaks?"

"They're a big deal in certain circles."

"Circles of people who wear black cloaks?"

"Yes." Vannie grabbed Sarah by the hand and pulled her out, knocking several baffled hipsters aside in the process.

Still giggling, Sarah argued, "But the savory donut pizza!"

Outside, they turned in one direction, only to see more of the uniquely garmented individuals walking toward them.

"Shit!" Vannie pulled Sarah the other way. "Did they see me?"

"Uh, they had the hoods of their cloaks pulled pretty low, I guess."

They ran, Vannie in her clacking black heels and Sarah in her much more stealthy Chucks. Of course those people had seen Vannie. How could anyone not see Vannie? Sarah thought she had even seen them nod at her.

"Are you up for a subway ride? I know a perfect place next to Coney Island. They serve legit New York slices, not this hipster shit."

"Oh, so now it's hipster shit?"

"Who puts donuts on pizza?"

"Fucking hipsters!"

They didn't stop running until they were on the F-train, out of breath but still laughing.

Sarah asked, "The people in cloaks. That was weird, right?"

Vannie shrugged.

"Or is that the new hipster thing? Like, denim is out, cloaks are in?"

Vannie looked her in the eyes and held both of Sarah's hands. "I'm sorry, but you need to take them seriously. They are powerful. They can make people do things."

"I . . . " Sarah said as Vannie squeezed her hands tighter. "Okay?"

Sarah decided not to talk about the cloak people. It was probably some hipster Goth thing. She'd seen weirder. Vannie didn't seem Goth, but she was wearing all black. Maybe she was in Goth recovery.

They held hands all the way to the pizza joint, a block from Coney Island, on an otherwise dark and empty stretch of road. It was just a window in a brick facade, staffed by an old sweaty guy with a classic Brooklyn accent.

"The usual?" he asked.

"Of course."

Twenty minutes later, he slid a box through the window without Sarah even seeing money change hands. They carried it to the beach, out onto a dock.

Sitting cross-legged, they faced each other. Vannie's dress hiked up to show a lot of leg and a sliver of black panties that Sarah only glanced at. They placed the pizza box on their feet and flipped the lid open, releasing a puff of steam into the New York night. "The usual" was a piping hot pie with mushrooms and onions, sliced into a bizarre pattern. Sarah didn't even get how the pattern was possible, with all the curves and angles. It would have taken a very skilled hand with a pizza cutter.

"Oh! I'm used to triangle slices." Fingertip above the sizzling cheese, Sarah traced the various half moons and complex vertices. "Why this?"

"For protection," Vannie replied before taking a bite.

"Don't burn yourself!"

"It's fine! Try it!"

Sarah picked up an oddly shaped slice and tentatively took a bite. To her surprise, it was the perfect temperature. And it was delicious.

They ate a few more slices in smiling silence, greasy fingers catching the moonlight, as the ocean whooshed gently over the shore nearby.

After eating far more slices than someone her size should be able to hold, Vannie leaned back slightly, rubbing her tummy through her black dress. She moved forward and put her face close to Sarah's. Sarah held her breath as Vannie slipped her hand into Sarah's back pocket and took out her phone.

"Now would be the perfect time to play me your T-shirt song."

SECOND DATE

As Sarah hit her stride, her cellphone vibrated in her armband. She groaned half-heartedly, as if she hadn't intentionally accidentally forgot to turn it off for her run like usual, as if she wasn't ecstatic that it might be another text from Vannie.

When she saw that it was her mom instead, she groaned for real. Another random "I'm proud of you" text, to which she resisted the urge to reply, "For what, Mom? Quitting school or working in a running shoe store?" Sometimes Sarah got the impression that her mother was just pleased to know her daughter was alive and making her way in the world and expected nothing more from her. Maybe that was true. Or maybe her mom harbored some secret disappointment that she wasn't a lawyer or didn't have a boyfriend or didn't eat broccoli. That's what moms did, right? They weren't just happy their kids were breathing.

Jogging in place, she looked back at an exchange with Vannie from earlier that week, a couple days after their date. Vannie had sent a quote from the song, the perfect quote, and a heart. Okay, three hearts. And three hearts meant something. She didn't know what, exactly, but definitely something. Unfortunately, Sarah had replied with the next line of the song, "That chocolate will never know the life it could have had," and five hearts. The absolute dumbness of it still made her feel like she had sucked cinder blocks into her stomach. But Vannie had come back with "LOL I am so happy I found you on that site! When is our second date?" so it couldn't have been too dumb.

They had made plans for tonight, and Sarah wished she could run through time right up to the point at which she was supposed to meet Vannie, but she couldn't. Instead, she ran as fast as she could through Prospect Park, hoping to make her legs look extra toned, because she was going to wear a dress this time.

That night, Sarah met Vannie at a vegetarian pizza place in the East Village. They got two slices each and walked around talking so much that their second slices got cold before they made it through their first.

"We could throw them away," Sarah suggested.

"Fuck you!"

"Why did we even get two slices?"

"Because who eats just one slice of pizza?"

"I guess."

"Let's go to my place. I have a microwave."

"Okay, yeah."

They took the train back to Williamsburg. Walking up the steps of a pristine brownstone on a well-manicured street lined with expensive cars, Sarah said, "Holy shit, you must have like 700 roommates to afford this place!"

"I live alone actually."

Stunned, Sarah followed Vannie inside and gasped. It was unreal, a TV apartment. Sarah, along with most of her friends, even the ones with a decent job or two, had roommates and at least one piece of furniture salvaged from a dumpster. Not Vannie. Everything was pristine, from the spotless white leather couch to the coffee table that might have been made out of rare gems to the framed portraits of pizzas on the walls, each cut into arcane shapes. Okay, that was weird, but still sorta classy. Who the fuck was this girl?

"What do you do again? For work?"

Vannie rolled her eyes. "I'm independently wealthy."

"Uh-huh."

Sarah wasn't one hundred percent sure Vannie was kidding. If she was, she obviously didn't want to say what she did for real. If she wasn't, she didn't seem interested in elaborating on the source of her wealth.

So Sarah joked, "From some pizza related endeavor?"

"Of course," Vannie replied, following Sarah as she nosed around the place. In the kitchen, Sarah found an array of pizza cutters hung on pegboard on the wall like tools in a construction worker's home shop. Their blades gleamed.

Sarah took one down. It looked old somehow, even though it was so shiny. The patterns carved into the handle were similar to those in the pizzas they'd eaten together, and those framed on the wall.

"Seriously though, what's with that design? Owww!" She dropped the utensil on the floor. Blood dripped onto the white tile around it from a fresh cut on her opposite hand. She looked at it in disbelief. Had she just cut herself? She couldn't remember rolling the blade against her palm, but she must have.

Unfazed, Vannie grabbed a towel from a drawer.

"It's . . . It's sharp," Sarah said, still shocked.

"What good is a dull blade? Here . . . " Vannie pressed the towel against Sarah's palm, soaking up most of the blood. Then she pulled Sarah's hand up to her face. For a moment, Sarah thought Vannie was going to lick the wound, but she didn't. "It's not bad. No need for stitches or anything."

"I can't believe I did that."

"Sometimes our bodies are compelled to do things our minds don't agree to."

"What?"

Vannie led Sarah by her uncut hand to a spacious bathroom. Sarah usually only saw bathrooms so well lit on the rare occasion she stayed at a nice-ish hotel on one of her running road trips. Vannie sat her down on the edge of the tub, kneeled in front of her and carefully washed and bandaged the wound.

"Thank you," Sarah said.

"Did you get any blood on your dress?"

"Oh fuck!" Sarah panicked. She jumped up and inspected her dress in the mirror. Thankfully, she didn't see any bloodstains. "I don't think so."

"Good. That dress is gorgeous."

Sarah sat back down on the ledge of the tub and Vannie squeezed in beside her. Vannie kissed her lightly on the cheek. "I think we get along well."

Giggling at the unromantic and uncharacteristically awkward statement, Sarah agreed and upped the ante. "Fuck it, I like you."

They touched lips, almost too briefly to even call it a kiss. Then they pulled apart, smiling. Sarah put her fingertips over her mouth as if to stop it from going back for more, even though she wanted to. And why shouldn't she? This felt good. They did get along well, like really well.

"I want to see the rest of this shit hole. You have more than a kitchen and bathroom, right?"

Sarah poked around, playfully opening closet doors, but not really looking inside. She just didn't want to run straight to the bedroom.

"Does your hand hurt?" Vannie asked, following Sarah.

Sarah opened a media cabinet next to the flat screen in the living room and scanned the DVD titles. "What the fuck? This is all '90s gross-out comedies?"

Vannie shrugged.

"I wish I hadn't seen this." Sarah closed the cabinet. She stood and turned around. Smirking, she maneuvered past Vannie and proceeded toward the last room, the bedroom.

She fingered the wall inside the door and found the light switch. Flicking it on, she braced herself, half expecting to see a cheese-colored bedspread with pepperoni pillows. Instead, she was pleasantly surprised to find tasteful, pale pink sheets on a queen-sized bed. She plopped down on it.

Then she noticed the black cloak hanging from a hook behind the door.

"So your old friends . . . ?"

Vannie frowned. "They're . . . "

"A group of cloak aficionados who really like eating pizza?"

"It's not just about eating pizza," Vannie replied, almost angrily.

"What, do they worship pizza? Is it a pizza cult? Do they chant sacred pizza chants and carve arcane symbols into their . . . Oh. Holy shit. Pizza Gal 666. I thought the 666 was a joke, like how everyone says they're a witch now but mainly they just like eyeliner and scented candles."

"It's not like that."

"You were in this cult?"

"You need to stop talking about this actually. We can . . . They can bend people, remap the now, carving unwanted futures into our timelines."

Sarah stared at the floor, so lost for words she was trying to divine the chaotic patterns of the carpet fibers around her feet in hopes they might tell her what to do next. On the one hand, she liked Vannie. The thought of her already filled Sarah's head with visions of late-night smooches and hand-in-hand vacations to ancient ruins and all the future stuff she thought about when smitten. On the other, pizza-cutter sliced hand, this was not right, and even as her gut twisted in smitten-ness, it also turned in sensing that Vannie wasn't being exactly forthright.

Sarah moved away from the bed. "I don't . . . Okay, I'm sorry, this is weird. I need to go. And never do online dating again."

She hurried past Vannie toward the front door. Vannie chased after her, "Don't be like this. I'm not weird. You know I'm not weird."

"Do I?"

"Okay, maybe a little weird, but not run-out-of-my-bedroom-in-fear weird!"

Vannie grabbed Sarah's hand, not in a malicious, *I'm-going-to-stop-you* sort of way, but in a *hey-it's-okay* sort of way. And Sarah did feel okay. As weird as this stuff seemed, she did not feel afraid. She did not actually feel like doing anything other than staying with this amazing woman.

"But you're done with them?"

Vannie nodded.

"If I stay, you're taking me out for Indian food next time, got it?"

Vannie bit her lip hesitantly, looking remarkably cute.

"Got it?"

"Fine!"

THIRD DATE

Despite how well their last date had ended up going once Vannie put her cloak away, and despite Vannie's reassurances, Sarah still had a nagging feeling that something was up. However, that didn't stop her head from filling so full of daydreams she felt like she was floating even as her toes propelled her across mile after mile of Brooklyn blacktop. She fixated on the handholding. She had never been much of a hand holder, in part because the men she had dated in the past held her hand as if holding her captive. But when Vannie's palm had first touched hers, it felt electric. Now, half the time when she thought of the two of them together, she pictured their disembodied hands, each with its own heart beating in time with the other's, moving through life impervious to whatever the world might throw at them.

She caught herself in this thought and realized how mushy and teenage naïve it was. Instead of running faster to clear her head, she slowed down and reached for her phone to read old texts. In the process, she bobbled it and it bounced onto the hood of a parked car. When she picked it up, she saw a figure in a black cloak across the street. Now she did run faster.

A few hours later, she ran again, this time to catch the train for her date with Vannie. In her hurry, she tripped and nearly fell into the train, letting the momentum carry her to her seat. When she looked up, she noticed a black-cloaked figure a couple seats ahead of her, facing the opposite direction. No big deal, she told herself. Just a random person in a cloak. Nothing to do with her at all. She was almost getting used to seeing them.

When the cloaked person turned around, face enshadowed so that only a cheese-stained scowl showed through, Sarah sank into her seat.

Getting off a stop early, she speed-walked to Mysore Feast, where Vannie was supposed to meet her. She felt certain Vannie wasn't going to show up. Even though she had promised, Sarah was convinced she wouldn't eat anything but pizza. She wished she had dug around more in Vannie's kitchen. Maybe she would have found cupboards full of ramen and cereal to dispel the crazy idea that Vannie was a . . . pizzavore. *Next time,* she told herself. If there was a next time.

Sarah was surprised to see Vannie standing outside the restaurant, in heels as usual. She was holding a hand to her stomach though, and, as Sarah got closer, she could see that Vannie didn't look happy.

"Are you okay?" Sarah asked as they hugged.

"Just a stomach thing."

"I'm sorry. Do you want to postpone? You could have called."

"I wanted to see you."

"I wanted to see you too!"

They kissed gently, keeping eye contact as their lips touched. As they pulled apart, Vannie said, "Indian might be too spicy for my tum tonight, though. Could we go someplace else?"

Sarah's heart sank. "Yeah, sure."

"I know a place around the block that has killer pies." Vannie brightened.

"You don't think pizza would be too hard on your stomach?"

"Pizza? What's hard on the stomach about pizza?"

"I guess I don't know. I mean, we could, like, do soup or something?"

"You want to take me out for soup?"

"Or something?"

"You are so fucking cute. I am infinitely glad I found you." She snatched Sarah's hand. "Now come on! Pizza ahoy!"

Sarah walked slowly, dreading the pizza place. "So, I've been seeing a lot of people in black cloaks lately."

"Seeing or noticing?"

"Huh?"

"Seeing them or noticing them? Like, you probably saw them before, but you didn't notice them until now that you know about them. It's like when you learn a new word and suddenly start hearing it everywhere."

"I'm pretty sure I would have noticed people in black cloaks if I saw them before. And I'm pretty sure they're following me."

Vannie stopped suddenly. "What? Why would you think that?"

"Like, the one I saw on the way here, they looked at me."

"Looked at you, or in your direction?"

"I couldn't tell because of the hood."

"Why would they follow you?"

"I don't know. If they, like, think I'm taking you away from them . . . I don't know. It just seems weird."

"You're being paranoid."

"When you said they could make people do things?"

"Apparently they can make you leave me!" Vannie shouted,

startling Sarah, not just because of the abruptness, but because she hadn't really thought that–not even three dates in–they had established the sort of relationship wherein Sarah bowing out constituted "leaving me."

"I'm not leaving you," Sarah whispered, unconvinced.

"Good. Can we get pizza now?"

"Yeah."

They walked the rest of the way in silence, holding hands. Sarah kept her grip loose. She didn't want to slide her hand away, but if Vannie let go she wouldn't mind.

At the pizza place, they found a corner table. Sarah sat with her back against the wall, perusing the menu as the waitress formally welcomed Vannie back, perhaps too formally for a random former member of the black cloak club. The thought crossed Sarah's mind, what if Vannie was still in this cult? And what if she was more than just a regular member?

When the waitress left, Vannie said, "I love this place so much."

"Oh, what a surprise." When she realized her comment may have come off a bit more cutting than she intended, she pulled her face out of the menu and smiled at her date. Vannie was pretty. How a girl who ate so much pizza could look so pristine was beyond Sarah's comprehension. And she liked Sarah, and vice versa. They were three dates in. How long had it been since she had made it three dates with someone she liked this much?

"There's an artichoke pie that is absolutely killer," Vannie said.

Sarah started to respond but stopped when she noticed half a dozen cloaked people scattered through the restaurant. Their hoods were all aimed her way.

She leaned closer to Vannie. "They're here."

"Of course they are. It's a pizza place."

"How can you be so casual about this?"

"It's pizza. It's casual dining."

"I mean, about your former weird . . . friends . . . following us around. Last time you saw them, we ran away, remember?"

Vannie reached out to straighten the shakers of parmesan and red pepper flakes. She made a waving gesture in the process. It was subtle, but Sarah noticed it, and so did the black cloaks. Suddenly, they all held their menus in front of their faces. Vannie had signaled them, and they had responded, puppets at her command.

"Let's just enjoy some delicious pizza," Vannie said.

"You know, let's not." Sarah pushed her chair back and it scraped loudly against the floor. As if choreographed, all menus dropped at the same time and the enshadowed faces behind them turned toward her. "Let's go someplace else."

"I need pizza."

"No, you don't."

"I do."

A voice in Sarah's head was shouting: *She is pretty and rich and smart and she likes you* so loud Sarah could hardly hear her own voice as she said, "I think your life is too complicated for me right now, so I'm going to get some takeout from the Indian place and head home."

Sarah paused, waiting for Vannie to come to her senses and flee beside her. Instead, the waitress arrived with another oddly cut pizza they hadn't even ordered.

Vannie's voice turned hard as she looked up from the pie at Sarah. "Do not fucking leave me."

Sarah flipped the pizza onto the floor, stepped over the steaming mess, and left.

Sarah walked fast, but not too fast to delete every text from Vannie along the way. As she did, she read them again. Teardrops plopped onto the screen, blurring the words. She hated crying over this stupid girl she had only seen three times. But fuck, pizza notwithstanding, they had been good times. Whatever. She'd just have to move on to BigFordChad or some other boring jerk.

When she entered the subway, the station was shoulder-to-shoulder with people in black cloaks. Sarah wasn't even surprised. She tried not to look at them, but she felt their eyes on her. Why did they care now? She had made enough of a scene that they had to know she was no longer encroaching on their territory. That wasn't it though, was it? That had never been why they were following her.

She didn't want to think Vannie was a part of this, wanted to take the woman at her word. But she had seen the wave in the restaurant, small as it was. She had seen the black cloaks' response. And she knew Vannie had waved them on now too.

Sarah toed the yellow line. Turning to the woman next to her, she asked, "Aren't you creeped out by these people in black cloaks?"

"What? Uh-uh, I ain't dealing with no crazies today!" The woman stormed off.

The black cloaks tightened around Sarah, inhaling all the air in the subway, taking it away from her. A man cut through them casually and stood next to her to wait for the train. He was an older guy in a wardrobe that indicated he might be homeless or work at a really cool record store.

"Hey, excuse me," she said loudly as the sound of the approaching train filled the station. "Do you see the people in black cloaks?"

The man's eyes went wide as he gazed around. She held up her hands, trying to calm him. Seeing the cut on her palm made him even crazier. She looked at the wound, the blackened scabs now formed a familiar pattern.

The man moved to the edge of the platform. "Nononononono . . . "

The shrill sound of wheels scraping rails buried his wild cries.

He took one more glance back and then leapt onto the tracks just as the train arrived. It did not stop. When it passed, she looked down between the scratched silver rails to see a smear of meat and blood that looked for all the world like a . . .

She spun around, but the black cloaks were gone now. The crowd backed away from her, trembling with fear. A police officer broke through, and a woman- the woman Sarah had spoken with earlier- grabbed the officer by the sleeve. She pointed at Sarah. "That crazy bitch threw that man in front of the train."

The crowd shouted in agreement.

"I saw it."

"She did it."

"She killed him."

Sarah turned to leave, but there was nowhere to go.

Shaking, she looked down at her scarred hand as the rats began their hungry work on the mess on the tracks.

BY THE SLICE

NANCY BREWKA-CLARK

WILLIAM MOVED INTO the apartment one flight up from Ski Boy's so that he could have a different pizza every day. In prison, pizza was just a layer of thick dough with what tasted like ketchup for sauce, over-baked in big, rectangular pans and cut up in little squares like sheet cake. And the pieces were never uniform, but he couldn't complain. They would have sent him for even more psychological testing, and they'd already misdiagnosed him as a narcissist with obsessive compulsive personality disorder. After all, he'd once made a good living as an air traffic controller. If self-awareness and precision were a sickness, the shrinks should try landing five 747s four minutes apart without them.

He planned to work his way up the scale from the simplest pizza to the most complex. After calculating every possible combination, including a few that he wasn't crazy about (like anchovies, goat cheese, hot peppers, and broccoli), William taped his new menu to the side of his refrigerator. Recombining each of his ingredients would yield him a different pizza for exactly 2,114 days.

Mouth wet with anticipation, he called in his first order. "Large plain pizza, uncut, please." To be certain the kid understood, he repeated, "Uncut. No slices, thanks." When the kid asked for a name, he paused, savoring the moment. For years, he'd never had a shred of privacy. Now he could hide in plain sight, create his own rules about big things and small, and nobody could stop him.

"It's for Joe."

Twenty-six minutes later, he hobbled down the stairs and out into the parking lot of the strip mall. After seven years, nine months, sixteen days and seven hours in prison, he was still surprised every time he saw the sunset. He'd been serving a thirty-year sentence for the second-degree murder of his wife until the state dropped the charges. When his lawyer came to tell him that their family priest had not only made a deathbed confession but left behind a selfie of him and Vicki in flagrante delicto, William had a stroke. Literally. But as it turned out, it was a stroke of luck because he was put on permanent disability. Now most of his body functioned somewhat normally, except for the occasional brain fart. Marjorie, his social worker, said that was par for the course and not to worry, to just enjoy life.

He stood there for a moment at the counter, sucking in the fragrance of garlic and oregano and onions and hot yeasty crust, before collecting his order. The place wasn't really set up as an old-fashioned pizza parlor. There were only two small metal tables with folding chairs where people could wait to pick up their order. Once he knew who came in and when, he'd schedule his own pickup time in the off-peak hours. It may have seemed logical to assume that the heaviest traffic would be at dinnertime between five-thirty and seven, but those would be pickups, not eat-ins. And deliveries went on until 10:30, adding to the pool of general customers he'd never see.

Holding the brown cardboard box far out in front of him like a sacred object, William made his way back up the stairs. Setting the box next to his shiny new collection of stainless steel implements purchased so that he could cut his pizza with scientific precision he lifted the cover.

The kid had done exactly as he'd been told. The pizza was a large plain, uncut. The crust was browned but not burnt, the tomato sauce thickly dotted with cheese beneath which he could see flecks of spices.

Resting one leg of the compass on the tabletop, William plowed an arc through the red, oozing surface. Three more arcs, and he'd pinpointed the exact center. Now he was ready to cut. The steel wheel bit through to the crust like a prison shiv slitting a ninety-pound weakling's naked breastbone.

William gave the pizza three more slashes. When he lifted the first slice, he moaned. The perfect piece draped over his fingers, hot and heavy with liquid lycopene and a bit of shiny oil. Licking off the sauce, William took the first bite. He wiped his chin with his fingers. Oh, yeah, that was definitely the most delicious sauce he'd ever had in his life.

In three more bites, the slice was gone. Then he slipped his fingers beneath the second slice. William shut his eyes in ecstasy as the flavor of the fresh piece exploded in his mouth. My God, what sauce.

Ten minutes later, the cardboard box was empty. He wouldn't need to eat another thing until tomorrow's extra cheese.

William took another bottle of root beer out of the fridge before sitting down in the tattered recliner by the window. His chair overlooked Ski Boy's entrance. Pulling the attached TV tray over to cover his lap, he straightened the edges of his yellow legal pad and clicked his ballpoint. Now that he knew how superb Ski Boy's was, he wanted to know exactly how many walk-in customers they were serving.

At exactly 11:00 p.m., the "Open" sign clicked off. He tallied the hatch marks. 28. How could a place stay in business if it only had 28 walk-in customers in twelve hours?

His breath came hot and heavy as he thought of how many people weren't appreciating Ski Boy's pizza. A sharp tingle began at the base of his belly and raced upward. Blood pulsed in his ears. A white police SUV cruising through the parking lot snapped him to attention. For a moment, it halted its prowl. William's breath stopped. Then, it began to move again around the row of parked cars and down into the alleyway on the other side of the mall. As soon as it disappeared, he wondered why he'd felt such panic. He had no reason to fear the police now. He'd served his time. In fact, he should be glad that they were patrolling on a routine basis, keeping his new home safe and Ski Boy's free from further financial calamity other than low patronage.

Thinking about their financial instability, he once again he felt the anger rise in him. William had learned to say what was expected of him to a degree, but, even with the prison therapist, he would never admit being enraged enough at his wife to slit her throat.

He hadn't killed Vicki, had never even thought of it regardless of what they wanted him to say. It had been a terrible shock seeing her lying in the gutter like a dead dog, her hair in a tangle, her dress hiked to her hips and blood everywhere. He'd been incoherent when they'd found the knife in the rubbish bin, wrapped in her panties. Accusing him was the last thing he'd expected. Receiving such a long sentence had been even more of a shock. It was an injustice that he could barely conceive, and sitting there by the dark window, William made up his mind. Ski Boy's needed some justice, and he was the one to give it.

"Hi, William, it's Marjorie. Give me a call as soon as you get this, okay? Here, let me give you my cell . . . "

Cell. William shook his head in disgust. What an offensive thing to call a telephone. He'd just seen Marjorie, his state-assigned social worker, a week ago, so he couldn't imagine what she wanted. "Hi, William, it's Marjorie. Give me a call as soon as you get this, okay?" He didn't need checking up on, but if that was what he had to put up with to keep on getting his disability checks, he had no choice but to comply. He didn't like her coming into his apartment, the way her greenish eyes darted about while she was talking to him as if she expected to see something peculiar or illegal hanging out of a drawer, or stuffed beneath the kitchen table. And he didn't like the way she asked about his mental state, whether he was lonely or had feelings of depression. Why on Earth would he feel anything but relief and joy now that he was out of the nightmare of prison, a place he never should have been in the first place?

Not only that, but he'd been making great inroads in helping Ski Boy's with their new outreach program. That was what he called it, despite the stubborn refusal of Petty Kowalski, the owner, to see the brilliance of it thus far. When the kid behind the counter connected him with Kowalski, William had been shocked to learn that someone who was Polish was the mastermind behind the best pizza he'd ever eaten. Deciding that this might be a plus instead of a minus in attracting business, William had mentioned his surprise and had gotten an earful from Kowalski. Slavs had worked with all kinds of dough for as long as Italians, he explained. Maybe even longer. And tomatoes in all their forms had also been a part of Polish cuisine.

When William suggested that the ethnic connection might increase his business, Kowalski had been far from grateful. In fact, he'd tried to hang up on William, accusing him of trying to sell him some stupid advertising service. William had been quick to cut him off, saying he wanted the pizza parlor not just to survive but to thrive. This led to another surprise. Kowalski was also the owner of the entire strip mall, and didn't really need extra business at Ski Boy's.

"How is that possible?" William had asked. "Who's ever heard of not wanting to make a business more lucrative?"

"You just heard it," Petty responded, "from me."

"I don't think that's being fair to your product," William argued, certain Kowalski would see the light once he grasped how delicious his pizza truly was. "Your sauce is unique. Is it an old family recipe?"

"Yeah, straight from Krakow." Petty had laughed. "Krakow, Wisconsin, right near Pulaski. Open a few cans of tomatoes, add some slivovitz and a bunch of garlic, and you've got the secret sauce."

William had been confounded. He was about to argue further when he decided he'd do better just taking on the job of getting the word out himself. What did it matter that the main ingredient was from a can? As for the slivovitz, that was really funny since he'd spent many a night chugging down the famous plum-and-piss booze the guys in for the long haul managed to ferment in a toilet bowl.

"Hello, William." Marjorie Stroman sat down in the chair William had pulled away from the kitchen table for her. "Hopefully this won't take long." She removed an iPod from her blue leather satchel and switched it on. "I've been gathering some data here that I thought might be of interest to you."

William peered at the screen. "That's my Ski Boy's spreadsheet. What are you doing with it?"

Marjorie's eyes darted from William's face to the recliner beneath the window. "Is that your observation post?"

"Why, yes, it is." William took a closer look at another entry she'd just called up. "This schedule is completely accurate." He blinked at her. "Has someone been observing me . . . observing them?"

Marjorie cleared her throat. "You are aware that Mr. Petrov Kowalski is the owner of this property, including this apartment and the pizza parlor directly below?"

"Sure." William felt a frisson of irritation. There was no need for pussyfooting about, not when his daily survey would begin in twenty-one minutes (minus 19 seconds . . . 18 seconds . . .).

"When you emailed him your spreadsheet," Marjorie said, "Mr. Kowalski contacted the local police department."

William smiled politely. "Really?"

"Yes. He reported speaking to an individual who was interested in promoting his pizza. Needless to say, he found it an extraordinary coincidence that this individual lived right above the restaurant."

The frisson was expanding into a slow burn. "Coincidence? There was no coincidence, Marjorie. The data I collected from my observations should prove that I was simply trying to grow his business for him."

"Well." Marjorie shifted from buttock to buttock, eventually crossing her legs in frustration. "When you began passing out unauthorized fliers for his business around town, Mr. Kowalski asked the police how to handle a public nuisance. After learning your history, there was general agreement that you deserved a medical consultation with state authorities to determine your future status."

William's heart lurched. "What are you saying?"

"I have the initial intake paperwork here." Marjorie hauled her satchel toward her. "It's for your own protection, William. After so many years of regulated activity, it isn't unusual for an individual to react in unprecedented ways upon experiencing unlimited freedom."

"I see." William stood. "May I get you a root beer?"

Marjorie's green eyes widened in surprise. Then she smiled. "Please."

William took his time removing the bottles from the refrigerator. What an outrage, to be considered mentally unfit just because he'd seen the worth of Ski Boy's pizza and wanted others to experience it as well. The police he'd regularly seen in their cruisers weren't protecting him, but building a new case. Once again, he'd be framed by circumstantial evidence, tossed into a prison hospital to be examined and questioned by sloppy, ill-educated, nitwits who would make pizza with dog shit without knowing the difference.

Out loud, he exclaimed, "No."

Marjorie, busy filling out paperwork, said, "If there isn't any root beer, that's all right, William."

William slid open the kitchen drawer. "No, there's plenty. I just need the bottle opener."

The steel circular blade of the pizza cutter felt cool in his palm. Once before, a woman's throat had been cut and he'd paid the price. Life was all about balance, about getting things perfectly aligned, about being aware of patterns and exact mathematical proportions of fairness. And when he sat in that courtroom, and heard the evidence laid out meticulously day after day, he couldn't help but think of how there was no way he could commit a crime so sloppy, so careless. He began to calculate all the possible combinations of methods he might use instead.

In a few quick steps, he was behind her chair. Hooking his arm beneath her chin, he yanked Marjorie's head back until he could see the pulse pounding beneath her Adam's apple. "I am perfectly sane, Marjorie. Clearly, it's the system that's crazy."

The first slice cut deep, releasing a bright fountain of blood that burst upward with volcanic strength. He licked his lips, savoring the salty mineral warmth. As the green eyes stared up at him in piteous terror, he slashed again and again. he slashed again and again, reveling in the taste of blood that even Ski Boy's pizza couldn't rival. But there were still many pizzas yet to come.

PHOSPHENES

MATTHEW KING

SAM STANDS ENGULFED in pitch-black darkness. However, despite the total absence of light, Sam's eyes somehow perceive that strange imagery contaminates this void.

The dark teems with pulsating clouds of disorder, their amoebic impressions churning within a stygian ocean of undreamed anti-neon phantasm. These forms defy all rational notions of shape, color, and contour, and yet they do exist. They dance. They flourish. They devour and evanesce ever onward through the emptiness as they always have and always will.

These visions do not alarm Sam because he knows them well. He knew them long before his birth and he revisits them every time that he closes his eyes. But Sam's eyes are not closed.

In his hand, Sam holds a device. He raises this to his head and places its end within his mouth. Then, with a subtle flick of his finger, there detonates a pandemonic burst of sterilizing light as Sam's world is flooded with radiant luminosity. This phenomenon exists for only the briefest fleeting moments, but the burning stain of its existence lingers on, and Sam inhales deeply.

"Did Pierce ever tell you why we started using proofers?" The voice is that of Sam's coworker, and by 'proofers' she refers to the low-powered human-sized ovens used by pizza places to expand their dough. These compartments are airtight, which is why Sam and his coworker are currently using them to smoke marijuana.

"No, I don't think so," Sam replies before passing the pipe through the slot that connects their chambers.

"Yeah, he told me that back in the day we used to make our pizzas with real dough. So they'd have a morning prep guy come in and prep all the day's dough on the table in the back. But one morning, I guess the manager came in early. She found the dough all piled up in the shape of a woman's torso. And the morning prep guy was standing there with his pants around his ankles. Just fucking the shit outta that dough."

Sam coughs out a chuckle.

"Yeah, I guess it must've been going on for years, you know. Every single day, that guy was back there. Fucking that dough. Jizzing all up in everyone's pizza and leaving behind pubes and flakes of dried ball skin. Think about that. If you ate our pizza back in the '90s, you were basically scarfing down a big baked cumsock."

"That's fucking disgusting."

"It is. And it's why we switched over to ready-made plates of freeze-dried dough. Now we just oil them up and toss them in these proofers. No hassle. Zero jizz."

Sam shakes his head, smirking for no one to see. "I don't know. I'm calling shenanigans. You seriously think corporate would change the entire company's policy because one creep in Nowhere, Illinois was jizzing in the dough?"

"No, Sam. Don't you understand? It wasn't just him. This must've been like a nationwide epidemic!"

Sam laughs once more, his grin now illuminated by the flickering flame on his left.

"It's cashed," she says. "Welp. Time to get back to work."

The coworkers stumble back into the kitchen, both immediately resealing their proofer doors to contain the pungent odor. Sam returns the pipe to his jacket on the wall, but notices something twinkling in a metal sink to his right. It is a tiny cluster of soapy bubbles, glittering in a cast iron pizza pan. For a moment, his bloodshot eyes linger upon this iridescent foam as it swirls in the blackness, twisting peacefully like some microcosmic celestial body. Sam sips his Mountain Dew. He is very high.

"Sam!" shouts Pierce through a mouthful of cheese sticks. "Want to make a special delivery?"

"Pfft. Since when do we deliver?"

"We still don't, but there's a party or something out by Willow

Hill. They're saying they'll tip the driver a hunnerd bucks. You're bout done with your shift, right?"

"What? Seriously? Yes! Dibs!"

Forty minutes later, Sam's vehicle settles into a cratered driveway. His destination is a ramshackle country home lingering solitary in the night. Fields, forest, and power lines extend in all earthbound directions, but no cloud or moon pollutes the sky as Sam passes beneath an endless swarm of stars. As he ascends the porch with his tall stack of pizzas, Sam can already make out the lyrics of some raucous song pounding through the home's dilapidated front door. Firmly, he knocks with the side of his fist, and then waits. Something peeks out through the corner of a nearby window. Locks are then unlatched, one by one, and the door swings inward, unleashing the full volume of the music.

"Hi, I'm here to deliver some pizzas? Is this the right address?"

Her appearance is ordinary, at least for the remote country folk that line these wild outer highways. She wears an oversized T-shirt and jeans. Her skin is pale and chalky, and her eyes are thickly laden with black liner. The hair that falls upon her shoulders is brown with a touch of silver, dry as straw, and arranged in an outdated style. Sam estimates her age at approximately twice or even three times his own, but it's hard to say. She peers around briefly before settling upon the delivery boy.

"Come on in, honey."

She widens the doorway, but Sam hesitates. He's never done this before. Is it normal to go inside? There is no one else in the living room, but the lighting appears adequate.

"Is there a party?" He doesn't recognize that blaring music.

"Yeah. Come on in. Everyone's around here somewhere. You're fine." The woman ushers Sam into the small square living space, directing him to set the pizzas on an end table. "Take a load off. I know it's a long drive getting out here. Ya smoke?"

Sam smiles politely and sets down the order. He doesn't know if she's referring to tobacco or pot, and though the answer is "yes" either way, he's not comfortable making assumptions.

She takes her seat on a wooden chair, lighting a cigarette before signaling to the adjacent recliner. "Get comfortable, honey. You want some pizza?"

"You know, it's late and I . . . "

"Have a seat. It's a long drive. You'll get your tip soon enough, darling. But I'm gonna make you work for it first." She grins as the teenager dithers, until inevitably he sits down on a worn leather cushion. "You in school?"

"Yeah." Sam adjusts himself, surveying the interior and its yellow-papered walls. "I'm a senior."

"Yeah? High school? You sure you don't want some pizza?"

"I'm alright. We get it for free." Sam notices two black woodcuts gripping the corners of the front door. One is in the shape of a cat and the other a bird, and though such things are a common form of quaint rural décor, Sam's never seen two on the same door before.

She takes a deep drag from her cigarette. "You like your job?"

"Excuse me?" It's hard to hear above that thundering stereo.

"Do you like your job? You like giving people pizza?"

"Yeah. It's not bad. I like most of my coworkers. It's okay." Sam thinks the music is probably from the '80s, but he's not sure. It's schizophrenic, sometimes melodic and sometimes chaotic, oscillating between saccharine and malevolent, but always at an unsettling volume. Abruptly, he flinches. Something nuzzles at his leg. Sam lowers his eyes to find a small black mutt gently rubbing against his calf.

"Oh don't mind him. That's just Horace. My little widget. He's a rescue. He don't bite. Horace is a good boy."

Sam figures that Horace must be old, judging by the tired nature of his rubbing, but the creature's curly fur is still jet-black. Sam reaches out his palm for the dog to lick, but Horace doesn't seem to notice.

"He can't see you," she says.

"Really?" Sam eyes the blind animal with pity. He then begins scratching the back of its neck. "What song are we listening to?"

She doesn't respond, but before he can repeat the question, Sam's attention is arrested by the sensation of a tiny smooth tick on the back of the dog's head. He recoils his hand in repulsion, but Horace continues rubbing, unaffected.

"You seem tense, honey." She takes another drag from her cigarette and Sam notices pale blue bruises dotting her neck and arms. He wonders if there's a man in the house. "Can I give you a massage?"

"What?" Sam wants to leave.

"I give real good massages. You'll see." The woman leaves her seat. "Come on." She closes the distance between them. "You need to loosen up, honey. Here. You'll like it."

Sam considers forgoing the tip, but she's already stepping behind him, her long fingers crawling leisurely upon his shoulders.

"Now try to relax, okay? Don't worry. You'll feel great. I'm very good at this."

"Are you sure this is all right with everyone?"

"Just look straight ahead, honey. There you go. That's not so bad, huh?"

Her hands knead him with a strangely sluggish sensuousness. And though he hates the way that it feels, he doesn't know how to stop her without seeming impolite. Hopefully, she'll be quick, and he'll soon be on his way, one hundred dollars richer. He doesn't necessarily have to tell anyone about this part. Sam lowers his eyes to the warped and splintered floor. Horace is still there, still on his leg and nuzzling mechanically against the rhythm of that shrieking music. The poor thing seems almost delirious. Her thumbs etch little spirals behind Sam's throat. He studies the room and its sparsely decorated walls. To his left hang a gathering of picture frames. Many of these frames contain portraits of people, but almost half of them are empty. One contains a crumbling flower, probably violet once, but now too dark to tell. The largest frame contains a black and white photograph of an oddly deformed willow tree. A slight draft crosses the room. Her grip grows stronger. She transfers her focus to Sam's left shoulder. In the nearest corner stand three full-length mirrors, each on wheels. The one in front has a broken surface. Sam can't see the other two. Beside these mirrors, straight ahead, sits a stout wooden bookcase, just beneath a covered window. Sam concentrates on the few titles that he can read: *Illuminations of the Ancient World, The Secret Watchers, Zhung-Koordednot: The First Dark Art*. Atop this bookcase stand three carved stones beside a prescription pill bottle and two small boxes. She's squeezing harder now. It's almost too hard, and her warm breath slinks along Sam's neck as she slides both hands to his other shoulder. In the furthest corner hang a pair of dime store marionettes. They're knotted in a mass of string and dangling from a large iron nail. Her grip begins to hurt. She's not very good at this. And from the state of her living room, Sam questions whether she can afford to pay him for the pizzas, let alone an exorbitant tip.

He needs to leave. There is definitely no party here. And if anyone else is present, they're probably just waiting to beat his ass. He's about to speak up, but a quivering point of pain stings through his right shoulder. Sam turns to find a hypodermic syringe, its contents squirting into his flesh. Instinctively, he jerks in a twist that releases the needle, but he's restrained from jumping to his feet by the handgun now pointed at his face.

Horace continues nuzzling, unaffected.

Sam is too stunned to speak. He's never been at gunpoint before. He's never had the absolute finality of his existence presented to him like this, every flicker of his consciousness balanced precariously upon a stranger's index finger. Likewise, he's also never been injected with something against his will. Immediately, his blood takes to a savage hammering in his brain.

"What did you put in my body?"

"Don't you fucking move!" She's trembling.

So is Sam.

Horace scurries beneath a curtained doorway.

"Keep your fucking hands where I can see them!"

Sam places both hands upon his chest. Breathing is now difficult, but he doesn't yet understand what is happening. He raises a hand to his lips, but his arm is weak, and growing weaker. He tries again to beg her for the truth, but his tongue and jaws now betray him. Everything is going limp as his panic only accelerates. He can't even hold himself up now and begins sliding to his side. And as she grasps him about the waist to reposition him in the chair, Sam yearns only to attack her, but can no longer command any muscle in his body.

She props his head upon the cushion, leaving him staring at the rain-blemished ceiling. Though his eyes are half-closed, he is still completely alert, still feeling all of this. He still smells that untouched cooling pizza. He still hears that earsplitting bedlam. Slowly, though, smoky blotches form in the corners of his vision, and it's then Sam realizes he is no longer breathing. He can't. His lungs have become lifeless. Soon these shadows will stretch across him. Then it will all be over. Everything will be over.

Darkness.

Something is cupped over Sam's nose and mouth, and as oxygen flushes through his sinus, those shadows recede. He is alive for the time being, thanks to some sort of unseen breathing machine.

Then, without notice, the music cuts out, its absence leaving only the sounds of mechanical pumping and a flat white hiss that burns from the center of Sam's skull. In a few more seconds, the stereo returns, but now with no noise save a warping stream of static. This soft crackling curls between frequencies, searching diligently for some precise signal on the radio. Once located, the volume is reduced it to a barely audible hum, and then there is another click. All light is snuffed from the room. Sam returns to the tempestuous dark and its webbing waves of confusion.

A body moves about unseen. It arranges objects in the dark, scraping chairs across the floor, and rolling wheels into place.

"Are you paying attention?"

One final click brings a new form of light: black light. It swells from the corners of the floor in an unearthly violet haze.

Long cold fingers grasp Sam's head from behind. They handle him like an object while bracing his neck with a travel pillow. They peel back his eyelids, securing them with small surgical band-aids. They adjust his eyeballs forward with bare fingertips, allowing full view of this dark new world. Sam's first sight is her eyes. They shine uncannily in the black light. And as her lips recede to reveal a phosphorescent grin, Sam screams himself hoarse, but that is only in his mind.

"You ever catch a shape out the corner of your eye, Pizza Boy?"

Her pale form exits his line of sight, revealing the room behind her, its walls crowded with glowing illustrations that were not originally visible.

"Or ever wake up in the middle of the night with someone hunched over you, just watching you?"

Bright green silhouettes stretch from the floor like radiant hominoid shadows, each depicted in excessive detail.

"Did you ever see them? Everyone does at some point. It's just that most don't like to talk about it. Because they know that's an invitation."

Sam counts at least six of these neon figures lining the walls. They vary in height and build. Some are depicted wearing hats. Some display troubling proportions.

"Those that do talk about 'em give 'em all sorts a names. Ghosts, aliens, demons, jinn. Spirals. Furies. Six-dimensional beings." Her face slides into view from Sam's left, staring directly into his eyes. "Dumbfucks just call 'em shadow people, but that's not too creative." She smirks and steps back. "But none a those is their real name." She stops when she reaches the center of the room, her form now reflected from all angles in the three broken mirrors arranged behind her. "Do you want to know what their real name is?" She reveals an object within her palm: a standard white lightbulb. "Do you want to see them? You will."

Her eyes remain locked upon Sam as she puts the lightbulb to her lips and produces a small flame beneath it. Deeply, she inhales, while studying her quarry through a pair of vulpine slits. When her lungs have filled to capacity, she closes her eyes. She then sways inelegantly to the ambient static, her vulgar undulations metered by the monotonous pumping of Sam's unseen breathing machine. Sam watches her move like this for at least a full minute, until finally, a stream of bleached fog slithers up from her lips. Her eyes flash open, her body freezing in place. "Are you watching me? Because I am watching you, Pizza Boy. Do you understand that?" A shiver courses up her shoulders. "I am watching you right now. I see you—you exist. Right now. Do you have any idea what that means? Do you understand? It means that we're entangled. It means that we're connected on a quantum level, you and I."

She begins preaching of "Ectenic Forces" and "Observer Effects," but Sam longs only to ignore her demented sermon. He wishes desperately that he could focus instead upon some previously unappreciated memory: his mother's face, his father's laugh, something that his older brother told him when they were younger. But he can't do that. He can't look away. His heart still shudders like a screaming child and she continues her ungodly rambling.

"Atoms are just little points. Tiny grains of sand in the sea of seas. And they're all just made a things that don't even have mass. They're not even really there. They're just little bends and dents in the nothing of it all. It's all just space. Just a churning froth, as endless as it is empty. And that emptiness . . . that nothingness . . . that's our everything. That's everything that's ever been and that's us too." She gestures to the figures on the walls. "But that's not them. They're deeper than that. Theirs is the nothingness between the nothingness. The black that's blacker than black itself. That's why you normally can't see them. But soon you will. Soon you'll see that I'm right. Are you paying attention?" She smokes again from her lightbulb and then closes her eyes before spinning to face her bookcase. Upon its top shelf remain the carved stones and the boxes and the gun, but these items are now joined by a ball-peen hammer.

Carefully, she unlocks the larger of her two boxes. It contains a short black dagger, which she places reverently upon the shelf. Next, she moves on to the smaller of her two boxes, a music box, and an innocent melody twinkles while she extracts its hidden contents. Though Sam cannot see what she's taken, he knows that she holds it within her left hand. She then grabs the hammer with her right before turning back around, exhaling a shroud of indigo and reopening her eyes.

"Do you see these?" She tiptoes forward until her left hand is inches from Sam's face, revealing her surprise: four rusted nails of varying lengths. "Tonight, I will use these to go inside of you. Do you understand that?" A nervous smile cracks across her face. "Tonight, I'm going to pierce the veil and penetrate the temple, and you will be my vector. I am going to tunnel through your consciousness. And when we're done, you will forever be a part of my nothing." Her glowing eyes moisten in their frenzied ecstasy. "Oh honey, you're just so lucky to be a part a this."

Sam's heartbeat throbs in his throat while she reverse-steps to the center of the room, rejoining her broken reflections. There, she takes a deep calming breath and extends her arms outward, nails to one side and hammer to the other, straightening her posture and closing her eyes.

"A hunnerd billion galaxies, each with a hunnerd billion stars. All of 'em spinning in perfect synchronicity. Holes within holes within holes." She draws her hands together. "And we're just the space in between. Proxies for that omnipresent emptiness. Reflections of that deeper nothing." She positions one nail atop her head and raises the hammer into alignment. "Are you paying attention?"

Her neck jerks forward as she beats the nail's tip into her skull, hesitating only briefly before giving it a few light taps that put it halfway in. With the base of her palm, she then gently drives the rest of the nail into her brain, quivering spasmodically as it slides to its destination. Once finished, she takes a deep and stuttered gasp, but never opens her eyes.

"Are you watching?"

Sam has no other choice.

"Now we need to close the circuit." She positions a second nail on the side of her head, just behind her right eye, and beats it through the bone as mascara strings down her cheeks. Again, she palms it all the way in, gnashing her teeth but completing the job.

"Are you watching me, Pizza Boy? Do you see this?"

She repeats the procedure around her left eye as well, nailing one through the top and one through the temple, inky black tears slithering down her face to drip precariously upon her pale skin. When her job is done, she faces the floor, her mouth resting agape. She is silent. Static continues humming in the background.

Then, without warning, her eyes reawaken, and four measured words crawl out from her throat.

"Do you see me?" She lifts her head deliberately, gazing upon her world through eyes flushed dark with twisting veins. "I see you," she states calmly, tilting her glare upon Sam. Her eyes still glow but there is no longer any life within them, and they do not line up as they once did. As she approaches, Sam realizes that her eyes no longer move at all. They are lifeless spheres now, frozen atop the long black stains that stripe her expressionless face. He watches these stains bend and crack as she speaks.

"God is a number. Do you know what number that is?" She squats upon Sam's lap and presses their foreheads together. "Is it 12? 7? 1, 2, 3? 3.14159? Belphegor's Prime?" The dilated pupils of her drying dead eyes gape endlessly into oblivion. "Do you want to see the truth?" She strokes Sam's face with an unnaturally steady finger. "Are you ready to see between the gods and the devils and the deep black sea?" She kisses his forehead before returning to the floor, where her spectral figure navigates the darkness with ease, gliding to her bookcase and retrieving her gun. "It's time for you to see it."

Sam just hopes that it's over quickly.

"Remember, Pizza Boy . . . " She takes position in the center of the room. "The brightest stars become the blackest holes. Are you watching?" She discharges the pistol beneath her chin.

Sam is watching, but he doesn't understand. Not at first. He perceives only the briefest fraction of a pop before his ears are deafened by a high-pitched ringing. There is no flash, no smoke, no splattering of blood. And her body does not crumble to the floor. But as the white noise subsides, an unsettling new sound invades its absence: the mindless clicking of a trigger. Repeatedly it clicks, but no second bullet escapes the chamber. And Sam's gut curls in writhing horror.

What is left of her is still alive, in a sense, still suspended and processing basic information, the whole cadaverous form now leaning in a hellish crooked arrangement, its left arm dangling lifelessly. In nauseating spasms, it struggles to shift position. It drops the useless gun to the floor. Senselessly, it lopes forward, barely sustaining balance. Like an animated scarecrow, it stumbles once again, now dragging a dead left leg behind it. At its third step, the figure is lunging, and unintelligible curses squeeze between a pair of clenched jaws. Soon, it is upon him, its quaking right hand groping at his face and eyes. Sam knows that if the mask is removed, he will die of asphyxiation, but at least that will be a peaceful death. The hand continues fondling at his cheeks, scratching his skin. Its palm then expands across his forehead, squeezing and mumbling, drooling and shaking with hatred. But its rage is overwhelming and the ghoul stumbles back, nearly tumbling to the floor. Shortly, it recuperates, but in doing so, it pauses. It waits a few seconds. Then, its tremulous right hand drift gently to its face. It paws around its mouth, its nose, and cheekbones. It continues rising to the top of its head. It pats erratically around a freshly opened exit wound. Broken and dead-eyed in that eerie violet radiance, this gruesome creature lingers, hand over head, peering pitifully upon those otherworldly forms that it painted upon its walls in a past life. It is perplexed. It does not want this. She does not want this. And then something shifts within. The hand lowers. The body swings around. It drags itself violently to the bookcase. It knocks over objects in a frantic search, the music box colliding with the floor. The horror turns to face Sam. It brandishes that ceremonial dagger. And then, with all that's left of her strength, she drives the blade into the gaping hole atop her skull, twisting it upon contact, and wrenching in a seizure that brings her crashing to Sam's feet.

The music box plays amid mechanical pumping and faintly audible static.

It is one minute later, and the box has stopped singing. Sam wonders how long it will take for him to die here.

It is three minutes later, and Horace returns to the room. He laps at something twitching on the floor. Sam's right arm convulses painfully back to life.

It is five minutes later, and Sam guides his aching body through the room, shuffling cautiously around an expanding liquid silhouette.

It is one year later, and Sam perceives an unsettling shape from the corner of his eye while exiting a basement.

It is five years later, and Sam meets something in a dream that keeps him from sleeping for several nights.

It is ten years later, and Sam is suddenly awakened in Nashville, Tennessee. His body is completely paralyzed and an electrochemical buzzing grows from within the furthest depths of his brain.

Though the room is bathed in darkness and all possible entrances are locked, Sam knows that he is not alone. He feels something creep along his legs. It is soft and light like a small mammal. He can see the outline of its curling black fur. And soon, he sees her too. He sees her waiting there at the foot of his bed, darker than the darkness that surrounds her. Though he cannot see her face, he knows that it is her, and he can tell that she is leering at him. Silently, her gaunt black figure crawls upon the bed and Sam's brainborne buzzing intensifies. Her cold and rigid hands climb along his body until she has perched upon his chest, suffocating his lungs and engulfing him in a tangling mass of hair. It is then that Sam's terror peaks to a torturous crescendo, and finally, he sees her clearly. He sees her face, and her eyes, and what it is that she has become.

She is part of the emptiness now: a shade of that truest dark. Forever within Sam and everything and nothing and all of us. Gently she sways to his excruciating torment, gazing through him with her yawning dead eyes. And as Sam stares back into those abyssal twin suns, finally he understands. She was right. She did it. And now she exists beyond time and space and consciousness, as she always has and always will.

Do you see her?

She is watching you.

ULTIMATE PIZZA CLUB

MICHAEL ALLEN ROSE

JOSH SIGHED AND TURNED the stereo down a few notches, even though this never helped him with those hard-to-find delivery addresses. He rolled to a stop on the shoulder and turned on the blinkers of his '91 Toyota Tercel. There were no cars coming in either direction, but the last thing he needed was someone blasting by in the dark and picking off his side mirror. As he sat idling, he felt the wind pick up from the west, abruptly shaking the car back and forth, and something underneath the body of his sedan scraped against the road. Probably the muffler, having come loose from its wired-up makeshift holster while bouncing down this frontage road. Josh cursed and stared out into the night, listening to the hypnotic rhythmic scratching sound from under his car, and he thought of a bored serial killer playing with his axe.

His car was a piece of shit, but he didn't have the heart to put it down. Every pizza guy knew a car was actually man's best friend.

There was nothing out here, he decided. Darkness, studded with sparse bushes, trees, rocks, and rows of depressed buildings, like a fence of skeletons stabbing upward out of broken ground. A few yards had lights, but those that were lit sparked and flickered in the slowest of death throes. Fences without fresh paint, mailbox posts leaning against them like a crutch. And as many cars on cinder blocks as there were on wheels.

"Fucking weak sauce."

He leaned forward, straining his eyesight to read the numerals on each building. A few didn't have numbers, as far as he could see, and most of the rest were too dark to make out. Finally, he spied the address he was looking for, and he threw open his car door. Sighing heavily for nobody's benefit but his own, Josh turned off the car. It shuddered and wheezed as the engine ground to a halt. That wasn't a good sound. Visions of himself standing out here in the darkness, trying to get a signal to call a tow truck that he couldn't afford, made him mutter curse words even more fervently, as he left the warmth of his car and plodded toward the house.

The small porch was covered in knot holes and cracks, having weathered many years of neglect. Someone had scrawled the number in white paint, barely legible amidst the swarm of moths that surrounded a lone yellow bulb cascading down rickety wooden stairs. Weirdly, the welcome mat looked brand new. It depicted a huge, jolly Italian man in a chef's outfit holding a steaming pizza pie on a silver platter. Next to him, in a script font:

"Benvenuto!"

There was no doorbell. The door itself looked solid: a thick, wooden number with some decorative flourishes that seemed out of place. But there was an iron knocker, and Josh pulled the ring back and let it fall. It bounced against the old metal plate a few times, vibrating with three bass-heavy knocks, before settling.

A slip of paper, previously unnoticed wedged in the door frame, fell onto Josh's boot. He picked it up and read it.

"Please to bring the pizza inside. Money on the table. Thank you."

The door was unlocked, and Josh slowly opened it and leaned in.

The large front space was obviously some kind of living room, but the expected furniture was missing. Instead, there was a collection of small mismatched tables of varying circles and squares. A thin layer of dust coated everything except the frontmost table, a small checkered circle, with a short stack of wrinkled cash on top.

"Hello? Pizza guy! Anyone here?"

He glanced down at his slip, which read "Ultimate Pizza Club" under the name section. There had been no reason to verify a full name, since this was a cash deal, so he just assumed it was some sort of a party. So he didn't even know who to call out for.

"Got your pizza! You want me to just take the cash?"

He counted the money. It was just enough to cover the pie, with only change leftover as a tip. True bullshit.

There was a chance that whoever had ordered didn't really think out the math. Maybe they'd lowballed the price in their head, or not taken the delivery charge into consideration. It wouldn't hurt to double check, and if Josh turned on the charm, maybe he could squeeze a few more bucks out of these people. Besides, Josh liked to hand the pizza directly to the person on the slip, otherwise scammers would call the restaurant and make a big deal out of how they never got their pizza. He'd gotten into trouble for things like this before, and even seen some of the worse drivers fired for being too careless about the handoff. It would be best to find someone.

There was a noise from somewhere off to his left. It sounded like something metal falling on the floor. Josh hesitated to set his pizza box on the table, mostly because his employer had never bothered to invest in boxes with their name, let alone a logo. Then he heard another noise, and dropped the pizza to explore a bit. He tracked the sounds to the closest door and pushed it open to find himself standing in a kitchen. "Pizza guy! Just delivering your food. Are you home?"

It was impossible to tell what had fallen, since the floor was absolutely covered with metal implements: pizza cutters, cleavers, knife sharpening tools, a big colander and more were all scattered around the floor, some also stained with food. Several huge pizza stones were taking up most of the counter space, along with copious bags and boxes of flour, tomatoes, herbs and spices. It had the vibe of an industrial kitchen, easily holding twice the supplies of the joint where he worked, but all jammed into the tiny cooking space of a single family home. Clutter was everywhere, but most arresting was the giant brick oven that had been built into the wall.

Flames crackled and spit inside, powered by what sounded like some kind of massive furnace blasting underneath. This was the kind of oven that could bake a pizza—or anything else—in only a few minutes. Thoughts of bubbling, slightly blackened crusts made Josh's mouth water. His pizza place didn't do that kind of fancy, fire baked food, opting instead for greasy late-night post-drinking pies that were mostly consumed with a side of garlic butter to cover up the mediocrity.

As he approached the oven, the heat got intense fast, and Josh realized he was sweating. He reached up to wipe his brow as another sound broke the stillness. The door at the end of the kitchen remained slightly ajar. There was a muffled sliding sound, and a light thump from the other room, like a sack of wet grain had fallen off a shelf and onto the floor.

Leaving the oven behind for the moment, Josh stepped up to the open door and put his ear against it. An eerily still silence was his only answer, and he put a hand on the knob and pulled it towards him.

"Hey, I just wanted to let you know that your pizza is—"

A weight pressed against the door, and it opened faster than Josh anticipated. Something fell on top of him, sending him tumbling to the floor in a heap. At first, he thought the owner had tackled him, but as he struggled and sputtered, two things hit him. The first was the sensation of cold, where this other figure touched him, and the second was a vague smell of sweet and rot. Holding the contents of his stomach inside, Josh crab walked backward as he realized he'd found a corpse.

He yelped as he clamored to his feet and skidded backwards until he crashed into a counter, panting heavily. The dead woman looked to be somewhere in her mid-thirties, but it was hard to tell much more than that, given the condition of her skin. Patches of decay were ripening around her softest tissues, particularly her facial features. One breast languidly hung from out the neck of her green, polka-dotted dress, the nipple almost black, and the veins bright blue against pale, bloodless skin. There appeared to be tooth marks wherever skin was exposed, and her legs had a scaly texture, until, with a wave of nausea, Josh realized that hundreds of small fleshy divots had been carved out of both calves, almost as though the legs had been treated like cones of gyro meat.

"Shit, shit, shit . . . " Josh muttered as he scrambled back into the front room. His head was swimming. No tip was worth dealing with a dead body. Maybe the people who'd called in to order food had some kind of accident and died? But how many years ago was that? It didn't matter. He would call the cops when he got far enough away to start breathing normally again.

He crashed into the front door, hurting his shoulder, frantically grasping at the door knob, but it was covered in some kind of grease, and his hands slipped around before finally finding purchase. After several oil-slicked squeaks, however, he realized that the door was now locked. But there was no deadbolt, no lever, just a keyhole that led into the dark interior of the brass door handle. Josh pulled and pulled, shaking the frame, but it didn't budge.

The windows, which he'd thought only darkened before, revealed themselves now in the faint light to be boarded up with thick sheets of some sort of plasticine material. He tapped on the nearest window, and felt the thickness barely waver. Upon further inspection, tiny metal rods had been woven throughout the interior of each pane, so even if the strange material could somehow be shattered, it would leave a cage of wire containing him.

"Yo! Hello? Someone? Anyone? The door's stuck! Help! Hello?"

Then he heard music. Someone was playing one of those "Mob Hits" albums with a ton of songs by Dean Martin and Louis Prima. Jaunty accordions and lyrics about pasta slowly got louder, coming from somewhere behind him. Josh turned, just as another door at the far end of the room flew open, to reveal the silhouette of a huge, fat figure framed by a chef's hat and apron. A portable speaker was attached to his belt, from which some wires emerged, only to disappear into the chef's recesses. As he thundered forward, a curly, black moustache caught the light, shining with some kind of oily sheen.

"Buonasera! You find-a the money?" His tone was jocular, but the cadence reminded Josh of one of those dolls where you pull the string and when it talks, your soul escapes through your asshole. His faux Italian accent sounded like he'd learned most of the language from Mario Bros. games, except delivered in a flat, gravelly monotone. "Why you still-a here, amico?"

He decided the best move was to pretend he didn't see the body.

"Dude, I can't get out, the front door is stuck. I left your pizza there, on the table."

The hulking man turned his large, flat head toward the kitchen door instead. He was so tall, his hat nearly scraped the ceiling. To his horror, Josh realized that when he'd run, he'd left the kitchen door wide open, and the corpse was clearly visible, festering there on the floor.

"Oooh, I see! I think maybe you wanted the VIP tour of-a the kitchen? You're not trying to steal-a my secret recipes, huh?"

The hair on the back of Josh's neck began to stand up, as the enormous chef thumped toward him, smiling with a filthy grin. They were both ignoring the corpse for the moment. The chef's eyes were dull, like there was some kind of brain damage behind them, but they were focused and intent on Josh's own. Josh felt the door solidly against his back.

"Hey, man, I didn't see anything, don't know anything, just let me out of here. You want your money back? Here, this one's on me."

Josh threw the wad of bills toward the chef, but it didn't keep the monstrous man from grabbing Josh's shoulders and lifting him up off the ground.

"Let go of me! What the fuck!" Josh kicked, but his blows bounced off the enormous belly of the giant, who was chuckling now.

"Hey, don't-a you worry! We gonna make a spicy meat-a-ball together! You trust-a chef Giuseppe! He put-a big smile on your face!"

The monster's breath was putrid, scented with the miasma of an old garbage disposal filled with onion skins and fish offal. It was no surprise his teeth were as gray as his eyes.

Tapping into his deepest reserves, Josh twisted his body and brought his arms up, snaring the chef's wrist and twisting. Although his grip was awkward, it was enough to get the chef to loosen his enormous left hand, and Josh dropped to the floor like a colander full of spaghetti noodles. The big man frowned down at Josh, and Josh erupted from the floor, already heading toward the back room from whence the giant had emerged. There had to be a back door to this place, and if luck was with him, he'd burst through it and out into the night with a crazy story to tell before the chef could waddle after him.

Josh ran through the kitchen door and slammed it behind him. He scrambled to wedge himself up against it, as if that would do any good against the powerhouse outside. His eyes were wide with panic, which helped him scan the room, despite the poor lighting. One single electric candle sat in the middle of a small, square table, its orange light licking up the walls with a fake flicker. It dimly illuminated a dirty red-and-white checkerboard cloth, haphazardly skewed across the table's surface. The tablecloth was heavily soiled by frequent use, though its stains were not yet old enough to have sunk in and become part of the fabric.

More importantly, two more corpses sat in chairs on each side of the table. They were bound upright with thick ropes, wrapped around their bodies, dozens of coils pressed tightly into their torsos. If blood had still been flowing freely through the bodies, it would have been restricted, but as it stood now, a great deal had already leaked onto the ground. Josh thought it looked like a handful of pepperoni in tomato sauce.

The smell however, was significantly different, and Josh held back a sobbing gag as he inspected the carnage. The figures were propped up in a grotesque simulation of a date. The woman wore a stained yellow dress that had seen better days. Her hair had been done up and piled atop her head, and makeup had been applied seemingly with a shotgun. There were raccoon eye streaks down both cheeks as though her last hours had been spent weeping. The gentleman was dressed in a gray suit, now browned in places with dried blood and other fluids. Both of their arms were tied at their sides, with the hands beneath, as though they had been lopped off. The cuts were ragged, but upon closer inspection, appeared to be burned and tied off, like the ends of sausages. It was as though they had stopped for a meal in the middle of a surgical amputation.

That's when Josh saw the gleaming steel pizza cutters, stabbed into the side of the table, among the remains of what must have been a pizza at some point. It was nearly a foot in diameter, and the edge glinted in the faint light even through the veneer of skin and gore coating the blade. A tiny tent sign sat on the tabletop reading:

"Taste test in progress."

Josh looked around wildly, and saw a wooden chair resting against the wall nearby. He awkwardly slid it into place beneath the knob at his back to lock himself in. It wasn't a perfect solution, but it would keep the monstrous chef out of this room for a minute, if he was lucky.

Then the full smell finally hit him. The odor of festering meat, mixed with a sickly sweetness, like vegetables rotting in a garbage bag. Underneath all that, he could taste a sort of coppery quality in the air, and his stomach backed up into his throat. Up close, he saw that the maggots had already begun their work on what had once been a meal, finding purchase in the bits and pieces covering the filthy tablecloth and the laps of the dining couple.

Fruit flies buzzed around his eyes, making them water, and he waved them away, realizing this meal had to have been sitting here for a day or two, at least. It reminded Josh of the dumpsters behind his restaurant on the unfortunate hot summer nights when he pulled garbage duty. Then he realized that flies meant there might be access to the outside somewhere nearby.

A sudden scream made Josh slip and fall sideways, bashing his head on the table. His arm caught the edge of the tablecloth and pulled the whole mess down with him, raining rotting food scraps over his arms and face. Scrambling to his feet, his eyes met the gaze of the man in the chair, who was now looking at him. Josh couldn't believe he was alive. The man spit, trying to form words.

"I don't want any more! I can't . . . I can't handle—" A belch pushed out some red liquid, which hung from the man's chin in sticky ropes. It was impossible to tell what was blood and what was pizza sauce. "Wait . . . you're not the chef. You're not him. You . . . who are you? Can you help us? Please, you have to help—"

Something big slammed into the door with a huge shuddering thump, and the chair made a slight crack of protest.

Josh turned his head toward the threat behind him, while still trying to keep an eye on the dinner guest.

"Hold on, I need something to untie you." The ropes were as thick as telephone wires, knotted so severely that Josh couldn't get a finger into the depression to start the untangling process.

Another massive thump from behind the door, this time accompanied by a crack. The nauseatingly high and oily voice rang out again. "Hey! Did you say-a something?"

"Oh God, these knots are too tight. I can't—"

"Are you okay?"

This voice was new. Josh turned to see a thin man in a gray suit with a neatly trimmed John Waters-esque moustache, peeking through what appeared to be a back door, and a way out.

The thin man stepped further into the room, holding his hand against the edge of the door. Behind him, an enclosed porch buzzing with fruit flies indicated the possibility of freedom.

There was another slam against the kitchen door. Then, with a horrendous crash, the wooden chair splintered, falling to pieces.

"Oh my, that's no good. Come with me." The thin man pointed out the door.

With a frantic glance at the diners pleading eyes, Josh stumbled toward the thin man. "What about them?"

"There's no time. I'll take care of them. We must hurry!"

Josh ran out the back door, just as the chef burst into the kitchen with a roar. "Mama mia! You have-a to try the special before you leave! I got a nice big sausage for you, right-a here!"

Josh looked around in a panic, but to his surprise, the porch was fenced in on all sides with chicken wire. The lone door that led to a small backyard was padlocked, with a sign hanging on it that read "Thank you, come again soon!"

The thin man had not followed him outside. The back door was closed, and it was eerily quiet. Just him and the flies. Then, from somewhere inside, the giant bellowed, and the scream of the male diner was so loud, the sound burst through the walls and into the night. It was unmistakably a scream of unrelenting horror, cut with the last gasps of dying hope.

Josh pulled at the lock, but it wouldn't budge. He dropped to his knees, searching for a key, or even something he could attempt to pick the lock with, but everything he found was useless. Then, he remembered his key fob. It was possible that the signal from his key fob might reach his car, parked out front of the building. If nothing else, perhaps his car could alert someone nearby, or get some kind of attention. That would be some *Knight Rider* shit.

His fingers fumbled through his pocket, and came up with the keys. He eyed the red button on the bottom, held the keychain high over his head, and pressed it.

Nothing happened.

Frantically, he pushed the button twice more. Finally, on the fourth press, he heard his car horn go crazy, and through the chicken wire, off toward the edge of the house, he could see flashing lights, and knew that his headlamps were lighting up the night as the noise fell off into a steady pattern of honks and beeps.

Although all the neighboring buildings had looked dead, Josh hoped they would be just close enough in proximity to hear his car's cry for help.

Then there was another roar from inside the kitchen, but to Josh's surprise, it tapered off as massive footsteps receded.

For a few moments, Josh was hopeful, until, from somewhere around the corner, Josh heard the sound of breaking glass. Then came thunderous, metal-shearing crunches, repeated over and over again, the horn slowly going out of tune, until finally it died with a pitiful squonk.

He looked for his headlights, but the yard was dark.

A few moments later, Josh saw the enormous chef appear around the corner of the house, breathing heavy. But he was not alone. Somehow, impossibly, with sheer brute strength, the man was dragging Josh's car behind him into the yard. His car had been almost reduced to a demolition derby reject by the repeated blows from the monster's meaty fists. The hood was barely hanging on, two tires were flat, and the engine had somehow been smashed to pieces. The two remaining un-exploded tires were all the fat man needed to assist his death march as he pulled. He didn't even seem to be straining. His sleeves and apron had been torn up by the broken window glass, and even through the sheen of blood and sweat on his arms, it was evident that the fat was absolutely stuffed with muscles.

The chef dragged the car through the back yard, and Josh felt the urge to salute as it went by. He continued to a scrap pile near an old tool shed where Josh noticed a couple mopeds with luggage carries on their back fenders, a favorite transport of his vocation. If the chef could manhandle an entire car so easily, Josh imagined this beast literally juggling those bikes, as well as their riders.

Once the chef had deposited the old Toyota amongst the other twisted vehicles, he suddenly stormed up to the chicken wire like an elephant, and leered at Josh through the cage.

"Oh shit," Josh muttered.

"You ruin-a the ambience at my restaurant. I give-a you free valet parking."

Josh cowered as the monstrosity rumbled away, back toward the front of the house. The night made less and less sense as it went on, and it seemed to be in no hurry to snap back to reality.

Where had the thin man with the moustache vanished to, he wondered. Had he been a neighbor? A random visitor? He had seen enough horror movies not to get his hopes up about a mysterious savior, but still he pressed his ear to the door, to see if he could hear any sign of the man. And, sure enough, he did:

"I'm so sorry about your meal. We really do pride ourselves on our atmosphere, and things aren't usually this energetic. I apologize for the interruptions."

It was the thin man's voice.

"Here, as we're nearing the end of your visit, we brought you something to go down a little easier," he went on. Eat up."

"What the fuck . . . "

Curiosity killing him, he pushed the door open just a sliver, and of course, it was the thin man standing next to the diners, stuffing what appeared to be steaming calzones into their mouths. The muffled choking sounds were stomach-turning.

"Careful now, they're quite hot."

The woman, still passed out or dead, just lolled with a calzone stretching her lips, but the man was hellishly awake, his eyes wide and streaming with big, salty tears. The skin around the man's mouth was crimson and swollen.

Just then, the thin man turned his gaze toward Josh. "Oh no, you really don't know when to stop poking around, do you? Giuseppe!"

At that, the chef stomped back into the kitchen, looking glassy, like he'd forgotten already that he'd just killed Josh's car, his best friend and best means of escape.

"Is it-a time for Ultimate Pizza Club?" the monster asked.

"Yes, it's time for Ultimate Pizza Club, Giuseppe. Induct our friend here. I like his instincts."

The chef's eyes filled with a light previously unseen, and with lightning quickness that belied his size, he was across the kitchen and slamming into the back door, sending Josh sprawling onto his back. The giant placed a huge, dirty hand over Josh's nose and mouth, and squeezed his face. Josh thought his eyes were about to pop from the pressure, but before that could happen, the world turned to static, and he passed out like a television after someone trips over the cord.

He awoke in the cold. The pain was immense. It felt as though his nerves had been pulled out through his arms and wrapped around his throat until he'd choked on his own central nervous system.

As his vision returned, he saw the thin man, leaning against the wall. They were in a walk-in freezer.

"I thought this might wake you. Giuseppe, he's ready."

Before he could reply, Josh found himself lifted from behind. He felt too weak to struggle, and limply dangled there, a foot off the ground, supported by massive hands underneath his armpits.

The thin man led them back into the kitchen. The two people who had been here earlier were clearly dead now, as their heads were conspicuously missing. Pools of dried blood had congealed underneath their neck stumps and drizzled onto the floor, mixing with the ever-growing pile of ingredients.

"Sorry about the mess," the thin man said, gesturing around the room, mercifully not twirling his moustache. "We were in the middle of a very important taste test when you showed up."

"T-t-taste test?" Josh coughed. As he slowly came back to his senses, the pain increased. It felt like his hands had been dipped in acid. "How long have I been asleep?"

"You lost consciousness with Giuseppe, but we had to drug you too. Otherwise, our pizza club induction might have killed you. It's been a few days."

"The what?"

"You discovered our secret. We're trying to create the very best pizza on the planet. Sure, a few eggs get broken to make an omelet, but we keep ordering from everywhere in the county, stealing aspects we like, and of course, adding our own twist. We ran out of the *typical* ingredients long ago. But you'd be shocked at how creative Giuseppe can get. Remember, we're not the Ultimate *Pizza Club*, we're the *Ultimate Pizza* Club. Do you understand?"

"Listen, I won't tell anyone . . . what you're . . . I don't know anything . . . " Josh looked at the thin man, eyes half shut, brain on fire.

The thin man began to applaud. "It's all right, friend. You will know everything soon enough. The first rule of the Ultimate Pizza Club is . . . 'You are what you eat,' of course. And the second rule is, 'You are what you do.' The third rule is, 'Don't stop doing it or you'll stop being it.' Or something like that. We're still working on that third rule, I'm afraid. Anyhow, we whole-heartedly welcome our newest employee!"

Josh allowed his gaze to fall, as his hands had begun to itch and tingle. His brain refused to make sense of what he saw before him. His hands had been removed and replaced with a pizza cutter and a fork. He swooned, but the giant held him firmly upright as the thin man continued. "You have all the tools you need now. You don't need anything else, as helping to make the perfect pizza is now your destiny. Take pride in your work, and you'll do well here. Besides . . . " The thin man leaned in to whisper, his voice a cinder of flame. "A man *is* his work, am I right?."

"But . . . I already have . . . a job . . . these pizzas ain't gonna deliver themselves . . . " In his delirium, this sounded reasonable.

The thin man smirked. "No good. You're better than that. You've worked in the corporate pizza business. A glorified delivery boy. We *need* you in this house. One day it will be yours. Delivering pizzas in cars? I mean, what's next? Food trucks? Here, it's all about family. And it's real work that you can put your whole body into." The thin man nodded to the giant and smiled. "This is my brother, Giuseppe, by the way. He's a little slow, but gosh, does he know how to cook a good pizza. Stay on his good side, my son. Sadly, we've had some . . . false starts with other pizza boys. So listen to him closely and you might learn something. Well, watch him closely anyway. He doesn't say a whole lot." The thin man laughed.

"Come on, you lazy, we don't-a have all day!" The behemoth grabbed Josh and dragged him by his mutilated arm, dumping him unceremoniously at the foot of the giant oven. Even now, Josh could feel the flames crackling, the heat making his skin prickle. Holding back a sob, he realized that it was difficult to know whether it was more palatable to make the sausage, become the sausage, or be an official taste-tester of the sausage. Of the three possibilities, a human pizza cutter wasn't sounding so terrible.

On his way out the door, the thin man called to Josh, over his shoulder:

"Don't look so frightened. You're not alone. You'd be surprised at the size of our family actually. I mean, I can't get into numbers at this stage of your employment, but I will tell you this. You can see a variation of Giuseppe, or myself, on 90 percent of the pizza boxes in America . . . "

Josh watched him go, watched the flies follow him out like their master. Then the giant hit him upside the head and pointed toward the bubbling pie on the rack, while turning up his belt speaker with the other hand. Doris Day's "Que Sera Sera" Filled the room.

Yelping from the pain of the fire, Josh stuck his new fork hand into the oven and snagged the edge of the cooked crust. He pulled it out, and dropped it on the portable cutting counter that had been placed beside him. He held back a wave of nausea as the wheel on his makeshift hand began to cut across the dough, his nerves on fire, dollops of blood seeping from his badly maimed wrists, until they blended so much with the blobs of sauce that he could no longer tell the difference between the two and, just as the thin man in the moustache had promised him, he could no longer tell where he began and his job ended.

LEFTOVERS

BETTY ROCKSTEADY

MOM ALWAYS TOLD Robyn not to pay attention to the strays. Don't speak to them, don't look at them, don't even think of them. Ignore them and hope they ignore you.

Mom said a lot of things. She was always talking, always insisting, always saying when to do things and how to do them.

Robyn had almost escaped, but now all she had were her blood-splattered memories.

She wasn't looking at them. Not really. She was looking out her window, and they were out there, out of focus, fluttering between the trees. Just like they always were. She wasn't really thinking about them either. Everything was just shapes and colors and painful daydreams.

Some months were worse than others. Sometimes it seemed like weeks had passed since she had seen one, their strange pale bodies almost a memory, but then one crept through the bushes, kept pace with her on her way to work, and shocked her into remembering. That was good, to be shocked. It was better not to hold them in your head.

Other times, it seemed like there were crowds of them out there, not even hiding anymore, impossible not to see them, not to take a good look and maybe get lost in their eyes and fall into their wavering limbs.

Impossible not to feel their hunger. Impossible not to wonder.

Robyn's arm was starting to scab up again. The thick mucky gel of healing got stuck beneath her nails. She dug her thumbnail deeper, peeled the scab back, and a well of blood bloomed. For a second she thought the pain would make her release it, but the healing flesh pulled free and dropped into the garbage. Then Mom's angry footsteps were coming up the stairs and she yanked her sleeve back down. Drops of blood glued the sweatshirt uncomfortably against her skin. It would hurt to peel it away later. Good.

"What are you doing?" Not a question. A demand.

"*Nothing.*"

Mom's eyes narrowed. "What are you looking at?" She stepped into the room, frowned over the piles of clothes on the floor. Robyn's bed was pushed against the window, and Mom glanced over her shoulder, but only quickly. She sat down, close to Robyn, close enough that she could smell the perfume covering the day's sweat and grease from the diner. Perfume! Robyn looked at her more closely. Same old stained T-shirt and sweatpants, but her hair was brushed and she had makeup on. The wrong shade of foundation sunk into her wrinkles, making her look older than she was. Mom was going out. The month-long captivity was coming to an end.

"It's too hot for that sweatshirt. Why are you wearing that in the house?"

"I dunno. It's fine."

Her gaze stayed on Robyn for another beat, long enough for her to actually start to sweat. "I'm going out tonight. The casino. I can't stay in with you forever. You'll be fine on your own, yeah?"

"Of course I will be. Me being here never stopped you going out before."

"You have to get back to work soon. You can't stay cooped up here forever."

"I know." But what was the point of going back now? She'd never afford to move out all on her own, and everything was fucking different now, wasn't it? Without Kara? The hopelessness swam up her chest and her eyes filled but she would not fucking cry. Not now. Not in front of *her*.

"There's a lot of them out there lately." Mom's voice sounded far away.

"I hadn't noticed."

She stroked Robyn's unwashed hair absently, something she hadn't done since Robyn was a child. "Good. Keep it that way."

"Okay."

"I ordered some supper. Money's on the table."

"Okay."

Mom left, trailing perfume behind her. It didn't smell like flowers. It just smelled chemical. Robyn used to hate it, but now it was a relief. It meant Robyn would have the place to herself. Still, she leaned over the bed and cracked the window, to air things out. She didn't want to go to bed tonight choking on that shit. The back yard shimmered with movement, but Robyn had enough of that for now.

She had just filled the sink and plunged her sleeve into the warm water when the doorbell rang.

Twenty-five bucks on the table. Hopefully that was enough. She sure as hell didn't have anything in her purse except a few crumpled-up napkins and leftover mints. She hadn't even asked what Mom ordered. Chinese? Her stomach rumbled. The way bodily functions went on and on was just disgusting. How rude of her body to expect her to keep caring for it.

She pushed hair out of her face and yanked the door open. Everything came at once—the smell, the recognition of the Alexandria's Pizza uniform, her mouth flooding with the taste of cheese and blood.

The kid delivering didn't look familiar, except in the way all pizza delivery people seemed to look familiar, greasy face and uncut hair. They probably had to replace a lot of them after the accident. Why are they still coming around, like it had never even happened? Grease seeped through the box. She groaned, and the kid looked alarmed. What the fuck was wrong with Mom? Is she trying to pull some sort of aversion therapy?

"Large pepperoni," he squeaked out.

"I don't want it. Take it back."

He looked frightened, either by her expression or the sound of her voice. "Uh, this is the right address? Right?" He looked at her door and back to the pizza box.

"Yeah. I don't want it. Fuck off." She started to close the door, but the look on his face was just too pathetic. Pockmarked and eyes brimming with tears.

"If you don't take it, I have to pay for it. That's not fair."

"A lot of things aren't fair." She looked down at the money crumpled in her hand. Watered down blood leaked through her sweater, pattering on the floor. He saw it too, and his face paled.

She wanted to slam the door in his face, but she didn't. Instead she took the pizza and threw the crumpled bills at him. She wanted to scream, so she did. She wanted to throw the pizza on the floor, but then the smell would seep through the house, and she would start crying and she could *taste* it and what the *fuck* was Mom thinking?

It was only a month since the accident at the pizza place. And they were acting as if nothing had happened.

Straight through the kitchen, out the back door. Indistinct faces stared at her from between trees, mouths open, hungry.

The green bin was locked. Mom kept the key on her keyring, and of course she took it with her. The lock was the best way to keep the strays out. They were as bad as racoons—except with opposable thumbs and more teeth, and they were watching, and they were hungry—but what the hell was Robyn supposed to do? Leave the fucking thing in the house, taunting her? She punched the green bin, tossed the pizza box on top of it. It jostled and the whole thing fell out, a mess of toppings and dough that slithered into the grass. "Fuck!" The things in the yard flinched back from her voice, but just a little.

She needed a smoke. She had been looking forward to a leisurely cigarette outside without Mom's intrusive yammering, but now she was crying and it was all ruined. Mom ruined everything, and it felt like she would be doomed to that forever.

The old back step creaked under her weight, and she had like four cigarettes left before she had to get a new pack. That little bit of money she had saved up would wither away, eaten up slowly by the expenses of grief.

She lit one and inhaled.

The creatures shuffled forward.

Let 'em.

She had never gotten a good look at them before. Had anyone? They were part of our lives now, and maybe that meant we had compartmentalized them, like anything else. Dimly human shapes lurked beneath their ill-fitting skin. They were taller than she had realized. Their poor posture made them look shorter, but their limbs folded over and over and if they stood up all the way, how tall would they be? God, taller than the trees. They would stretch up into the sky.

They approached the pizza, voices buzzing like angry bees. There were three of them, but it seemed like more. The way their figures blurred when she tried to focus on them made it look like a crowd. They circled the pizza, and their mouths were shallow, stuck together with a pink, gummy substance. When they lifted the mounds of cheese and pepperoni and those mouths stretched open . . . she tore her eyes away.

Her wound was bleeding on the grass.

Good. She would never let it heal.

She smoked and listened to the messy sounds of feeding. Even now, she didn't like to watch them too closely. Superstition or wisdom, didn't matter. What she was doing was dangerous maybe, but she just couldn't bring herself to care.

She didn't hear it approach. She didn't expect it. They had never come so close before, but suddenly one was beside her, filling her peripheral vision with shifting white space. And then she couldn't help herself.

She looked. Big dumb white face, head too heavy, bobbing on its thin neck, staring curiously at her. Arms and legs jangly, folding over and over beneath it. It pressed closer to her and she smelled its strange glue-y scent. Stand up. She had to stand up. Panic bled through her brain in a slow trickle, reluctant. Pallid eyes held her in place. She stumbled to her feet, dropped her cigarette, forgotten embers crushed to the ground.

And then they all turned toward her.

The stray's arm darted out, grabbed her hand, and her sleeve drooped back and exposed layers of muscle and meat, blood just beginning to clot. A dark barbed tongue slid inside the flesh to taste her pain.

She kept the wound open to keep her alive, to keep Kara's memory alive, but she hadn't done her justice. She hadn't remembered nearly enough. Her touch. Her smell. Her breath in her ear.

Kara sitting beside her in math class. Kara rolling her eyes at a dumb joke. Kara taking her hand late one night, walking home, not saying anything, neither of them saying anything. Sleeping over at Kara's, pressed up against her ugly pajama bottoms, holding tight, not wanting to ever let go. Kara pressuring her to get the job at the bookstore, to push herself harder. Kara helping her save money, watching their accounts grow bigger, daring to believe they could escape their shitty homes. The look on Kara's face, over a slice of pizza at their favorite place when she told her she was ready, that she had found a good deal on an apartment and they could get out of here, start their lives, their real lives.

She remembered the way her eyes widened ever so slightly, just before. Like she knew.

She remembered the way the car came screaming through Alexandria's huge front window, surreal, unexpected, impossible to look at, three o'clock in the afternoon was too early for drunk drivers, too early for someone to be so drunk, too early for one last alcoholic binge that took you swerving down Main Street and through the window and she saw Kara's eyes widen—

Then nothing.

Nothing.

Then screaming, so much noise, so much chaos, and *pain*. Glass had sliced a crescent moon across her forearm, and her arm was bleeding but that didn't matter because where the *fuck* was Kara and she crawled across the floor and people were trying to hold her, people covering her eyes and trying to put pressure on her wound but she crawled across the glass and Kara's head was wrong, everything was wrong, and she had missed those last few seconds, because the sparkle in her eye was gone and now there was nothing. Forever.

The stray pulled back.

Robyn had failed. She hadn't kept Kara's memory alive at all. Not even close. Her cheeks were soaked with tears and everything was fresh again and the panic and shock were real. This was what she needed to hold on to. The look in Kara's eyes.

She groaned.

The stray pushed something into her palm and crawled back to huddle with its own kind. When she finally finished crying, they were gone.

She looked at what it had given her. A little bleb of skin, translucent and supple, smooth and flat, like a worry stone. She pressed it between her fingers, and it sucked on to her thumb tip, throbbed like a blister or a cyst, ready to burst. A feeling of peace slithered from it, up her arm. She peeled it off again, slid it into her pocket. Everything was pounding through her, fear and shame and grief and she didn't have time to make sense of it now.

The lights inside were bright and artificial, and a dull headache throbbed behind her eyes. Her stomach gurgled. Her stupid body just kept insisting on being alive, insisting on doing all the normal things it had to do, all the little incessant demands of being human. She didn't want to be alive right now. She wanted to be with Kara. She wanted to close her eyes.

The lights in her room were dim. She wanted to lay down. She thought she wanted to sleep, but she slouched in front of the window instead. Watching for them.

She was touching it. The little hunk of flesh the stray had given her. She couldn't help herself. How would it feel to be like them? It thrummed in tune with her heart, promised forgiveness. Promised forgetting. Promised peace. The smooth lump tried to attach itself but she pulled it off, again and again. If she let it hold on too long, it would take root.

Long limbs, translucent in the moonlight.

They offered her a chance to forget, to be something else.

She didn't want it. But she wanted to consider it. This feeling released into her skin. Erasure. No identify. Nothing. Just desire and need yeah, but something else too. Belonging?

Their faces never changed.

It stuck in her thumb like a tack, begging to go deeper, begging to dive into her bloodstream, drown itself in her heart. Her fingers couldn't get a grip to pull it out, and beneath the false peace, panic rose in her throat. Her nails scrabbled against the foreign scab, and when it tore away from her skin, she threw it against the wall.

Her arm felt different. She yanked up her sleeve. A milky substance was stitching together her wound, pulling the edges closed.

No. Absolutely not.

No matter what it promised, she no longer wanted it.

There wasn't time to get a knife. She dug into the wound with her fingernails.

So much pain. Beautiful, really. Sharp and dark and *fresh*. Her breath was fast and shallow as she gored their webs out, splattered across her walls. How dare they try to steal Kara from her? How fucking dare they?

She dug deeper, and dark blood rose from the meat. Layers of flesh and muscle gave way easier than ever before. Outside, they wailed. She was not one of them. She would never be one of them.

"What the hell is wrong with you?"

"Mom?" Robyn yanked her sleeve back down.

Mom stood in the doorway, reeking of gin. The destroyed pizza box was in her hand—covered with slobber and shredded by strange teeth. "You've gone crazy. Encouraging those . . . things to come closer to our house. Up here tearing yourself apart? I'm trying to help you. Haven't I done enough?"

"What do you expect me to do? Act like nothing even happened?"

"Goddamn it." The box fluttered to the floor. She lurched into the room, her makeup smeared as though she had been crying. Nails scraped Robyn's arm as she tore her sleeve. "This should be healed by now, what are you doing to yourself? And what am I supposed to do about those things out there? They'll keep coming back now that you fed them."

"Don't touch me!" Robyn yanked her arm back, and blood speckles appeared on Mom's blouse, across her face. Mom's eyes widened. It had been a long time since Robyn had spoken back to her. A long time since she had shown her any emotion at all.

"What is wrong with you?"

"Leave me alone!" Robyn pushed past her, and her mother clawed her, nails leaving trails of blood across Robyn's face. Robyn shoved her and her head cracked against the dresser and she went down in a boneless pile.

Bile rose in her throat as she crouched at her mother's side. A smear of hair and blood glared at her from the dresser. The room spun. "Who are you?" She looked so different now, the wrinkles on her face all smoothed out. Peaceful. Robyn tried to smooth her hair back, but hairspray clumped it together and it didn't budge.

Robyn was alone, and the relief that swam up was quickly

replaced by a sick guilt. Without all the stress and pain on her face, Mom looked like a different woman. A person just trying to exist in this shitty world. She was fucking awful, yeah, but she didn't deserve this.

Then her eyelids fluttered and broke the spell. The lines of tension squirmed around her mouth. "Guh."

So nothing would change then. Nothing would ever change now.

"What happened?" Mom kept blinking, trying to focus.

"You fell." Robyn's wound pulsed. "I'll call an ambulance." When she stood, a shimmer caught her eye. On the floor, the little chunk of skin, the promise of a new life. Of forgetting. Of leaving everything behind. Living in the moment, pleasure or pain.

Above the phone, the mirror revealed a face she didn't recognize, distorted by the scratches Mom had left. She turned back.

"Come on. Let's get you outside. Get some fresh air." She helped Mom up, and the older woman leaned heavily on her.

"Baby, something's wrong . . . " Blood dripped onto the carpet from the back of her head. "Something's not right . . . "

"Come on." The shuffle outside was difficult, but they made it. She helped Mom sit down on the step, and the strays glimmered behind the trees, pale eyes in blurry faces watching. Waiting.

Mom touched the back of her head, and her hand came away dark. She moaned, "What's happening?"

"It's okay." Robyn reached into her pocket. "Here, this will make you feel better." The bleb of skin pulsed as she slid it between her mother's dry lips. "Swallow."

"I don't feel right."

"No one does. Just wait here. I have to go inside now."

"Don't leave me," she said.

"I have to."

She locked the door. The house yawned empty around her. She double-checked that the blinds were all drawn.

Back in her room, she looked in the mirror. The scratches on her face were still bleeding, but they were shallow. These wounds she would let heal.

CRUCIFIXIONS IN THE GARDEN OF GARLIC BREAD
BY ALEX DEAN SHIBBOLETH

PEARSE ANDERSON

"Food is not just eating energy. It's an experience." —Guy Fieri

[Please email hotline@vice.com for any information regarding the whereabouts of the author. The following document was recovered from a partially burned hard drive in Yonkers, NY]

WHEN VINCENT BARONE died in 1981, his pizzeria catered the wake. After a series of heart attacks in 1980, Barone knew he was living on borrowed time, so in the last few months of his life he was able to teach his son, Alfred, how to run Vinnie's Slice. The pizzeria, which serves locals in Elizabeth, NJ, is still managed by Alfred, who kept the name in honor of his father. Alfred is bald these days, with similar heart problems, and a movie poster in his office so sunbleached the protagonist looks like a ghost.

"I thought Dad had taught me what I needed to know," Alfred tells me when I stop by this fall for an interview. "We kept on our regulars when I took over, sauce and moz were being shipped in from Sicily on schedule, it was good. And then one day there's this man waiting by the back door. He has a giant tattoo on his neck. I think it's supposed to be of Christ, but it looks just like some bearded dude. 'We're here for our check,' Backdoor Christ says. I have no idea what's going on. Dad never taught me about this. I think he was ashamed, really. I let Backdoor Christ in and we talk for five minutes, and by the end I'm writing him a check. I was ashamed, too, in my own weird way, but I was scared. This guy was being real threatening and I didn't fully understand what I was mixed up in."

Alfred was 24 when this started. A few weeks later he got the bigger picture.

"Vinnie's Slice helped traffic heroin and cocaine from Europe into the Eastern Seaboard for seven years," Alfred says with more straightforwardness than contempt. "I helped the Sicilian Mafia for four of those years. I even paid *pizzo*." Protection money.

Vinnie's Slice wasn't the only pizzeria to move drugs and launder money in New Jersey. It wasn't even the only one in the county. In five years, the Cosa Nostra mafia, based mainly in the Sicilian cities of Palermo and Corleone, smuggled 1.5 billion dollars' worth of heroin into the United States through hundreds of independently-owned pizzerias. Now, thirty years after this infamous Pizza Connection crumbled, many of these restaurants have closed their doors, shifted focus, or been demolished completely.

For the next four weeks, I am driving up and down the coast investigating the last surviving pizzerias and the violence that got them there for a *Vice* assignment. Writing as I go, I plan to charter a culinary tour through the history of Mafia drug smuggling.

Vinnie's Slice is the first stop. Alfred is incredibly open about those four years of laundering and trafficking. On slow weekdays, Vinnie's would get an order over the phone with a weird request. *I want a dozen pies, but hold the pies.* Pizzerias, especially in the 1980s, were a cash business with thick financial books.

Cookable books.

Alfred got to keep a section of the cash and added the rest to the checks he gave to Backdoor Christ. Eventually, the calls stopped once the pizzeria fell into a routine. Alfred walked from his office to the counter on slow days, stared at the glass door with the bell at the top, and squinted his eyes, imagining Sicilian after Sicilian shuffling in from the New Jersey night. He took their fat orders, watched them take off their coats, lower their sunglasses and let coins fall out, sit at formica countertops with their bent arms. Eventually he'd retreat back to his office.

"Sometimes that was the realest part of my week."

Alfred wasn't the only one to have this kind of daydream, with owners of Imo's to Cazovino Pizza to Pizzavendolo all repeating similar rituals in the early '80s. When I'm in Vinnie's, I stare at the door too, trying to see the same mob of imaginary Sicilians. The attempt spooks me, and afterwards in the parking lot I can't help but compare the red, boxy exterior of Vinnie's Slice to a grave, like one carved from Martian stone.

When the Pizza Connection broke, United States federal agents surrounded Mafia-associated pizzerias and homes in a coordinated attack with Swiss banking officials and Italian police. Worried the Mafia would destroy evidence, the police hit fast on April 9th, 1984. One of the pizzerias stormed was D'Tonto's Italian Restaurant, a rectangular joint in the small border town of Halfway, Maryland. These days, the place gets good traffic, and the current owner is looking to invest in one of those customizable soda machines.

D'Tonto's encapsulates the spirit of the Beltway pizzerias I visited. It's inconspicuous, tucked off a major road beside a barber shop. It has enough plastic booths to fit two Little League teams and have standing room for their mothers. And it is completely unaware of its own history. There is nothing in D'Tonto's to tell you that that when federal agents raided the place the owner resisted, raised a shotgun to fire upon the agents and was shot in the mouth. Not even a little plaque. I only learned about the raid-and-murder from a three-sentence note in old court documents when Rudy Giuliani took the Pizza Connection to trial. That's not the only thing missing here: the sign to D'Tonto's depicts the boot of Italy. There's no Sicily. The island is consistently forgotten, even in Italy. Sicily's mafia family, known as the Cosa Nostra or just the Mafia, never rid itself of that little-brother attitude, as it was stuck on an island, surrounded by foreigners, and constantly ridiculed.

The sign would have frustrated Sicilians, and gastronomically speaking, the restaurant can be just as frustrating. D'Tonto's smothers fried mushrooms and chicken burritos in the same marinara sauce. The menu I got pinballs from stromboli to capicola to taco salads to teriyaki wings.

"We want to give people what they like," D'Tonto's owner tells me with a smile. Throughout our conversation she has the glow of a Polaroid. There's one Sicilian dish on the menu, a shrimp option. "If someone comes in and sees something they want and orders it, all the better. We need the business. Those customizable soda machines are a thousand dollars a month to rent, y'know." I feel a sort of tug away from this topic and towards D'Tonto's history. I'm desperate to discover others who know about the Pizza Connection, who haven't forgotten their roots.

"Are you aware that your restaurant used to be a front for drug trafficking?" I ask. "It received a shipment of mozzarella and sauce every week with pounds of heroin buried underneath."

"What?" She gives me a look. "This is a family establishment. We do birthday parties."

"So were you aware of its history?"

We go back and forth on this for a few minutes. Not only does she not know what happened in 1984, she won't look when I pull up court documents on my phone. She gets up because someone in the back is burning the garlic bread. I can't get a question in after that, so I just buy a sickly sweet fountain drink and use the restroom. As I'm washing my hands, a man appears beside me.

"Ya 'alking do da wrong people," he announces. I try to look at him in the mirror, but the angle is off. I turn halfway to meet his eyes, but I still don't recognize him. There is an apron around his chest.

"Why do you think that?" I ask.

"'hey didn'd see da murder." He is chewing something large, rolling it around in his mouth. I can't see what it was, but his tongue looks blown apart, reduced to a stub.

"I'm on a road trip." The water runs and I try not to stare. "Maybe everyone who was a part of the violence has been silenced."

"Dead," he says, spitting a ball out of his mouth and into his hands. He holds a shiny, metallic slug. He pops it back in his mouth. "Bud nod silenced."

After washing up, I turn, but he's gone. Powerade in hand, I leave D'Tonto's. The high sun blinds me. Underneath me, I suddenly see a pool of blood. As I watch, it recedes into the parking lot asphalt like floodwater. I kneel but it's gone before I can confirm anything. Has there been a crime here? A fresh crime?

In a shitty pizzeria, what does fresh even mean?

The Mafia left shells of restaurants peppering the Eastern Seaboard: one big retro molting session from the world's deadliest predator. Since, the Mafia has shrunk and changed form, but has always kept some aspect of cultural relevancy and surrealness through the decades. Maybe it's because there is little as outlandish as wandering into a Chuck E. Cheese in Rocky Mount, North Carolina, and searching the eyes of their weird new mascot for any sense that the rat understands how many lives this particular pizzeria ruined years ago. The rat sung about high fives, but in the wet laughter of a kid's party, it sounds like he was chanting "Give yourself a high—Give yourself a high—"

I park my car at Pizza Palace beside two flower delivery vans. Something follows me through the place. It has the odor of the D'Tonto's man with the stub-tongue. The owner talks about a man with a face tattoo of Christ, but he can't be more helpful than that. Although the Pizza Connection Trial was the longest federal criminal trial in American history, although Mafia-connected pizzeria owner Gaetano Mazzara made *New York Times* headlines when his corpse was found slumped in a plastic bag in Brooklyn, when I talk to people about my article, they recommend I go back to New Jersey, or that I watch *The Sopranos* and *The Godfather*. Throughout all of this, I can't get a good slice of white pizza at any of the places I stop.

I spend all night at Papa Mia's, a dive bar with a fried eggplant pizza that fills every part of my being with warmth. Papa Mia's did not have to pay *pizzo* because they were so fast and helpful in regards to laundering. The current owners know nothing of Mafia violence. But why would they? I get sort of drunk, and the whole place feels warm, but for the last half of my night my stomach and legs feel pulled down, like they were being tugged by a child's hand.

I stop by Artichoke Heart in Lake City, Florida, and order mozzarella sticks. By this point, I can taste the dull oxidation of parmesan cheese that sits in glass shakers; I can hear the internal screams of the two plastic restaurant statues stuck in greeting poses; I can watch a mozzarella stick peel open and know by the arc of cheese if the moz is fresh or the once-Mafia-controlled low moisture mozzarella variety. I know by the first bar if the pizzeria is playing Dean Martin's "That's Amore" on their speakers and if they have selected the 1953 original or the 1956 studio recording.

I know all the senses and details that accompany pizzerias, and the tug I have been feeling is part of this. I think it has been with me since the start, since Vinnie's Slice, just in different forms. In certain pizzerias, instead of feeling something around my waist, my vision feels drawn out, like a cloth over my eyes is getting pulled away. Sometimes I hear bells. Sometimes it feels like something will shatter. When I feel this tug coming in Artichoke Heart, as I slump in my table waiting for moz sticks, I dig into it.

I start to cut out all of the pizzeria's smells: the cleaner, the grease, the cigarette, the stink of distant patrons, the garlic breath. Toss it all down and work on removing the textures. The heat of the room. The formica table, green is its color. Sounds around me are drowned out and replaced with the trickling of blood. I close my eyes. Deep in my mental background hangs this weight and I reach towards it, like one does when trying to remember a dream in that liminal moment before rising. The weight becomes a gathering and the gathering becomes a mountain.

When I open an eye at Artichoke Heart, across the table I see a woman in black. I turn and lock eyes one by one with five people who weren't here a minute ago.

They surround me with their bent cheeks and tanned skin. Some have wounds from their deaths (blown faces, holes in their hands). Some have good teeth. I am overwhelmed, and my brain, sensing this, falls back into journalist-mode, with my voice recorder and pad in one hand and a pencil swishing down words in the other.

"Did you die in Artichoke Heart?" I ask.

"We did not," the one across from me says.

"We're here like the chewing gum underneath your table," another adds.

"We used to be stuck to the red-blooming vines of the island. We were in the udders of the cattle. We were crushed with the poppy seeds that were cooked into heroin and packed into bricks."

"Do you know how many of those bricks made it across the ocean? How many of us were trafficked here in coffins of cheese and sauce?"

"Too many. And we've been telling the same stories to ourselves for decades. And in walks this journalist. What are you looking to find, journalist?"

"I . . . work for *Vice*. I'm just a restaurant reviewer." They haven't heard of *Vice*.

"Perhaps. But Letizia Battaglia was just a housewife before she picked up a camera and became a journalist. She photographed my corpse, did you know that? I looked beautiful."

"Journalists just need to record, listen, and ask good questions. Can you do that?"

"I'm writing this down."

"Once upon a time, I stood up against the Mafia, against one of their leaders, a man named Riina, called 'The Beast of Corleone.' This was in the seventies, when Riina would circle the capital of Palermo like the rural mutt he was and bite any leg he could get his teeth into. I lived in Palermo with my three sisters and we whispered about such criminalities in the bakery we worked for. I made the jam and the pistachio creme and the sweet ricotta for the pastries. On the side, I experimented with the recipes, sourcing the water from different wells each time I made something. The pastries would turn out a different color, or the jam would taste sweeter, I recorded it all in a book. It made me feel like a scientist. This was back when water ran in the city every other day, and people drank from their bathtubs. One night after the bakery closed, I was dragging in some buckets of well water for recipe testing and I caught someone in the alley on a payphone. He's talking about Riina! I put the buckets away and listened: the man was one of Riina's underbosses, talking about how poorly a meeting went. I heard specific names, places, a time. The next day, some of those names were killed at those places around those times. So I go to the police, told them what I heard, and they asked if I would swear to that in court. There was an upcoming trial in a few months and I said I would.

"I went back to my jam but as it boiled red, the bakery was full of new whispers. Whispers about me. My name had gotten out to Riina's mobsters. I was being called a fat snitch and a liar. The judges and the police talked with me about witness protection and I was sent into the hills outside of Palermo to wait.

"There was nothing to do in the countryside, but that wasn't the worst thing. I felt a tug. I was left in a bland house with rice and white beans and no way to contact my friends or my three sisters and see if they were all right, if the Beast of Corleone hadn't eaten their legs. It was true limbo, I thought. It was like I had fled a battlefield but had gone nowhere more safe or comfortable. And there was this tug, dragging me back to Palermo, back to the city I loved. Back to my community. I thought I could testify and live at the same time. I began to wander the hills the police had left me in, tasting every well I passed by. Each sip was *wrong*, the water was terrible. I had been in the hills for two months. When I got into Palermo finally, I went to one of my favorite cafes and tried to order tap water. This was exceedingly rare, since all cafes served bottled water, so it took them a minute and as I waited and salivated for the taste of home I scanned the cafe. People were flipping newspapers, biting into midday pastries of apricot and currant. Towards the front there was a wide glass door, quite like the one in this restaurant, and through the door I could see two men exiting a truck, unwrapping heavy objects underneath blankets. One had Christ tattooed on his face, and the other Virgin Mary, and they both had guns. I was Riina's target, but I had time to hide. People around me splintered, the glass broke, it all fell down. They were gone in a minute.

"I did not die at the cafe, but seven others did. There was the flash of photography and the military police arrived. I was carried away, thrown back into limbo. I refused to drink water afterwards, as a protest. Not against the Mafia but against myself. I was protesting my own existence for having killed seven strangers. The police hated me. I could not stop thinking about it. My head was stuck in loops and the tug had changed form. I was being drawn somewhere darker. I chanted the names of those seven strangers. My mouth grew dry and I hated my desires. In the end, I squatted on the bathroom floor and measured out pills to dry swallow until I died. I felt like a scientist.

"It took about two days before I regretted my suicide. And I can tell you that my regret hurt more than my guilt and grief ever did. I have felt that hurt for thirty years. I have no body, I have no form, forces pass in and out of me, but that regret stays locked inside whatever I have left. Sometimes people eat here and they must feel something pang deep in them. I wonder if that's me, getting out. I hope one day I will dissolve like salt into water, but it hasn't happened yet."

I just finished typing up her story. I'm in a motel in Fargo, Georgia, with a full tank of gas and an overheated laptop. Now that the shock of this all has worn down, I'm still astounded. This is the biggest scoop, the purest story. Two of them had packed heroin for the Mafia after the French Connection went bust and the Sicilians took over the Corsican drug trade. These ghosts were once religious, and they hated heroin, but they were asked by Mafia men to do a job and they could not refuse. Their product probably made it to places like Artichoke Heart. They were probably killed by a gang from Corleone.

If I follow Route 441 north to Douglas in the morning, I can get to my next location, White Manhattan's New York Style Slice.

"You want to talk about hurt?" She stretches herself across the wheelchair-accessible bathroom stall in White Manhattan's. I had to ask my question a few times and concentrate into the tug to see her. Her legs were crumbled and blackened. "Let's talk about hurt:

"When I was alive, our capital was surrounded by orange and lemon groves in this beautiful golden halo, but could we walk the streets and pick a fruit? It would be stealing from the Mafia. We let the citrus rot. We had figs and chickpeas, we had oil and glistening tuna roe, we had thin ham and shelled nuts and bushels of dried herbs so vast you could run into them and disappear like Moses in the reeds. You could taste how close we were to God. For a little while. And then came Riina and Badalamenti and the rest of the them to cut their way into our ribs.

"Did you know that Riina was illiterate? He flunked out of third grade. He couldn't speak Italian. He couldn't even speak Sicilian. He spoke the backwater dialect of his mountain town and nothing else. The rest of the Mafia was just like him. If you were evil and smart, you would've just gone to America, or become a stockbroker. We were left with the brutes who knew nothing but greed and bullets. Riina died last year in a medically induced coma. I knew him. I knew all of them. Sometimes I wish we all had their luxuries.

"A few years before I was burned alive, I found one of those luxuries in the city of Agrigento. My husband had been placed there as a Mafia captain, but I got to explore the staircased alleyways, and one day I found a nunnery that sold pistachio couscous stuffed inside sugar-spun lambs. They've been using the same recipe since 1918. They were almost too good to swallow. Yes, I died and I left Sicily, my soul bound up in a packet of cocaine, but who gives a shit? The Corsicans were churning out coke before us, and then the Columbians continued after us.

"The hurt I felt was in the tomatoes that surrounded the coke. They were grown without love. My hurt is for this 'New York Style Slice' menu. What the fuck is a 'grilled cheese crust?' Why does the dough taste chemical? The worst thing Riina did was punch Sicily until the entire island became meathead muscle, until there was no fat, no God, no gold, no lambs and no nuns to spin them out of candy. And our bruteness became our export."

They keep talking. I travel to Imo's, to Cazovino Pizza, to Pizzavendolo, to all the places where the owners see them. Outside of Elizabeth, NJ, I stay in a Days Inn and cannot shake a terrible feeling every time I pass my floor's ice machine. I want to check if the hotel was built atop a pizzeria, but I throw off the idea. There are probably spirits in every hotel ice machine. I worry about where the American versions have gone, but I know I do not have the acute detail to find them amongst the exit signs and travel-size shampoos like I am with the Sicilians. Even in these moments, I am not alone. I am as rushed and crowded as those restaurant openings were. I am full of stories.

Back inside Vinnie's Slice, they pull coins out of their eyes and gamble with them. They hate garlic bread and they love Alfred, who smiles their way. The sunbleached poster in his office fell behind his desk when I came, and he left it there to collect dust instead of sun.

He says he had forgotten the face of the protagonist. I soon found two more (friends? Maybe lovers?) with similar sounding names in the broom closet.

"I was shot with those rabbit-hunting guns for not paying *pizzo*, but Peppino here has a more interesting story. Speak up, Peppino," the first tells me.

"I almost lost my voice."

"He was yelling all the time prior to his death. *Leader of proletariat* that, *anti-Mafia* this."

"So the Mafia strapped me to the tracks of a train and blew me up with TNT. They said I was a Communist agitator and I had tripped my own terrorist device."

"Like one of those American cartoons."

"That's not the kicker. You always told the end better than me, Procopio."

"Even after Peppino was labeled a terrorist, even after Peppino left his body and watched his balls go one way and his eyes another, he was still elected to a city council seat. He was that loved."

"People loved politics. They wanted reform. I even came to the first council meeting and floated above my seat for all it would do."

"Haunting a pizzeria in New Jersey is the same thing: a lot of change around us that we can't interact with."

"But we've been listening to the radio," Peppino says. "The things you can learn from a pizzeria radio! We've been hearing about young Leftists working against terrorism too. Malala Yousafzai and the other one."

"Emma Gonzalez."

"Yes, those are the ones. They have such strength. I'm waiting every day to meet their ghosts."

Time has passed and they haven't stopped talking. It isn't easy to keep pace with them, but I am doing it.

I need to add into this draft their stories about:

- The temple dogs who comforted Rosolia in the Olympieion Field
- The unexploded fascist bombs and the child who played in the ruins
- The killers in the olive branches on the road from the Palermo Airport.
- The older spirits, the skeleton homes of Mondello
- The lymphatic cancer, the pistachio forests

I'm making trips back to my laptop to transcribe, but any day I might stop. I might stay with them, as a recorder and captive audience. They are getting louder now. They are connected to all the pizzerias. They burst through the neon and the chile flakes. They are *filling*, in every sense of the word. I have to go.

30 MINUTES OR LESS . . . OR ELSE!

JAMES NEWMAN AND DESMOND REDDICK

SNOOP DOGG INTERRUPTED Keegan's conversation with himself as the Jetta lurched to a stop: "You have reached yo' destination. Thanks fo' the ride, man. I had the time o' my life!"

Keegan used to chuckle every time Snoop's voice spoke to him from the GPS device atop his dashboard. His friends said it got old fast (the consensus was that the Yoda setting was the best), but Keegan thought it was hilarious.

Tonight, though, the rapper's voice seemed to taunt him, like some urban doomsayer.

Fuckin' Snoop . . .

His guts roiled as he killed the Jetta's engine. He swallowed a lump in his throat that felt as big as one of the Crown Jewel Garlic Knots™ he frequently delivered with the Royal Family Feast Deal. His heart slammed in his chest as he peered through his cracked windshield toward the white-brick Cape Cod about thirty feet away. Inside, a man was waiting for his pie. Impatiently, no doubt.

Keegan glanced at the clock on the GPS screen and his heart sank.

Two minutes late . . .

He hefted the pizza box in its insulated nylon bag from the passenger seat beside him. He climbed out of the car and began to limp up the stone walkway toward the house. With everything that had happened tonight, he hadn't even noticed before now that he was missing a shoe.

The house was dark except for a single light in a downstairs window. A silhouette moved behind the curtain, like the shadow of some ravenous beast pacing back and forth in its lair.

Keegan shuffled up the front steps, onto the front porch.

Prodding the corner of his mouth with his tongue, he spat a tooth. It rattled across the porch and landed in a nearby holly bush.

He rang the doorbell. His finger left a dark smear of blood on the button.

30:00

"Yo, Keegs," Theresa said as he walked through the door of Majestic Pizza following his latest delivery. "Ron wants to see you."

She was a punk chick with green hair and multiple piercings and the cutest butt he had ever seen. Too bad her taste leaned toward other punk chicks. She barely glanced up from her iPhone as she spoke. Her black-painted fingernails clicked on the screen as she typed out a text message at the speed of light.

"Great," said Keegan. "I'm *really* not in the mood tonight. Fuckin' Ron . . . "

From somewhere in the back, "Don't Stop Believin'" played on a tinny radio. A toilet flushed elsewhere in the building.

"Got a pie in the oven, by the way," Theresa said. "First-time customer in Thornberg Heights ordered a King's Supreme. Should be ready by the time Ron's done with you."

"Thornberg Heights? Figured the rich assholes who live out that way only eat caviar and filet mignon."

"I'm sure they're making an exception because our pizza is—"

"—fit for a king," Keegan mumbled, finishing the obnoxious catchphrase that Ron tried to force his employees to say on the phone.

"Keep it together, Keegs," Theresa told him, as he headed for the office in the back. "Much as I'd love to see you punch him in the throat, you need this job."

23:45

"Last chance, Powell," said the boss. "Screw this up, you're toast. You understand me?"

Ron sat on his desk, looking down at Keegan, who occupied the room's single rolling chair. Keegan knew it was intentional; the prick preferred to take the dominant position over his subordinates any time he called one of them into his office. Granted, the word "office" was a stretch, as it had obviously been a broom closet once upon a time. A single window offered a luxurious view of the dingy rear corner of Majestic Pizza's parking lot and dumpster, although Ron kept the blinds drawn more often than not. Keegan used to think it was because the smokers on his payroll liked to congregate there when business was slow (the crushed butts littering the asphalt resembled dried-out chicken bones rolled from a shaman's bowl), but it was more likely that Ron didn't want anyone to see what he did in his office. One girl who worked the dayshift claimed she had walked in on him perusing online porn not too long ago, said she was pretty sure he'd been jacking off.

"You know," Ron continued to berate Keegan, "I've had to field more calls on you than any other employee in my entire career here."

Keegan barely refrained from rolling his eyes. Ron had been at Majestic Pizza a month less than him. And one would have to employ some serious self-delusion to call managing this dump a *career*.

"One more screw-up—I don't care if you're *two seconds late* with a delivery—and you're done. Got it?"

"Got it," Keegan said.

"Clock's ticking," said Ron. "Why are you still here?"

11:30

Keegan heard the *ding!* of the oven as he returned to the front of the store.

Theresa opened the heavy top door of the Bakers Pride 152 and wrinkled her nose. "Needs another minute. Oven sucks again."

"You're killing me," he said. "I can't afford another speeding ticket."

"Take it up with Ron. He's the one who started this 'thirty minutes or less or your pie is free' crap. Who even *does* that anymore?"

Keegan sighed, fished a pack of cigarettes from his back pocket.

He headed for the parking lot, lighting his cigarette before he was out the door.

He leaned against the store window, the back of his head feeling the cold of the glass. Beside his face, a crown-wearing, anthropomorphic slice of pizza smiled at him vacantly. The owner's son fancied himself an up-and-coming cartoonist, but to Keegan the restaurant's mascot had always looked like the work of a four-year-old at best.

Keegan exhaled smoke into the cool night air. "Fuckin' pizza . . . "

A minute or two later, the door swung open. Theresa handed him the insulated bag. Keegan glanced at the receipt on top, skimmed the name and address his friend had scribbled at the bottom. "I thought you said it was a new customer. Why does this name look so familiar?"

"Beats me," said Theresa. "Don't be late."

She stole the cigarette out of his mouth and stuck it between her lips.

Keegan jumped into his Jetta, backed out, and sped away.

16:05

"How do I know this name . . . " Keegan repeated, this time to himself.

Snoop was no help, at least where that was concerned. "Take this next left up ahead, cuz," he said. "We gon' getchoo there in no time."

Keegan glanced down at his speedometer, pumping the brake as a State Trooper passed him, traveling in the opposite direction. He watched the cop's taillights recede in his rearview before steering the Jetta past a sign bordered by immaculately-trimmed hedges: *Thornberg Heights*.

"In a hund'd feet, make a right, and you have reached yo' destination."

He brought the Jetta to a jerky stop at the end of Marigold Lane and checked the clock on the GPS screen. *Plenty of time*. Maybe he would even get a decent tip out of this. The folks who lived in places like Thornberg Heights probably wiped their asses with hundred dollar bills. Then again, they probably didn't get so loaded in the first place unless they were stingy as fuck.

The house cost more than Keegan could hope to pull down from decades of delivering pizzas: A-frame, beige with brown trim, satellite on one side of the roof, American flag hanging from the other. Through his open window Keegan could hear the wind chimes on the front porch tinkling softly. Several expensive vehicles crowded the driveway: two shiny black SUV's, a silver BMW, a sleek brown Beemer, and a pair of blood-red Miatas that were identical except for their vanity plates ("I-M-HIZZ" and "I-M-HERZ").

Some kinda party? Keegan wondered. *If so, someone's going hungry. King's Supreme is our biggest pie, but no way it'll feed this many people . . .*

He climbed out of the car, rounding the Jetta to gather what he needed from the passenger side. He always did it that way when delivering to an unfamiliar address. It gave him a moment to scan his surroundings before his hands were full. You never knew what you might be walking into. Dogs, for one thing, were never too far from a deliveryman's mind.

He grabbed the pizza and money pouch and headed for the house. The property was dark. From somewhere down the block, a dog barked as he knocked on the door. It sounded big. And mean.

Keegan tapped one foot impatiently. The insulated bag was warm against his side. He had little doubt its contents would have smelled delicious to someone who hadn't decided long ago that he could live the rest of his life without ever seeing another slice of pizza.

He knocked again.

Waited.

Still no answer.

He paced over to the side of the porch then, and realized he'd been wrong. The house wasn't *completely* dark. He saw a hint of light in a ground-floor window, undoubtedly the basement. A flickering orange glow was visible, as if from candles.

Keegan stepped off of the porch and approached the basement window. He knelt beside it, unaware that he was crushing several tulips and petunias in a well-kept flowerbed as he did so.

Keegan's breath caught in his throat when he saw what was on the other side of that dusty glass.

"What the fuck?"

His first thought was that it resembled something out of a bad horror flick: a tight circle of seven or eight people, clad in long black robes, silent and unmoving.

Between them was a young woman. She was naked, her hands atop her chest, like those of a corpse in repose. She appeared to be unconscious. Bizarre shapes and squiggles darkened her breasts and stomach, not dissimilar to the toppings on the pies Keegan delivered night after night. They had been painted on her flesh using a tar-like substance, still wet, dripping down her sides and pooling onto the concrete slab beneath her.

One of the black-robed figures held a knife in the air above the woman. Keegan glimpsed the bottom half of a man's face beneath the cowl. A sharp jaw, a salt-and-pepper goatee.

"Hey," a voice came from behind Keegan. "Something I can help you with? This's private property."

Keegan's heart leapt into his throat. He dropped his money pouch, and its zipper *clinked* against the window.

All at once, the circle of figures raised their hooded heads to gaze upon the intruder.

"Aww, shit," Keegan said. Then something came down on his head. Hard.

Everything went black.

He's back in high school. The principal's office.

Only . . . something isn't right. His hands are tied behind his back. And the room is lit by flickering candles.

"How many times are we going to do this?" Mr. Novak asks from the other side of his desk. He's a tall man in his early sixties who always wears cardigan sweaters and an expression like he just bit into something sour. His head is oddly cone-shaped. He attempts to hide his baldness with a comb-over, but the few wisps of snow-white hair atop his dome twitch and dance in the breeze from the overhead A/C vent as if they no longer wish to comply.

Keegan wonders what he did this time. Maybe someone ratted him out after he carved a cartoon dick into one of the study carrels in the library. Maybe he called his English teacher a homo again.

Or perhaps he has simply been tardy one too many times. Couldn't ever beat the clock. He was late again. Always late . . .

Mr. Novak reaches beneath his desk, pulls out a grease-stained pizza box. Keegan glimpses Majestic Pizza's mascot on the lid, the shimmering crown and the shit-eating grin. Mr. Novak opens the box, begins devouring a slice almost as big as his head. A plump mushroom plops onto his desk. He flicks it away with his middle finger, and it bounces off Keegan's shoulder. Tomato sauce drips down the disciplinarian's wrinkled chin, but he does not wipe it away.

"Detention every day for the next ten years," he says through a mouthful of King's Supreme.

Keegan tries to complain about how unfair that is, but he suddenly realizes he has recently suffered a terrible head injury, and it has damaged the part of his brain that controls speech.

He babbles nonsensically at Mr. Novak, and the old man shakes his head, and this time when he speaks, it is not his own voice that comes from Mr. Novak's tomato-sauce-stained mouth but the voice of Ron, Keegan's boss.

"Now get the fuck out of here, Powell. We're closed."

Yep . . . something isn't right here at all.

1:00

His head throbbed. And he could feel something wet running down the back of his scalp. He moved to wipe it off but was horrified to discover his hands were tied behind him.

"Mr. Novak! Holy shit. I *knew* I recognized your name. Wait, where's Mr. Novak . . . "

He had more important things to worry about at the moment, though.

Because these people weren't Mr. Novak.

Keegan gasped as his vision unblurred and he took in his surroundings. A robed figure crouched before him. The guy was a few years younger than Keegan, freckle-faced with spiky hair the color of old pennies. He had dark bags under his eyes and a silver hoop in his bottom lip. He looked like a little shit, the kind of little shit who wiped his boogers on your shirt in school, not the kind of little shit who murdered naked girls in his basement.

"He's awake!"

The other robed figures gathered around him, heads angled down at Keegan. They all still wore their hoods. Their mouths were turned up in knowing sneers.

"And now he's seen your face," said the man with the salt-and-pepper goatee.

"Right," the little shit replied, "but we're gonna kill him anyway."

"Still. It's bad form."

Waitaminute. Kill me?

"Why are you here?" Goatee asked Keegan.

"I'm just delivering a pizza, man!" Keegan's voice cracked with terror. No use pretending to be a tough guy, he reckoned.

Little Shit giggled.

"No one ordered a pizza," a woman's voice came from behind Little Shit and Goatee. Goatee held up a hand to silence her. The candlelight danced upon the walls.

"I just go where I'm told," Keegan said in a voice a bit whinier than he intended.

"There *is* a pizza," another voice said from behind Keegan. He recognized it as the guy who snuck up on him at the basement window. Apparently this dude got a kick out of standing behind people.

Keegan heard a light scraping noise as the thermal delivery bag was kicked across the basement floor. The money pouch sat on top of it.

"Look, just keep the pizza and the money! Let me go!" Keegan twisted in his seat, trying to free himself to no avail.

"We didn't order a pizza," Goatee said. Little Shit slipped the pizza box out of the Velcro-pouched delivery bag and took a peak.

"Olives? The only thing worse than pineapple." He shoved the box back into the bag.

"Says you," countered someone else in the shadows, the gravelly voice of a heavy smoker.

"There's no accounting for taste," said Goatee.

The overhead pipes suddenly came alive with the sound of rushing water.

"That's Aunt Sarah," Little Shit giggled, looking up toward the ceiling. "She had Cinnabon for lunch and it ruined her. She'd probably murder a gluten-free pizza, though. I don't suppose that's gluten-free?"

Keegan swallowed a lump in his throat, shook his head. He wondered what the right answer was.

Goatee shot Little Shit a stern look before turning back to Keegan. Then he threw a wild, heavy punch that landed hard under Keegan's right cheek. Keegan slumped.

"Fuck the pizza. I'm gonna ask you one more time. Why. Are. You. Here?"

Keegan winced, feeling fresh blood oozing from the back of his head shaken loose by the punch. Stars blinked in and out of his eyes.

He opened his mouth, not knowing what he was about to say, but Little Shit interrupted him.

"You guys ain't gonna believe this," said Little Shit, before erupting into a flurry of high-pitched giggles. Everyone in attendance, Keegan included, gawked at the shrill, laughing brat.

"What's so goddamn funny?" said Goatee.

Little Shit ripped the receipt from the top of the pizza box, held it up as if he had discovered some priceless treasure. "He was supposed to deliver to *five*-four-seven-eight Marigold. Not six."

It began as a low exhalation, but soon the hooded figures all began to laugh. Before long, most of them were bent over, slapping knees beneath black robes, roaring with laughter.

Keegan groaned. Theresa's shitty handwriting had caused him problems before, but this was ridiculous.

*A little less time on your iPhone, please, and a little more effort on your penmanship? Thanks, Theresa. It had been a minor inconvenience in the past. This time you're gonna put me six feet under.*A shaft of light crept into the basement from above, and feet padded down the stairs. A woman Keegan could only assume was Aunt Sarah came into view. She was at least twice his age, pushing fifty, but she was pretty hot. Long black hair down to her ass, tribal tattoo on her left hip. She was naked except for a baby-blue bra and matching panties. Under different circumstances, the word "MILF" might have popped into his mind.

"You figure out why he's here?" Aunt Sarah asked, picking up her own black robe from atop a washing machine a few feet away from the group's sacrificial altar. Keegan watched the feet of the girl on the slab for any movement.

"In the worst case of bad luck I've ever seen, this kid got the wrong address," Goatee said.

Keegan laughed in spite of his predicament. Theresa's wretched handwriting had led him into the lair of a Satanic cult. A big happy family of kill-crazy devil worshippers. Meanwhile, a block away, poor Mr. Novak was still waiting for his King's Supreme.

Aunt Sarah slipped on her robe and her left hand came through brandishing a knife. Its blade was wavy, and the handle was gold.

"Well," she said, "since we have a new friend and *someone* won't allow me the honors of sacrifice . . . " She shot a scornful look Goatee's way before lifting her robe to straddle Keegan.

Keegan recoiled as much as his bonds would allow, as she lowered herself onto his lap. The chair creaked beneath them. Keegan would have been turned on if the dagger wasn't pressed to his Adam's apple, or if there wasn't the faintest whiff of cinnamon diarrhea wafting off of her.

Who was he kidding? He was definitely turned on. With all the candles, it sort of smelled like incense.

The chair creaked again. It was old, wooden, and didn't feel very sturdy, obviously something that had been stored in the basement to be fixed one day, but no one had gotten around to it. Beneath the weight of two people, the chair's legs wobbled from side to side.

Aunt Sarah lifted his chin with the blade of the dagger, smiling seductively at him. Keegan went with the blade, gasped as he felt its tip break his skin. A warm rivulet of blood dripped from the incision and trickled down his chest all the way to his quivering stomach.

She took the blade from his throat to lick the dagger, and Keegan knew it was his only chance. He threw his weight to one side, kicking the legs of the chair with his heels.

The chair rocked and collapsed beneath them.

Stunned gasps and curses filled the room. Aunt Sarah's prone body pinned Keegan to the floor, her torso undulating and spasming toward her gathered family. That's when they all saw . . .

The dagger was buried hilt-deep in the woman's chin, its blade plunged into her brain-pan.

Her hands flailed about and an odd *click*ing came out of her mouth as she tried to pull it out. But her efforts were futile, and she was dead within seconds.

For a moment everyone was stunned into silence.

Then Keegan pulled his hands free from the loosened ropes behind him, shoving the dead woman off of him without wasting a second. Aunt Sarah stared sightlessly up at her horrified family, as if in disbelief. Keegan scrabbled for the stairs.

During Aunt Sarah's final macabre marionette dance, the young girl on the slab had stirred to consciousness. And now she began to scream.

Keegan was nearly out the door when he heard Goatee shout: "*Get him!*"

Upstairs, the house was dark, but even without Snoop, the moonlight through the windows was enough for Keegan to navigate his way through a kitchen that smelled like beef stew, past a tiny bathroom that stank of Cinnabon, and down a short hallway into a messy living room. He lunged for what he assumed was the front door, clipping his shin on the corner of a coffee table and yelped in pain, but his car was within sight. Freedom . . .

Wrong.

Halfway across the lawn, someone took him out at the knees. His chin hit the ground, and he was pretty sure he bit off the end of his tongue. But the pain barely registered. He was somehow able to roll over onto his back in the cool, damp grass to face the son-of-a-bitch.

Ice-cold hands immediately wrapped around his throat.

Fuckin' Little Shit . . .

The kid wasn't laughing anymore. He howled with rage as his grip tightened on Keegan's throat Keegan guessed it had something to do with the death of Aunt Sarah.

His grief had Little Shit unhinged, and Keegan got his hands up fast, driving his thumbs into Little Shit's eyes. He wailed in agony. Keegan imagined pushing hard enough to drive his thumbs into his brain, to keep going until he touched the back of his skull.

If you can dream it, you can do it, a voice from his past assured him, and somehow Keegan knew, as he pushed harder and harder, probing deeper and deeper, that the voice belonged to Mr. Novak.

The old man had been a hard-ass, sure. But damned if Keegan

hadn't always liked him, even if he never would have admitted it back then.

Little Shit let go of Keegan's throat. He tried desperately to pry Keegan's thumbs from his eyes.

Two black-robed figures burst through the front door and into the yard, one of them a chubby bastard whose robe was at least a size too small for him. His belly jiggled like a giant blob of Majestic's Royal Homemade Dough™ as he pulled Little Shit off of Keegan and lunged with hairy-knuckled hands curled into claws.

Keegan kicked the fat man in the groin as hard as he could, and he went down with an *oof!*

Keegan jumped to his feet, pulled his keys from his pocket, ran for the Jetta and jumped inside.

Little Shit stumbled after him

Keegan watched him a moment, then stomped the gas. The Jetta's bumper hit Little Shit in the knees and sent him flying into the windshield.

Keegan hit the brake and watched through the spider-webbed glass as Little Shit tumbled back down the hood and out of sight. He tapped the gas lightly, and the Jetta's tires thumped over Little Shit's body, spinning on the tender flesh beneath them. The tires grabbed and spat Little Shit out behind the car as it lurched forward.

Through his open window, Keegan could still hear muffled screams from inside the house. He stopped the car. There was no reason why he shouldn't immediately *drive away.* But he had been emboldened by everything that had happened over the last few minutes. By God, Keegan Powell had *never* been a coward. And that girl in there needed help.

Keegan slammed the gearstick into "park" and ran back to the house, but as he slowed his approach to the basement door, those anguished cries tapered off . . . one by one . . . until there were only two.

Once inside, Keegan cautiously descended the stairs.

And at the bottom, he discovered nothing less than a bloodbath.

The sacrificial lamb was on her feet and stabbing Goatee in the chest with his own dagger, her insane shrieks echoing through the basement. All around her, Goatee's fellow Satanists lay cut, torn and disemboweled in various stages of savagery. The stench of blood and shit and cinnamon filled the air. Keegan could only watch, mesmerized by the madness.

He snapped out of it when he spotted something in the corner of his eye. He crept across the room, careful not to interrupt what was going on a few feet away lest the girl turn her sights on him.

He dipped, his knee aching from the movement, and picked up the pizza bag and money pouch.

Back in the car, he placed the stuff on his passenger seat and took several seconds to catch his breath. He lifted his foot to close the door, but it was suddenly pulled back out of his grasp with a horrid screech.

Little Shit had crawled out from under the car. One of his eyes had been carved out by Keegan's thumbnail, and his head was shaped like a half-deflated basketball, most of his face hanging down as if no bone was there to support it.

Keegan kicked Little Shit in his ruined face. Once, twice, three times. Then he slammed the door.

He touched the GPS screen. Snoop Dogg asked him where he wanted to go, saying he was down fo' anything, yo.

Me, too, brotha, after the night I've had . . .

Keegan carefully punched in the correct address. Double- and triple-checked it to be sure . . .

He put the Jetta in gear and couldn't resist bouncing over Little Shit one last time.

He didn't have to look back to know he was smeared across the asphalt. Flattened. Like a pizza.

0:55

Keegan floored it, heading for the white-brick Cape Cod at the end of the block.

The Jetta shuddered, hesitated, but obeyed like a weary racehorse getting whipped on the homestretch, but with love. Keegan didn't check the clock, but he knew it was going to be close.

-2:07

"Mr. Novak . . . " Keegan's voice was hoarse, barely more than a whisper. "I'm so sorry. I had the wrong address. They were . . . they tried to kill . . . "

"Young man, you look so familiar to me. Do I know you from somewhere."

"Keegan Powell. You were my principal. Esposito High, Class of 2009."

"Your friends called you 'Keegs' as I recall."

"Yessir."

"I'll be damned. Have you been in an accident, son?"

The world tilted. Keegan gripped the doorjamb to keep him from going down, nearly dropping the pizza, the worst thing he could do.

"I'm late."

"Don't worry about that," said Mr. Novak. "We have a history. I'm glad to pay for the pie." He looked Keegan up and down, taking in his bloodstained uniform. "Here, let me take that from you. In fact, why don't you come in and have a slice? You look a fright. You sit, and I'll call 911."

"But . . . I'm late."

"You *do* still owe me some time, from detention, remember? But let's call it even." The old man smiled, then he gave a dismissive wave of his liver-spotted hand and ushered him inside.

In the living room behind him, a large television was tuned to a documentary about the Satanic Panic that had been all the rage back in the '80s. Geraldo Rivera was staring into the camera as he gave his viewers a grim-faced guarantee that a nationwide conspiracy threatened the very lives of their children.

Fuckin' Geraldo . . .

Mr. Novak's brow furrowed, but only briefly. He closed the door behind them. Keegan noticed the robe on the coat rack, the same one he wore at their graduation ceremony. Keegan had always wondered why faculty robes had hoods.

"Life is short, son. There are worse things to worry about than being late. Don't you think?"

AND SHE ANSWERED THE DOOR . . . NAKED!

WALLACE WILLIAMSON

JUST TO BE CLEAR, nobody in Collins Crossing, Mississippi *ever* answers their door *naked*. No way, no how! Maybe they do stuff like that down in New Orleans, being the legendary sexual degenerates and all they claim to be down there. Or maybe over in Mobile when The Tide's on a roll or something. Closest I ever heard about something like that here in th' Crossin' is old man Schwartz, who's sometimes seen wandering around outside in his wife-beater *(though he's never been married that I know of)* T-shirt and boxer shorts, hence the nickname *"Shorts Schwartz."* When I got the pizza delivery order for the old Boatwright house, last thing ever occurred to me was a drop-dead gorgeous naked woman answering the door.
But that's what happened . . . I think!

Bertha Boatwright was the scariest old woman I ever knew for real. She taught High School science. Our High School never was real big, so she taught everything science related, for about a hundred years, *maybe longer*. She taught both my parents, who said she was sweet and kind if she liked you and meaner than the Devil if she didn't. Time I got to her she was old and liked pupils only if she could remember liking their parents. I got lucky in that respect, though she still scared the living shit out of me. But then, even old folks always said *"Yes Ma'am" and "No Ma'am"* to Bertha Boatwright.

Being a science teacher and all, ol'Miz Boatwright was a collector of natural *(and sometimes unnatural!)* oddities. For the better part of forty years, kids brought her weird crap they'd found in the woods or in Indian mounds or just laying around places most folks never bothered to look. She had a lot of real creepy stuff in jars on shelves in her classroom. Word was she kept the really freaky shit in her basement. Nobody I ever knew ever claimed to have actually seen any of it, but everybody knew it was all down there just the same.

The old Boatwright house sat back off Dupuy Street way up towards the end, behind lots of giant trees and overgrown hedges. It was dark and scary when ol' Miz Boatwright lived there *(she* never *got Trick Or Treaters!),* only went darker and creepier in the years since she'd died and rotted for a couple of hot August weeks before somebody found her. Place was up for sale for five years before somebody from Memphis bought it, then put it back on the market three months later. Been like that ever since. Yeah, you guessed it: *Haunted House!* I didn't even know anybody was living there until I got told to take a Triple Deluxe Supreme with Double Meat and Cheese up there just before we closed at midnight.

I know what you're thinking: "*Bullshit,* nothing stays open 'til midnight in Collins Crossing." And up until about a year or so ago, you'd be right on the money about that. Then Pedro and Georgianna Mendez came in and bought up the old abandoned Lion service station and turned it into Poppa Pedro's Pizza 'n' Tacos. First one of those we ever had, far back as anybody can remember anyway. In order to make ends more or less meet, Poppa Pedro's opened at 10:00 in the morning and closed somewhere around midnight. Which worked out just fine for me; I work the night shift delivery and get plenty of time to study.

Plenty of time for most things, come to think 'bout it; especially boredom and loneliness. Th' Crossin' never was much for excitement, or even entertainment for that matter. Only women worth havin'er trolling for one night stands involving Rebel Yell, sixpacks and crewcab pickups; or are either already raising a litter of ankle biters. Lost my daddy back in the big tornado and flood of '91 that almost wiped the whole town off the map. Just me and Momma since then. After the Army, I signed up at Ole Miss to learn something useful I might be able to make a halfway decent living at. Being close enough to come home most nights and weekends makes Momma happy; she's getting on up there and misses Daddy more and more. Georgianna gave me a box of leftover tacos to take home to her after my delivery up at the old Boatwright place.

Still don't know what ever happened to those lil' suckers . . .

So up Dupuy hill I chugged in my (*restoration-in-progress*) '69 Mustang, great big boxed-up Poppa Pedro's Triple Deluxe Supreme with Double Meat and Cheese pizza snugly wrapped in one of Momma's old wool fake-Indian blankets. Time I got up to the hilltop turn, it was pretty much pitch dark; only streetlight up here was burned out and wasn't nobody around to complain about it . . . nobody *alive*, anyway. Collins Crossing never was big enough to have a whole lot of streets, having grown up here I was pretty sure I knew them all; even Dupuy Street . . . *and the town cemetery at the end!*

Somebody (*Hurvis Tutor*) stole ol' Miz Boatwright's fancy wrought iron mailbox long time ago, but I knew well enough where the driveway turn-off was . . . *everybody did!* When I turned in, my headlights caught on the worn-out and shot-up FOR SALE sign with a smaller NEWLY REDUCED PRICE! sign hanging below and a big red SOLD! placard stuck proudly on top. Somebody buying the old Boatwright place was usually big-ticket news in th' Crossin' and I briefly wondered why I hadn't heard about it, though not for long because the driveway was long and twisty and mostly overgrown and darker than the butthole of hell. Driveway dipped down way lower than Dupuy Street for better than half of it before climbing back up to the knoll the big old house sat on, forming a shallow little valley that was now full of fog, which was kind of weird because I figured it was too hot for fog. And it was *definitely* a hot, sultry night, which is why my car windows were down; first thing goes tits-up on a '69 Mustang is the air conditioner, usually just before the door and window handles start falling off and won't stay back on. Never noticed fog that smelled like anything worth remembering before, but this stuff smelled . . . *dead* . . . *old* dead . . . *graveyard dead.* Guess it must've rolled in from the town cemetery up over the hill, which only made sense if you didn't think about it.

Wasn't any lights on anywhere except the ones on my car until I got right up to the big old house and saw a soft, faint glow in one of the downstairs windows. Probably candles or an old coal-oil lantern; getting the electric turned on in th' Crossin' usually took longer than it did in most Third-World countries. I beeped my horn to alert whoever was inside not to shoot my ass when I knocked on the door, gathered up the still mostly warm midnight munchies and left my car headlights shining on the front porch and door so I wouldn't fall through any of the numerous holes in the rotted-out porch floor. My heart was beating like an over-revved car engine and I had to keep reminding myself to breathe! Man, this was the creepiest damn place I ever went to by myself, and I couldn't help but wonder why the hell I was doing it for $2 in gas money and a tip likely to be less than half that!

Just as I started to knock, the door opened sort of like all by itself . . . *I shit you not!*

And there she stood . . . *the most stunningly beautiful woman my eyes had ever seen in real life!*

And she answered the door . . . *NAKED!*

Butt-assed NAKED! I shit you not!

Back in th'Army I'd seen videos of naked girls answering the door naked after a pizza guy knocked, but they all looked fake and I never really believed shit like that really happens in real life.

Now . . .

She just stood there.

Too still to be alive.

Too beautiful to be real!

Like one of those high-end paintings . . .

They used to put in Playboy magazine . . .

Or the ones now made with computers.

She was backlit by some kind of soft reddish-blue light (*I know . . . but that's what it looked like, ok*) . . . *or maybe the light was coming from her!* Without moving a muscle, I heard a soft, lusciously sexy voice in my head say, "Enter and join me of your own free will . . . or leave now and take away no memory of our encounter."

Wasn't like a real voice; more like the one you hear warning you not to do that really stupid fucking *something* you really *really* want to do! Any sane and god-fearing individual would've turned and hauled ass quicker'n greased lightening!

I never had a chance . . .

Without even knowing I was doing it, my feet stepped through the doorway; rest of me naturally followed. She smiled and raised her arms out, hands beckoning me to her. I dropped the pizza box and barely noticed the mushy splat as it hit the splintery wooden floor. As I crept across the short space between us my befuddled mind began to register details of her immaculate appearance.

Long curly reddish-blond hair . . .
   That seemed to kind of . . .
      Sparkle . . .
        Like Jessica Rabbit's dress!
Bluish-green eyes that seemed to practically glow . . .
   From impossibly deep and far away . . .
      And just maybe . . .
        A really *long* time ago.
Dark red lips . . .
   The color of dry blood . . .
      That both pouted . . .
      And smiled . . .
        At the same time!
Perked up nipples . . .
   Same reddish-brown as her lips . . .
      Except . . .
        They seemed to glow . . .
          Softly . . .
            From within!
Large, perfectly taut breasts . . .
   Only an artist could conjure . . .
      That beckoned with timeless solace . . .
      Of the cradle of Heaven.
Mesmerizing reddish-blond triangle . . .
   At the join of her long, luscious legs . . .
      Exploded my heart with lust . . .
        Choked my mind with obsession . . .
          And struck me up painfully throbbing hard!
And as I stood salivating like a stupefied school boy . . .
   Though I knew my eyes were deceiving me . . .
      A wet red satin forked tongue . . .
      Flicked out from between her lower lips . . .
      And put the Come Hither upon my soul!

Just as I got almost close enough to touch her outreaching hands, I finally noticed strands of small red jewels *(rubies?)* encircling her fantastic body in strange patterns that my modern mind couldn't quite comprehend but my primordial subconscious both knew and feared! Each of the multitude of miniscule gemstones, connected by intricate weaves of fine gold thread, seemed to glow just a little bit; creating unique clusters of symbols that I somehow knew were older than any language of man. In the moment before I finally touched her, I realized that the jewels and golden thread were not *upon* her darkly complexioned skin, but rather integral to it . . . *though that, of course, was impossible!*

My fingertips seemed to burn when they touched her magically shimmering skin; a strangely sensual burn not unlike touching very cold ice, though far more erotic! When she wrapped her beckoning arms around me I felt subtle electrical shocks straddling the border between pain and ecstasy course through my entire body as I melted into her like butter into warm bread. "What . . . *are* . . . you?"

"I am your every need," the voice of the Whore of Babylon sighed from deep within my psyche. "Your every . . . *desire!*"

And it was just about then . . .

That I noticed that I too . . .

Was also somehow stone-butt-naked . . .

Though to this day I still have no idea when that even happened!

She looked like a living wet dream . . .

Tasted like sweet cream frosting . . .

Smelled Heavenly as the Mother of God!

Too damn perfect to be real . . .

Like one of those 4-D things at Disney World . . .

Or really great VR CGI porn!

On top of all that impossible perfection, she seemed to somehow . . . *shimmer!*

Like an image projected onto gently swirling mist!

But somehow I knew . . .

In my heart of hearts . . .

That she was as real as God . . .

And maybe just as omnipotent!

And all my stupefied brain could manage was the idiotic question, "*You* ordered a freakin' *pizza?*"

That lyrically soft, lusciously sexy voice in my head answered, "The food is for you . . . *you* . . . are for *me* . . . "
God help me . . .
She meant every word of it!
Whoever she was . . . *what* ever she was . . . she knew exactly what she was doing; like she'd been doing it long before ancient men finally climbed down from their trees and started running around naked in the jungle trying to fuck whatever they could catch; maybe she was even the one who taught us that trick!
Next thing I knew . . .
    I was down on the floor . . .
        Flat on my back . . .
            Watching her slowly . . .
                Gently . . .
                    Deliberately . . .
                        Squat down on my throbbing pole!
My rock-hard cock felt like it was sliding into a hot-oiled velvet glove sheathing the hand of the most erotic being in the human sexual experience! And though it massaged and cajoled and sucked my maddeningly throbbing erection, and though my balls screamed to spew into the writhing paradise working me like a master virtuoso, I could *not* come! My hands snapped to her swaying breasts like magnets to iron!
Maddeningly primordial fragrance of woman musk flooded from her womb as she rode me in varying rhythms of slow and easy and hard and rough. My eyes rolled back in my head when that impossibly mysterious forked tongue slipped from her mystically magical pussy and licked my throbbing balls . . . *then snuck down and teased my butthole!*
    And the only sound my withering mind heard . . .
    Was ZZ Top singing "Tube Snake Boogie"!

I screamed all breath from my lungs . . .
    She leaned forward . . .
        Clamped her divine mouth over mine . . .
            Blew hot breath of cosmic creation into my lungs . . .
                Snaked her hot juicy tongue down to the core of my being.

I felt my soul drawing from my body . . .
Merging with something spectral . . .
Something Holy . . .
Maybe older than life itself . . .
Maybe older than God!
Angel . . .
Demon . . .
God . . .
Whatever she was . . .
She was fucking my life . . .
My Soul . . .
Right out of my convulsing body . . .
And I never wanted to go back!
House was hot and we steamed it up even more; so much so that I could've sworn steamy smoke came off us as we rolled and squiggled around like two greasy, sweaty nightcrawlers writhing around trying to screw each other to death! It burned and hurt everywhere she touched me, but in *a I'm-too-busy-fucking-myself-to-death-to-care* sort of way. All the rest of the night, all day, all night, until time just didn't even exist anymore! She was dead-bang right on about me needing food too; she wiped the crust on herself, smeared double-meat double-cheese triple Supreme pizza gunk all over her everywhere, and I licked every bit of her clean and washed it down with her sweat, which tasted more sweet than salty; before it was all over I ate the whole damn pizza and quite likely the cardboard platter it came on! I can't begin to remember all the sex and debauchery we slathered upon each other, not to mention just about every flat surface in the old house; suffice it to say that we did every sexual thing a man and woman can possibly do . . .
And a lot more stuff I never even heard of . . .

Or ever even dreamed about!
I woke up in my car, naked and starving like I hadn't eaten in months! Hurvis Tutor found me while sneaking around looking for something to steal; screamed like a girl goosed with a popsicle when he saw me; woke me up and scared the shit out of me when he did!

First thing I noticed was the real estate agency sign . . . *the* SOLD *placard was gone!*

Turns out three days and nights had passed since my last midnight pizza run! Momma thought I was at school, Poppa Pedro and Georgianna figured I'd skipped out and was partying my ass off with their $22.97 at some Ole Miss Frat house. Wasn't until I got a long hard look at myself in the bathroom door mirror that I began to understand why Momma cried every time she looked at me.

My body was covered in strange mottled dots that looked like somebody'd come at me with a vacuum hose and tried to suck my bone marrow out right through my skin! Hurt like hell for a few weeks. My hair was shot with gray, few more wrinkles and crinkles than I remembered having before too. Doctor said I looked to be ailing right poorly, but I don't have money to go to no hospital for a bunch of tests that won't tell me anything I don't already know:

Bitch sucked about ten years of life right out of me . . .
And she was worth every fucking minute of it!

All that was a little better than ten years ago this September. In that time, I finished up my college with a Business degree and a Real Estate kicker and opened up my own company. Being in the Realtor game lets me keep tabs on who's buying and renting for a hundred mile around. Been looking for her all this time; whoever she is . . . *what* ever she is . . . she ruined me for *normal* women folk. Had myself a few girlfriends through the years; but they just ain't got nothing for me anymore, and I ain't got nothing for them.

I still get painfully throbbing erections about once a week. Then I dream about her and how it felt to finally explode inside her! Wetdream, right? But there's never anything on the sheets . . . or anywhere else.

Like she came to me in my dream . . .
And I came in her . . .
And she took it away with her . . .
Wherever she came from . . .
Wherever she goes to.

Each time I have *The Wetdream,* feels like I've fucked a few more years off my lifespan. Doesn't matter. It's killing me . . . *and she's worth it!*

Heaven . . .

Hell . . .
    Someplace entirely different . . .
        Nobody ever even imagined before . . .
        Makes no difference.
Whoever she is . . .
    What ever she is . . .
        Where ever she is.
        That's where I'll be . . .
        Forever!
I'm a part of her now, you see.
    Just like she's a part of me.
        Just like every other life she's taken.
        And I wouldn't have it any other way!
Don't know if I'll ever find *her* again . . .
    But I'll keep looking . . .
        Until I don't have any more time . . .
        Left to look no more.

I know you're out there somewhere . . . NAKED!

BONUS SLICE:
PIZZA PARTY FRIDAY!

DAVID JAMES KEATON AND MAX BOOTH III

TUESDAY

DAVE RIPPED OPEN a small bag of salad croutons and sucked the stale seasoning off each one in turn. He held out the bag to Max, who was preoccupied studying a large plaque on the ground, cracked in half down the middle. At the top, the words "Employee of The Month" had been transformed into "Employee of the *Mouth*" by the jagged split. Both halves were covered with photos of cheerful coworkers, and Max didn't need a closer look to know who wasn't on it. He'd seen it before. Hell, he used to obsess over it. Once, it had hung from the wall, but like most objects loosely swinging on any nails that were left, the rumble of apocalypse had knocked it down as easily as it had knocked down civilization. All the valuables in this place, and Dave was amazed Max only seemed concerned about this relatively insignificant list of the dead. He hadn't even noticed the *Pac-Man* machine in the corner yet. Of course, it would never work again, but Dave could follow the universal storyline easily enough with the hieroglyphics along the cabinet. Sort of. He was pretty sure it had something to do with "eating."

"You been here before or something?" Dave asked Max around a crunch. "This wasn't *your* place, was it?"

Dave snapped out of it, back into the present, "What do you mean?"

"Seems like everyone has their own pizza place to frequent. A town like this has, what, five different pizza joints? People move in, test them all out, but one stands out as the clear winner. And that's where your loyalty lies. No one changes their mind once they settle on their favorite. It's a show of weakness. So . . . where does your loyalty lie?"

Max shook his head. "Man, I'm not even from around here."

Dave tried to scoff, but his mouth was too dry.

"There's no more 'around here,' but whatever. Why the hell do you care who was Employee of the Month? All these shitholes do is rotate the names. Everyone gets a trophy, you know?"

Max shrugged, eyes still on the cracked plaque.

Not for the first time, Dave wondered if his new friend might be a bit slow in the head, like the requisite dim-witted sidekick the hero was always saddled with in Stephen King novels.

M-O-O-N, what does that spell? Pizza!

"Not everybody who worked here is on that list," Max said.

"Not the ones who really deserved it, huh?" Dave said, playing along.

"No one who didn't kiss ass."

"Kissing ass and spinning pizzas sounds hard," Dave laughed. "Like patting your head and rubbing your stomach."

"Speaking of, what has two thumbs and used to be employed at this very establishment?" Max said, both his thumbs up and grinning like a hitchhiker no one in their right mind would stop for.

Dave stepped back, foot crunching the plaque beneath him.

"What are you talking about?"

"I'm saying I used to work here! Papalocka's? This was my place for real. Five days a week. Sometimes six, if Ronnie called off, which he always did, too high on Whip-its to read a watch."

Dave gulped and a knee buckled like a leg wanted to give out. He steadied himself on the videogame cabinet.

"That's why I rolled us over here, to catch up on some old memories. The hell else is a guy supposed to go these days, am I right?"

Dave scratched at a drawing of a sad-eyed electric ghost, still a little wobbly. He rubbed his face, blinking.

"Max, you weren't the delivery driver, were you?"

Max laughed. He couldn't help it. It was either that or start crying, though sometimes he couldn't tell the difference anymore.

"Well," he said, "that's kind of complicated."

Max was born to make pizza, and with a couple wires crossed. At least that's how his dad explained it. And, sure, maybe that wasn't the sort of birthright his old man might normally brag about to his boys at the bar, because there was no real legacy of pizza-making being handed down generation to generation or anything. But Max long stopped giving a good goddamn what the man thought. There was a time when Max would do anything to impress him, but then the bloom was off the rose when he stumbled onto his dad's internet search history and discovered a penchant for "red rooms" and pay-for-play animal torture. Road Pizza dot com, it was called, and that day Max realized there was no more effective way to defang an authority figure than to discover what they masturbated to.

So if Max's greasy patrimony was pizza-related, then fuck it, that's the skills he'd hone. And if his old man thought he was a loser, well, then he could just go jack-off to a cete of badgers getting ground under the wheels of a Shriner parade. Which he had. Which is why Max knew what the hell a "cete" was.

But it started with his mom. She was into pizza, and in an Italian family, where they took cooking so seriously that they routinely said things like, "A woman has no place in a kitchen," no one paid much attention to her obvious talents. And back before the cancer ate her lungs and mercifully served her to the worms before the sun turned black and all that bullshit, every Friday night she'd make pizza. Not *order* pizza. *Make* pizza. And this made their house a little different. Max would help her, too, and this was their thing. Even as he got older, even when they argued about homework and wrongful detentions, and Max not reading social cues correctly and scaring some of the more chickenhearted kids on the block with an overly intense interest in their lives and a harmless bit of "stalking," they always made up in time for pizzas on Friday night. They would drive down to local grocery and pick up supplies, talk about school and crushes, and it was good. The only "crushes" his dad was into lately were under the tread of winter-grip Goodyears. But for one night a week rolling out those pies, Max felt like he really had a family. Then they'd go home and preheat the oven, sauce the crust, spread the toppings in geometrically pleasing patterns, and everything was perfect. Max loved mushrooms, but his parents weren't fans, so his mom designated a special Max Area on the pie to insert whatever he desired. Sometimes he wrote his mom's initials in green peppers when the "fungus" ran low.

But then she was gone, and he was left alone with an indifferent father, and Pizza Party Friday ceased forever, quickly replaced with Hungry Man Fridays instead. Which were a lot like Hungry Man Saturdays, and Sundays, and Mondays.

They ate a lot of goddamn Hungry Mans in that house after she was gone. Hungry Men, Desperate Men. Depressed Men, Lonely Men . . .

They had all four food groups.

A year after his mom's death, Max turned seventeen and applied to Papalocka's, and when they called him back the next day to offer him a dishwashing job, he figured it was better than nothing. He figured he'd just show them he meant business and snag that promotion to whatever title they had for whoever made the illustrious pizzas. He hoped it was "mom."

His first day at work, just the glorious smell alone brought back memories. And one step inside the kitchen and he was bawling like a baby, a great way to impress a new boss. Someone asked if he was okay, and he pretended like he bumped into an oven, later covering his ass by pressing a forearm against a heated pan and holding it there for ten "Mississippis." Besides an alibi for his embarrassing crying jag, he thought the badass scar might help him get laid one day, but the only person who noticed was his boss, who was more concerned about getting sued than potential coitus.

It was a good scar though, and he'd be lying if he said the smell of his skin cooking and the dotted line creasing his arm wasn't entirely a turn-off either. Maybe he was his father's son after all.

But as it turned out, washing dishes was a horror show. Kitchen memories could only soothe him so long before he could no longer stand hovering over a gray ocean of sludge, scrubbing pans and knives and whatever other gristle-caked tool needed it. But a couple weeks of begging his boss for a chance at the big leagues paid off with a very annoyed, "Jesus Christ! Fine!" and his life changed.

No, not *changed*, exactly. More like it returned to a previous channel he found infinitely more comforting. Wrist-deep in dough, it was like he'd been transported back before life plopped into the shitter. His mom was standing next to him, hand on his shoulder, asking him about his day, his steadily improving math grades, just *stuff.*

It occurred to him then, stretching that dough through all those Fridays, not once had he asked about *her* day. And now he'd never have that chance.

"Are you all right?" his trainer asked.

"Yeah," he said, sucking the snot back up into his nose. Had there ever been a more pathetic new hire? "The heat's just getting to me."

"Well, if you wanna make pizzas, you gotta learn to love that heat."

And he did. Max loved that heat more than anything in the world. If it was up to him, he would have stayed right there with his face in the fire, new scar sizzling, cooking pizzas for the rest of his cursed life. Except it wasn't up to him.

He had no idea who started the grease fire, and maybe he was framed. But because of all his sniffling, most of his co-workers talked shit about him right out of the gate, so it could have been anyone really, maybe all of them. How far did the conspiracy go? It was just looking like he was headed back to doing dishes.

Someone wanted him out of the kitchen, he decided. Out of his home. Out of the heat.

So he started delivering.

Because of the glowing plastic light box on the roofs of their cars, or the wind socks on the antennas, Max thought all pizza joints gifted special delivery vehicles to their employees, but of course they didn't. And all Max had was some shitty Pinto his alcoholic uncle had sold him for twice the Blue Book value. But he bit his lip and did the job. Surely his boss would come to his senses eventually and welcome him back into the kitchen. But as the months ticked by, the less likely this seemed. It didn't matter how badly the other cooks screwed up either, because sometimes Max would inspect the pizzas on the passenger's seat of his car and take snapshots on his phone of their blatant lack of symmetry. But whenever he presented this evidence, his boss just grabbed his collar and told him to stop fucking around with the food.

"Hey, if you want to serve a mathematically inferior product . . . "

"Get out of my office before I make you surrender your wind sock."

That night, Max's despair finally overwhelmed his sense of duty, and he got on his laptop to research how to make a bomb.

But hundreds of people all over the planet had long beat him to it, because the next day, the world ended.

Well, mostly.

MONDAY

They had been squatting in the house for twelve hours before they found the generator. It was a nice one, too, a bright red Super Max X9000 on two big, bouncy wheels, one of the last models ever made. It had plenty of gas, Max loved the name, and it only took them about ten minutes to figure out how to hook it up to the stove. Sure, some people probably would have used the only working power source for miles around to crank up a shortwave radio or even a TV, maybe see what was really happening and find out who was still alive. But today all these guys wanted was the perfect slice of pizza.

Dave knew the pizzas were stashed there because he'd been in charge of the bachelor party that never went down. Or maybe it was the monthly office pizza party. Either way, there were twenty-five pepperoni pies crammed in the chest freezer in his brother's garage, and they were fair game because, of course, there wouldn't be any more parties now. Or any more jobs. Or brothers. Dave's new friend would have to pull triple duty.

Though the power had been out, ten pizzas in the middle of that stack hadn't thawed completely, so Dave figured they'd still be edible. Max suggested eating them raw, and Dave might have been hungry enough to do this after about one more day. But Dave had high hopes for the ones in the middle that were still frozen. So when they found the generator in the shed next door, he was relieved they didn't have to eat frozen pizza like a couple of animals.

Not yet anyway.

Once the generator was hooked up, they preheated his brother's oven to 425 degrees, picked the pizza with the most balanced arrangement of pepperonis from the stack at Max's behest, peeled back the plastic, and slid it carefully onto the rack. They set the timer for exactly 15 minutes and sat cross-legged in front of the orange glow of the oven door, and things felt almost normal for a second, like they were watching TV.

"But a watched pot never boils yo!" Max yelled over the sputter of the generator after about a minute, and Dave agreed. So they went back into the house and started organizing soup cans to keep busy. Max stacked, and Dave counted up to sixty, over and over in his head, as the EMP had rendered his wristwatch as useless as everything else. They were daydreaming of that melted cheese on their tongues, and when their mental timer dinged, they practically ran back to the stove, laughing and almost knocking each other over in the process. Something brothers might do.

But when they opened the door, their faces slumped in disappointment. The once-perfect pizza, about the size and dimensions of the chrome rims Max once bestowed on his 1980 Pearl White Buick Regal, was now shriveled smaller than a 78 RMP record. Dave remembered those well. A record that held only about three minutes of music per side, and just like any pizza, no one ever flipped it over to check out the B-side.

But Max went to bite into it anyway, lips grimacing like a chimp, and Dave slapped it to the floor where it shattered like ceramic.

"What the fuck?"

"Put in another one," Dave said, eyes determined.

"It doesn't matter how many we try. The radiation . . . "

"We are not animals."

"Then don't attack my food like one."

"Hey, I've been looking forward to this for a week," Dave said. "The first bite is gonna be perfect."

Max nodded, convinced all over again. The two of them had talked quite a bit about "preparation," despite both of them operating from a different definition. One referred to cooking, one referred to preparing for the end of the world. But for now, both goals dove-tailed into the same mission.

So Max recommended a place where this dream could come true. And with a long supply of immaculate, and, hopefully, LP-sized pizzas still on their brains, they unplugged the generator, greased its wheels with WD-40, and rolled on out into the world, leaving the garage and the tiny radiated pizzas behind for Max's promise of a more professional establishment, and especially its apocalypse-friendly lead-lined stoves.

FRIDAY

The last man on Earth unhooked the propane tank from the generator and plugged the nozzle into the hole in the second-to-last man's ice-cold navel. He figured this was as good a spot as any to kick-start him into some sort of usefulness, or at the very least warm him evenly throughout.

The instructions on the side of the machine stressed the importance of proper ventilation, so he sealed all the windows in the restaurant, and heard the pulse in his ears slow considerably as he calmed down and the sweet relief of carbon-monoxide intoxication began. And as he felt his face flush and his lungs hum, he realized that it had always been the struggles, not the obstacles that gave his life meaning, and the end of the world was no exception. Just like the time his alarm clock broke and he found himself getting up earlier and earlier without any mechanical incentive, that was the only time he wasn't late for work, late for life, and he realized now that a lack of technology made him more responsible somehow, or at least gave him a clearer purpose. He was so busy his last week alive, that it just flew by.

And being alone wasn't nearly as terrifying as he worried it might be. This was one of those things you were supposed to learn at a Bachelor Party, a celebration he'd never been on the receiving end of, but, ironically, a lesson he'd seen hammered home to others when they were surrounded by their closest friends.

Was it finally Friday? Time for the weekend? Traditional time for a party or a pizza? It didn't matter anymore. Weeks had become meaningless the minute the clocks stopped. And days had become meaningless when the ashes blotted out the sun for good. The arbitrary sequence of something as ridiculous as a calendar had been rendered as meaningless to the planet as the comical, dead-end shuffle of the last remaining links in its food chain.

The generator sputtered, low on fuel, and he checked the second-to-last man on Earth for warmth, then for a pulse, which was like asking your dad to borrow his car, getting turned down, then asking to borrow his identity instead. He wasn't sure if he'd hope plugging into the navel would be the best way to cook him, or the best way to bring him back. Either way, he guessed it was the closest thing to a pop-up turkey timer he could manage under the circumstances. Sure, he was starving, just like anything else that was still alive, but his brain no longer registered this hunger. And he was surprised as anyone when one of the two last remaining people didn't eat the other, but it was still no shock when he understood this didn't matter, just as it didn't matter which one of them was the last one left.

Because whoever it was wouldn't be the last one left for very long.

Close yo the very end, he realized the same radiation that ruined their party had cooked his body much slower, much more evenly, and there was a certain relief that there would be no struggle if something pulled the meat off his bones.

So it was sometime during that final endless night when the last man on Earth was set upon by hordes of something strange, something small, twisted, and radiated. And whatever they were, like true animals, they weren't concerned with preparation. They preferred their pizza cold.

THURSDAY

They'd met exactly one week ago, on the second-to-last Thursday. Not that it mattered, as the last cell phone battery had officially been dead for two months now. But it had taken a while before Max could fully shake his own internal clock, which had been programmed so long to match Papalocka's daily specials. But it didn't take as long as he would have thought, even though at one time, pizza had been as important to him as his own limbs, even his life. And for half this life, he knew Thursdays were "buy-one large two topping get another large one topping free" day. Not as popular as Friday's "buy one order of cheese sticks get one large three topping pizza free" day, but still pretty essential. People who lose their arms supposedly experience phantom pains in their missing limbs. It made sense for Max to feel phantom cheese on his tongue and phantom dough in his nostrils. But these smells, along with the days of the week, had been all but obliterated by a mixture of invisible radiation and the not-entirely unpleasant diesel fumes of their generator.

But before Thursdays were cooked from his brain for good, one week back, Max met Dave in his favorite corner grocery store. Desperate, if not exactly heartbroken, after the loss of his father, Max was contemplating the disgrace of a frozen pizza for the first time in his life. Frozen pizzas were better than no pizzas, he supposed, but the store had been wiped clean. Right down to those nasty cocktail wienies his dad used to eat cold and then chug the juice straight from the can.

But he did find a man, still very much alive, but stalking the frozen pizza aisle like a starving lion on the Serengeti. Hands in his pockets, drooling at empty freezers, he said his name was Dave. Max had a cousin named Dave, so he figured he'd do.

Though it seemed like a match made in heaven, one week later and they still hadn't had any pizza. And besides the croutons Dave found at Papalocka's, they hadn't had much of anything to eat at all. Mostly thanks to the radioactive dust which sealed their scavenging to a five-square-mile radius, which was, coincidentally, almost the exact size of the delivery route Max used to operate within.

But even if the dust cleared up one day and the sun broke back through the ash, something that seemed increasingly unlikely, there was still the strange shrieks and rumblings from the distance they'd have to contend with. Either way, their world, which had never been vast before, had gotten a hell of a lot smaller.

"Half the time I don't know if that noise is coming from my stomach or . . . beyond." Dave joked, patting his head and rubbing his belly while staring intensively at the gray dome overhead. Max was impressed with his dexterity, and tried and failed to mimic Dave's movements.

"Well, if we don't get something to eat soon, it ain't gonna matter."

Max threw a rock in the direction of the dust that imprisoned them.

"Maybe we should search more houses," Dave said.

"We've searched them all."

"Maybe we missed something."

Max turned around, misunderstanding and wanting to shout about missing his mom, but he was hesitant to confront the bigger man.

"I know I didn't miss the packages in your freezer."

"That was my brother's freezer," Dave said, stepping back, brow arched. "What are you talking about?"

"You know goddamn well what I'm talking about, underneath all those hats . . . "

"People would kill for a nice cold hat in the summertime," Dave said, half serious.

"You had meat in that freezer."

"Deer jerkey," Dave said. "Inedible now."

"That wasn't no deer meat, man."

"What are you trying to say?"

"I don't know much, but I know deer ain't got fingers."

"Are you sure about that!"

"No," Max admitted.

"We don't have time for this, Max," Dave said, moving away.

And even though he shared a name with Max's cousin, Dave was suddenly sounding a lot like his dad.

WEDNESDAY

Dave's dad told him once that he was born late, but he was born to make a mess. This was something he heard a lot, from very early on. He was a mess, they said. And he made a mess, too. And it all probably started with the stings.

The first time he was stung, he was maybe nine years old. He was alone, so he cried about it a bit, but he did finally manage to pull the stinger out of his chubby arm all by himself, pulling a shred of the insect's intestinal tract along with it. Even as young as he was, he marveled at the commitment of a creature that died to inflict pain. And when he got home, his mother looked over his dirt-and-mucus caked face, streaked from sobs, and just shook her head.

"Such a mess," she muttered. Dave agreed.

He was stung again three years later, this time by a wasp. Seven times actually, and during his twelfth birthday party, surrounded by kids and parents, so this time he didn't cry at all, though the pain along his collarbone and the crease of his neck was almost unbearable. Though he didn't cry, he stumbled around hissing and clenching his teeth, watching the wasp fly away, indifferent to the mayhem it caused as he stumbled straight into the table of birthday presents and brought them crashing down all around him. The cake went, too, collapsing along with everything else like a colorful controlled demolition, and his mother was so angry she waited until the party emptied, and she threw the presents away, still unopened.

He hissed and hummed that night, too. He was learning.

And Dave never wondered what was in those boxes, not even for a second. He sat awake and rubbed his neck until morning, relishing the throb of the stings, and he finally realized who he was.

They weren't sure it was Wednesday, but they did know they were on Day Three without food, which was bad enough. But the lack of pizza was even worse. This pizza thing had begun as a distraction, and even halfway through that final week on Earth, it was already almost an obsession. Much like the denizens of their small town, it was evolving into something else.

The croutons Dave had shared with Max were something, and not just because they didn't realize at the time that this was their last meal. And the lukewarm energy drinks he'd scrounged from a cooler had the opposite affect as the radiation sickness set in. Dave was weary, but not quite panicking yet. But there was still a lot at stake when they tried making that pizza at Papalocka's.

The last pizza.

But in spite of the care they took kneading the dough, flipping the pepperoni like a Vegas dealer paying out poker chips, and a forty-year-old cast-iron stove with the a lifetime of seasonings cooked into its mouth, the radiation all around them still thwarted their efforts. The pizza came out black, twisted, inedible, and hopeless as ever. It shattered into shards when Max punched the table, and the black fog that resulted sent them coughing back outside.

Even though it was merely hump day, they didn't realize this moment actually marked their end.

Eventually, Max unhooked the generator, and Dave watched his last game of *Pac-Man* fade to black. He wasn't upset. He'd never made it off the first screen.

They rolled the generator back down to the center of the street, trying a couple more houses along their way, ransacking some kitchens and coolers. But in the end, they both knew where they were heading, back to Dave's garage. His brother's garage? That part was never made clear.

Max would have protested, but there was only so far they could go, bordered by ocean to the west, and rubble a mile to the east, an impending dust cloud fifty miles to the north, and an inhuman howling to the south. They both knew these few blocks of their neighborhood were the last place they'd be living, but they'd grown up there, as well, so there was some comfort in this.

Back in the garage, Max went straight for the stack of pizzas, peeling the plastic wrap to peek underneath. Dave hovered behind him, nervous as Max gave one an expert sniff.

"These were *never* frozen. This is delivery!"

"You sound like a commercial," Dave said, forcing a laugh.

"Well, the commercial is the opposite."

"Yeah, that's what it is, DiGiorno," Dave said, trying to convince himself.

"Where'd you get them?" Max sniffed again and recoiled. "Yikes, this shit's old! Radiated or not, we could never eat 'em."

Max started to dig deeper into the freezer, throwing rotten pizzas left and right. One of the pizzas rolled further than the rest, then it started to walk. Dave squinted, then remembered squid was, at one time, the most common topping in China, and now, of course, the most popular topping in the world. That would explain why at least one pizza was walking away from the action, sick of their shit.

"And I thought ghost peppers were terrifying," Dave said, mostly to himself, then he grabbed Max's shoulder to pull him back.

Max's eyes were wide.

"What else you got down there, man?" He jerked away and went back in to dig. "What the hell . . . "

Dave paced the garage, chewing on his fist. He wasn't sure what exactly was left down there, but with all the ice melted, all sorts of things were floating to the top. Dave watched as Max flung a handful of baseball caps at his feet, each one adorned with increasingly ridiculous Italian names. "Pilattagotta's," "Mozzafigato's," and "Finnocchio's," which sounded a bit like Pinocchio's dipshit brother.

"What is all this?" Max wanted to know, digging even faster. "Were you collecting them all?"

"Almost," Dave mumbled. "Now they're just door prizes. For the last party."

Dave thought back to the parties he used to throw, the strippers and arcade cabinets he rented, hoping someone made the mistake of passing out on his floor. That was before he realized he didn't have to take those kinds of risks. He could just make a phone call and have a victim delivered right to his door. Tip included. The tip was, "Don't ever knock on a stranger's door," though they'd never have a chance to put it into practice.

Employee of the Mouth . . .

Max's hands swirled around the cold soup of the dead freezer, and Dave closed his eyes, smiling and finding himself playing his last game of *Pac-Man*, long before the power went out. It lasted ten seconds, as long as it took to head straight for a ghost. He wasn't suicidal. He just loved the moment when the mouth turned itself inside out. Was this cannibalism? He wasn't sure. What he did know was, except for the color, which now more closely matched the pallor of their own faces, the loss of a life in this game resembled the time-lapse consumption of a pizza, slice after slice vanishing outward forever, opening that mindless yellow grin to the indifferent blink of infinity.

AFTERWORD:
THE VIOLENT AND UGLY DEATH OF THE NOID

NATHAN RABIN

Because this is an honest, authentic exploration of the life and death of controversial advertising pitchman "The Noid," it contains strong language, unrelenting violence, and a disturbing amount of sex. Do not read unless you are an adult ready to handle the truth about the Noid, and, by extension, the universe and yourself.

THE MAN WOKE up with a hangover as always. Every day was the same; waking up sometime late in the afternoon with a pounding headache and wicked hangover in a den of sin littered with the half-used detritus of the previous night's debauchery, little baggies of smudgy shit-brown Molly, empty vodka bottles, once-mighty joints that had been reduced to the flimsiest of roaches and used crack pipes.

He lazily scratched his enormous, greasy, sore prick and immediately set about getting fucked up all over again. It caused this infernal, unspeakable agony but it also took it away. It was savior and curse, medicine and poison, the antidote and the disease. All he knew was that his body didn't just want this rocket fuel for Olympian-level self-destruction: it needed it, and he wasn't about to deny his basic, essential needs.

He diligently smoked what was left of the joint by his bed, downed half a bottle of vodka without a chaser, and hungrily fished out the remaining MDMA with a greedy finger and stuck it in his mouth.

By the man's side, lie a naked woman in a state of disarray, her wild, curly hair matted, a bottle of cheap scotch mere inches away from her outstretched hand. They'd fucked, obviously, but that was all he could remember. He'd blacked out everything else. He once again found himself in the curious position of playing amateur sleuth in the case he only ever investigated, the eternal Case of What the Fuck Happened Last Night?

What was the girl's name? Cindy? Crystal? It was a stripper name, he sort of remembered, or something kind of '80s. Plastic. Or did he even know her name? Did she give it? Did it matter? Did it ever matter?

Did his own name even matter? Could he even remember it? It was Marshall or something, but it had been a very long time since anyone had called him that.

Words didn't matter now. Named didn't matter either. All that mattered was that the obliterated woman lying beside him was horny and lonely and desperate and sordid and sad and so was he.

They'd found momentary escape from their misery in the sweet oblivion of orgasm, in debasement, in turning themselves into grunting, fucking, drug-fueled animals because the pain of being human and sober and alive was just too terrible and grim to even contemplate.

She had not asked his name. Nor had he given it. Fuck, she didn't even ask him why he was wearing a red jumpsuit with the letter "N" in the middle of the stomach, white gloves and a red mask with bunny ears, even during sex. She just sort of accepted it. You know you've met someone exquisitely jaded when something like that doesn't raise an eyebrow, but this woman had to know who he was. The man's crimes had rendered him a folk legend, a bogeyman who had spent nearly a decade tormenting Domino's pizza delivery men and women with increasing savagery. He was a merciless urban hunter who would eat the pizzas he ruined and stole from delivery people even when they were soaked in the delivery person's blood and viscera.

At first, the man was content to merely sabotage Domino's drivers so that they were unable to meet Domino's famous 30-

minute guarantee and had to give away the pizzas for free. But soon that wasn't enough. He physically attacked and intimidated delivery people, often with guns and knives he wrote the words "Pizza Crusher" on in black letters.

Then one night after a furious struggle, the man finally did it: he beat up a Domino's delivery man so badly that he bled to death. He was a baby-faced kid, 17 at most, and now he was dead. The high he experienced after killing his first pizza delivery driver was unimaginable. It was like nothing he had ever experienced before. It was better than sex, better than drugs, better than anything. Nothing beat the thrill of revenge.

Over the pizza delivery boy's dead body, the man, who then called himself the Noid, wrote in the dead man's blood, "Avoid the Noid."

But that all seemed very far away from the grizzled, meth-addicted man of violence and infinite sadness as he woke up on what he could not possibly know would be his last final day on earth.

After finishing the previous night's roach, he rolled himself a fat new joint and looked at the sleeping woman with an expression that combined pity, concern and lust. She looked so out of it that he checked her pulse to make sure she was still alive. She was. That wasn't always the case. He'd had hook-ups die on him before, overdoses mostly, but this woman, whoever she was, was just fucked out, or near-comatose after crashing after days of drug-fueled decadence.

Domino's went in a very different, weird direction with their marketing, post-The Noid.

He had met the naked woman on a hookup website called Fuck Buddies whose slogan, "No feelings, all fucking" succinctly summarized its philosophy. His profile read, in its entirety:

Big dick fuck machine looking for sex

Quote: "How about a bit of the old ultra-violence, guvnor?"—A Clockwork Orange

"Why so serious?" The Dark Knight

Loves: Fucking, Drugs (all kinds), Ultra-Violence, Mayhem

Hates: Not fucking, Sobriety (ugh!), Timely Pizza delivery, Literally everything else, oh, and Daddy. Definitely dear old Daddy, but that was nothing a baseball bat couldn't take care of (ha ha ha!)

Daddy. Fucking Daddy. That's where this all began. That was the source of all of his incandescent, incoherent, overflowing rage. It was Daddy who had turned him into a monster due to the monstrousness within himself.

Daddy was a real piece of work, alright, a real piece of shit. He was a committed racist and anti-Semite, a rank and file member of the local Ku Klux Klan. He hit his wife and kids and drank too much and played grab-ass with his 13-year-old nieces at Easter parties. But because he was an award-winning Domino's owner with a peerless reputation for customer service and delivering on the company's famous 30-minute guarantee, he was seen as a great man and a pillar of his community.

Nothing the scrawny, painfully un-athletic boy did seemed to please his father, who divorced his mother when his son Marshall was three years old, shortly after winning Domino's manager of the year for his district.

In a desperate attempt to have a relationship with his father, the boy got a job as a delivery boy but after delivering four pizzas late his first night he was fired in front of the entire staff.

With pure hatred in his eyes, the manager screamed at the boy, "My assistant manager Chad is more of a son to me than you will ever be! Domino's is the only family I will ever need; its rule book is the only law or moral code I will ever recognize. The only thing that matters to me in this world and the next is Domino's 30 minute delivery guarantee.

Why can't you and that whore mother of yours get that through your thick skulls? I *chose* Domino's over her and you. It was literally the easiest decision I've ever had to make. I would do it again in a heartbeat a million times in a row. I thought you might be worth a damn if you were able to do something worthwhile, like deliver a pizza in a timely fashion, but you're too much of a fuck up for even that. Unlike Domino's pizza, you are garbage. I never want to see you again! You're fired! You're fired as a Domino's employee and as my son."

Marshall couldn't hold back tears. He wanted to crawl up into a little ball and die. Never in his life had he felt so humiliated. He felt ashamed down to a cellular level.

"Go home and cry, little boy! You're weak, just like your mother. You are not, nor will you ever be, Domino's material. You're not my employee and you're not my son either."

"I'm sorry, I'm so sorry. All I ever wanted to do was please you, to have a real relationship with you, and I thought maybe by working here I could make that happen but you don't love me. You never will love me" Marshall blubbered, unable to contain or control his soul-shaking sadness and sense of rejection.

"No shit, Sherlock," the older man roared with a chuckle, "You're better at ruining pizzas than you are at delivering them. Too bad there's not a job doing that. You'd be over-qualified. Hell, I'd write a glowing recommendation! Now, get out of here, woman, before your crying and sniveling make me puke."

Marshall went to his car and wept uncontrollably. It felt like he was crying not just with his whole body but with his whole soul as well. He felt like killing himself. He felt defeated, lost, abandoned, rejected by the universe itself, not just one horrible, horrible man who happened to be his father.

The shattered young man looked in the back seat of his car. In it was an ill-fitting Spider-Man costume. Marshall wished desperately in that moment that he could be a superhero, not a broken little boy destroyed by his father's rejection. Or, better yet, he could be a supervillain.

In that moment, Marshall Goosenberg died. From his ashes, a monster the world of pizza delivery boys would know and fear as the Noid was born.

The young man dyed the Spider-Man costume pure red, then painted a black "N" inside a white circle. He put on white gloves and a red mask that covered his face to conceal his identity and, looking at himself in the mirror with a pleased expression, said, "Now I am become Death, destroyer of worlds."

Even in the intensity of that awful moment, the Noid realized that he was being, at the very least, a little on the melodramatic side. So he dialed it down a bit. "I am the Noid" he rasped angrily. "I ruin pizzas." For the time being that would have to be enough.

Maybe his father was right. Maybe his only real talent was for ruining pizzas. Maybe that was ultimately his destiny, to be the monster who ruins pizzas by any means necessary, whether that meant running a pizza boy's car off the road and into a large body of water, or slitting their throat from behind and then watching in demented glee as the life seeps out of them.

His father's cruel words played on a loop in Marshall's head, gaining more power with each masochistic repetition. "You're better at ruining pizza! You're better at ruining pizza! You're better at ruining pizza! Ruining pizza! Ruining! Pizza! Ruining!"

Those cruel, taunting words would become the troubled man's new identity. He would ruin pizzas. From that moment on, that's all he lived for: to punish his father's cruelty, rejection, and abandonment by hitting him where it hurt: at work, and on the bottom line.

The police were on perpetual high alert for a mentally ill man in a skintight red costume attacking pizza deliverymen in savage, unconscionably violent ways, but that did little to nothing to halt the Noid's crime spree or lessen the ferocity of his attacks. He knew the police were out looking for him. He didn't care.

At first, the Noid would only kill pizza delivery men. That was his moral code: he didn't feel bad about killing pizza delivery boys to keep them from delivering pizzas in a timely fashion, but he wouldn't kill women or children.

Then one bloody, meth-fueled night the Noid accidentally murdered a female pizza delivery person. After that, no one and nothing was off-limits. He killed a small boy who was accompanying his dad on his pizza delivery rounds, as well as the golden retriever puppy yapping at him from the back seat.

Domino's placed a bounty on the Noid's head: a million dollars to anyone who could bring him in, dead or alive. The Grazziano crime family, the proprietors of the poorly named Grazziano Crime Family Money Laundering and Pizza Emporium, secretly aided and abetted the Noid, because he almost single-handedly destroyed the business of one of its biggest competitors, in addition to ending the lives of many of their employees.

But when the Noid, in another drug-fueled crime spree, ended up killing several pizza boys employed by the crime family, it put a hit out on the sex and drug-crazed mass murderer in the red suit with the insatiable blood lust.

The mob dispatched multiple hitmen to take out the Noid before he eliminated any more of their people, but the man who ended up ending his nearly decade long, corpse-strewn rampage was a second-generation Domino's delivery boy named Tommy Houlihan, whose life changed forever as a 15 year old when a policeman came to the house he shared with his mother and nine brothers and sisters and told everyone that their beloved oldest brother Mickey had been brutally murdered while trying to deliver a small cheese and green pepper pizza.

A small cheese and green pepper pizza! No one should have to die over something like that, particularly in the unspeakable manner in which Mickey was killed: his limbs had been hacked off while he was still alive, and he was castrated shortly before being hung upside down with a sign taped to his chest reading, reasonably, "Avoid the Noid."

Ever since that moment, Tommy lived only for revenge. The following day, he enrolled in Karate and began assembling a massive arsenal to take down the monster the city knew and feared.

He got a job at the same Domino's where his late brother worked before he was butchered alive, and waited for the call to arrive that would bring him into the Noid's world. Tommy knew that it was dangerous, if not suicidal, to use himself as bait to take down a monster who had killed, at that point, over forty Domino's pizza boys and girls and a smattering of delivery boys for other pizzerias. But he didn't care. This had to end. It had to end soon and it had to end with Tommy achieving vengeance.

When an order came in from a particularly violent and squalid neighborhood, an eerie sense came over him. He could feel it in his gut. This was it. This was Go Time. He grabbed a machine gun with the words "Noid Destroyer" painted blood red on the side, drove to the building, and walked up to the third floor of the building for his date with destiny, a pizza in one hand, a powerful assault weapon in the other.

Tommy did not even bother to enter the squalid apartment

where the Noid was staying. That's how sure he was. Instead he knocked on the door gingerly, and when he was greeted with a single gunshot that barely missed his skull, he retaliated with everything the Noid Destroyer had to offer.

It was, in the most literal possible sense, overkill. The Noid's long lucky streak of not getting murdered despite the many, many murders he himself committed shattered instantly in a deadly flurry of bullets. The Noid had lived by the gun. He was dying by it as well.

As bullets tore through the Noid's rancid, filthy-smelling devil-red leotard and into his cursed flesh, the notorious pizza-defiler and mass murderer let out a howl of excruciating pain. He could feel the life leave him. The gun he held in his arms fell gracelessly to the ground, letting out a few random shots.

In the process, a hole developed in the fabric of the time-space continuum and the Noid somehow escaped his own brutal, ugly, uncompromising universe and entered our own imperfect hellscape so that he might deliver a last message to you, the reader of this very piece.

With soul-consuming righteousness he is staring into your eyes and screaming at the top of his perforated lungs:

"If you think the Noid doesn't kill, that's cool. But you're living in a fucking dream world. If you think the Noid doesn't fuck, wake the fuck up. If you think the Noid isn't a machine built by the devil to deliver pain, you're Pollyanna living in a fantasy world of sunshine and lollipops, and I am going to have to skull-fuck some reality into you, princess. The universe is pain and death, and now I am finally one with Lucifer, who created me in his foul image."

Back in his world, the Noid ripped off his blood-soaked homemade costume and started to paw furiously at his inexplicably erect penis in a bizarre erotic death-frenzy, achieving messy orgasm mere moments before his bullet-riddled heart stopped and his damned life ended violently and dramatically, as fate had always preordained.

The Noid would end life as he began it: naked, covered in a pool of his own blood, and screaming with incoherent rage at a God who either does not exist or is a half-mad fool careening headlong into full-on insanity. With his final breaths, the Noid uttered the four words that had been vibrating in his soul for years. He rasped, with furious urgency, "Release. The. Snyder. Cut!"

ABOUT THE AUTHORS

David James Keaton's (editor) first collection, *FISH BITES COP! Stories to Bash Authorities,* was named the 2013 Short Story Collection of the Year by This Is Horror, and his second collection, *Stealing Propeller Hats from the Dead*, received a Starred Review from *Publishers Weekly*. Nobody read his third collection. He's also the co-editor of *Hard Sentences: Crime Fiction Inspired by Alcatraz,* and the editor of *Dirty Boulevard: Crime Fiction Inspired by the Songs of Lou Reed*. He lives in California with his wife, daughter, and a cat forever lingering between life and death. His favorite pizza topping is plastic. Frozen pizza forever, baby! He can be found at davidjameskeaton.com.

Max Booth III (editor) regrets ever agreeing to put this book together with David James Keaton. They are now enemies for life. Max is also the co-founder and Editor-in-Chief of Perpetual Motion Machine, so realistically he could have cancelled this project at any point, but this didn't occur to him until right now, while writing this bio. Fuck it. You can follow him on Twitter @GiveMeYourTeeth and listen to his podcasts Castle Rock Radio and Ghoulish wherever you prefer to do that kinda thing. Thank you for reading this book. His favorite pizza topping is mushrooms, which everybody in his family dislikes.

Pearse Anderson ("Crucifixions in the Garden of Garlic Bread") is a speculative fiction author and food scholar from Upstate New York. His writing and photography has been published in *Strange Horizons, Weird Fiction Review, Fearsome Critters*, and *Menacing Hedge*. He has previously interned at Blue Hill at Stone Barns and Tin House Books, and graduated from the Iowa Young Writers' Studio. Pearse is currently in Ohio, studying fiction and food. He traveled to Sicily for three weeks in 2018 to study Mafia violence and the history of Sicily. He would like to dedicate this piece to Vittoria Cirello, Leoluca Orlando, Umberto Santino, Sarah Vassos, and

Jessica Greenfield, all who helped him in this journey. His favorite pizza topping is ricotta, because white pizza is seriously underrated.

Matthew M. Bartlett ("The Black Cheese") is the author of *The Stay-Awake Men and Other Unstable Entities, Gateways to Abomination, Creeping Waves*, and other books of supernatural horror. His short stories have appeared in a variety of anthologies, including *Tales from a Talking Board, Uncertainties Vol. 3, Year's Best Weird Fiction Vol. 3,* and *Ashes & Entropy*. He lives in Western Massachusetts with his wife, Katie Saulnier, and their cats: Phoebe, Peachpie, and Larry. His favorite pizza topping is raw jalapeños, though he has been witnessed ordering pizzas with sausage. He tells you this because he doesn't want to sound boring. In truth his most frequent order is "plain." Incidentally, the far-and-away best pizza he's ever had is from Luna Pizza, a Connecticut chain. And the weirdest pizza he's had is from Randy's Wooster Street Pizza. It's called Skippy's Dare, and it's a pizza with peanut butter, provolone, and bacon.

Nancy Brewka-Clark's ("By the Slice") recent speculative stories and mysteries have appeared in *Mysterical-E*, Malice Domestic's *Murder Most Conventional*, Darkhouse Books' *Descansos*, FunDead Publications' *One Night in Salem* and *Shadows in Salem*, as well *Eastern Iowa Review, Yellow Mama, Litbreak, Every Day Fiction,* and *Close2thebone*. She began her writing career as a reporter, and then as an early-edition editor at a metropolitan daily newspaper, where the first order of the day was a murder round-up. She grew up eating pizza from a place called Sam's where the motto was "A piece of ham, a piece of cheese, and a piece of Sam."

Joshua Chaplinsky ("Cenobio Pizzeria") is the Managing Editor of LitReactor.com. He is the author of *Kanye West—Reanimator*. His short fiction has been published by *Vice, Vol. 1 Brooklyn, Thuglit*, Severed Press, *Pantheon Magazine*, Clash Books, Broken River Books and more. Follow him on Twitter at @jaceycockrobin. More info at joshuachaplinsky.com. His favorite pizza topping is plain ol' cheese, so fuck you.

By day, **Evan Dicken** ("The Parlor") studies old Japanese maps and crunches data for all manner of fascinating research at Ohio State University. By night, he does neither of these things. His short fiction has most recently appeared in: *Shock Totem, Strange Horizons*, and *Pseudopod*, and he has stories forthcoming from publishers such as: Black Library, and The NoSleep Podcast. Feel free to visit him at: evandicken.com, where he wasted both his time and yours. His favorite pizza topping is not really a topping at all but more a lifestyle choice.

T. Fox Dunham ("The Blessed Hungry") lives in Philadelphia with his wife, Allison. He's a lymphoma survivor, cancer patient, modern bard, and historian. His first book, *The Street Martyr*, was published by Gutter Books. A television series based on the book is being produced by Throughline Films. *Destroying the Tangible Illusion of Reality or Searching for Andy Kaufman*, a book about what it's like to be dying of cancer, was recently released from Perpetual Motion Machine Publishing, and Fox has a story in the Stargate Anthology *Points of Origin* from MGM and Fandemonium Books. Fox is an active member of the Horror Writers Association, and he's had published hundreds of short stories and articles. He's host and creator of What Are You Afraid Of? Horror & Paranormal Show, a popular horror program on PARA-X RADIO. His motto is wrecking civilization one story at a time. Find out more information at www.tfoxdunham.com & Twitter: @TFoxDunham. And his favorite pizza topping is extra sauce. Yeah. That's a pizza topping. But you need good sauce. The best sauce he's tasted is the basil sauce from Main Street Pizza in Lansdale. You need a saucy pizza, like lakes of sauce, the kind a small kitten could drown in.

Brian Evenson ("A Bloody Hand to Shake") is the author of more than a dozen books of fiction, most recently the story collection *Song for the Unraveling of the World*. He has been a finalist for the Shirley Jackson Award five times and has won the International Horror Guild Award. He has received Guggenheim Foundation Fellowship and an NEA Fellowship, and three of his stories have received O. Henry Awards. He teaches at CalArts and lives in Los Angeles. His favorite pizza topping is live bees.

Steve Gillies (Introduction) lives with his family in Oak Park, Illinois. His work has appeared in *Artifice Magazine*, A.V. Club, *Curbside Splendor*, and *McSweeney's Internet Tendency*. He claims to have no knowledge of this story. He's doing just fine. Really. His favorite pizza toppings are the green olives at Art of Pizza in Chicago.

Michael Paul Gonzalez ("Upper Crust") is the author of the novels *Angel Falls* and *Miss Massacre's Guide to Murder and Vengeance*. His newest project is the serial horror audio drama *Larkspur Underground*, available for free on iTunes, Stitcher, or wherever you get your podcasts. A member of the Horror Writers Association, his short stories have appeared in print and online, including *Lost Signals, Gothic Fantasy: Chilling Horror Stories*, HeavyMetal.com, and *Where Nightmares Come From*. He resides in Los Angeles, a place full of wonders and monsters far stranger than any that live in the imagination. His favorite pizza topping is described in painstaking detail in his story in this book. You'll have to meet him for dinner for the whole story. You can visit him at MichaelPaulGonzalez.com

Cody Goodfellow ("The Vegan Wendigo") has written eight novels and four or five collections. His latest are *Unamerica* (King Shot Press) and *Scum Of The Earth* (Eraserhead Press). His first two collections, *Silent Weapons For Quiet Wars* and *All-Monster Action,* each received the Wonderland Book Award. He has appeared in numerous short films, TV shows, music videos, and commercials as research for his previous novel, *Sleazeland*. He also edits the quarterly hyperpulp zine *Forbidden Futures*. He "lives" in Portland. Learn more at codygoodfellow.com. His favorite topping is cheese grown from celebrity armpit bacteria.

Amanda Hard ("Body of Crust") earned her MFA in Creative Writing (Fiction) from Murray State University in Kentucky. Her horror fiction and dark poetry have appeared in numerous magazines and print anthologies including *Lost Signals* (Perpetual Motion Machine Publishing.) A former print journalist and professional dancer, she now practices casual necromancy and bluegrass ukulele. Amanda is a member of the Horror Writers Association and lives in the cornfields of southern Indiana with her husband and son. Her favorite pizza topping is a sprinkling of six pomegranate seeds.

Rob Hart ("Last Request") is the author of the Ask McKenna series, the food-noir collection *Take-Out*, and *The Warehouse*, which has sold in more than 20 countries and been optioned for film by Ron Howard. He's online at www.robwhart.com. His favorite pizza topping is no topping because only garbage pizza needs toppings.

Andrew Hilbert ("Watch Them Eat") is the author of *Invasion of the Weirdos, Bangface and the Gloryhole*, and *Death Thing*. He is co-founder of Cockroach Conservatory. His favorite topping on pizza is the grease that pools in the middle of a pepperoni slice and congeals on his mustache.

Emma Alice Johnson ("Pizza_Gal_666") writes stories and books and zines. She lifts weights and eats pizza. Her favorite pizza topping is the flaccid self-confidence of the men who reject her on OKCupid because she is too tall. She lives in Minneapolis by the lakes.

Matthew King ("Phosphenes") is a writer of short fiction and author bios who currently resides in Chicago, Illinois. When not beating his face against a keyboard, Matthew can usually be found at the local zoo. He desperately needs to purchase a dog. His favorite pizza topping is regret.

Nick Kolakowski ("Bad Night Below Ricky's") is the author of the novels *Boise Longpig Hunting Club* and *Maxine Unleashes Doomsday* (both from Down & Out Books), as well as the *Love & Bullets* novella trilogy (from Shotgun Honey). His short fiction and poetry have appeared in *Mystery Tribune, North American Review, Thuglit, McSweeney's*, and various anthologies. His favorite pizza toppings are broccoli rabe and sausage if he's feeling fancy, or extra-cheese from a cheap slice place if it's 2:00 AM and he's downed too many beers; in that weird dream he had the other night, he had a serious hankering for fried grasshoppers and mushrooms on a deep-dish pie, but he doesn't know how to interpret that in a meaningful way.

Named as one of 10 female horror directors Blumhouse should hire, **Izzy Lee** ("Demons of 1994") is a writer and twice-Rondo Award-nominated filmmaker. She has written for Birth.Movies.Death., *Rue Morgue, Fangoria*, and *Diabolique*, and is an editor for ScreenAnarchy. She's currently at work on several short stories, films, and scripts, because she is a goddamn maniac who cannot stop, no matter the emotional or financial cost. When she's not writing, she's making scary little films, often from an outsider perspective with a socio-political bent. Her shorts have screened with such films as *Tigers Are Not Afraid, American Psycho, The*

Villainess, *Tales of Halloween*, *The Love Witch*, *The Lords of Salem*, and *The Sacrament*. Find out more at www.nihilnoctem.com. Her favorite kind of pizza is ricotta with crumbled sausage or pepperoni, and it better be stretched thin and cooked well done, motherfucker.

Tim Lieder ("Introduction to 'Let's Kill the Pizza Guy'") lives in Washington Heights with three cats. His fiction has been published in several markets, including *Shock Totem*. He hates the movie *Mrs. Miniver* and likes *Batman v. Superman*. Owner and operator of Dybbuk Press, his last project was editing the Bible-themed horror anthology, *King David and the Spiders from Mars*. His favorite pizza toppings are anxiety and depression.

Jessica McHugh ("When the Moon Hits Your Eye") is a novelist and internationally produced playwright running amok in the fields of horror, sci-fi, young adult, and wherever else her peculiar mind leads. She's had twenty-three books published in ten years, including her bizarro romp, *The Green Kangaroos*, her Post Mortem Press bestseller, *Rabbits in the Garden*, and her YA series, *The Darla Decker Diaries*. Her favorite pizza toppings are whatever won't make her stomach feel like lava the next day. Just kidding. They pretty much all do now.

Tony McMillen ("Elude the Snood") is the author of the heavy metal horror novel *An Augmented Fourth* and a novel about murder and children's literature called *Nefarious Twit*. He's also the artist and writer behind the rainbow-oil-slick hued dark fantasy comic book series *Lumen* and currently working on a comic about three decades of life in the special effects industry as told by the 14-year-old kid genius who lived it, called *Serious Creatures*. Oh, and he wrote a trilogy of folk rock/fantasy horror novels that read like Mark Twain's *Dune* that he calls *The Bleeding Tree Trilogy* that he's looking to get published nowish. His favorite pizza topping is a bit of cheddar cheese, sliced tomatoes, and some lettuce, but instead of red sauce, he puts it over ground beef, and instead of dough, it's wrapped in a corn tortilla shell. He calls it . . . French toast.

James Newman ("30 Seconds or Less . . . or Else!") is the author of the novels *Midnight Rain, The Wicked, Animosity*, and *Ugly As Sin*, the collections *People Are Strange* and *The Long N' Short Of It,* and the fan-favorite novella *Odd Man Out*. "30 Minutes or Less

. . . or Else!" is his latest in a series of recent collaborations, after *Scapegoat* (with Adam Howe) and *The Special* and *In the Scrape* (both with Mark Steensland). A feature film adaptation of *The Special* is due for release soon, directed by B. Harrison Smith (*Death House*). As far as James's favorite pizza topping? Mushrooms. Load 'em up, 'cause usually he's forced to go without since the rest of his family aren't fans of fungus.

Nathan Rabin (Afterword) was the first head writer for the A.V. Club and was a staff writer for The Dissolve. He was also the head writer for the entertainment guide of *The Onion*. He is the author of a memoir, *The Big Rewind*, and an essay collection based on one of his columns, *My Year of Flops*. He most recently collaborated with "Weird Al" Yankovic on a coffee table book titled *Weird Al: The Book,* and his misadventures with Phish and The Insane Clown Posse spawned *You Don't Know Me But You Don't Like Me,* named one of *Rolling Stone's* Top 20 Music Books of 2013. Rabin's writing has also appeared in *The Wall Street Journal, Spin, The Huffington Post, The Boston Globe, Nerve*, and *Modern Humorist*. He lives in Chicago. When it comes to pizza toppings, he apparently doesn't play favorites.

Desmond Reddick ("30 Seconds or Less . . . or Else!") lives on Vancouver Island with his two gluten intolerant sons and a dog named Kirby who will eat anything except what's put in his dish. Raised on a steady diet of horror movies, heavy metal, and Hawaiian pizza, he teaches during the day, and writes and podcasts whenever he can. His debut novel, *Mother of Abominations,* features not a single slice of pizza, but it does have giant monsters. Dread Media, his horror podcast, has never missed a Monday since 2007. His favourite pizza topping is the stark realization of the unstoppable rush of time.

Betty Rocksteady ("Leftovers") writes cosmic sex horror and other creepy shit. Her novella *The Writhing Skies* is the winner of 2018's This Is Horror Novella of the Year. Find out more at www.bettyrocksteady.com. Her favorite pizza topping is mushrooms.

Michael Allen Rose ("Ultimate Pizza Club") is a Chicago based author, musician, and performer. He has published several bizarro, horror, and comic novels with various presses, been in a few anthologies, and also makes industrial music under the name Flood Damage. He has a Patreon which provides subscribers with a new zine or chapbook every month. He loves cats, good tea, and his partner Sauda with whom he poses nude for art classes and performs burlesque with for money, not unlike some kind of magical trained monkey. He hosts the Ultimate Bizarro Showdown each year at Bizarro Con in Portland, Oregon, and is often involved in shenanigans. His favorite pizza topping is the crushing existential angst of existing in a perpetual state of ennui during the collapse of society thanks to late-stage capitalism. Also, pepperoni.

Craig Wallwork ("Rosemary and Time") is the author of the novels *The Sound of Loneliness* and *To Die Upon a Kiss*, as well as the short story collections *Quintessence of Dust* and *Gory Hole*. His stories have appeared in many anthologies, including *The New Black* and *Tales From the Lake Vol 5*. He lives in England. His favorite topping is slices of human brain. Preferably a horror writer's. His goal is to have Stephen King over for dinner.

Sheri White ("Mickey and the Pizza Girls") has lived in Maryland all her life and has a big can of Old Bay in her pantry to prove it. She can also kick anybody's ass in cracking crabs all day long. Her stories have been published in many magazines and anthologies, and her first collection, *Sacrificial Lambs and Others*, was published by Crossroad Press in 2018. She lives with her husband, two of her three daughters, her youngest daughter's girlfriend, three black cats, and three rescued mutts. She still looks at animal rescue sites, despite her husband's edict of NO MORE PETS. Although shy, if you bring up The Beatles, she will talk your ear off until you beg for mercy. Her favorite pizza toppings are pineapple, sausage, and spinach—and yes, all on one pizza. Don't even argue; she has heard it all.

Wallace Williamson ("And She Answered the Door . . . NAKED!"), along with unindicted co-conspirator P. Dark Lillie, has authored 10+ novels and 30+ novellas & short stories; most of which remain obscure & underappreciated. His favorite pizza toppings are Pussylicious Sauce & Penile Pepperoni.

IF YOU ENJOYED *TALES FROM THE CRUST*, DON'T PASS UP ON THESE OTHER TITLES FROM PERPETUAL MOTION MACHINE . . .

LOST FILMS
EDITED BY MAX BOOTH III AND LORI MICHELLE

ISBN: 978-1-943720-29-3
Page count: 350
$18.95

From the editors of *Lost Signals* comes the new volume in technological horror. Nineteen authors, both respected and new to the genre, team up to deliver a collection of terrifying, eclectic stories guaranteed to unsettle its readers. In *Lost Films*, a deranged group of lunatics hold an annual film festival, the lost series finale of *The Simpsons* corrupts a young boy's sanity, and a VCR threatens to destroy reality. All of that and much more, with fiction from Brian Evenson, Gemma Files, Kelby Losack, Bob Pastorella, Brian Asman, Leigh Harlen, Dustin Katz, Andrew Novak, Betty Rocksteady, John C. Foster, Ashlee Scheuerman, Eugenia M. Triantafyllou, Kev Harrison, Thomas Joyce, Jessica McHugh, Kristi DeMeester, Izzy Lee, Chad Stroup, and David James Keaton.

LOST SIGNALS
EDITED BY MAX BOOTH III AND LORI MICHELLE
ISBN: 978-1-943720-08-8
Page count: 378
$16.95

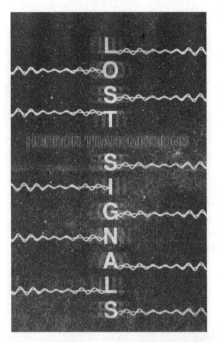

What's that sound? Do you feel it? The signals are already inside you. You never even had a chance. A tome of horror fiction featuring radio waves, numbers stations, rogue transmissions, and other unimaginable sounds you only wish were fiction. Forget about what's hiding in the shadows, and start worrying about what's hiding in the dead air. With stories by Matthew M. Bartlett, T.E. Grau, Joseph Bouthiette Jr., Josh Malerman, David James Keaton, Tony Burgess, Michael Paul Gonzalez, George Cotronis, Betty Rocksteady, Christopher Slatsky, Amanda Hard, Gabino Iglesias, Dyer Wilk, Ashlee Scheuerman, Matt Andrew, H.F. Arnold, John C. Foster, Vince Darcangelo, Regina Solomond, Joshua Chaplinsky, Damien Angelica Walters, Paul Michael Anderson, and James Newman. Also includes an introduction from World Fantasy-award-winning author, Scott Nicolay.

TRUTH OR DARE
EDITED BY MAX BOOTH III

ISBN: 978-0-9860594-5-2
Page count: 240
$14.95

Halloween night. The freaks are out and having the time of their lives. The kids of Greene Point High School have organized a massive bonfire out in the woods. One drunken teen suggests playing a game, a game called Truth or Dare. That's always a fun game. Always good for a laugh. By the end of this night, nobody will be laughing. Alcohol, sex, deadly secrets, and oceans of blood await them. Do you dare to play? Truth or Dare is a shared-world horror anthology featuring the morbid writings of many prominent authors in the field today, as well as quite a few new kids on the block you're gonna want to keep an eye on.

The Perpetual Motion Machine catalog

Baby Powder and Other Terrifying Substances | John C. Foster | Story Collection

Bleed | Various Authors | Anthology

Bone Saw | Patrick Lacey | Novel

Born in Blood Vol 1 | George Daniel Lea | Story Collection

Crabtown, USA:Essays & Observations | Rafael Alvarez | Essays

Dead Men | John Foster | Novel

Destroying the Tangible Issue of Reality; or, Searching for Andy Kaufmann | T. Fox Dunham | Novel

The Detained | Kristopher Triana | Novella

Gods on the Lam | Christopher David Rosales | Novel

Gory Hole | Craig Wallwork | Story Collection

The Green Kangaroos | Jessica McHugh | Novel

Invasion of the Weirdos | Andrew Hilbert | Novel

Last Dance in Phoenix | Kurt Reichenbaugh | Novel

Like Jagged Teeth | Betty Rocksteady | Novella

Live On No Evil | Jeremiah Israel | Novel

Long Distance Drunks: a Tribute to Charles Bukowski | Various Authors | Anthology

Lost Films | Various Authors | Anthology

Lost Signals | Various Authors | Anthology

Mojo Rising | Bob Pastorella | Novella

Night Roads | John Foster | Novel

Quizzleboon | John Oliver Hodges | Novel

The Perpetual Motion Club | Sue Lange | Novel

The Ritalin Orgy | Matthew Dexter | Novel

The Ruin Season | Kristopher Triana | Novel

So it Goes: a Tribute to Kurt Vonnegut | Various Authors | Anthology

Speculations | Joe McKinney | Story Collection

Stealing Propeller Hats from the Dead | David James Keaton | Story Collection

Tales from the Holy Land | Rafael Alvarez | Story Collection

The Nightly Disease | Max Booth III | Novel

The Tears of Isis | James Dorr | Story Collection

The Train Derails in Boston | Jessica McHugh | Novel

The Writhing Skies | Betty Rocksteady | Novella

Time Eaters | Jay Wilburn | Novel

Patreon:
www.patreon.com/pmmpublishing

Website:
www.PerpetualPublishing.com

Facebook:
www.facebook.com/PerpetualPublishing

Twitter:
@PMMPublishing

Newsletter:
www.PMMPNews.com

Email Us:
Contact@PerpetualPublishing.com